# Viper

MICHAEL MORLEY

PENGUIN BOOKS

PENGUIN BOOKS

Published by the Penguin Group
Penguin Books Ltd, 80 Strand, London WC2R ORL, England
Penguin Group (USA) Inc, 375 Hudson Street, New York, New York 10014, USA
Penguin Group (Canada), 90 Eglinton Avenue East, Suite 700, Toronto, Ontario, Canada M4P 2Y3 (a division of Penguin Canada Inc.)
Penguin Ireland, 25 St Stephen's Green, Dublin 2, Ireland (a division of Penguin Books Ltd)
Penguin Group (Australia), 250 Camberwell Road,
Camberwell, Victoria 3124, Australia (a division of Pearson Australia Group Pty Ltd)
Penguin Books India Pvt Ltd, 11 Community Centre,
Panchsheel Park, New Delhi – 110017, India
Penguin Group (NZ), 67 Apollo Drive, Rosedale, North Shore 0632, New Zealand
(a division of Pearson New Zealand Ltd)
Penguin Books (South Africa) (Pty) Ltd, 24 Sturdee Avenue,
Rosebank, Johannesburg 2196, South Africa

Penguin Books Ltd, Registered Offices: 80 Strand, London WC2R ORL, England

www.penguin.com

First published 2009
1



Map of the Bay of Naples by Damien Demaj



Set in 11.75/14pt Garamond MT
Typeset by Palimpsest Book Production Limited,
Grangemouth, Stirlingshire
Printed in England by Clays Ltd, St Ives plc



ISBN: 978–0–141–03122–4

*This is a work of fiction. Names, characters, places and incidents are either the product of the author's imagination or are used fictitiously, and any resemblance to actual persons, living or dead, business establishments, events, or locales is entirely coincidental.*

www.greenpenguin.co.uk

Penguin Books is committed to a sustainable future for our business, our readers and our planet. The book in your hands is made from paper certified by the Forest Stewardship Council.

To Billy – our magnificent surprise

# Acknowledgements

*Viper* is influenced by the criminal activity of the Camorra in Naples. Most of the places mentioned genuinely exist and most events are drawn from real Camorra activities. Some, however – for reasons that will become obvious – did not happen and do not exist.

I was helped in my research by new-found friends in the carabinieri in Naples, who need to remain anonymous, and by members of the Neapolitan Camorra whom *I* prefer to keep anonymous. I must also express my gratitude to Guy Rutty, Professor of Forensic Pathology, East Midlands Forensic Pathology Unit, University of Leicester, UK, for his advice on matters of pathology – any deviations from hard cold facts are not his errors but my deliberate fictitious inventions.

Thanks to everyone at Penguin, particularly: my editor Bev Cousins, who made so many great observations that I lost count, and to Alex Clark, Tom Chicken, Shan Morley Jones and Ellie Smith, who all added their own special polish. Thanks also to Julia Bauer in Germany for her many ideas and as always to Jack Barclay for his invaluable advice.

I'm blessed with having Luigi Bonomi as my agent

and literary guru, and in the international field there's no one better than Nicki Kennedy and Sam Edenborough at ILA. A big, fully interactive thank you to Ronald Goes for decoding the mysteries of the web, helping me set up *www.michaelmorleybooks.com*, and providing more than one or two laughs along the way.

Finally, my wife Donna and son Billy deserve a special mention for their support, especially during that bizarre moment when I got arrested by the carabinieri in Castello di Cisterna while taking research photographs of their barracks. The phrase 'Daddy has been arrested *again*' still causes us amusement.

## *La Baia di Napoli (Bay of Naples)*

# Prologue

*La Baia di Napoli*

Francesca Di Lauro had the kind of eyes you never forgot. Hypnotic, almost translucent. An indefinable shade between blue and green. More hologram than optic.

They were fixed on the man in front of her. Fixed very firmly on him as he watched her naked body. Francesca's faultless skin and tumbling black hair were backlit by the golden flicker of a newly lit fire. The two of them were alone. Outside, in the pine-smelling woodland. No one to disturb them. Perfect privacy.

Only this was no romantic encounter. This was the worst moment of her life. The flames around Francesca's feet crawled up the metal stake she'd been tied to. Wind tugged her hair and suddenly the jaws of an orange dragon were chewing her flesh. Francesca twisted hopelessly, the agonizing heat searing her paraffin-soaked skin.

He stood a few metres away, mesmerized by the slow murder, stroking himself pleasurably. His eyes fixed on the curtain of flames. *This would take time. A deliciously long time.*

Francesca had been tied with coils of wire around her feet, hands and neck. He'd learned from past mistakes.

*Rope burned, then they tried to get away.* He didn't want any more messiness. *No mistakes this time.*

Bricks were stacked waist-high, all around her. A kiln to funnel heat up her body. Rags stuffed in her mouth and then bound around her face to choke off any screams. Though sometimes he liked to hear them. Liked to hear the air leave their lungs for one last time.

Francesca's head slumped limply on her chest. She was a quiet one. Flames ate her hair. The smell of burning flesh, sweet and greasy like a hog roast, carried in the cold night air. He sucked it in. Savoured it. Fed on it.

Amid the crackle of the fire he waited. Listened now for the moment when he heard her skull crack and sizzle. *Popping chestnuts! How he just loved to peel away those crisp, burned outer shells.*

He'd removed all her jewellery and, while he watched, he played with it in his pocket, turning the trophies in his hand like beads on a rosary.

The blaze illuminated the pit that he stood in. It was almost three metres deep, seven metres wide and fifteen metres long. It had been dug by the landowner as foundations for a house that never got built. *Dead dreams.* These days it was more commonly used to burn some of the overflowing stinking rubbish that clogged the city's vermin-infested streets.

He stayed until darkness had faded seamlessly into the dawn, then he raised a gleaming stainless-steel spade and began softly singing. He sang in English, complete with a near-comical Dean Martin accent.

*When the stars make you drool joost-a like pasta fazool, that's amore;*

He scraped Francesca's bones from the blackened wood, grey ash and red embers. Slammed the blade of his spade across the snake of her spine.

*When you dance down the street with a cloud at your feet, you're in love;*

The metal sliced through her pelvis –

*When you walk in a dream but you know you're not dreamin', signore,*

– through her skull –

*'Scusa me, but you see, back in old Napoli, that's amore.*

– through her hips and ribs and any other major bones that had survived the inferno.

He searched the scorched ground. Made sure he'd been his usual thorough self.

And then he chopped again.

This time he used a small hand-axe on the troublesome hip, cleaving through the sacrum, coccyx, ischium and pubis.

He was dripping with sweat when he climbed out of the pit, carrying Francesca's young life in two dented steel buckets, her total existence reduced to ash and broken bones; ash that blew away in the wind as he walked to his car.

*Would her beauty have stayed with her into her thirties, forties or fifties? Would her children have inherited those hypnotic eyes?*

The ponderings amused him as he drove to the sacred spot where he laid them all to rest.

He dug again. The blood-red sunrise painted his skin as he upended Francesca's remains into a shallow grave.

He slapped the old steel buckets with his hand. Cleared the last of the dust – the last of Francesca – that stuck to the sides. A couple of smashed bones were still larger than he liked. He stomped them into the earth.

The first coral-blue hues of morning fought their way into the angry sky as he completed the burial. He bent his head, closed his eyes and slowly prayed: *Domine Jesu Christe, Rex Gloriae, libera animas omnium fidelium defunctorum de poenis inferni et de profundo lacu.*

Before leaving, he urinated on the freshly dug grave. Partly because he needed to. Mainly because he liked to. As he zipped up, he wondered whether God would indeed heed his prayer to free the soul of the faithfully departed from infernal punishment and the horrors of the deep pit.

But then again, he asked himself, did he really give a fuck?

He sauntered back to his car, singing in Italian this time: *Luna rossa lassù, mare azzurro quaggiù: questo è amore!*

# ONE
# Five years later

# I

***Prigione di Poggioreale, Napoli***

Camorra mobster Bruno Valsi got a five stretch for frightening the life out of people due to testify against his gang boss father-in-law. It was a walk in the park compared to the life sentences he should have served for several murders and countless sadistic assaults.

Few had cheered when he'd gone down. Few had been that brave. Maybe the fact that three of his arresting officers had been shot in the legs, and the local carabinieri headquarters had been burned to the ground, had something to do with the silence.

The Camorra message had echoed around every street corner. Cross the Family – get brutally punished. No one needed telling twice.

As witnesses withdrew, even the local cops heeded the warnings. Vital evidence vanished from inside the station house. The case against Valsi's father-in-law crumbled. But the young Camorrista wasn't so lucky. One young woman came forward and testified about being threatened. It was enough to get him the five years. One day – soon – he would find her and make her pay.

Three guards marched the Camorrista into the discharge area for him to collect his personal effects and change out of his prison clothes. He gave them the finger as they watched him strip. Above his left breast a tattoo declared who owned his heart. Not a woman. No way. It belonged to the Finelli clan. The guards' eyes were drawn to the distinctive image of a red viper, slithering down a switchblade. From its mouth dripped three blood-red words: *Onore. Lealtà. Vendetta.* Honour. Loyalty. Vengeance. The Finellis were one of the few Camorra clans to wear gang markings. Valsi jabbed a finger at the word *Vendetta* and his jailers looked away. '*Andate tutti a fanculo – fuck you all,*' he called to them as he struggled into his old, grey Valentino suit. Prison life had made the trousers too big in the waist and the jacket too narrow across the chest. That's what happens when you pump iron twice a day, every day for 1,827 days behind bars. You get hard. Jail rock hard. Prison had changed him in other ways too. He was meaner. And better connected than he'd ever been.

One of the bigger and more senior guards walked him the final distance to the front gates. Valsi stood inches from his face. '*Caccati in mano e prenditi a schiaffi.*' The insult was well known, *shit in your hand and then hit yourself*, but until now, no one had ever dared say it to a prison officer.

Jacket over shoulder, he blinked as he walked into the sunlight. To the far east rose the slopes of Vesuvius and Mount Somma. Up close and all around him inner-city slums skulked incongruously in the shadows of the slick and shiny skyscrapers of the city's business district. Hardly anything of value had been built here without kickbacks to the Camorra clans – the Families who ran the System – an invisible web of corruption that supported and strangled the socio-economic life of the Campania region.

Valsi gave the guards the finger for a final time. Prison gates creaked shut behind him. Giant bolts slammed. Heavy keys turned. In the safety of the jail the guards cursed back at him. Across the road, locals cheered and clapped as he walked free. He smiled for them and they cheered even louder. Journalists flashed cameras from a polite distance. Valsi's notoriety and good looks sold papers, the Camorra was akin to celebrity. Within hours his new images would become screensavers on the cellphones of thousands of teenage girls across Naples. He was the ultimate bad boy. The rebel whom girls couldn't help but fantasize about. The man even their mothers glanced twice at.

Almost in unison the doors of five waiting Mercedes swung open and a legion of black-suited Camorristi stepped out. It was more than an act of respect, it was a public display of defiance. Heavily armed, their weapons were brazenly on show. No one dared challenge them.

Valsi soaked up the sight. Cameras clicked again. Another smile for the press and his public. Then he coolly walked towards the one car that stood out

– a new chauffeur-driven Mercedes Maybach – the type of limousine that cost more in extras than most Neapolitans earned in a year. Only when he was a metre away did his proud and grateful father-in-law step out and embrace him.

If Don Fredo had known what was on Valsi's mind, he'd have had him shot dead before the prison gates had even shut.

# 2

***Carnegie Hall, New York City***

A howling nor'easter had bowled up the coast and airdropped a thunderous delivery of snow and ice on a New York City that had complacently thought it was in for a mild winter. Rosy-cheeked kids stretched cold hands at falling flakes. Yellow Cab drivers snarled from rolled-down windows. Their cursing breath froze in the early December air as traffic hit gridlock. Winter was going to be savage.

Jack King, his wife Nancy and four-year-old son Zack had arrived at her parents' house in Greenwich Village barely two days before the biggest pre-Christmas snowfall since 1947 had shut down both JFK and Newark airports.

Nancy had closed Casa Strada, her booming hotel and restaurant business in Tuscany, for two months to enable extension work to be done. Straight after New York she'd be in Umbria, buying property to convert into a second hotel. Jack, meanwhile, was mixing business with pleasure. *Pleasure* being the chance to catch up with old friends and family that he and his wife had left behind when they'd emigrated to Italy. *Business* being a well-paid keynote speech in his capacity as a freelance psychological profiler.

He commanded the stage of Carnegie Hall as surely as any entertainer who'd trodden its famous boards. 'Given the inclement weather, I want to leave you with some chilling thoughts,' Jack told the International Serial Offender Conference. 'People are like icebergs; we only ever see ten per cent of them. The really interesting – and sometimes deadly – ninety per cent lies mysteriously hidden in the dark waters of personal secrecy.' He peered out from the stage in the Isaac Stern auditorium. Almost three thousand people, spread five tiers high, peered right back at him. 'Bergs are pieces of ice that have broken off from giant glaciers. Similarly, serial killers are people who have broken off from civilized society. Some bergs are small fry, they're maybe only a metre high. Others are massive and murderous, reaching up to a hundred and sixty-eight metres, about fifty-five storeys high.' The select audience, comprising law enforcement officers, psychologists and psychiatrists, hung on his every word. 'You mustn't let those killer bergs grow. You've got to be alert, every step of your long journey, through each investigation.' Through the stage lights he could see people scribbling, fidgeting and frowning. Some, he guessed, were recalling encounters with their own bergs.

'Serial killers, like those bergs, come in all shapes and sizes, and all of them are potentially lethal. You have to spot them early. Catch them after murder one, while they're still small fry. And remember, to do that, you have to concentrate damned hard on the ten per cent that's on view above the surface.'

Jack took a final look around. His gaze stuck for a second on the front row, where one man, thin and pale, stared up at him with black empty eyes that seemed to be hunting for his attention.

'In your investigations, please pay particular attention to these three things. *Thought, Feeling* and *Action.* Right now, right at this moment, you're all doing the same thing. You have a uniformed, shared *Action.* You're all just sitting and watching. That's your visible ten per cent. Your action is very much in full public view. But *Thought* and *Feeling* are complex masses that make up your private ninety per cent, and that's what we can't see; that's what you're keeping hidden. A few of you may still be *feeling* shocked or sickened by some of the murder-scene slides we looked at earlier. Some of you may have been bored or fascinated by them. Whatever your emotions, you've all kept those *feelings* hidden. Similarly, as I come to a close, I know you are almost all *thinking* different things. I hope many of you are *thinking* that your time at this conference has been worthwhile. I'm sure some of you are worrying about how you're going to get home through the snow tonight, and I'm confident that there'll be several of you who are hoping that your own dark secrets of infidelity, sexual deviation or petty theft from work will never be discovered. Well, don't bank on it, they might well be.'

Embarrassed laughter rippled through the audience. Jack let the tide settle, then finished his speech. 'Remember, *everyone's* an iceberg, and only ten per cent of each of us is on show. You can't spot a killer berg without looking beneath the surface. Search for that hidden ninety per cent. Find it and destroy it, before it destroys us. Thank you for your time. I wish you all a safe journey home and a peaceful and merry Christmas.'

Applause rang out. Jack mouthed several 'thank yous' left and right of stage. As he clapped back and started to head for the exit, his eyes caught again on the thin, pale-faced man staring up at him from the front row. The man with the blank, unblinking gaze. The only person in the auditorium not clapping.

# 3

***Centro città, Napoli***

The black snake of Mercedes slithered north through the rubbish-strewn side streets of Naples.

Bruno Valsi swivelled in the backseat and glanced through the rear windshield. 'We're not heading home?' He tried not to sound suspicious.

Don Fredo, sitting alongside him, smiled reassuringly and lit a Cuban cigar. 'It is your first day of freedom and we are going to honour you. I know you are anxious to be alone with your wife and son, but my daughter and grandchild will have to wait a while longer.'

Valsi relaxed a little, though the incident made him realize his vulnerability. He was unarmed and at anyone's mercy. Five years in jail had left his street instincts rusty. He made a mental note to sharpen up.

'Don Fredo, it is not necessary to *honour* me. To have served you as I did was honour enough.'

The sixty-four-year-old Camorra *Capofamiglia* raised the palm of his right hand, signifying that protest was futile. 'Bruno, you gave up many years of your life to protect me. You broke the case that the police were assembling. All their allegations of false accounting, tax evasion and corruption have been withdrawn. All of them. You made a personal sacrifice for the Family, and tonight it is time for the Family to show their gratitude.'

Valsi bowed his head in respect. 'I am moved by your generosity. I only did what any of your soldiers would have done.' His heart thumped double quick time, a physical reminder that this was a moment he had long pondered over during the endless dark nights in his cell. *Would Don Fredo welcome him back as a hero? Or have him killed because he might emerge as a threat?*

The Don lowered the side window and exhaled a long breath of hot cigar smoke into the chilly air. 'Do you know Positano?'

Valsi shrugged. 'Not well. All my life has been spent in Naples.'

'Then you should. It is very beautiful. Very romantic. You must take my daughter there. Legend has it that the journeying Ulysses was drawn to Positano by the sound of irresistible sirens.'

Valsi smiled. 'The only sirens I've ever heard were from the polizia.'

Don Fredo ignored him. 'There is a hotel near Positano that is special to me. It is where my wedding reception was held, many, many years ago.' He paused and made the sign of the cross in memory of his wife Loretta who'd passed eight years back. 'Tonight it will hold another reception. In fact, it will hold two.

If I recall correctly, you were taken from us the night before your son's first birthday.'

'That's correct.'

The Don nodded. 'Quite. So, tonight, we will start with Enzo's birthday party. One big one to make up for all the ones you missed. I have jugglers, clowns, acrobats; everything needed to light up his life.'

'I'm sure he will love them. That is very kind, very generous of you.'

Don Fredo took another pull on the Havana and looked at his son-in-law through the smoke. 'And then, when Enzo has been put to bed by Gina, we will be joined by members of our *other* Family and we will have *your* reception, a very special "welcome home" party.'

'Thank you, Don Fredo.' Valsi sounded distant as he contemplated for a moment what life would be like again with his wife. He'd forbidden Gina to visit him in prison and knew things were going to be horribly strained as they started over.

The Don had smoked only a fraction of the cigar but he was already finished with it. As a teenager, he'd struggled to break into the tobacco-smuggling racket rooted in the port of Naples. Fifty years later he had the lion's share and could afford to be wasteful. He pushed the Havana through the gap, glided the window shut and turned to Valsi. 'Now, there is something else, Bruno. Something a little more serious that I have to discuss with you.'

Valsi felt a shiver slide down his spine.

# 4

***Carnegie Hall, New York City***

Jack escaped a pack of flesh-pressing professionals who swamped the stage following his speech. He headed out of the auditorium and searched for a washroom.

A hand touched his shoulder. 'Can I please speak with you a minute, Mr King?' The request came from the thin, pale-faced man that Jack had spotted on the front row. Standing, the guy was barely five-five. Jack guessed he was in his late twenties, though the dark shadow of his beard made him look older. His frame was almost skeletal. Eyes black and empty. Teeth so poor you could tell straight away that he wasn't American. And there was something else; a bitter-sweet stink of salty body sweat that made Jack wince. 'Sure. Will it take long? Only, I need to find the men's room.'

The man looked over his shoulder. 'It's around here.' The accent was now recognizably Italian. 'Come, I'll show you.' He headed off so quickly that Jack had little option but to follow.

'Thanks,' said the profiler, as his escort held the

door and then followed him in. Jack used the urinal, all the time conscious of the strange Italian standing by the washbasins, watching and waiting for him.

*Think I've hooked myself some serious creep,* he thought as he washed, then dried his hands beneath a blower.

'You want to talk here? 'Cause I thought maybe outside would be better?' Jack motioned outside, his patience already wearing thin.

The Italian got the message. He opened the washroom door and found a space in the crowded lobby. 'I am Luciano Creed.' He extended his hand.

Jack shook it. It was limp and sweaty. 'Pleased to meet you, Luciano. Now, how can I help?' He fought an impolite urge to wipe his hand on his trousers.

'I work in Naples. I'm a psychology graduate . . .'

A female theatre worker in tight red jeans walked by. 'I am being, how you say . . .' he stammered, 'on attachment to the police there.' He was so distracted by the woman that he dried up completely. His head even swivelled as she walked past.

'*How* can I help?' repeated Jack, irritation now obvious in his voice.

Creed gathered his thoughts. He unzipped an unfashionable blue checked cardigan and pulled out a polythene document case that had been tucked partly down his pants and pressed close to his chest. 'I came all the way to New York to hear your lecture and to show you these.'

Jack grimaced. Work was supposed to end today.

One speech and then a chill-out Christmas at Nancy's mom and dad's. That's what he'd promised her.

'I'm sorry, buddy, you're probably about to show the wrong thing to the wrong guy at the wrong time.'

Creed ignored him. 'Five women, all reported as missing. I think there's more to it than that, more than just missing.' He unzipped the case and produced a map of the Bay of Naples. 'I've mapped seventy different aspects of behaviour in the five cases, used Multidimensional Scalogram Analysis to combine variables and connections in the incidents. I'm sure they are connected.'

Jack was well versed in geographical profiling. He'd studied what the Brits and the Germans had been doing with Dragnet and he'd been particularly impressed by the Canadians and their Criminal Geographic Targeting programmes.

'Look at these papers and tell me what you think.' Creed held them out. Jack tried not to look. Finally, he took them and glanced down at the map.

Red dots marked Casavatore, Santa Lucia, Barra, Soccavo and Ponticelli. At first glance there was no obvious connection. Then, like old-fashioned photographic paper developing in a darkroom tray, Jack saw the links. None of the women's homes were very close together; they probably didn't know each other. The marked sites were spread across the outskirts of Naples, and all were served by fast motorway routes spreading north, south, east and west. Their killer

– if indeed there was one – most likely met them in Naples itself, offered them lifts home. Maybe he picked them up at nightclubs, perhaps he was a cab driver, or even knew them personally and they felt comfortable enough to travel willingly with him. The A56 beltway bisected the map. He guessed that at night you could travel fast down there and likewise along the A1 and A3 that ran off it. Jack looked up at Creed. 'In non-scientific, non-sociolinguistic language, just tell me straight, why do you think these women aren't just walk-aways?'

Creed stepped forward and talked excitedly. His voice, basted in garlic, was hushed and confidential. 'Five women, all within a twenty-kilometre radius of each other; none prostitutes, all respectable; none showing any previous signs that they wanted to leave the neighbourhood.' He paused and saw the interest register in Jack's eyes. He took a slip of paper with their names written on it and pressed it into the profiler's hand. 'Mr King, none of these women, not a single one of them, took any clothing or personal possessions with them when they disappeared.'

Jack's face showed surprise. He didn't want to get sucked in, but he couldn't help seeing red flags. He looked down at the slip of paper and the list of five names. 'What do the cops in Naples say? If your case is that convincing, then I guess they're all over it?'

'Mr King, every day there are so many murders in Naples that there is no time to look for those who are merely missing.'

Jack made one last effort to block him off. He glanced pointedly at his watch. 'I'm sorry, but I have to go. The weather's really bad and I've gotta make a family dinner.'

Creed snatched the mapped papers and returned them to the plastic wallet. His face was red with anger. 'I have come all the way to New York to ask for your help.' He nodded in the direction of Jack's hand and the list of names. 'Those women are dead. I *know* they are dead. And if you turn your back on me now, then more will die and both you and I will feel like we have blood on our hands. Of that I promise you.'

# 5

***Hotel Le Sirenuse, Positano***

Ten thousand euros' worth of fireworks exploded across the Bay of Naples. Italy's hottest boy band sang their own special version of 'Happy Birthday'. Under patio heaters beside a shimmering pool, crowds laughed and cheered as streamers and balloons filled the night sky. But none of this made six-year-old Enzo Valsi crack a smile. Most kids would have thought they were in heaven, but the only moment light came to the youngster's eyes was when a waiter slipped while carrying a tray of white wine. The birthday boy's life, young and tender as it still was, had already been corrupted and bled of its innocence. He lived in a world where the bogeymen were real. So real that it was inevitable that one day they'd turn up, spilling out of cars with smiles on their faces and machine pistols in their hands.

Another volley of fireworks exploded in the pitch-black sky, illuminating the jumble of multicoloured houses that climbed up the hillside of Positano. The boy band signed napkins and made eyes at waitresses. Across the pool, Bruno Valsi ruffled his son's hair and kissed him goodnight. His wife Gina, the boy's nanny and an armed bodyguard the size of a garage took him away. His father didn't even look back as he joined the other men filtering into the brightly lit hotel.

The private dining room of the eighteenth-century palazzo had been electronically swept and declared clean of any listening devices. Armed Camorristi stood at every doorway. More sat in cars on the driveway and approach roads, pistols and sandwiches on their laps.

Inside the elegant dining room, gang boss Fredo Finelli chimed a spoon against a crystal champagne glass. The table had been laid for fourteen people, the most trusted and highly rewarded of the Finelli Family. To Don Fredo's right sat Salvatore 'The Snake' Giacomo, a strongly built, grey-faced man in his late forties. A man who for more than two decades had been Fredo's *Luogotenente*, his fixer and personal bodyguard. No one was quite sure whether his nickname had come from his association with the clan and its distinctive viper tattoo, or because he once chose to slowly and sadistically strangle a victim using a length of metal chain. On Fredo's other flank was his consigliere, his business and legal adviser, Ricardo Mazerelli. The forty-eight-year-old lawyer had been a senior official in the city's mayoral office until he'd lost his job during a rare but successful police clampdown on local authority corruption.

'Gentlemen, please fill your glasses,' commanded

Fredo, 'for tonight there is much toasting and much celebrating to be done.'

Bruno Valsi sat at the opposite end of the table. He studied the faces of his fellow Camorristi, wondering how they felt about his return.

'The first of my toasts,' continued Fredo, 'is to loyalty. My father once told me that friendship is like silver but loyalty is like gold, and the years have proved him right. Gentlemen, your loyalty to our Family and ours to each other is golden; please raise your glasses in honour of our collective loyalty. *Salute!*'

Across the white linen tabletop Valsi joined in the responding chorus and noticed Ricardo Mazerelli's piercing blue eyes looking him over, assessing him for future reference. They both nodded amiably at each other, but neither broke their gaze until Don Fredo spoke again.

'Five years ago, my son-in-law Bruno showed the depth of *his* loyalty. He made a personal sacrifice to protect me and to protect this Family. That sacrifice cost him half a decade of his life. Today, he is returned to us and tonight we recognize that sacrifice and we reward it. Bruno, please come here.' The old man extended his hands. Valsi rose from his seat and walked towards the top of the table. Clapping broke out and became hard and tribal, the crowd timing their slaps to match Valsi's steps, then accelerating the rhythm into a crescendo as he and Finelli warmly embraced each other.

Finelli patted down the applause. 'In recognition

of his loyalty to all of us, I am pleased to announce that Bruno Valsi is now elevated to the rank of *Capo Zona*.'

Again the applause rang out, harder and warmer. But Valsi could see coldness in the eyes of a few of the older soldiers. Being made *Capo Zona* meant you had a specific geographic region to exploit. You could raise money for the Family and take a healthy share for yourself. It also meant being given the chance to assemble your own crew, a sort of family within the Family, and this was what worried the older Camorristi.

Don Fredo was also watching. His expert eyes examined the other *Capi*: Angelico d'Arezzo, Giotto Fiorentino and Ambrogio Rotoletti. They were impassive. Their hearts and minds still needed winning. They were older, *much* older than Valsi, but they would give him a chance, albeit a small one. Finelli broke from his assessment and addressed them all: 'Bruno Valsi will take over the Family's eastern sector, the one richest in what we call our *entertainment* business. These are the responsibilities that were carried out by Pepe Capucci, before his heart attack last month. Bruno has been given the right to assemble his own crew and he has told me he will announce who they are within the next few days. So, my *Uomini d'Onore*, my dear gentlemen of honour, please raise your glasses and toast the successful future of my son-in-law, Bruno Valsi, this Family's youngest ever *Capo Zona*.'

Chairs slid back, the men rose and held their glasses high. '*Salute*, Bruno!'

Don Fredo embraced Valsi again and then clapped him as the toast finished. As the smiling *Capo* returned to his seat, Don Fredo added one final footnote to his speech, something he hadn't previously discussed with Valsi in the drive from Poggioreale jail. 'Bruno, I have another gift for you; something to help you with your new business interests.'

Valsi's smile slid away. In his line of business there was no such thing as a pleasant surprise.

Don Fredo extended his right arm and put his hand on the shoulder of Sal the Snake. 'Salvatore, my personal friend and loyal *Luogotenente*, has generously volunteered to join you in your new business team. He will help you establish yourself. I know his special experience and skills will ensure everything goes according to both our plans.'

# 6

***Carnegie Hall, New York City***

Luciano Creed was still smiling when he slipped into the Starbucks next door to Carnegie Hall. Jack King had grudgingly relented and agreed to see him again. One more meeting – tomorrow, for one hour max – then they'd be done. Well, Creed was certain Jack wouldn't be *done* so quickly. The Italian took a double espresso and sat in the window to drink it. He enjoyed staring out of the big glass pane, watching people flood by.

*Not people, just women. Men were mere flotsam.*

King had been right; you could never judge people from the measly ten per cent that they showed in public. *It's the ninety per cent of ourselves that we keep hidden that is most interesting.*

Creed liked the idea of comparing himself to an iceberg. Cool. Surprising. Powerful. It summed him up perfectly. He ran King's lecture over in his head. It had been worth travelling over for. Well worth meeting the great Jack King. What was it that he had said that had most impressed him?

*Thought, Feeling, Action* – the three things to concentrate on. Creed let the words swim in his head. He was *acting* like most everyone else in Starbucks, just sitting there getting warm, hiding from the bitter blizzard blowing outside. But right now he was *thinking* about how you would abduct and kill a woman.

His eyes settled on a petite blonde who'd stopped in front of the window. She was trying to find a cellphone ringing in her purse. *Nice face. Nice shape. Easy prey.*

Her long blue coat was tightly tailored, hugging her waist and flowing fashionably down to knee-length black boots. He imagined her naked but with the boots still on, his hands around her slender hips as he pressed her against him. *Skin on skin. Skin on leather.*

He was sure she would have a small tight ass and firm legs. An ass he'd want to slowly explore with his tiny bony fingers. Legs he'd love to run his tongue up and down before unzipping those boots.

*Taste. Touch. See. FEEL.*

Creed was already *feeling*, feeling fully aroused. He had to shuffle positions on his window seat to shake off the fantasy.

*Thought, feeling, ACTION.*

ACT like a killer. Wasn't that what he was supposed to do? What all profilers were trained to do? Well, he could certainly do that – better than anyone dare imagine. He had great talents. Skills people still needed to recognize.

Creed wiped coffee from his lips, but his smile still lingered, and so did his own strange thoughts and fantasies.

# 7

***Hotel Le Sirenuse, Positano***

*Damn Don Fredo! May his soul rot in hell!* Bruno Valsi slapped a hand against the wall of the hotel's honeymoon suite.

The old man was cleverer than he'd given him credit for. Elevation to the rank of *Capo Zona* was generous repayment for the loyalty he'd shown. But having Sal the Snake forced upon him – well, that was something else. It was humiliation. It was distrust. It was an insidious way of controlling him. It was damned clever.

'Bruno. Is that you?' called a hopeful voice from the bedroom of the luxury suite. As a teenager, Valsi had taken up with the young and plain-looking Gina Finelli. He'd done it purely as a way of ingratiating himself with her father, perhaps getting a little work, some protection in his life. Then Gina's accidental pregnancy had changed things. The obligatory wedding that followed proved a blessing in disguise and Valsi's ambitions vaulted. But now – to be honest – the Don's daughter was another problem he could well do without. What little feelings he'd had for her had disappeared as surely as her waistline had vanished during his years inside. He couldn't believe how she'd piled on the pounds.

*A woman's disrespect for her body is disrespect for her husband.*

The bedroom lights were out and the room was lit only by the flicker of candlelight. Enzo was sleeping in an adjoining suite with his nanny and a bodyguard ouside the door. Gina was reclining against a mountain of cushions and pillows on the bed. 'Did it go well for you?' Her voice was soft and calm.

'Well enough,' said Valsi coolly. He swept his jacket around the back of a chair, like a matador swirling a cape around a bull, then sat on the edge of the bed to untie his shoelaces. 'Your father, he sees fit to give me my own crew, but then he as good as tells everyone that he has me on a lead and that Salvatore – his trusted, thick-headed Salvatore – will walk me like a young pup that doesn't yet know when to bark or when to sit.'

Gina grimaced. This wasn't what she'd hoped for. For five years she'd faithfully waited for this night, for the very moment her husband would return to her bed. She'd not only personally chosen the suite, but the red and pink silk lingerie she wore had been specially made for her. No woman alive could have tried harder, or been more nervous about creating exactly the right mood for them to restart their marriage.

Valsi stripped off his shirt and dropped it on the

chair. He stood to undo his belt and could feel her eyes trace the sculpted muscles of his shoulders, chest and abdomen. He slid off his pants and folded them, as he'd done every night in his cell. Gina could see that his thighs bulged from endless squats performed in the prison gym.

'Let me help you,' she said, a girlish lightness in her voice as her fingers slid around the waistband of his Calvin's.

'Let me piss.' Valsi brushed her hand away.

He left her stranded on the edge of the bed. Her outstretched arms still held the air where he'd been. Her eyes followed him to the bathroom. He walked like a panther, taut and muscular, dangerous and exotic. She ached to dig her nails into his skin and feel the rush of him inside her. He was back, and she wanted him again. 'Uncle Sal really likes you,' she called, hoping to lift his mood.

'He's not your uncle. Why do you call him that?' Valsi urinated noisily as he spoke.

Gina picked at her fingernails. 'He's like an uncle. He's been around my family since I was a young kid.'

'So has the mailman. Maybe you should call him uncle too.'

Gina tried to stay positive. 'Maybe it is good that my father wants Sal to look out for you. Maybe this is a good thing?'

'And maybe not. Maybe it is a stupid and dangerous thing.' He flushed the toilet. 'Maybe it is the worst thing that could be done to me – and maybe your father knows that.' He stepped into the shower. Enough of the maybes. His wife and her bed could wait. He had no desire to be with her.

At Poggioreale, showers were dangerous places. Places where people got fucked in the ass. Places where people got knifed and killed. Places you were never safe. Now, he stood under the steaming waterfall, trying to relax, trying to clear his mind. One question bothered him more than most: *How long can I stand living with this fat bitch?*

Eyes closed, head tilted back, he turned up the heat but still couldn't soak the smell of Poggioreale from his pores nor banish the jail's demons from his memory. Prison didn't just affect you, it seeped through your skin and twisted itself into your DNA. It altered you forever.

Valsi felt edgy. Permanently edgy. One blink away from an outburst of violence.

He pulled on a white towelling robe and struggled to get used to its softness as he headed to the bedroom.

Could he fuck her? Should he fuck her? Hell, did he even need to bother with this shit?

Gina sensed his dark mood. 'You look tired, baby, come here and let me look after you.' She pulled back the crisp white bed linen so he could slip in beside her.

Valsi could smell the sheets, sharp and fresh with a tang of lemon. Again this unaccustomed luxury rankled. He sat on the edge of the bed. He and his wife were only inches apart, but there may as well have been miles between them. 'We need to talk.' He bowed his head and focused on the strange-smelling sheets. 'I don't want there to be any confusion about how things are between us.'

She reached out to take his hand. Wanted him to know that she understood his awkwardness. Valsi moved it away.

He had made up his mind that he was going to put the record straight, lay down the new rules, right from the start. 'Gina, I think you know I will always be a good father to Enzo, and I will always provide for you and for my son.'

His wife smiled. 'I know you will, Bruno. You are a good man and we both love you so much . . .'

'Let me finish!' His dark eyes grew wide and cold. 'We both know that a marriage is forever. But you have become a fat ugly woman while I have been in prison. So fat that you sicken me. Have you looked at yourself?'

Gina was shocked.

She knew she wasn't the shape she'd been when he was arrested, but surely she didn't deserve this? The rejection stung. She pulled the covers up over her arms, an involuntary sign of retreat that she hated as soon as she realized she'd done it.

'Yes, please do that. Cover yourself up, you disgust me. *Chiattona.*' Valsi contemptuously flicked the rest of the covers up at her.

Gina's temper snapped. No one insulted her like that. 'How dare you fucking speak to me like this!' She jumped out of the bed and stood right up close to him. 'Who the hell do you think –'

Valsi grabbed her face. The fingers of his right hand dug into her skin as he squeezed hard. 'Shut the fuck up and listen. And don't talk back to me.' He pushed her on to the bed.

Gina sprang at him. Inches from his face. Her eyes flashed defiance. 'Don't you *ever* touch me! You bastard! You so much as lay a fucking finger on me and my father will kill you.'

Valsi laughed at her. Laughed and then slapped her with the back of his hand. A hard flat blow across her stomach. It knocked the wind out of her. She doubled up over the bed and wheezed to catch her breath.

'Have you learned nothing from the last time I had to punish you? Are you now stupid as well as fat and ugly?'

Gina's pain was deep and dull. The blow ached all the way through to her spine. She struggled to breathe.

Valsi sat down and leaned over her. 'Your father has just promoted me, made me *Capo Zona*. He's done that because he fears me and respects me. Now is the time for you to be a good daughter and wife and respect him and fear me as well. Because if you cause any problems between us, if you become a *scissionista*, then you could end up getting both yourself and your father killed. You understand what I mean, don't you?'

Gina Valsi fully understood. *Scissione* was the Neapolitan term for a split within a Family, a scissored division, brought about by *scissionisti*. *Faida* was the result – internecine warfare – usually bloody, brutal and relentless.

*You can't be foolish, Gina. Don't create a bloodbath. This outburst is understandable. Bruno is adjusting to life outside prison. Don't make too much of it. Imagine how difficult all this must be for him.*

Bruno could see her thinking things over. He brushed hair from her face and spoke more gently. 'If you are asked, you will tell your father, your family and our friends, that we have the model marriage, and that I am the perfect loving husband and father. And I will tell everyone what a wonderful wife and mother you are. This is a marriage of convenience. Nonetheless it is a marriage, and marriage must be forever. Have I made myself clear?'

Gina Valsi nodded. She didn't want to be beaten again. She'd learned the hard way that Bruno would hurt her in places where the bruises would never show. And there was another thing she knew. For some mad, crazy reason, deep down she still loved him, and probably always would.

# 8

***New York City***

Shiny's restaurant was famous for its truffle-flavoured sturgeon and Kumamoto oyster and quail egg shooters. And those were the main reasons Jack had picked it for his rendezvous with Luciano Creed. His restaurant-owning wife had given him strict instructions to sample as much as possible and come away with both lunch and dinner menus. 'Steal them if you have to!' she joked as she kissed him goodbye. 'And if you can get tips from the chef on how he makes the shooters, then tonight I'll put a smile on your face wider than the Hudson.'

It was smack on one o'clock when Creed walked through the door. He stamped snow on the doormat. Jack – always early for meetings – sipped still water without ice and watched him squint around the room before spotting him.

'Hi, I didn't see you at first,' said Creed enthusiastically, as he settled into a chair and put a plastic folder on the tabletop.

'*Buon giorno, come stai*?' said Jack amiably, noticing Creed wasn't only wearing exactly the same clothes as the day before, but he smelled as though he'd been in them for the past year.

'Aah, *parli Italiano*?'

Jack laughed and raised a defensive hand. 'I understand quite a lot, but I'm not so hot on the chat. All those irregular verbs and rule exceptions, they finally saw off my patience.'

'So you don't help out in your wife's restaurant – in San Quirico, isn't it?'

Jack's warmness faded. It was no secret that the former FBI man and his family had taken on the restaurant, but it certainly wasn't a big or famous hotel, so Creed must have been doing personal research. 'Yes, it is. But how do you know about it?'

'Like I said yesterday, I have come to New York to see you at the conference, and for you to look at this case.' He tapped the plastic document folder in front of him. 'So I do my research on you. I use Google, and I look at your website. And I see lots about you, then I use the MSN and the Yahoo and the Lycos and –'

'I get the picture,' said Jack, growing bored. 'Shall we look at the menu and order?'

'I take the spicy crab as an appetizer and the *robata* – the skewered meat – they recommend that as a house speciality.'

'You Googled this restaurant too?'

'Yes. I didn't want to waste time looking at a menu. You said you would give me one more hour of your time, and now . . .' Creed glanced at his watch, 'we have only fifty-seven minutes left and I want to make every second count.'

Jack motioned to Creed's document file. 'Then let's get going.'

'*Sì*.' The young Italian quickly produced papers and passed them across the table. 'I made copies in the hotel. You have a map of the area in Naples marked with all the places the girls lived. And you can see also the times when they were seen.'

Jack looked at the papers and saw dates for the first time. It made his blood boil. Creed had been holding back on him. 'Luciano, I now understand why your cops in Naples aren't giving you house room. These disappearances are all cold cases. In fact, they're so damn cold they're deep-frozen. They go back, what, five, maybe six years?'

Creed was unflustered. 'Yes, some more than six. From memory, the first disappearance was a little over eight years ago. But why is this important? A murder is still a murder, no matter when it happened.'

Jack was exasperated. 'Can you prove that even one of these women has been killed? Were any homicide investigations launched at the time of any of the disappearances?'

Creed remained unfazed. He shook his head, then dug in his file and produced more paperwork. 'Victimology,' he announced. 'Please listen to me and then tell me *this* is only coincidence.' He handed over another sheet of paper and counted off his points on outstretched fingers: 'All of the women had long hair, lived within twenty kilometres of each other, probably went to the same clubs and bars in Naples.' Creed stopped to make sure Jack was following him. 'As I said to you yesterday, Mr King, none of them packed clothes, none withdrew money, none told any friends they were running away and none seemed to have anything to run away from.'

Jack softened. 'And the police haven't investigated this? I don't believe that.'

'Separately, yes,' said Creed, 'but not as one single case. Not with the thought that one person might have abducted and killed them.'

There were lots of details still missing. 'I imagine many young women run away from Naples. No doubt the prettier ones run furthest and have more chance of staying away. No disrespect, but I'm told Naples is not exactly the nicest place in Italy.'

Creed shrugged. 'In Naples there are no jobs. Many people live in what you call slums. Their homes are likely to be broken into, their cars stolen. And the Camorra kills many people every month. What sane young woman would not want to grow wings and fly from this city?'

'Indeed. That's exactly my point.'

'But, Mr King, this pattern that I have shown you, this does not happen all the time. These kind of women don't just vanish in this way.'

As food came and went Jack gave him room to build his case. 'You mentioned the Camorra – you think the mob is involved in this?'

Creed huffed out a laugh. 'They are involved in everything. They *run* Naples. They control everything from the milk you drink to the rubbish you toss away. Do you know anything about them?'

Jack didn't show his offence. 'It's some time since general crime intel reports fell on my desk but I know about them.'

'Without the Camorra, Naples and Campania would fall apart. They're not just a crime organization, they're a social welfare network. They're the brains and wallet of most businesses. That's why we don't talk about the Camorra, we talk about the System. Where I was brought up, you had more chance of getting a job from the System than from the state. For every member of the Cosa Nostra in Italy there are now half a dozen Camorristi. They are everywhere. Everyone is somehow connected. And they want to be connected. If you're part of the System you don't worry about jobs, paying the rent, feeding your family. You're made for life. The man who killed these women may be in the System, he may not. The point is, he's a killer and he's still free.'

Thoughts clicked into place in Jack's mind, a confusing Rubik's cube of criminal puzzles. *Were the women just missing, or were they dead? Was this so-called System responsible for their disappearances, or just a backdrop to everything? Was Luciano Creed really what he seemed, or maybe something even more unpleasant?*

Jack picked up the bill from a white china plate. As the waitress slotted his credit card into a reader, he noticed Creed openly checking her out, his stare so intense it almost sucked sweat from her skin.

*Hunter's eyes. Cold and hungry, no softness, not even a flicker of warmth.*

The machine buzzed. Jack signed. The waitress smiled and thanked him for the tip. As she walked away, Creed swung round in his chair and drank in the last of her before she disappeared into the kitchen.

'Some women might think that rude,' said Jack, unable to let it pass.

'There is no harm in me looking.' Creed grinned a yellow smile. 'And no shame in it. We all think about fucking; it is our basic instinct to find a mate and breed. I don't believe it is healthy to deny it.'

Jack sipped at his San Pellegrino. 'You sound like a caveman. I think most of us have become a little more advanced than that.'

'As you said in your speech, Mr King, our fantasies and feelings are hidden like icebergs. But you and me, well, we're profilers, aren't we? We *know* what hidden thoughts men have. We divide the world into women worth fucking, and women who we'd rather die than fuck.'

Jack was uncomfortable, but stayed polite. 'I think we're about done here. Can I keep these documents you copied for me?'

Creed leaned over the table. 'I want you to come to Naples with me. I just need two days of your time to show you things.'

'Can't be done, sorry.'

'Five women, Mr King: Luisa Banotti, Patricia Calvi, Donna Rizzi, Gloria Pirandello and Francesca Di Lauro. The last of these, Francesca, I knew her *personally*.'

Jack stood up from the table and picked up the papers. The emphasis on *personally* explained a lot. He could well imagine why anyone who was the object of Creed's attention might want to vanish from his life and never be traced. 'I'll ask one of my friends in the national profiling unit in Rome to look into your findings. If you're right, then they'll help and I'll give my opinions. If you're wrong, then thankfully, you and I will never speak or meet again. Now I'm going. Enjoy the rest of your stay in New York.'

# 9

***Hotel Le Sirenuse, Positano***

Salvatore Giacomo, aka Sal the Snake, and his boss, Fredo 'The Don' Finelli sat by the restaurant window, talking in hushed voices while looking out over the bay of Positano. Bruno Valsi weighed them up as he walked their way.

The old man, dapper in blue Prada pinstripes, raised his hand and summoned a waitress as Valsi sat down. 'I don't have long. I must attend meetings in the city, so let's discuss only what matters.'

'As you wish, Don Fredo.' The newly appointed *Capo Zona* respectfully nodded.

'Operations in our eastern sector will now be run by you. These are mainly the entertainment and the garbage collection and disposal businesses. Sal will take you through the books and show you the revenue splits that will come directly to me and what may be kept by yourself and your crew, when you have picked them.'

Valsi let the offer sink in. Garbage collection and disposal in Naples had long been Camorra controlled and it was profitable. The economics were simple.

The more toxic, the more deadly, the more profitable. But even the bottom-end business of just clearing factory and business trash was also booming. Right now, garbage was piled two metres high on many street corners as the clans in the System battled with councils for control of contracts and areas. 'I know this business is profitable. Good money, no doubt, and I will take care of it. But please tell me of the entertainment interests that we have. I need some glamour as well as sacks of garbage.'

Finelli smiled. 'There are five nightclubs and six restaurants. Pepe's accounts will be sent over to you. There are also several escort businesses, including two new online agencies. Our porn output is small, but we have both film pirating and magazine production.'

'Glamour aplenty.'

'Indeed. There are also some run-down businesses that need attention, particularly camping and holiday-villa sites. They are spread between Naples and Herculaneum, and Herculaneum and Pompeii.'

'My favourite place as a child,' said Valsi. 'I know so much about Pompeii that I could get a job there as a tour guide.'

'Let's hope it doesn't come to that,' the Don smiled. 'It's a good time for you to take over these businesses. Pepe Capucci was going soft. We need to squeeze the margins, generate some more cash. If Pepe hadn't given himself a heart attack I'm sure, in the end, he would have given me one.' The old man put his hand on Valsi's arm. 'But squeeze gently. Do it with charm, Bruno. Our Family are not known as bullies. We provide jobs and incomes in many parts of our district. I want to keep respect and goodwill.'

'I understand,' said Valsi.

Don Fredo dipped into his jacket and produced a small, slim brown envelope. 'There is something in there to get you on your feet again.'

Valsi looked surprised. 'You were very generous when I was in prison. I know Gina is your daughter as well as my wife, but we were more than well provided for.'

'Bruno, please don't insult me by questioning my gift.'

Valsi took the hint. He used a table knife to slit the envelope.

'You will find something more than money in there,' added the old man.

Valsi pulled out four undated cheques totalling €200,000. He quickly did some calculations. On top of the monthly wages of €5,000 that he'd received while in jail, he'd now pocketed a total of half a million for his five years inside.

*Loyalty money. Money to buy you. To curb your ambition.*

'You are most kind,' he said, nodding politely as he folded away the cheques.

'You missed something.' Don Fredo spoke over the cup as he sipped his espresso. 'I think you will find another enclosure in there.'

Valsi tipped the envelope and shook it. A slip of

paper fluttered on to the table. On it was a name that was painfully familiar to him. And an address that he'd been long searching for.

Finelli dabbed his lips with a white linen napkin. 'It can be done quickly. Salvatore has the men ready and waiting for you. I'm sure you'll feel much better when it's over.'

# 10

***I Quartieri Spagnoli, Napoli***

One-week-old Alicia Madonna Galotti screamed at the top of her tiny lungs as new aunt, Alberta, took her from her mother and gently rocked her.

The 38-year-old shushed her sister's baby, then raised the tiny head in the palm of her left hand and lovingly kissed it. Babies smelled so good. Well, at least they did when they'd just been washed and powdered. The child's skin was wonderfully wrinkled. As soft and warm as velvet. She had pale hazelnut eyes, the colour of the teddy bear that Alberta Tortoricci had brought her, along with three irresistible dresses and a gel teething ring. Alberta stroked a fuzz of jet-black hair that would one day cascade through the hands of besotted boys who would pledge their lives to her. Or, at least, that's what Alberta hoped as she sat in her sister's lounge. During the five years she'd been in the witness protection programme, set up for her since Bruno Valsi's conviction, she'd only visited once. Such isolation made her feel like she'd been punished for her bravery. Alberta had been a junior partner in one of the city's oldest accounting and auditing firms. She'd made the near fatal mistake of turning to the police when her bosses had refused to explain, or let her correct, a series of worrying entries in the books of several Finelli businesses. Her diligence had put her at risk and, on one occasion, brought her face-to-face with Valsi. Playing with a cut-throat razor in his hand, he'd told her that there was no point her having a good head for figures if he had to hack it off and feed it to a pen of pigs.

'I think *Mamma* should have you back, my darling.' Alberta surrendered the still crying child to Pia.

'She'll get used to you,' replied her younger sister, glancing at her watch and then immediately putting the child to her left breast.

Alberta flinched as she watched the greedy baby latch itself into position. 'Doesn't that hurt?'

'A little. Sometimes she gets too eager and chews with her gums.'

'Oh, my God! It's too painful to even think about.' Alberta rubbed her own breast as though she could physically feel the pain. 'I think I'll go for a cigarette.'

Pia thought of saying something but checked herself. She'd only managed to kick the habit after she'd found out she was pregnant, so she knew she didn't really have the right to preach. She smiled dotingly at her baby as her sister grabbed her coat and headed outside.

The street was short and filled with cheap apartments that wouldn't argue at being called slums. The Spanish Quarter had beautiful historic homes but they were not in the area where Pia lived. The engine of an unmarked police Fiat idled not far from the front door, two cops in the front, as always, drinking coffee, eating junk and chain-smoking. For once they were early. It made a change. She lit up and smiled at them; the driver raised a hand in acknowledgement, blue-grey smoke clouding his face.

*Alicia Madonna was beautiful.* If Alberta had a child, she wanted it to be exactly like her niece. Though, given the state of her life, she knew there was little chance of her meeting someone and settling down.

The driver's door of the Fiat opened and a detective waved her over. Dangling from his right hand was a police radio, pulled tight on a coil of black curly wire attached to the dashboard. Alberta saw a dozen cops a week, and they all had that same edgy, scruffy look to them. She'd liked the one who had driven her over from Assisi, where she'd been relocated after the Valsi trial. His name was Dario and he'd been as big as a house and smelled of pine and fruit. This new one looked similar but had an even nicer smile and wore old-fashioned Ray-Ban Aviator sunglasses. It made him look like a tall Tom Cruise from his *Top Gun* days.

'*Buon giorno, mi chiamo Satriano, Detective Paolo Satriano.* My *Capitano* needs to talk to you.' He shrugged his shoulders. 'We have a little problem with your transport.'

'What do I do?' asked Alberta, staring at the police radio he put in her hand.

'You press here. Keep it pressed while you talk.' He created a burst of static as he showed her how to click a button on the side. 'Please sit in the vehicle, so you can hear through the speaker.'

Alberta slid into the driver's seat, noticing the cop's eyes roam over her legs as she adjusted her skirt and squeezed in.

He smiled politely and closed the door. Not as handsome as the last cop she'd seen, but that smile already had her hooked.

'*Pronto?*' she said, holding down the button in the way he'd shown her.

It didn't work.

The radio was a fake.

So too was the policeman.

The driver leaned against the car door and drew on his cigarette. His big frame blocked any view from outside. In the same movement, a hand snaked from the rear seat and clamped across Alberta's mouth. Simultaneously, the other man in the passenger seat slid out a gun, clicked off the safety and pushed it into her stomach.

# 11

***Greenwich Village, New York City***

'No more Dr Seuss, not tonight,' insisted Nancy King, doing her best to look serious as Zack begged for another bedtime story.

She kissed him on the tip of his nose, then swung her legs off his bed in the spare room at his grandparents' home.

'Sleep well, baby, and I'll read you some more tomorrow.'

'Night, Mommy! I love you.'

'Love you too, honey.' Nancy blew a kiss from her hand as she reached the doorway but didn't turn out the light. Zack would no longer sleep in the dark. Not since his nightmares about Daddy's work and the Black River Killer.

Downstairs, her father Harry sliced a slab of beef while her mom added roast potatoes and vegetables to willow-patterned plates that Nancy had been eating off since she was Zack's age.

'You have any mustard?' Jack was rummaging among the dishes, glasses and bottles that filled their old mahogany dining table.

'French and English. Behind the gravy,' said his mother-in-law.

Nancy joined them. 'That little guy doesn't look too sleepy. We might have a visit in a few minutes.'

As they finally tucked into the food, Nancy and her folks spoon-fed nostalgia to each other and Jack's thoughts slipped to Luciano Creed.

*Was Creed a bungling amateur profiler who'd wrongly mistaken runaway women for murder victims? Was he the jilted lover – or, more probably, the unwanted admirer – of Francesca Di Lauro – and was he obsessed with finding her? Or was he something even worse – was he right? Were there a number of unsolved disappearances that the police in Naples for some reason – scarce resources, lack of interest – hadn't properly investigated?*

'Could you pass me the wine, honey?' Nancy pointed to a bottle of Brunello that had come from a vineyard less than ten kilometres from their home in Tuscany.

A further thought distracted Jack. He remembered working a case in Queens – a hospital porter had called in at a precinct house with a tip-off on where to find a murdered youth. Said he'd overheard two out-of-state youths talking about a murder while they ate in a burger bar. Cops had followed up and dug a thirty-year-old black man from beneath steel in an old warehouse. Eventually, the white porter turned out to be the killer. And the dead guy hadn't been his first black victim. He'd contacted the cops with the bogus story of the youths because he'd killed three times before and '*wasn't getting the recognition he'd deserved*'. The world was full of weirdoes, and those who killed for fame sometimes went as far as injecting themselves into the heart of the inquiry.

Nancy tried again. This time waggling a wine glass in her fingers. 'Could you *please* pass me the wine, honey?'

'What? Yeah, sure.' Jack grabbed the bottle and poured its rich red liquid into the sparkling glass. 'Sorry.'

His wife smiled, but he was already far away again. Tomorrow morning he'd go and see Creed. There were questions he just couldn't leave unanswered.

# 12

## *Napoli del nord*

Scampia's hollow-eyed skyscrapers cast slim shadows over the old Fiat gliding through town. Alberta Tortoricci took in the grim vista as she headed into her darkest nightmare. By the time the real cops had arrived to escort her back to her home in Assisi the fake ones had pulled into the grounds of one of the area's many disused factories. The huge building was derelict and bare of branded signage. Buckled and broken chain-link fencing ran all around it. Dogs sniffed garbage and lifted their heads as they passed.

Alberta's hands had been tied and her mouth gagged. But they'd made no attempt to blindfold her. There was no need. She wasn't going to live to identify them.

They dragged her down the side of the old factory. Her feet slipped on sodden cardboard boxes that had rotted in the rain. A metal door jerked back in rusted spasms and they pushed Alberta into the cold, damp twilight of the factory. Grey light drizzled through dozens of small windows high off the ground. Across in the corner of the room, in soft silhouette, she saw a man sitting on a slatted fold-up chair.

'*Buon giorno, Alberta,*' said a voice that leached the blood from her heart.

She recognized it as Bruno Valsi's.

'Please, sit down. I've been waiting. Waiting five years for you.'

Valsi stood up and stepped away as his men forced Alberta down on to the chair. Unseen fingers refastened her hands around the back of it and then bound her feet to its front legs.

'I'm sorry to be so impolite, but you've got to be tied. Otherwise, the sheer amount of pain that I'm going to inflict upon you will throw you to the ground.' Valsi snapped his fingers, summoning one of the two henchmen who'd brought her.

Alberta never saw the hammer in his hand.

Without any backswing he crashed its flat metal head into her gums and teeth.

The shock was instant. A dull crack. An explosion of pain in her skull.

Pieces of broken teeth jammed at the back of her mouth. She had to swallow jagged bone in order to breathe. Other teeth were hideously bent back at their roots. Blood and saliva drooled down her chest.

'*Cantante!*' spat Valsi. His eyes were on fire.

Alberta knew what was going to happen next. The police had warned her about it. She'd seen it in her nightmares. The hand of the henchman reappeared. His fingers fumbled in her mouth. And then, she felt the acidic tang of metal on her tongue. Pliers. She could see the end of them as he squeezed tight and pulled the tongue through her smashed teeth. Punishment for the *cantanti,* those who *sang* to the authorities, was always the same. They had their tongues cut out. Then, almost as absolution for the sin of speaking to the police, the sign of the cross was razored across their lips.

The pain was unbearable. Her vision fogged as a switchblade clicked open and the henchman sawed off as much of the pink muscle as he could.

'*Vaffanculo!*' he swore as Alberta's blood spurted on to him. He slashed a crucifix across her skin, backed away and deposited the severed tongue in a handkerchief held for him in the leather-gloved palm of Bruno Valsi. Blood dripped and balled up on the dusty factory floor.

Valsi studied his new pink present, then folded the white cotton gently around it. '*Va bene*,' he said unemotionally. 'Sal, bring me her present.'

The grey man at his side smiled and disappeared into the shadows.

'You like jewellery, don't you, Alberta?' Valsi grinned as he circled her bloodied face. 'Of course you do. All girls like jewellery. Well, you'll *die* for this piece – literally – it was designed just for you.'

Alberta Tortoricci couldn't see what they were

doing. The room was too dark and her eyes were blinded by tears and pain.

'It's a special designer necklace.' Valsi hovered over her.

She was more frightened now than she'd ever been in her life. But she was determined not to show it. Alberta shut her eyes and tried to distract herself from what was happening. She conjured up images of her first day at school.

*Blue dress, white top, hair in pigtails, new brown shoes.*

'It's a necklace; our Frankenstein necklace.' He looped a thick steel collar around her neck. Wire flexes trailed from both sides.

*Her first kiss – Roberto Bassetti, thirteen years old – his mouth tasted of liquorice.*

'This jewellery is unique, Alberta, rather like the testimony you gave in court, you being the only witness against me.'

Valsi fell silent as he concentrated on fastening two bolts at either side of what were semi-circular steel strips that overlapped each other and had been punched with holes to accommodate the bolts.

*First boyfriend – Armando Rossi, seventeen – they rode his Lambretta. She'd leaned her face against his back and wrapped her arms around his waist.*

'Beautiful. *Bellissimo.* It fits perfectly. You'll look a dream. Well, my dream at least. You see, five years is a hell of a long time to think about revenge. Because that's what this is about, Alberta, revenge – pure and simple . . .'

*First true love – Bernardo Santo – a man ten years older than her, a man who'd always smelled of forests, a man she should have married and had children with.*

'Sockets, please.'

Wires were handed to two goons. Valsi squatted, so that he was at Alberta's eye level.

'I hope the voltage is good. We've rewired it especially for you. Too little and the current will cook slowly through your neck until your head drops off. Too much and it may explode. Pop! Neither is a nice way to die.'

*Die!*

Alberta's powers to distract herself were gone now. There was no past to dip into.

No more *firsts* to go through.

Only *lasts*.

The last moments of her life.

Valsi smiled in mock sympathy and touched her cheek. 'Hey, enough of these sad looks! You know you have to die, Alberta. I must show the polizia what happens when they exploit people like you. All *informatori* must know what awaits them if they ever try to do the same.'

Valsi paused and watched for fear on her face. He was saddened that there was none. Brave bitch. Brave, *arrogant* bitch.

'Sal, throw the switch!'

The air buzzed and hummed.

Alberta's body went into spasm. Her eyes bulged and her head sagged as her nerves became paralysed.

'Jesus, what a stink!' Valsi wafted a hand playfully in front of his face. The room filled with the smell of burning flesh. The henchmen coughed and laughed. Coarse, meaty sounds like they were choking on beer during a good joke. Alberta was dribbling blood.

But she still wasn't dead. Even as her internal organs baked from the electric charge, life still flickered within her.

Valsi squatted on his heels again. Stared into her eyes. 'Not long now, you're frying nicely.'

Alberta's skin was crimson.

Her flesh was starting to split.

Suddenly, a gush of blood and boiling stomach contents bubbled from her mouth.

One of the goons gagged.

Sal the Snake had left the electric box and stood beside Valsi. He shook his head and smiled. What a sight.

'She's dead,' said Valsi. 'Don't waste any more juice on the bitch. Sal, get her body out of here and destroy what's left of it. Set fire to it so the cops don't find any of our traces, then leave it where it'll be found within the next few days.'

# 13

***New York City***

Jack seldom slept past six, so it was no chore to cross town and be at Creed's hotel before seven. He stamped snow on a large rubber mat opposite a cheap reception desk staffed by a plump woman in her forties. 'I'm looking for a guest of yours – Luciano Creed. Could you call his room for me?'

Brenda Libowicz had worked receptions in fifteen different hotels in New York City and she could smell *cop* all over her early morning visitor. 'NYPD?'

Jack smiled in due appreciation of her observational skills. 'Ex-FBI. Is it that obvious?'

'That it is,' Brenda smiled warmly. 'Only cops and feds get to the point that quickly. *Normal* people usually manage a hello, a *please* or even a remark about how cold it is.'

'*Normal* people?' laughed Jack.

'No offence. You know what I mean.'

'None taken.' He nodded at her computer. 'Any chance of ringing my Mr Creed?'

'None,' she said, flatly. 'He left town last night. We called him a cab for the airport.'

'You remember when?'

'Let's see. I think it would be about eight. Yep, that's right. JFK was still shut but Newark had reopened a runway around five.'

Jack frowned. 'Was he due to check out so soon?'

Brenda finally needed the computer. She typed an entry and pulled up his record. 'No, he was down originally for another two days. Only told us yesterday that he was leaving early.'

'Can I see his bill, please?' He stressed the *please.*

She pulled a printout from a tray and handed it over. Jack made a note of the home address, though he doubted it was real. There was no CAP– *Codice di Avviamento Postale* – the Italian equivalent of the postcode, and the province was Ogliona, which he was certain didn't exist. 'He pay cash or card?'

'Cash. Big wad of Uncle Sams.'

Jack read the rest of the bill. 'Media services. What's that, Internet?'

She shook her head. 'No. It's a nice way of billing a fella for the porn channels.'

'You know what he watched?'

'Sure. He was here four days and he bought the twenty-four-hour non-stop adult service. Watched the lot.'

Jack raised an eyebrow and passed the bill back.

'He was a real sleazeball. Gave me the shivers. He done something?'

'Not sure.' Jack glanced at the clock behind her head. 'I guess his room's not been cleaned?'

She laughed. 'You guessed right. Maid don't start til ten. You want to look, I suppose.'

'You mind?'

'Not at all.' Brenda bobbed beneath the counter and eventually produced the key card to Creed's room. 'Second floor. Number two-twelve. Stairs right behind you and to the left.'

'Thanks. I appreciate this.'

'Enough to buy me coffee sometime?'

Jack took the key, but not the bait. 'Would love to, but my wife wouldn't approve. And anyway, I really don't know if I would be safe with someone who reads people as well as you do.' He winked and headed for the stairs.

'Safe?' she shouted. 'Oh, believe me, mister, *safe* is the last thing you'd be!'

He could still hear her laughing when he reached the landing of the second floor and let himself into Creed's old room. It was small and stank of an unflushed toilet, old carpets and no ventilation. In the tiny en-suite bathroom he picked up a plastic waste bin. He collected another from near a big old-fashioned boxy TV that virtually rested on the edge of a sagging single bed. He pulled off a dirty duvet and emptied the bins on to the grey-white base sheet.

There were sweet wrappers, empty Coke and beer cans, a half-empty plastic bottle of hotel body lotion, numerous tissues that looked stiff from semen, several pages from magazines that had been ripped out and then torn into small pieces. Some hotel paper that had been written or drawn on had also been torn up into pieces no bigger than a postage stamp. *Anything ripped this small had to be of significance.*

Jack was desperate to examine the pieces of paper and magazine but had no evidence gloves. He returned to the bathroom and found what he was looking for – a shower cap. He opened it up, put his hands inside and used it like clumsy mittens.

Working through the cap, it took him almost an hour to assemble just one largish section of the hotel paper and a single page of the magazine. But what he saw was enough to convince him that Luciano Creed could indeed be everything he feared.

By the time he left the hotel, salt and grit had chewed like rats through the city's blanket of white snow. The sun was high and dazzlingly bright as traffic crawled back to normal – or as normal as New York City ever gets.

Jack holed up for a while in a nearby deli. Black coffee and a skinny blueberry muffin quelled his hunger and fed his thoughts.

'You want a refill?' The question came from a surly sumo wrestler masquerading as a waitress.

'Thanks.' Jack proffered his mug.

She walked away and he speed-dialled the cellphone of Massimo Albonetti, *Direttore* of Italy's Violent Crime Analysis Unit.

'*Pronto, parla Albonetti,*' said a deep, Roman voice. He sounded distracted, maybe even annoyed at being interrupted.

'*Ciao, Direttore. Come stai?*'

There was a brief pause, then an eruption of laughter. 'Jack, my friend, you speak little Italian and the few words you have learned, you murder with your horrible American tongue. How are you?'

'*Vaffanculo*, buddy. I'm fine.'

More Italian laughter. 'Aah, the bad words you *can* pronounce properly. Fuck you too! You are like a small boy, using such language. Still, it is good to hear you.'

'Thanks, but you might not think so in a minute. I'm in New York, been speaking at a crime seminar, and came across someone from your neck of the woods. Guy called Creed, Luciano Creed.'

Albonetti was on his way into a community meeting. He'd been forced by his boss to address a holy order of brothers about the changing face of criminality in modern Italy. 'This name, it rings no bells.'

'Didn't expect it to. He's from Naples. Says he's a psychologist attached to the carabinieri. Been digging into some Missing Persons files and reckons he's detected a series of murders.'

'Murders in Naples?' Massimo faked surprise as he scribbled Creed's name on the front of a stack of files he was carrying. 'Now, that's a real shock.'

'Yeah. I know they have more killings than Iraq. The local force apparently has them down as MPs but Creed's done some low-level profiling on them and it all comes up looking like a serial murder file.'

'You think so?' Massimo sounded more serious now.

He nodded politely at one of the brothers entering the conference room for the planned meeting.

'It's more a *perhaps* at this stage. But I've seen enough to make me think there's a good chance we're not just looking at runaways. Can I give you some names?'

'Sure, shoot.'

Jack peered at the notepaper that Creed had forced on him. 'Luisa Banotti, Patricia Calvi, Donna Rizzi, Gloria Pirandello and Francesca Di Lauro.'

Massimo read them back to make sure there were no mistakes.

'Do you think you could have a little dig around and check out Creed as well?'

Massimo spelled out his name. 'C-R-E-E-D, and first name, Luciano?'

'You got it.'

'Okay. I am this second starting a meeting – with a bunch of priests, believe it or not – but I'll start digging around within the next hour or so.'

'Thanks. I've got a bad feeling about this guy. He's a bit of a weirdo and he claims to have been *personally* involved with the last girl to have gone missing.'

Massimo entered the room with his hand over the phone and apologized to his distinguished audience. '*Mi dispiace. Un momento per favore.*' The twelve brothers seemed to understand – the officer was a busy man – they would wait patiently.

Massimo spoke to Jack again. 'You'd have him as a suspect? He claims he's working with the police, but you think he might be the offender?'

'That's too big a stretch. But he makes me uncomfortable. I found some pornography and also personal sketches he'd made. He'd ripped them up and left the pieces in the bin in his hotel room. The photographs were hard-core sadism, much edgier than your usual hand-party stuff. They showed a naked woman, cuffed to a metal pole, being whipped and branded with hot irons.'

'*Mannaggia!*' The Italian's emotions made him forget the company he was in. 'God Almighty, why do people find such things a turn-on? Whatever happened to a stolen kiss, a hand on the knee and the sweet hope that it might lead to a little more?'

'Not for this guy, Mass. The sketches he'd made were of mutilated genitalia – multiple, obsessive drawings, too far out even for the Guggenheim.'

'*Porca Madonna!*' exploded Massimo.

The twelve holy brothers looked sharply at him and crossed themselves.

Massimo cupped the phone and whispered to Jack, 'I'll get back to you. I think I'm going to have to say an act of contrition before I start this meeting.'

# 14

***Centro città, Napoli***

Nine-year-old Mario Gaggioli mumbled the instructions as he ran. This was an *errand* that he knew he mustn't get wrong. His long black hair trailed from a specially customized woollen rapper's hat. His wiry body zigzagged fearlessly between the honking mopeds, cars and trams that fought for space down Naples' potholed streets. He was Ronaldinho, side-stepping a sliding tackle. He was Henry, ready to sell a dummy and unleash a fireball from his foot. Above him, wet washing flapped from lines strewn from one balcony to another. Down at his level, old people swore as he bumped and barged his way past them. His foot flashed at a stone and thundered it into the path of traffic. *Henry scores!*

True to his word, Mario didn't stop running until he reached his given destination. His body zinged with excitement. It was like Ronaldinho taking a penalty in the last minute of extra time. Now was the moment. The time to step up – to be brave – to deliver!

Pounding towards the front steps he remembered the drill. He flipped the woollen hat round so it concealed his face but still allowed him to see through a slit he'd cut in it.

*Ronaldinho places the ball and takes three steps back.*

Inside the building, he spotted his target.

*The Brazilian begins his run.*

Behind the reception desk, a man in uniform looked up from paperwork he was helping a pensioner complete.

'*La bagascia è morta!*' shouted Mario. He threw the small soft parcel he'd been given into the chest of the carabinieri receptionist and bolted for the door.

*Ronaldinho scores! It's all over!*

Mario had no idea why he'd been told to shout *the bitch is dead*, and he had no clue as to what was in the handkerchief. The carabinieri officer picked it up from the floor and opened it.

He wasn't sure what sickened him more, the sight of a severed tongue or the sure-fire fact that another young child's soul had already been lost to the Camorra.

# 15

***Capo di Posillipo, La Baia di Napoli***

The fortified home of the Finelli family, known to the carabinieri as the Viper's Nest, was in a rocky, wooded height at the western end of the Bay of Naples.

The spacious, sprawling structure was the product of two generations of Camorra activity. Fredo's father Luigi had been a young Neapolitan recruit to Vito Genovese's end-of-war smuggling activities. After *helping* re-route thousands of tons of army grain to the black market that was run from Nola, in the east of Naples, he went on to serve the Families of Lucky Luciano, set up after the mobster arrived in 1946. Luciano lived in the region until 1962 and by then Luigi Finelli had risen through the ranks and was running his own Camorra clan.

Despite bitter differences between father and son in later life, Luigi's portrait still hung above the table where three generations of the family ate dinner on a giant oak table. Many years earlier, Fredo had paid a local sculptor to fell the tree, slice it in two, treat the timber and then hand carve the bespoke piece that he hoped would be handed down from generation to generation.

Fredo's two younger brothers, Dominico and Marco, had come tonight with their wives, their sons and daughters and grandchildren. In all, the great tree had just finished hosting eighteen people, ranging in age from four to sixty-four.

There was no formality to what happened after dinner. Everyone went their own way. The children – mostly the same age – raced each other round the corridors until they were red-faced. Meanwhile, Gina Valsi and the rest of the adults took coffee and desserts in a giant L-shaped garden room that opened into a pool house where the kids would scream and splash once their dinners had settled.

Her husband and her father didn't join them. There was business to discuss. Don Fredo apologized and begged their understanding.

The *Capofamiglia* put his arm around his son-in-law's shoulders and guided him to his study. The den was large but warm and had a carefully crafted cosiness. The walls and floors were panelled in cherry wood, with floor-to-ceiling shelving filled with antique books on three sides and a custom-built desk and drawer area occupying the other wall. Three green antique leather settees formed a horseshoe around a giant cherry-wood table scattered with legal documents and company accounts. The centrepiece was a silver ashtray. Don Fredo lit a Toscana cigar. 'Please, sit,' he said, waving a hand at the settees. He heard Valsi settle noisily into the leather as he produced a bottle of Vecchio brandy and two crystal glasses.

'Salvatore tells me you managed to renew your acquaintance with our old friend from Assisi?' He chose the couch across the table and poured generous measures.

Valsi took a glass. 'Yes, it was good to catch up, but we won't be seeing each other again.'

They clinked crystal.

Don Fredo gently swirled the amber liquid, smelled it and took a warming sip. 'We mustn't be gone too long. It is impolite with family in the house. But I want to share a concern with you, and it is best we talk now before it grows into a problem between us.'

Valsi made a point of sitting upright. He wanted the Don to know he had his full attention.

'When you were in prison, you formed some friendships with people who, now you are free again, it would not be appropriate for you to continue having relationships with.'

The young *Capo* put down his brandy. 'When I went to jail, you told me that survival in Poggioreale would be all about relationships. You were right. Many people were good to me. I feel it would be wrong now to forget them.'

'I know. But despite how you feel, forget them you must.'

Valsi tried not to show his annoyance. 'But please, tell me, who exactly are you suggesting I turn my back on?'

Don Fredo looked directly into his son-in-law's eyes. 'It would not, for example, be good for you to associate, or be linked in any way, with the likes of Alberto Donatello or Romano Ivetta.'

Valsi stared back. The Don was well informed. These were men he wanted. Soldiers to form the backbone of his crew. 'They are good men. They would join our Family if we asked. And if we do not ask, then they will join someone else's Family and that will be our loss.'

'They are not good men, Bruno, and they are no loss!' The old man's eyes blazed with anger. 'They are heroin dealers who got caught, so they are not even good at that.'

'They were not caught. They were betrayed,' insisted Valsi, 'by greedy cops who wanted more than their fair share in kickbacks.'

Don Fredo sighed wearily. 'All cops are greedy. It has been that way since the first of them pinned on a badge. These friends of yours are stupid if they do not understand these things and make provision. But that is not my main point.'

'I don't understand.'

'Bruno, heroin and coke are not our things. Narcotics we leave to the Cicerone Family. They, in turn, leave the garment business to us. They do not tender against us when we produce for the big fashion houses and that gives us a rich advantage. Contrary to what the press say, we do cooperate with other Families and we do respect each other.'

Valsi took a hit of brandy to calm himself. 'Do you really believe that Cicerone does not supply counterfeit clothing to the houses in Milano? You think he does not own designer warehouses and outlets in Germany stacked with clothes made under your nose? With all due respect, his Family is worse than the cops who betrayed Alberto and Romano.'

Sal had warned him that Valsi was bold. Nevertheless, the young man was even more stubborn than Don Fredo had bargained for. 'The matter is closed.' He picked up his cigar and for a second or so had to work hard at bringing it back to life. Finally he inhaled and slowly blew out a long thin cloud. 'There is another issue. You and my daughter, everything between you is all right?'

'Of course, why do you ask?' Valsi was angered by the question.

The old man's eyes weighed his answer. He could see the unrest. 'You seemed tense at dinner. I know it must be difficult for you both after being apart for so long, but I don't like what I am seeing. It does not look like Romeo and Juliet to me. You young lovers should be overjoyed to be together again.'

Valsi feigned embarrassment. 'You are right, it is not yet easy.'

'We should go back to the others.' Don Fredo collected the cigar and creaked himself out of the leather. They both walked together but, as Valsi stepped towards the door to open it, the old man put his hand on his shoulder again and this time squeezed tightly. 'We've spoken tonight of important things, but nothing in the world is more important to me than my daughter's happiness. Make her joyous and you will be very richly rewarded. Break her heart and I will have you buried so deep no one will find you for centuries.'

# 16

***Sunset View, South Brooklyn, New York City***

On the way back to Nancy's parents' house, Jack swung by the home of his ex-FBI partner Howie Baumguard. An expensive divorce and an expansive booze problem had moved him from West Village, SoHo, to rented-room squalor. Jack climbed the garbage-strewn steps outside his friend's building, and made his way upstairs to a third floor that had never seen a working light bulb.

He had to bang four times before Howie eventually slid the bolts and opened the paint-peeling door on a chain thick enough to tow a truck.

'Hang on, I've got it,' he said, squinting at Jack in the hallway.

A warm, sour smell of beer and fried food hung in the air. The tiny room was so untidy it looked as if it had just been burgled.

'Great to see ya, man. Great to see ya.' Howie bear-hugged his former partner until he heard him gasp for air.

Jack slapped his buddy's back, then stepped away

a pace. 'Wish I could say the same about you. My friend, you look like a bag of shit.'

'Man, ain't you the charmer!' Howie scratched the start of a bald spot appearing in his nest of unwashed hair. 'Sit yourself down, Mr Smoothtongue, I'll fix some coffee.'

Jack watched him waddle away. Howie had just hauled himself out of the sack and was dressed in blue boxers and an old grey T that only half covered his paunch. He'd never been one to watch his weight but it looked as though recently he hadn't even given it a passing glance.

'I ain't got milk. Black okay?' Howie's head was inside a fridge that smelled as though something old had crawled in there and died.

'Just fine. You want some help?'

'Yeah, sure do. I want that you shoot my ex-wife, so I don't pay alimony. I want that you get me a new job paying half a mill a year. Oh shit, I nearly forgot. I want that Lindsay Lohan blows me twice a day and tidies up a little before she goes.'

'That all?' said Jack, moving dirty dishes and crumpled cans from around the foot of the couch. 'Should be a breeze.'

Howie eventually reappeared, his giant knuckles wrapped around the handles of two mugs of black coffee. 'Man, I'd diet for Lindsay. Hell, I'd go to a fat farm and have a blubber-suck for her. You know, where they stick one of those friggin' hosepipes in your gut and – voom! – in a schlurp they've siphoned off forty pounds. Yep, for Lindsay, I'd lose the weight!'

Howie handed over the coffee and slumped in a chair. 'Anyway, how have you been keeping? How's your catcher's mitt?'

Jack flexed the fingers of his left hand. It had been badly cut during his final encounter with the Black River Killer. 'It's getting there. Seems some nerve got damaged.' Jack fell silent for a moment. Memories of BRK flooded back – the nightmares that had haunted him for years, the victims he'd been unable to save and the personal danger that BRK had exposed him and his family to. 'Doc says I probably won't ever have a hundred per cent feeling back but, with physio, I think I'm gonna get close.'

'At least it's not your right hand,' said Howie, a twinkle of mischief in his eyes.

'Yeah, thank God for small mercies. So, exactly what happened at the Bureau? I can't believe you quit.'

Howie shrugged his huge shoulders in a way that made him shrink. He looked like a jilted teenager who didn't want to talk about it. 'I was a mess, man. It was jump or be pushed, and I didn't want the Push Monkey on my friggin' back.'

Jack tried the coffee. Cheap instant. Too hot to drink. Too bad to swallow.

'You should have claimed some lost time, taken a spell of compassionate. I'm sure they'd have understood that you needed a little breathing space.'

'Maybe,' said Howie, sounding defeatist. 'Truth is, I can't even walk straight, let alone think straight. I'm best outta there. I couldn't bear the thought of fucking up in the field.'

Jack put down the coffee. He could see his friend had been more depressed by the divorce than he'd realized. 'You've got to kick the booze, Howie. You know that, don't you?'

'Booze helps me snooze,' he joked. 'Without it I just lie awake at nights and drive myself friggin' crazy.' Howie put his hands behind his head and stretched his neck, trying to ease the tension that seemed to be always with him. 'Every minute of the goddamn day I can see Carrie getting balled by this punk at the gym that she went to. Christ alive! I was so fuckin' stupid not to realize she was playing away.'

Jack tried to get him focused. 'What exactly is bugging you? Is it that you found your wife cheating? That you discovered she wanted to be with some other guy? Or just that you got divorced?'

'All that and then some.' Howie scratched at his head again and then checked his fingers to see if he'd lost more hair. 'You know, I think what pisses me most is that I still love her. Even now, I'd forgive her and try again, but she don't want none of it.'

Jack tried to counsel the depression out of him but it was deep-seated, like a bruise that was yet to show its colour. It was going to take time to work through. He was still hurting for his friend as he said goodbye and caught a cab back. He'd promised they'd do lunch soon and he'd help him get sorted.

A couple of hours later, back at Nancy's parents' place, Jack was still thinking about Howie as he took a call from Massimo Albonetti. The *Direttore* cut to the chase. 'Jack, I called the Criminal Investigations Unit in Naples. Turns out they know your Luciano Creed, and he is a strange young man.'

'That I knew.'

'Creed is late twenties, single, came to them on secondment from the university, with good recommendations. A top graduate in criminal psychology and on paper the perfect recruit to the Crime Pattern Analysis and Research Department. But that's where the good stuff stops.'

'I figured it might.'

'That's what makes you such a good profiler, Jack,' joked Massimo. 'A month ago they terminated Creed's contract and escorted him off the premises. He shouldn't even have been at that conference, let alone claim that he was there on behalf of either the university or the police.'

'They give a reason why they let him go?'

'Sexual harassment. No specific incident, but several female admin staff went to Personnel and complained about him.'

'For doing what?'

'Pestering them. Asking them out.'

'Since when was *that* a crime in Italy?'

Massimo laughed. 'Since it was done by ugly, creepy

guys who smelled like sewage. Women complained of his lack of personal hygiene and said they felt he was mentally undressing them. Even when they told him to get lost, he kept coming back.'

'*Anyone* have a *good* word for him?'

'From what I learned, I don't think his *Mamma* would even have a good word for him. Given your comments, Jack, my colleagues in Naples would very much like to meet Creed. And they'd also like to talk to you about him. Do you know where he is?'

A bad feeling stirred inside the profiler. 'He's disappeared, Massimo. Hotel receptionist said he headed out to Newark just after it reopened. Maybe he's back in Naples, maybe he's on the other side of the world.'

Disappeared. The word resonated with both of them. Disappeared, just like the women had.

Just like killers do.

# TWO
# Three days later

# 17

***Parco Nazionale del Vesuvio***

Chief of Homicide *Capitano* Sylvia Carmela Tomms stood outside the crime scene in the damp clearing of parkland and blew cigarette smoke high into the evening air.

A local man walking his dog had found blackened human bones and now it seemed like half a forest was being excavated. An age-old murder was the last thing she wanted just before Christmas.

The 35-year-old was one of only a few female captains in the carabinieri, an organization that until the new century hadn't even admitted women into its ranks. She certainly looked the part. Striking black hair and dark eyes, good cheekbones and trim enough to turn heads whether she was in or out of uniform. She was also multilingual and had her sights set on the top. Sylvia was her German grandmother's name, chosen for her by her father, a diplomat from Munich working in Italy. Carmela was her Italian mother's name, a classical musician who'd met her father in Rome. And Tomms, well that was the marital name that she was about to get rid of, as soon as her divorce came through from the no-good Englishman she'd been foolish enough to marry.

The cigarette break was her first since arriving at the scene and cranking up the slow engine of a murder inquiry. It was probably something and nothing. A domestic, no doubt. Angry husband kills unfaithful wife and buries her body in woods. No big deal. Nevertheless, Sylvia was determined that it be investigated every bit as thoroughly as if a rich politician had just been killed. That was her style. Never cut corners.

The site had been taped off, an officer was in place to log visitors and a photographer had just arrived. An exhibits officer was on standby. A medic had pronounced death and the ME was on his way. The CSI had already established a safe corridor down which every man, woman and dog that had a right to be there could freely walk without fear of contaminating anything.

She'd also instructed officers to *grid* the scene, mark it off in zones with tapes and poles, so that the whole area could be scrupulously searched and accurate notes kept of whatever was found.

The crime-scene photographer began clicking away on the other side of the tape, getting wide shots of the location where forensic scientists were seemingly panning for bone.

Sylvia's Number Two, Lieutenant Pietro Raimondi, swigged from a small, green plastic bottle of *Rocchetta Natura*. 'In case we find skull fragments, you will want an orthodontist. Shall I contact Cavaliere?'

'No. Talk to Manuela in the office. She told me she found a hot new guy who studied at the UCLA School of Dentistry. Married, but gorgeous and prone to straying.'

'Remember we are carabinieri!' teased Raimondi. 'Our motto is *Nei Secoli Fedele.*' He melodramatically thumped his fist against his heart as though making an oath.

'Well, Pietro, let me tell you, I stayed *faithful throughout the centuries* that I was married to that English dog. Now I'm free and I need some fun. And as for the dentist, well I think he probably took the Hippocratic Oath, and that means he's sworn to secrecy.'

She relaxed a little, blew the last of her cigarette away. 'As well as DNA profiling, let's get CT scans on those bigger pieces of bone. And we'll need some anthropological and archaeological experts to look in detail at what we've got.'

Raimondi, who at six-four was what Sylvia deemed 'unnecessarily large for an Italian male', reminded her of a problem. 'We have no state forensic anthropologists available at the moment. Bossi and Bonetti are both still in Rome.'

'Great! When are they going to be free, do you know?'

Raimondi shrugged. 'Not for some time. I think they have other work backing up.'

Everyone had other work. Cases were backed up as far as Sicily. It seemed to Sylvia that you could double police resources and within a month they'd still be understaffed.

'What about going private? Sorrentino or De Bellis?' suggested Raimondi.

Sylvia thought for a moment. Sorrentino was a top anthropologist and archaeologist, meaning he wasn't just a bone man confined to the labs, he had expert field skills and could supervise the excavations. But he was also a bag of trouble. De Bellis, on the other hand, was probably a better osteologist, his anthropology was superb, but he was older than a dinosaur and could never be rushed to a deadline. 'Sorrentino, but stress the confidentiality. Tell him we don't want to be reading his report in *La Repubblica* before it's on our desk.'

Sylvia dropped her cigarette butt and ground it into the hard earth with the heel of her boot. She looked again at the excavation site and had a bad feeling. Something in her gut told her this wasn't going to be routine. She shivered for a second. Sure, it was cold. But that hadn't been what chilled her. What she'd felt wasn't the weather. It was the presence of evil.

# 18

***Greenwich Village, New York City***

It was one of those icy nights when the sky looks sharper than a sixty-inch plasma screen and the stars shine so brightly that kids try to touch them. Jack spent most of it walking around, while the rest of the house slept. The house was cold. The heating was off. He sat in the kitchen and brewed coffee. While he waited, he looked again at the slip of paper Creed had given him. *Luisa Banotti, Patricia Calvi, Donna Rizzi, Gloria Pirandello and Francesca Di Lauro.* Their deaths in his hand. It had been clever of Creed to imply that, to write them down and press them into his palm. Stigmata of responsibility. It made it hard for him just to screw up the paper and forget them. The coffee boiled and Jack drank it black, warming his hands around a Yankees mug. Five missing women, their disappearances stretching back more than half a decade, linked by a strange pervert who had crossed continents to try to get him involved. It was no wonder he couldn't sleep. His mind was churning with thoughts about Howie too. The big fella was all beat-up. The divorce had knocked him sideways, and then the bottle he'd sought solace in had laid him out. Punch-drunk.

Jack crept back into bed sometime before five and the warmth and close comfort of his wife's body sent him to sleep.

Less than two hours later his cellphone woke him.

He'd forgotten to mute it and by the time he found it in the dark, it had tripped to voicemail.

'Sorry,' he said as Nancy turned over and stared at him.

The message was from Massimo Albonetti, and it wasn't the kind that anyone should start the day with.

'It's okay, put the light on,' she said. 'I'm awake now.'

She watched as he listened to the call, and didn't like what she saw on his face.

He clicked off the phone. 'Massimo.'

'This Naples thing?'

'Yes, this Naples thing. Massimo wants me to go out there.'

Nancy ran her hands through her hair to untangle it. 'Oh, he does, does he? And when exactly does he want you there?'

'Early next week. Just to talk to the local cops, brief them on Creed, share the documents he gave me, that sort of thing. It could all be important.'

Nancy did little to hide her exasperation. 'Is there any point me pleading that we're supposed to be on holiday? That this is our one break together? That it's almost Christmas and I still have to help Mom and Dad prepare?'

Jack put his arm around his wife so she had to lean on his chest. 'Listen, honey. I feel bad about this guy Creed going AWOL. I feel even worse about things I found at his hotel and comments he made to me. I have to do this.'

'Like what?' she snapped. 'What did he say?'

Jack recalled Creed's comment . . . *more will die and both you and I will feel like we have blood on our hands.* 'Stuff, Nancy; just stuff.'

She screwed up her face.

'Listen, he might be a killer. If he is, then I don't want to think that I could have done something to prevent someone dying, but didn't.'

'And if he's not? What if he's just a weirdo, like you said?'

'Then there's no harm done, and I'll be back before the weekend.'

Nancy pulled herself from under his arm and headed for the bathroom. Sometimes her husband drove her crazy. Why didn't he just come straight out and say he *wanted* to be involved, admit that he ached to be out there in the thick of the action, racking his brains and testing himself? 'You'd better come home soon, even if he turns out to be Charlie Manson's murderous twin brother.'

Jack swung out of bed, smiled and told his first lie of the day. 'Don't worry, I'll be back on time, I promise.'

# 19

***Campeggio Castellani, Pompeii***

Antonio Castellani's eighty-three-year-old face looked like it had been shaped out of saddle-leather. Skin sagged around a once broken and now entirely toothless jaw and fell in wrinkly folds down his scrawny neck.

Alone since his wife had died a decade ago, he spent most of his time in the old, rusting caravan that was both home and office. From here he ran the family holiday camp business and from the leaky window that let in the winter wind he watched what remained of his family go about their chores.

Outside, hauling garbage, were his grandsons Franco Castellani and Paolo Falconi. Both twenty-four, they'd been best friends since they crawled on a rug together. That was back in the days before Franco's father went to prison and his mother ran away to Milan with Paolo's father. Paolo's mother had looked after Franco for two years before she'd then upped and left as well.

Antonio gazed sadly at his grandsons heaving sacks out of an old van, straining to earn extra money by burning trash that gathered on the streets. Was that what his life had amounted to? Garbage. Was this the best he could provide for his family? It certainly hadn't been what he'd planned half a century ago as he'd fought his way out of the slums and worked two jobs a day so he could start his own business. And years ago – more than fifty to be precise – well, he'd even hit the big time, for a while. He used the cash he'd saved to buy land and move in a fleet of shiny, new caravans. Then, by targeting those not rich enough to stay in hotels, he'd made money, good money, from tourists bound for Pompeii and Herculaneum.

It had all gone well.

Until he'd met Luigi Finelli.

Antonio had been full of bravado, ambition and cash. He'd cut quite a dash in the city's most popular ballrooms, bars and clubs. But such success didn't just catch the eyes of the ladies. It also turned the heads of the city's predators.

Camorra kingpin Luigi Finelli had been born with an instinct to spot easy prey. One long spring night, when Antonio fell into a game of high-stakes poker with fickle friends and ruthlessly rich strangers, Luigi scented blood. With a wave of his hand the strangers gave up their places to his Camorra soldiers. A day later, Antonio left at dawn, a broken man. All of his savings and a third of his business had been surrendered to settle his debt.

If you looked closely into Antonio's face, you could still see the lines of shock that had been seared into his skin half a century ago when the game ended and reality sank in. Past, present and future – all had been lost on the turn of a card. But this momentous event was not what was troubling him as he stared out of the caravan window this dour December day. It was something more personal. More painful.

Young Franco Castellani looked towards the caravan, caught his grandfather's gaze, smiled and waved. Antonio returned the gesture along with a gap-toothed smile. It had been years since Antonio had cried, but when he looked at Franco he couldn't help swallowing hard and blinking. It wasn't just that he had his grandmother's eyes, and Antonio remembered her every time he saw him. It was that the child had been cursed with something worse than death. A disease that was cruelly robbing him of the life he should have.

Car tyres crunching dusty gravel made the old man jump like a lizard in the sun. He hoped the arrivals were tourists, plenty of them, packed with cash.

But they weren't.

The black Mercedes S280 was undoubtedly a Camorra car. The Finelli Family normally sent their weekly collectors in more modest vehicles, but sometimes one of their distinctive Mercs rolled up. An under-boss usually slouched in the back while he despatched some young leech to come and bleed Antonio of his hard-earned money.

'*Buon giorno*,' shouted a man that most of Antonio's generation recognized as Sal the Snake. The Camorrista stood and waited for someone to appear from around the other side of the car.

'*Buon giorno*,' replied Antonio, respectfully dipping his head.

The muscled form of Tonino Farina slid out from the passenger seat and opened the back door for his boss.

'This is *Signor* Valsi,' said Sal, moving towards Antonio. 'He'd like to come inside and talk to you.'

The old man slicked back his hair and tried to fuss himself smart. 'Of course. Please, come in. This is an honour. A great honour.'

Valsi nodded, buttoned up his black suit jacket and climbed two metal steps into the van. He looked around contemptuously. The air stank of male sweat and cigarettes. It reminded him of his first day in prison.

'Sit down, *please*,' said Antonio. He hurriedly moved newspapers and a plate glazed with stale pasta sauce. Farina checked out the rest of the van. He opened the toilet door and almost gagged.

'I'll stand,' said Valsi. 'This won't take long.'

Antonio felt his chest tighten. He wiped his hands on his crumpled old trousers and hoped the Camorristi couldn't sense his fear.

'My father-in-law tells me that you pay us a third of all your earnings and, with only one or two unfortunate lapses, you have always met your debts promptly.'

'Yes, sir. That is the case. I do my best, even when times are difficult.' Antonio hated calling this young weasel 'sir'. There had been a day when he could have bought and sold scum like him.

‘How old are you?’

Antonio smiled. ‘I am eighty-three, almost eighty-four.’

‘Then you do not have long left,’ said Valsi coldly. ‘Do you have any illnesses, anything wrong with you?’

‘A little angina.’ He patted his thumping heart.

‘Then maybe you have two to five years,’ said Valsi. ‘What will happen to this place when you die?’

‘I will leave it to my grandsons. They will run the business. It will be their livelihood.’

Valsi smirked. ‘Oh, no. No, I really don’t think so.’ He placed his hands either side of the window and looked into the camp yard. ‘I am going to buy the land off you, and you can have some money for the last of your years. I will be generous, so there will be some cash to pass to your grandsons.’ He turned to face him. ‘*Signor* Giacomo here will come back with a lawyer and you will sign all the legal papers transferring ownership to me. We will build on here. Perhaps housing. Perhaps a restaurant and apartments. You will be compensated and move out. Do you understand?’

Antonio wanted to say no. With all his broken heart and all his broken spirit, he burned with the urge to say no.

*One last stand.*

‘*Signor* Valsi, this is all I have left. My wife died many years ago and my business has been difficult to run. But I have done so, because it is part of my family and I want to pass it on to the next generation. It is not worth much, but still it is an inheritance. And, in leaving an inheritance, we old people find some respect and dignity. Please don't take that away from me.'

Valsi's eyes lit up. The old man's fear excited him. '*Signor* Castellani, you speak of your own family and your own respect, but in doing so, you show only *disrespect* to me and my Family. I am not interested in how you, or your grandsons, feel. I am a businessman, and this is purely a business matter. I will pay you fifty thousand euros. It is enough to rent an apartment – no doubt until your death – and even put some food in your mouth. In return, you will sign over all the land to me. You can take anything you want from here, I demand only the earth. Building starts in six months' time.' Before Antonio could react, the caravan door opened.

Franco Castellani blundered in, his voice full of youthful excitement. 'Grandfather, I've finished the garbage and toilets. What do you want me –' He stopped when he saw the three sharp-suited men in front of him.

Farina grabbed Franco by the chest and pinned him to the wall of the van.

'Please, don't hurt him!' pleaded Antonio. 'He didn't know you were here, he didn't mean anything –'

'*Fuck!* What is this shit?' Valsi grabbed at Franco's chin. 'What the fuck is *wrong* with you? You've got the face of a fucking hundred-year-old.'

Antonio pushed himself between his grandson and Valsi. 'He's ill. He has Werner Syndrome. It makes him look old. It's not his fault. Please, don't hurt him.'

'Enough!' said Valsi. He let go of Franco and brushed his hands together, as though wiping filth from them. 'This shit better not be catching.'

'It's not!' Franco stared straight into the man's eyes.

Valsi sized him up. 'Fucking weirdo.' He turned back to the grandfather. 'Be ready to sign the documents my men bring you.' He pushed Franco to one side. 'Stay out of the fucking daylight, Freak Boy; it's not Halloween for another year.'

Valsi and his laughing henchmen left. The door swung loose and banged in the wind.

Antonio ignored it and wrapped his arms around his grandson. 'Ignore them, Franco. I love you and God loves you. Everything will be all right.'

Franco fought back his rage and nodded as his grandfather held him.

'It will be all right, I promise,' repeated Antonio. But they both knew that it wouldn't be.

Everything was going to be far from all right.

# 20

*JFK Airport, New York City*

The United flight rose in slow motion above the insipid winter whites of snowbound New York, then disappeared into the dark December night.

Ten hours later, Jack King dejectedly peered through the window at rain-sodden clouds barrelling across the Bay of Naples. Dozens of container ships swayed slowly in a sludge of polluted foam beneath him. On the dockside, metal cranes bent their iron beaks and pecked poisonous cargoes of illegal drugs, counterfeit goods and smuggled immigrants. This was one of the world's busiest ports, a crossroads of global criminality.

Thunder boomed as the plane touched down at Capodichino. Rain beat like ball bearings on the metal roof of the 737. They surfed to an air bridge on a wave of runway water.

Naples is Italy's third largest city, the birthplace of pizza and home to more than a million people. On passing Customs, Jack thought each and every one of them had turned up at the airport for what must be *National Talk as Loud and as Fast as You*

*Can Day.* He caught a cab and watched the city unfold before him. His mind soaked up the surroundings that may have shaped the psyche of a serial killer.

The journey was long and depressing. A few fields of denuded cherry trees and ranks of industrial greenhouses reminded him of Naples' agricultural heritage. The rest looked like urban wasteland. Traffic was as bad as, if not worse than, New York, and there was a palpable anger and aggression in the way people drove. Driving was combat. Parking was territorial. Pedestrians were prey.

Management at The Grand Hotel Parker's told him with pride that they'd upgraded him to a luxury room with a sea view. The description was only partly right. The view across the bay was indeed stunning, but the room fell short of luxury. Modest and clean were the kindest descriptions he could come up with. Like the city, the hotel lived on past glories.

He unpacked, hung his shirts over a hot bath to let the creases fall out and was fighting off the first wave of jet lag when Massimo Albonetti rang and said he was in reception.

Even in the most fashionable crowd, his old friend always stood out. Today he wore a bespoke mid-length black calfskin leather jacket, evocative of Marlon Brando's motorcycle days. He matched it with understated charcoal-grey trousers of wool and silk, a cashmere jumper and a grey cotton T-shirt.

'I curse Naples. Driving in this city is now completely impossible! How are you, my friend?' Massimo extended both arms and Jack surrendered to the inevitable cheek-kissing. If the truth be known, it still made him feel awkward.

'I'm fine. Red-eyed, but good. You got time to grab a bite?'

'Hey, I'm Italian; I always have time to eat. In here, or we go out?'

They settled on a table upstairs, at the hotel's famous George's restaurant. Jack's body clock was already out of kilter. Jet lag reduced the distinctions of breakfast, lunch and dinner into a simple desire to eat. They drank fresh orange and espressos while they perused the menu. Massimo put his glass aside and from the look on his face Jack knew something was troubling him.

'What's on your mind?'

'It's your friend Luciano Creed and his missing women.' Massimo Albonetti interlocked his fingers and cracked his knuckles. 'I received a phone call on the way over to you. It was from Sylvia Tomms, a carabinieri *Capitano* here in Naples.'

'And?'

'She's been working a case out near Pompeii, not that far from where a couple of Creed's women lived. Some human remains were found in a stretch of woods, way off the tourist road that leads up to the top of Vesuvius.'

'The volcano?'

'Yes, the volcano,' Massimo smiled. 'It is the only Vesuvius we have.'

Jack raised an eyebrow to acknowledge the levity. Humour always surfaced when cops got down to the blackest aspects of a case. 'Were they bagged? In a sack, a case, or anything that might give forensics?'

'You think Italian killers are more stupid than American ones?'

'I live in hope.'

'Sadly not. No container. They were just dumped in the soil. Not much chance of trace evidence from the killer, though the labs are sifting through samples. Let me get to the main point, though. Tomms has had a local anthropologist and his team piece together the bones recovered from the site. These people are good. They're used to digging up corpses that are centuries old, so they put this skeleton together very quickly –'

'And?'

The last of the levity left Massimo's eyes, 'And, it's a woman, one of the ones you mentioned.'

Jack took a slow breath. 'Which?'

'Francesca Di Lauro.' The lines on Massimo's forehead rippled again. 'Her jawbone had been smashed in more than a dozen different places but they pieced much of it together again. One of Sylvia Tomms' team managed to get some X-ray transparencies from her last dental check-up. The fit is identical.'

'You got a time on when she was buried?'

'Not yet. But we're talking years, not months.'

Jack voiced what was in both of their heads. 'So Creed was right about her being missing and being murdered. And if he's right about her, then he may well be right about the other missing women as well.'

'Why was he right, though?'

'Because he killed her?'

Massimo fell deep in thought. 'I don't know, Jack. The only thing that I'm certain of is that we're going to have to reopen all those damn cases. And believe me, that's going to cause a hell of a lot of work and generate huge political opposition. We're not going to win any friends with this one!'

## 21

***Centro di Visitatore, Pompeii***

Franco Castellani and his cousin Paolo Falconi slipped past the glass-screened kiosk without paying. Within seconds they'd vanished in the labyrinthine ruins of Pompeii.

They were serial non-payers and knew the place like the back of their hands. Pompeii was their playground. First stop, as usual, *Forum Olitorio.*Through iron bars, Franco stared into the old granary, studying every inch of the plaster casts of victims engulfed in the torrent of lava that erupted from Vesuvius back in 79@c.

When the site had been excavated in the 1800s, imprints of the dead had been found in the hardened lava. By pouring plaster into cavities left in the bed of ashes by the gradual decomposition of a corpse, it had been possible to recreate a near perfect replica of the victim's form.

The figure that always fascinated Franco was that of a young man, sitting with his knees tucked up and his hands on his chin, his moment of thought preserved forever by the awful lava flow that had consumed him.

Franco stared intently at Ash Boy, as he called him. He had the frame of a youth, but the plaster and the pose suggested someone older. Someone old before his time.

*Dead before his time.*

The observation resonated with Franco. The disease that had engulfed his own body – slower but just as deadly as the lava – had already stolen his youth. It had cruelly taken the years in which he should have been most attractive to women, the years in which he should find his soulmate.

Inevitably it would kill him. Just like Ash Boy. He would be *dead before his time.*

Franco walked with his hood up. Dark sunglasses not only hid his face from prejudiced eyes, they also made him feel safer and calmer. His doctor had recommended them. Partly as a cosmetic aid. But also to help rein in his explosive temper. He'd once almost beaten to death a teenager who'd made the mistake of taunting him. It had resulted in a suspended prison sentence for Franco and a long stay in intensive care for the mocking youth.

Five feral dogs followed them as they stopped at the junction of Via del Tempio d'Iside and Via del Teatri. The cousins sat on the cobbles that had once been stepping stones over Pompeii's open sewers. They drank water and ate the cheese, ham and bread they'd brought with them.

'Get lost, go away!' Franco kicked out at the dogs as they hassled for scraps.

'Hey, they're okay, let them be.' Paolo tore off some of his bread and threw it to the pack.

The dogs scavenged as the boys ate. Crowds flowed past, heading to the Doric Temple and Great Theatre. A group of schoolgirls sauntered by. Multicoloured rucksacks swung low over tight blue jeans. Pretty hands marked off worksheets.

'*Francesi,*' whispered Franco, picking up their accents as they gabbled to each other.

'*Bonjour,*' shouted Paolo in poor French, then added in English. 'You ladies need a guide?'

The girls giggled.

Franco's Anglo-Saxon was less subtle. 'Show us your cunts and we'll do your schoolwork for you.'

The giggling stopped. A young male teacher appeared from the back of the group. The cousins hadn't spotted him. He was suntanned, fashionably dressed and had the kind of confidence that only teachers have. As he strode over he'd probably weighed up the two young men and, being several inches taller and far more muscular than either of them, no doubt felt confident about his task.

He shouldn't have done.

Franco got to his feet. Before the teacher had uttered a word he adjusted his balance and thundered a kick between the man's legs. More followed. Rapid, vicious kicks, delivered with all Franco's hatred for the world and for what good-looking young men like this one stood for.

The teacher doubled over, hands clutching his

groin. Franco drop-kicked him in the chest. The impact made a dull and muffled sound. Ribs cracked like ice on a lake.

The girls screamed. Franco felt jolts of power and energy surge through him. Violence made him feel good. Feel complete.

'*Bastardo!*' swore Franco. He took a final kick at the man's head as he lay unconcious on the ancient cobbles.

Everyone looked away. A collective wave of nausea washed over them. Paolo pulled at his cousin.

'Now, we go. It's done. Come on!'

Franco was in a trance. Fixated by the sight of the pain and chaos that he'd created.

'Now!' shouted Paolo. Finally he got Franco to move. Dragged him down Vicolo del Menandro. Through an ancient block of houses that pre-dated Christ, then right into the wide, ancient thoroughfare known as Via dell'Abbondanza. At the end of it they ducked out of sight and Paolo exploded. 'What the fuck was that for? *Why* did you do that?'

'Because I wanted to,' wheezed Franco. 'Because he's a French cunt and he deserved to have his French cunt-face beaten to a pulp.'

'Hell, the guy hadn't even said anything.'

'He didn't have to. You saw the way those bitches looked at us.'

Paolo let out a sigh. '*Stupido*, they only looked at us because we spoke to them. Nothing would have kicked off if you hadn't asked to see their cunts.'

The criticism stung Franco. 'It was a joke. If *you'd* have said it they'd have laughed. But because *I* said it, they looked like they were going to be sick.'

Paolo let it rest. When his cousin was in this kind of mood there was no point trying to explain that the world wasn't always against him.

Franco's temper was snapping again. 'Bitches. Fucking little bitches. They think they're too good for me. Too pretty for me, all because of this!' He slapped his hands on either side of his face then scratched up and down at his wrinkled and mottled skin.

Paolo saw blood coming from his cousin's cheeks. 'Hey, stop it! Come on. Don't do that.' He pulled his cousin's hands away from his face.

'Too good? Huh!' said Franco. 'They're no better than the bags of trash we burn every day. That's what they are – trash. I'd like to take them down to Grandfather's pit, fuck them one by one and then burn them all.'

The pit was Franco's private place. No one went there but him. And nothing seemed to calm him more than spending time alone there, burning things.

'Fine. Whatever,' said Paolo, 'but unless we get moving again, the only burning you're going to be doing is your backside on a prison bench.' He put his hand on his cousin's shoulder and tried to push him into a jog. 'C'mon, let's move.'

'I'm not coming.'

'What?'

'I'm not running any more. I'm going to the *Orto*.'

'Don't be crazy. You nearly *killed* that French guy. Come on!'

'No.'

'Yes!' Paolo tried again to move him, but Franco wheeled away from his hand. 'Those kids will have told another teacher by now. The guards and polizia will be all over us in a minute. C'mon.'

'No! I don't give a fuck. I'm going where I want to go. I always go to the *Orto* and I'm not leaving today until I've been.'

Paolo stopped and thought for a brief moment. 'Well, I'm not. Crazy fucker! You get caught by the polizia if you want. I'm gone.'

Franco didn't even watch him head off. Instead, he cut slowly back through Vicolo dei Fuggiaschi and wandered towards an area of Pompeii that had been a vineyard before Vesuvius erupted.

Franco Castellani looked at the haunting sprawl and tangle of plaster mummies lying in the grey stony dirt of the Orto dei Fuggiaschi, the Garden of the Fugitives. More than a dozen adults and children had been found dead, huddled together, seeking the solace of human touch in the last moment of life.

*Human touch.* Something he craved.

He raised his eyes to the sky and felt a strange spiritual connection with the dead.

What had killed them? The boiling flow of lava

and the billowing fires? Or the choking whirlwind of pumice, ash and volcanic dust?

Had they been good people? Bad people? Had they deserved to die? He doubted it. No one deserved to die such a horrible death. No one but those little French bitches. Such an end would have been perfect for them.

Franco took his time wandering around. Paolo was right, the cops were soon everywhere. Swarming all over the place, like roaches. No problem, though. He knew the ruins like the back of his hand. He slipped outside the gates into the town of Pompeii. Disappeared down by the railway line heading east. He curled up behind a giant old hoarding advertising sanitary towels, and slept for several hours.

It was dark and late when Franco Castellani crept back into the rusty caravan he shared with his cousin.

Paolo looked up from his bunk, an old football magazine on his lap. 'You okay?'

'Yeah,' mumbled Franco, his head down in shame.

'Grandpa brought us two beers. I saved them till you came.' Paolo nodded at the small second-hand fridge that buzzed and clanked beneath a worktop in the tiny galley kitchen.

'Fuck!' swore Franco as he opened the door and sharp white light blazed into his face. 'Why does it have to be so bright?'

'Opener's on the top. Come sit with me.'

'Peroni. He spoils us.' Franco popped the caps. Foam fizzed over the bottle necks. 'He say anything to you about the Camorristi?'

Paolo took a beer from his cousin's hand and clinked bottles. '*Salute!* They want the place. Plan to move us out. They're going to build here, or something.'

'What? You fucking joking?'

'No. That's what they say. They are going to send *the guys* round. Grandpa has to sign, and that's it.'

'*The guys.* I hate the fucking *guys.* Where we supposed to go?'

'Like they give a fuck? It would have been different if *we* were *guys.*'

Franco started to peel the label off the bottle. He always tried to get it off without tearing, but never managed. 'Camorra soldiers. Us? You think so?'

'Why not? We can do stuff. We can run messages, do deals, scare the shit out of people and that.'

'Well, at least, I can. I'm not sure you can scare a fish.'

Paolo laughed and took a long swig of the beer. It wasn't as cold as it should have been; the fridge was playing up again. 'Grandpa would never let us work for the System, you know his feelings.'

Franco knew them well. The Camorra was the thing that he hated most. The thing that had ruined his life.

'You going to stay in tonight?'

'No. I'll have another beer with you, then I'm going out. You know I have to.'

Paolo avoided his eyes. He never knew where his cousin went, or what he got up to. He just understood that sometimes he had to be on his own. It was better that way.

# 22

*Stazione dei carabinieri, Castello di Cisterna*

The wet morning air tasted of stone and flint. Jack King clacked his tongue against the roof of his mouth and prayed he'd find decent coffee inside the local carabinieri HQ.

It was a rectangular, purpose-built, brick barracks. Four storeys high and home not only to the investigation division but also more than a thousand soldiers. Grey metal gates opened as Massimo flashed his ID. They were ushered across a gravelled driveway, past a frayed but still fluttering Italian flag, into a small, cool dark reception area tiled in cheap, dull marble.

'Wow, this place is depressing.' Jack squinted down a warren of dimly lit corridors decorated in spirit-sapping greys and faded blues.

'Not all of Italy is an art gallery,' remarked Massimo stoically, as he led them past a series of closed doors. They were still several offices away from that of *Capitano* Sylvia Tomms when she appeared from the depths of the warren. Mass kissed her lightly on both cheeks.

'Sylvia, this is Jack King. It's best we talk in English

but his Italian is quite good – especially the bad words – so be careful what you say about him.'

Sylvia laughed and stuck out a hand. 'Hope the jet lag isn't too bad. Thanks for coming.'

'I'll survive. Please call me Jack. It sounds like you have quite a puzzle on your hands.'

She smiled. 'Step by step, little by little, we will solve it. Come to my room. I'll get you both something to drink and show you what we've got.'

The office was tiny and cluttered. Her desk was covered in papers, photographs, memos and maps. In the middle, a flat-screen monitor rose from a heap of plastic water bottles, sandwich wrappings, old cigarette packets and coffee cups.

'Please take a seat. Just put those anywhere on the floor.' Sylvia motioned to two hard wooden chairs and the skyscrapers of files she'd built on them. The floor was also stacked with documents. Jack and Massimo had to place the papers they'd moved under the chairs.

'I'm sorry about the mess. I have an office three times smaller than any male *Capitano*, and whenever I try to order bookshelves or filing cabinets they never come. I think they're trying to tell me something, no? Anyway, this is how I work, and for me it is no longer a problem.'

Jack liked her. She seemed smart and didn't let shit get her down. A good way to get through life.

Sylvia pulled papers from beneath a thick teetering stack. 'An old man walking his dog in Mount Vesuvius National Park discovered what he suspected might be a human bone. He was right. We recovered more than a hundred smashed and fragmented bones from the site.'

Jack made a mental note of the severity of the destruction. The multiplicity of broken bones indicated a high level of rage and an urgent need for gratification.

Sylvia ploughed on. 'Local anthropologists managed to piece together the outline of a human skeleton. Here, look at this.' She handed over a series of glossies showing a partially reconstructed skeleton.

Jack was impressed. He'd seen experts back in the States struggle with similar cases. 'It's a good job. I'm amazed they got so much done so quickly.'

Sylvia looked pleased at the compliment. 'They are among the best in the country, maybe the best in the world. From the jawbone we have managed to get a conclusive match with dental X-rays. Our skeleton is that of Francesca Di Lauro, a twenty-four-year-old woman from Casavatore, last seen about five years ago.'

Jack scanned the shots again. 'The bones are black – I take it that's from some kind of burning?'

'Total burning. We don't know how or where or when, but all the bones were like that.'

'Anything from Tox?'

'Not much. Seems a regular accelerant was used to burn her. Paraffin.'

'What kind?'

Sylvia looked puzzled. 'Paraffin is paraffin, no?'

'That's what I used to think. Have them dig deeper. I worked a case in New York and found there are dozens of types of paraffin. Some comes as wax, some is cheap and imported from places like India. I guess there's locally produced stuff as well.'

'Italian factories use paraffin a good deal,' added Massimo. 'Industrial paraffin, chlorinated paraffin oil, that type of chemical. There will be records, health and safety documents, batch numbers.'

Sylvia scribbled a note to herself and Massimo wondered if she'd ever find it again amid the mess. Jack turned back to the photographs, fanned them out and looked for a close-up of the bone fragments. 'You got any better blow-ups? Ones of the end of the bones, the splintered parts?'

Sylvia slid Jack a BCU – a Big Close-Up – of a shattered hip.

'What are you looking for?' asked Massimo.

'I'm trying to work out when our killer set his fire. Looking at this shot, the hip is blackened, though there are traces of cream bone at the edge, where it's been bludgeoned, chopped with something. If it had been chopped first, then none of the cream of the bone would be showing; the splintered end would be as blackened as the rest.'

Massimo followed his train of thought. 'So Francesca's corpse was dismembered *after* it was burned? That seems unusual. I would expect a killer to try to dispose of a body, and any evidence attached to it, by dismembering it first, then burning it and all the clothing and anything else that he'd come into contact with.'

Sylvia Tomms had worked gangland shootings, a rape murder, and numerous messy domestics, but this was new ground. 'Go slow for the lady police officer,' she said. 'Let me get this right. You're suggesting someone killed Francesca, doused her in paraffin, burned the corpse, then chopped it up and buried it?'

'Maybe,' said Jack carefully. 'But even that doesn't quite make sense to me. Your ME should be able to set things right.'

'What? What am I missing?' asked Sylvia.

Jack turned to Massimo. 'You've got a dead body – what do you do with it?'

'Dump it,' suggested Mass, 'in the woods or in the sea. Chop it up, bury it in a forest, or on some land that you own.'

Jack wagged a finger. 'Okay. So what's with the burning?'

'Like Mass just said, to get rid of forensic evidence, in case the body or part of the body is discovered,' suggested Sylvia.

'That makes sense if it's *after* the dismemberment,' said Jack. 'Burning pieces of a corpse is easier than burning a whole body. Not many people have the space and privacy to light a giant bonfire and burn an entire corpse.'

'Or the time,' added Massimo.

Sylvia was now in sync with their thinking. 'Another explanation. One that fits with the cream ends to that burned bone, is that the fire was not only pre-dismemberment, it was also ante-mortem.'

Jack nodded. 'You've got it. That's the next assumption. In fact, the most likely one. I suspect the killer set her on fire while she was still alive. Perhaps he even wanted to *watch* her burn to death. And if that's the case, then the guy you're hunting is not just a killer – he's a sadist and a serial killer.'

'Bad combination,' said Massimo.

Sylvia glanced down at the pictures of bone. Less than a week ago she'd taken charge of a low-level inquiry. Now, all of a sudden, it was turning into a manhunt for a serial killer – and, by the looks of it, one of the worst Italy had ever seen.

# 23

***Casa di famiglia dei Valsi, Camaldoli***

The two six-year-old boys sat cross-legged in the corner of the lounge. White, black and red Lego was spread all around them. Small hands and big imaginations built space shuttles and heroic astronauts.

The mothers of Enzo Valsi and Umberto Covella sat at the opposite end of the room. Coffee, cigarettes and the criminal world of the Camorra were their playthings.

Tatiana Covella was two years older than Gina, and her husband Nico ten years older than Bruno but ten times less successful – as she kept telling him. Nico was still a *guaglione*, a *guapo*; one of *the guys* that bosses like Bruno would send to do their dirty work.

'The problem with Nico,' explained Tatiana, passing a lit cigarette to her hostess, 'is that he is *troppo spavaldo.* He is always happy with whatever he has, but sometimes, you know, he is just, just a . . .' Her hands grabbed at the air as though trying to pluck the right word from somewhere.

'*Pagliaccio*,' offered Gina with a straight face.

They both burst our laughing. 'All men are *clowns*,'

said her friend, 'but Nico, he is so gullheaded and macho. He is interested only in fucking me, not making our life better in any way.'

Gina looked across at the children. Umberto was banging the two astronauts together in some imaginary intergalactic battle. Enzo was stealing pieces from his pile to finish the side of the space station. 'I wish that, just once, Bruno would be a little more romantic,' said Gina, not meaning to. The thought had just tumbled out, and was now lying there for her friend to see.

'Give it time. When men are locked up, it messes with their minds. Bruno wasn't just in jail. Nico says *prigione di massima sicurezza* is awful. The isolation, the brutality . . .'

Gina laughed. 'Not for Bruno. My father saw to it that he was no more in maximum security than you and me sitting here in this lounge. No one stood in his way. A hand was never raised against him.'

'Still – *prison* – it poisons minds. It's not natural to be locked up, you must give him time.'

'He doesn't want time,' she snapped. 'What he wants is nothing to do with me. He's said as much.'

'He doesn't mean that. He's just confused.'

'Ha! Bruno, confused? Have you heard yourself?'

The sharpness in her friend's voice silenced Tatiana. *Tra moglie e marito non mettere dito*, she told herself. *Never interfere between husband and wife.* But curiosity is a terrible thing and she ached to know more. She lit a cigarette for herself. 'Have you – you know? Sex – have you at least tried?'

Gina looked sad. '*I've* tried. He hasn't. He doesn't want to come near me. Says I'm fat and I disgust him.'

'Fuck him! *Figlio di puttana!*'

Gina smiled at her friend's support. She was embarrassed, but it was good to get it off her chest, have someone to talk to about it. 'I don't know what to do. I'm not a weak woman. At least, I certainly don't think I am –'

'Of course you're not, don't be stupid.' Tatiana thought for a second. 'Has he got someone else?'

Gina shot her a knowing look.

'Okay. They always have someone else. But someone *special*, someone you think he favours?'

'There were – in the past – many *specials*.'

'Did you confront him about them?'

'Sure. Every time I found out.'

Her friend didn't ask *how many* times that was. 'And what did he say?'

Gina looked at her nails. Looked anywhere but in her friend's eyes. 'I went to see the women first. Paid them off.'

'What?'

'*Sì*. I *am* that stupid and that desperate. I paid the women to leave Napoli.' There were tears in the corners of her eyes. 'But at least the money came from our joint account and so at least my bastard husband paid as well.'

They both laughed.

'And now? Do you think he has someone now – so soon after being released?'

'I don't know.' She played with her cigarette and then shook her head, 'No. No, I don't think so.'

'Check his phone. Text messages *sent* as well as those received. They always forget to delete the ones they send.'

Gina smiled. Men were certainly stupid.

'Do you still love him?'

'What a question!' It settled on her mind like oil on water. As she thought about it, she glanced again at Enzo. He'd completed his task and had now confiscated one of Umberto's astronauts. 'He's the father of my child, the man I married. That's everything, isn't it?'

Tatiana shook her head. '"*Per amore, hai mai fatto niente solo per amore*?" You know this song?'

'Andrea Bocelli. "*For love, have you done anything only for love? Have you defied the wind and cried out, divided the heart itself, paid and bet again, behind this obsession that remains only mine?*" Yes, I know it. It is very beautiful. Beautiful and sad.'

*Beautiful* and *sad* – words that Tatiana thought also summed up her friend. 'But do you still love him like that? Do you love him so much you will do anything and everything, lose it all and then try again, knowing you could lose, lose and lose again?'

Gina looked up from the cigarette she was nervously flicking in an ashtray. 'I *do* still love him. But I wish I didn't. Does that make sense?'

Tatiana reached out a hand. 'Gina, you can't go on like this. You must protect yourself. If you want to avoid years of madness and tears, you only have two possible choices.'

Gina's eyes begged Tatiana for answers.

'Leave him. Take Enzo and leave him.'

'Not an option,' she sighed deeply. 'You know our way. You know my father. Marriage is for life; families are sacred.'

'Your father doesn't want to see you unhappy.'

'He doesn't want to see me divorced either. You *know* how things are.'

'Then you must choose the second option.'

Gina tapped her cigarette, the filter red from her lipstick. 'Which is?'

Her friend raised an eyebrow. 'Find yourself a lover.'

A cry from the corner of the room turned both of their heads. The boys were fighting.

'Hey, hey! Stop it!' Gina got up and went over to separate them.

Blood poured from Umberto's nose. He was crying. Tatiana pulled him close to her, wiping blood, tears and snot from his face.

'Say sorry, Enzo,' insisted Gina. The six-year-old pulled his shoulder free of his mother's hand. Then he smiled and spat in his playmate's face.

*Like father, like son? Is the die already cast?* Gina asked herself. Was her beautiful boy already destined to grow up to be as cruel as his father?

# 24

***Stazione dei carabinieri, Castello di Cisterna***

The winter light faded early and temperatures plunged way below zero. Heating pipes in the carabinieri barracks coughed and banged into life like the lungs of a geriatric smoker. Sylvia, Jack and Massimo continued their case conference over the best pizza Jack had ever tasted.

'A lady in Cisterna makes it for us,' explained Sylvia. 'If she could only take the calories out then I would eat this five times a day.'

'It is good – really good,' enthused Jack. 'But tell me a little more about Francesca.'

Sylvia raised her eyes. 'You've seen the photographs, I'm told in real life she was even prettier. A quiet girl. Lived alone in a rented apartment. Had a degree in art but that only got her a job as a hairdresser. The salon had shut down just before she disappeared. Neighbours thought she'd moved elsewhere to find work. No trace of a boyfriend. At least, not in the block. She comes from a good, respectable family, nothing untoward there.'

'Not like her namesake?' asked Massimo.

Sylvia smiled at the suggestion. 'Not at all. Her parents are about as law-abiding as you can get.' She turned to Jack. 'Di Lauro is an infamous name in Naples.'

'Let me guess. Camorra, the dreaded System?'

'You got it. Paolo Di Lauro bossed the Secondigliano sector throughout the nineties. He was a real wise *wise guy*. He established strong trading links with gangs and businesses in China, helped exponentially extend the System's power base. He ducked out before the end of the last century but the Di Lauro dynasty lives on. Some years ago they were involved in an incredibly bloody battle with other clans. They won because they're the bloodiest. They beat a sixty-year-old Camorrista to death with baseball bats, shot a woman *Capo* in the face in public.'

'A *woman Capo*?' queried Jack.

'Certainly,' said Sylvia. 'Women have been getting top jobs in the System long before they got even lowly ones in the carabinieri.'

Massimo raised an eyebrow. 'Like the Black Widow.'

'He means Anna Mazza,' explained Sylvia. 'She bossed the Moccia clan for at least two decades.'

It was an eye-opener for Jack. The Camorra regularly made the headlines in newspapers around the world, but he hadn't realized the full length and breadth of its activities. 'To be clear, though, our girl, Francesca, she has no Camorra links at all?'

'None whatsoever,' said Sylvia. 'It's just pure coincidence that she shares the same surname. It's also the name of a famous Italian fashion designer and a well-known photojournalist.'

Jack moved on. 'And how have her parents taken the latest news?'

'I've seen them recently. They're devastated. They'd feared something bad but had always hoped the phone would ring and she'd breeze back into their lives. Her father's a sales manager for some computer company. He and his wife split up some time before Francesca vanished.'

'No record. No hint of abuse, or anything?'

She shook her head. 'Not a thing. He's a decent man. I'm sure of it.'

Massimo opened a second box of pizza and ripped off a small slice. 'You said Creed knew Francesca *personally*. Did he give you details about their relationship?'

Jack shook his head. 'No. It was right at the end of our meeting. To be honest, I was keen to get away from him and was losing interest until he mentioned that he knew her. I thought about that overnight and then when I returned to his hotel he'd already gone.'

Sylvia jumped in. 'I don't see them as a couple. She was gorgeous – truly beautiful. Creed, on the other hand – he looks like a sewer rat.'

'Beautiful women have been dating ugly men since the dawn of time,' said Massimo.

'Thankfully,' added Jack.

Both men laughed.

'Sure, but the ugly men usually have more charm or cash than Creed,' added Sylvia. 'I could more easily imagine him *stalking* Francesca than dating her.'

'My thoughts entirely,' said Jack, 'and that's what worried me. If Newark hadn't got a snowplough down their runway so quickly I might have had another meeting with him and been able to shed some serious light on this.'

Massimo's willpower snapped. He went back for a bigger slice of the pizza. 'This is my last piece; no one let me take any more.'

'Me too,' said Jack, 'I'm stuffed. When I think of Creed I think of him as being inadequate. He seeks power and control and he has traits that indicate an inferiority complex . . .'

Massimo nodded as he chewed. 'But that doesn't necessarily mean he's an offender. If it did, then we'd be carrying out surveillance on at least half the male population.'

Sylvia poured Coke. 'You say *inadequacy.* That worries me. Inadequacy is the kind of thing that can drive scrawny men like Creed to rape and murder.'

'I'm not saying Creed *is* killer material,' stressed Jack. 'Inadequacy and inferiority are more stalker's traits.'

'But sometimes stalkers become killers,' countered Sylvia.

'Sometimes, but it's rare,' conceded Jack. 'There's

something about him. Something about this case that just kicks my gut, and I'm old enough to know that I shouldn't ignore being kicked in the gut.'

Sylvia glanced down at the thick pad of notes she'd taken during their hours together. 'You said in your statement to one of my officers that you thought Creed might be a competent psychological profiler.'

'The stuff he showed me was smart. He knew all about Criminal Geographic Targeting techniques, jeopardy areas, overlapping distance-decay functions. He'd certainly done some studying.'

'So we can't rule out that he's just genuinely interested in solving these cases?'

'No, we can't. At this stage, I don't think it wise to rule anything out – or rule anything *in*, for that matter.'

'Which makes him one of two things –' said Massimo.

Jack finished the sentence for him. 'I was thinking the same. Misunderstood or murderous.'

All three reached for more pizza. They needed the comfort food.

# 25

*Centro città, Napoli*

The black Mercedes S280 slid silently through the streets. Its heavily glazed windows stifled the snarls of city traffic.

Bruno Valsi rode in the back, Sal the Snake beside him, Tonino Farina up front and Dino Pennestri behind the wheel. Farina and Pennestri were both *made men* in their late twenties. Trusted members of the Finelli Family who'd been delighted to become the first members of Valsi's own crew. In the mind of the new *Capo Zona* there was nothing that Farina couldn't extort with his brutal fists, and no wheelman that Pennestri couldn't better.

But Valsi's mind wasn't on them. As they drove to his first business meeting of the new week, he was preoccupied with the growing tension between himself and the Don. Having Sal the Snake as a shadow was bad enough, but being denied the right to recruit Alberto Donatello and Romano Ivetta was much worse. It was disrespectful. And then there was the old man's less than coded warning about making sure his fat daughter wore a permanent smile on her face. Prison had taught Valsi to be patient, but he wasn't sure how much longer he could bite his tongue and swallow his pride.

'This is it, boss,' said Pennestri, pulling up outside one of Italy's biggest call girl agencies. The driver stayed put as Farina peeled out of the passenger door. He opened a rear door, his eyes scanning the street before Valsi eased himself out and put on his black suit jacket.

The building in front of them was made of crumbling unpainted stone. It was five storeys high, each storey boasting a row of windows that opened inwards behind rusty iron shutters.

The stairs stank of dog piss. The lighting was so dim they couldn't see their feet. The Finelli Family owned the entire block, spending little on appearances while maximizing the money they milked from sex lines and escort bookings.

Valsi had stayed up all night, studying the operation's payment books. The manager, Celia Brabantia, was on the take. The accounts showed an unusually steady flow of income. There were no ups and downs. No surges during times when the hotels were filled with conventions, exhibitions and tourists. No falls during the bleak winter months. Valsi figured that Celia passed on what she thought was a reasonable whack and then had the nerve to keep the rest for herself. *Mussa!* Now he'd teach her a lesson. One she'd never forget. The thought pleased him. Excited him. Violence was his drug. It didn't matter whether it was a man or woman who was suffering, just providing he got his fix.

Farina didn't so much open the office door on the top floor as bang it off its hinges. Half a dozen bored and bedraggled women slumped over silent phones jumped in their seats.

'Where's your boss?' hissed Sal.

The girls looked terrified. They all guessed who their visitors were and understood this wasn't a social call.

A Czech woman with short blonde hair and a long nose that spoiled an otherwise pretty face slid out of her seat. 'I'm Kristen. Celia's in the office at the back. Shall I get her for you?'

'We'll get her ourselves.' Sal pushed past her. Farina followed.

Valsi smiled. Sal had no style. No flair. 'You have to excuse him – Mondays are not his good days,' he said as he drew level with her. 'In fact, he doesn't have any good days.'

Kristen smiled back. He had a nice mouth. Good body too. 'Shall I get you some drinks?'

Valsi shook his head. 'Not now. But I'll get *you* one, when I'm done here.'

Kristen tried not to look too interested. 'I'm working late, and I'm not sure my boss will give me time off.'

Valsi laughed. 'By the time I've finished with your so-called *boss*, believe me, you'll be able to take the whole damned week off.' He turned away, cracked his knuckles and headed to the office.

# 26

***Laboratorio di Scienze Sorrentino, Napoli***

Forensic anthropologist Bernardo Sorrentino put his freshly manicured hands around the back of his head and shook out his long, black curly hair. The shoulder-length mane was his trademark. That and the black Gucci sunglasses he always wore whenever there was a photographer or TV camera around. The forty-two-year-old double divorcee had recently had one ear pierced, and wore a small thousand-euro diamond in it. Much to his disappointment this hadn't attracted a single column inch of comment.

The man the media called *Il Grande Leone* stared down at the monstrous mosaic of blackened bones laid out before him. On one brightly lit, large white marble table, lay the partially articulated skeleton of the woman who had been identified as Francesca Di Lauro. On an adjacent worktop were more of her blackened and splintered bones, some as small and fragile as pieces of eggshell. Given that the police had an ID there was now no point in piecing them together, but Sorrentino would do it anyway. To him it was like not completing a five-thousand-piece jigsaw, you didn't give up just because you could see what the picture was halfway through. His personal assistant, Ruben Agut, was already exhausted but was also committed to finishing the job. Sorrentino had picked the twenty-four-year-old straight from university. He was gay and Spanish and the anthropologist considered him to be yet another exotic accessory that would draw attention to himself. 'I'm going to get a lab coat,' he told him. 'Then we'll take those photographs and shoot more video.'

Ruben let out a deep and telling sigh. He was bored rigid with being the Great Lion's not-so-great gofer and was planning to quit and return to his native Barcelona. He and Sorrentino had had sex once. 'Purely an *experiment* in bisexuality,' his boss had called it. It had left Ruben feeling cheap and worthless. Before getting the camera he opened the recently arrived lab reports. He and Sorrentino had managed to unearth not only bone, but also dried organs and semi-fried muscle. These had been testable, they'd both been certain of that. It was a common mistake to presume that fire was the best means of destroying a body – far from it. The flames never destroyed *everything* of evidential value. Nothing did.

Ruben flipped open the paperwork. The results lifted his mood. He'd correctly identified pieces of liver, kidney and lower intestine.

But what he saw next almost brought him to his knees.

The young assistant slumped over the documentation and double-checked the summary. His stomach turned. At times like this, he was sure he should be doing something else.

Ruben was still catching his breath when his boss returned. Sorrentino was buttoning up his newly starched and pressed lab coat, watching his own reflection in the window as he walked past. 'What is it? What's wrong?' he asked, almost sensitively.

Ruben moved back from the worktop and pointed towards his discovery. 'You were right. The material you picked out was from a uterus. The extra DNA profiling confirms that Francesca Di Lauro was pregnant.'

# 27

***Campeggio Castellani, Pompeii***

The black waterproof anorak and trousers that Franco Castellani wore for garbage collection helped him disappear into the rainy darkness of the night. He slid from shadow to shadow around the campsite, *checking* on the safety of the guests. Or, at least, that's what he told his grandfather he did. For years he'd been prowling. Feeding on any flash of naked female flesh that he could find. Summer was best. Many young couples came to the site to be alone and he'd often see them lost in their lovemaking. He longed for the same. Ached for the sensation of sex. The mysterious closeness he'd witnessed.

In the past, Paolo had brought him hookers. The first had been his age, maybe even younger. She'd fled as soon as she'd got a good look at him. The second had been in her forties. As old and cold as his runaway mother. She was drunk and ridiculed him. Laughed at his withered face, his buck teeth and birdlike body. Asked if *Bird Boy* had got a worm for a cock? He'd have killed her if Paolo hadn't stopped him. At times like that – times like now – he felt more dead than alive.

Franco was poor and he was ill, but he wasn't stupid. He understood much of what the doctors had told him. Werner Syndrome was a rare and cruel disorder caused by missing proteins and damaged genes. It made him look old – very old – long before he should. It was responsible for him being smaller than most kids at school, but it hadn't really kicked in and done its terrible damage until he'd reached puberty. Then it had turned his body to Plasticine. Reshaped him in its own terrible way. His hair was already greying and thinning. His hands were becoming clawlike and mottled. The sickness would only get worse with age and would soon make him vulnerable to a range of cancers, heart disease and diabetes. Doctors wanted to carry out regular checks and tests on him, but he shunned them. The worse it got, the less care he took of himself. The more he needed to stay warm and infection free, the more he desired to wander in the freezing rain.

Tonight the downpour was so cold it made his face burn. Through the gap in the curtain of a caravan that people had just moved into, he saw the most beautiful woman in the world. Her hair was damp from the shower and she wore a white towelling robe. Franco slid back and felt his heart pound. From inside the van he heard someone shout her name. 'Rosa. Rosa, your dinner is ready.'

*Rosa.*

Franco spoke her name in the dark, cold wetness of the night. *Rosa.* His breath smoked white in the light from her window. *Rosa.* Even saying her name excited him.

His thoughts ran wild.

*Rosa.*

He knew exactly what he wanted to do to her. And he could barely wait for the chance to do it.

# 28

***Grand Hotel Parker's, Napoli***

Jack kicked off his shoes and slumped on to the hotel bed. It needed new springs or a better base. He'd barely slept last night. Before he'd left New York he'd filled Howie in on Creed and why he was heading to Naples. As he dialled his number he hoped his old partner wasn't too juiced to remember.

'Hi there, H. You sober?'

Howie Baumguard croaked a laugh back down the line. 'You joking? I left sober 'bout the same time you left charm school.'

Jack checked his watch, it would be just after seven p.m. in New York. 'What wild evening are you cranking up for yourself?'

'A couple of trays of Chinese slop. A few Buds. And I'm twenty minutes into *Apocalypse Now*.'

'Terrific. "*I love the smell of Napalm in the morning.*"'

'"*Smells like victory,*"' returned Howie.

'Man, that's a grim movie.'

'Grim, but brilliant. You wait two friggin' hours for Marlon Brando to come on screen and, when the thing's over, all you can remember is him.'

Jack recalled the classic Coppola epic and Brando's chilling Colonel Kurtz. 'Wouldn't you be better with something lighter?'

'Only other thing I've got is *The Grinch Who Stole Christmas*,' said the big guy. 'My son left it on top of the TV after his last sleepover.'

'You up to helping me with something?'

'Sure, what d'you want?'

'Remember the creepy Italian guy I met at the conference – Luciano Creed?'

'Kind of.'

'He stayed at the Lester. You know the place?'

'Yeah, I know it. Not exactly Trump Towers.' Howie found a pen down the side of the settee and used the cardboard lid from the Chinese food tray to write on.

'And that's a bad thing?' Jack would rather sleep on the street than at Trump. 'Would you take a ride out there and have a look around the nearby bars, clubs, check out the hotel again? See if he had any friends, visitors, such like while he was there?'

'You mean friends that get paid by the hour and never stay for coffee?'

'Yep, those are the ones I mean.'

'Okay. What's he look like?'

'Shit. He looks like shit. Small, thin, bony, five-five maybe, a hundred and ten to a hundred and twenty pounds, really dark beard line –'

'Designer stubble?'

'No, more Bluto black. Like this guy could never

shave clean. I've got a picture from the cops over here; I'll email it to you.'

'Fine. I'll hit the street tomorrow. That okay?'

'That's great.' Jack's voice grew serious. 'Howie, I need a break here. Girls have been going missing. Maybe even getting murdered. It would be good if you gave up the sauce – good for you too.'

His friend let out an exasperated sigh, the kind he used to reserve for his nagging wife – now his nagging ex-wife. 'Don't worry, I won't screw up on you. My fat ass will be on the case and will do good.'

# 29

***Secondigliano, Napoli***

Luciano Creed stood by a window in a slum apartment he'd rented in an area that the locals call Terzo Mondo, the Third World. It bore no relation to the false address he'd listed at the Lester in New York. For the moment he wanted to stay away from the cops. Soon he'd be ready to show himself again. But not yet.

His mind drifted as he watched neighbours in the street below. They were all dressed in their best clothes, heading off to church for a wedding.

Secondigliano was a poor, drug-infested neighbourhood in a north-eastern suburb where unemployment and crime were high and cops never came unless their sirens were wailing, their guns cocked and they had a big supply of body bags. This was a neighbourhood where drive-by shootings weren't uncommon. Where any attempted arrest could result in officers facing a mob of hundreds of violent protesters. Put simply, for many cops, this area was out of bounds. A strict no-go zone. Creed had grown up here. He knew its alleyways and escape routes better than any cops, even the carabinieri. Naples was an obligatory posting for most of the military, a rust-belt city that they were sent to for a year or two while they clawed their way up the promotional ladder towards the big jobs back in Rome as *Colonello*, *Generale* or even *Comandante Generale*.

Years back he'd dreamed of being a law enforcement officer, using his brain and his energy to catch the bad guys. Now, well, now things were different. Very different.

Loud cheering and clapping in the street broke his thoughts. The bride appeared from the neighbouring building. Confetti blew in the chilled air. Voices shouted their best wishes. Kisses on her cheeks. A considerate friend gathering the train of her long white dress. A proud father waiting in the back of a rented black Bentley, ready to give away the apple of his eye. Creed turned his back on the merriment. On the floor of the rented apartment, beneath an unshaded light bulb dangling from an exposed flex, lay his *collection*. Photographs of all the missing women, old photocopies of police reports dating back years, a map of the Bay of Naples marked with the places where they'd lived and small faded clippings from local newspapers reporting their disappearances. None of them had even warranted more than a paragraph in the local paper, let alone made the headlines. He thought long and hard about the women, their murders and what the police were now doing.

Nothing.

That's what they're doing. Nothing.

And that big-shot Jack King had no idea what he was up against.

No idea at all.

Well, he'd teach him. Teach him and the carabinieri not to ignore him. He'd give them a lesson they'd never forget.

# 30

*New York City*

Howie Baumguard woke with a hangover the size of Grand Central Station. It was so big he reckoned it could be seen from space. But despite the pain, he hit the streets. All day he pressed flesh and pounded pavements. He re-interviewed the Polish receptionist who had taken a shine to Jack. He bought coffee for beat cops who worked the neighbourhood. He shook up informants who infested the local strip joints and pick-up bars.

By mid-afternoon he wasn't only clear-headed, he was enjoying himself. *Back to your roots, Big H, this is what you do best.* And he wasn't just bragging, he really was good at it. Somehow people opened up more to fat guys with a sense of humour. It was something he'd learned long ago and he'd regularly shared these words of wisdom with every FBI medic that had tried to get him to diet.

As the afternoon clouds darkened, he was satisfied that he had enough scraps of information to start to put together a good picture of Luciano Creed.

Then things took a turn for the worse.

Three blocks from home he cut through a back alley to save time. And that's where it all went wrong. He stumbled straight into a good old-fashioned New York mugging.

Two black teenagers in hooded sweats had cornered a tall woman with short, spiky blonde hair. One was barking orders and holding what looked like a gun. Howie knew the hoodies had at least theft on their minds. If they felt lucky, then they might just roll the dice and go for rape as well.

The woman was holding a thin cardboard carton, literally hanging on to it for dear life.

Howie took a deep breath. No longer an FBI agent. No longer the bearer of a badge or a gun. All he had was fifty pounds more weight than both of the punks put together. *That*, he decided, would have to be his weapon of choice.

'Give it up, an' your fuckin' money!' screamed the bigger perp. 'Fucking bitch. Give it me, lady, or I'll put a fucking cap in your shitty white head!'

Howie slid along the shadows. Stuck to the cover of some overflowing dumpsters. He could tell the muggers were as jittery as hell, no doubt crackheads desperate for their next score. 'Jus' fuckin' whip the bitch and get her money!' shouted the smaller one.

Howie was still pinning down a game plan when his cellphone rang.

The hoodies' heads cranked towards him.

He had no choice but to break cover. Rush them now or get shot at.

Howie found he had all the speed of a rhino with a hernia. But, fortunately, about the same weight and strength.

'*Fuuuuck!*' was all the guy with the gun could manage as Howie crashed him into a brick wall, taking down his buddy at the same time. He heard the gun scatter across the ground and took the chance to pound a meaty fist into the face of the youth trapped beneath him.

Somehow the kid wriggled free and was damned well upright while Howie was still struggling to get up off all fours.

Howie knew a blow was coming but couldn't stop it.

A boot smashed into his face. A screen of eggshell-white light slammed down behind his eyes. More blows battered his body.

'Get the fuck outta here!' shouted one of the hoodies. Their feet slapped off into the distance.

The big guy lurched to his feet. Vision blurry, heart trying to bust through his chest. He rocked unsteadily. Caught half a glimpse of the woman – running safely the other way down the alley.

Then it hit him.

Sharp and hot. A numb pain that caused him to cramp before it exploded into white-hot agony.

Howie staggered. Put a hand on a wall to stop himself passing out. Reached back to find the source of the pain.

He'd been stabbed.

The smaller punk, the little bastard without the gun, had stabbed him in the ass. And the blade was still there. This was both good and bad. Bad because someone was going to have to pick the metal out of his butt, and that sounded a long way from fun. Good because he guessed the wound was so deep that if the knife had come out, then he might already be bleeding to death.

*I mean*, Howie asked himself, *how the fuck can you put a tourniquet on your own ass? In fact, how can anyone put a tourniquet on an ass?*

He steadied himself against the alley wall. Realized he was barely able to move, let alone walk. He had to think his way out of the jam.

'Are you all right?' asked a woman's voice.

Howie peered to his side. It was the dame with the big package. She'd obviously seen her attackers hightail it and come back to help.

'Sure,' he grunted through clenched teeth, 'apart from this blade in my butt, I've never been better.'

The woman looked around, and then disappeared behind him.

'No! Don't touch it! For fuck's sake, don't lay a finger on that friggin' knife.' And to make sure, he awkwardly turned himself away from her.

'You don't want me to pull it out?'

'No, no! I most definitely do *not* want you to pull it out.'

'Okay, okay!' she sounded panicky.

Howie could see the shock of the attack starting

to roll in on her. 'Take it easy, lady. They're gone. Everything's fine. But I'm gonna need your help now. Okay?'

'Christ!' she spluttered. 'They could have killed us. I mean, they had a gun and I don't know if it was real but it sure looked real and I never even saw the knife, but God, that's real, I mean, you . . . they've stuck a knife in you . . . and you're bleeding, and . . .'

'Yeah, lady, I'm bleeding – like a stuck pig,' said Howie, cutting her off, 'and you think we might be able to do something about that? Like maybe call an ambulance and get a paramedic here?'

'Yes, oh yes. God, I'm sorry. That must hurt, doesn't it?' She glanced to her left and right. 'Oh my, oh no! They've taken my purse! My phone, my cell was in that bag. With my keys, my house keys and things, personal stuff and pictures, and . . .'

'Whoah!' shouted Howie. 'Use my phone and ring a goddamn ambulance, and please be quick!' He painfully produced his cell from his jacket.

'They could have killed me. They could have raped me, or anything.'

'Lady, the phone!' Howie held it out to her, then steadied himself against the wall again.

The woman looked as though she was in a trance. She extended her hand in slow motion and took the phone. She flipped it open and stared at the keypad, like she'd never used one before.

And then, just as Howie thought she was about to punch in 911 – she fainted.

# 31

***Campeggio Castellani, Pompeii***

*Rosa Novello.*

Franco had seen her full name written down in his grandfather's Visitors Book. He kept suggesting they get a computer but he was told they were too expensive. A computer would be a relief for Franco. He'd had a stolen laptop for a while, bought it cheap from a Romanian gypsy staying on the camp. It had an aircard and pre-paid Internet access. But the real owner had cancelled the subscription after a few days and Franco had thrown it away in case the police traced it and caught him. For the brief time he'd used it, it had been a window on to the wider world. He'd looked in detail at his own disease, without the staring faces and probing lights of doctors around him. And he'd also tentatively explored the cyber underbelly of sex sites and chat rooms.

Rosa emerged from her caravan carrying a black sack of garbage. It was full and sharp corners of hidden trash were stretching it to bursting point. He wanted to go over and offer to carry it for her. That's what would happen in the films. That's how the hero would break the ice and get to know the girl of his dreams. Only real life wasn't like that. In real life she'd look at him and be scared. The shock would show in her eyes and she might even drop the whole sack. That's what others had done.

Rosa wore blue jeans and a red jumper. They didn't meet in the middle and her tummy showed. It stuck out like the top of a muffin, peeping above the rim of its greaseproof paper. He longed to touch her. Press his cheek against her muffin top. Smell it. Lick it.

The garbage bin was full so she dropped the sack alongside it and sashayed away. Her tight jeans showed her firm legs and what looked like the top of some tattoo on her back. Franco wondered what it was. Whether it stretched down into the crack of her bottom. What it would be like to run a finger over.

He was still thinking about the tattoo as he picked up her sack of trash and took it away. Precious treasure. He couldn't wait to be alone with it. To be able to secretly touch parts of Rosa's life.

# 32

***Ristorante di Rossopomodoro, Napoli***

Lunch was a *first* for the three eleven-year-old street kids. Before today, none of the *boy soldiers* had ever eaten in a restaurant.

The three friends forked pasta and meatballs into their mouths, barely pausing to gasp for air. They looked at the parents and kids around them, laughing and chatting. They couldn't believe that people lived like this. Happy, full, fat. Stealing from bins at the back of the kitchens was the closest to restaurant food they'd ever been. Opposite them were their heroes, Alberto Donatello and Romano Ivetta. The Camorristi were not eating; they were sipping espresso and talking in hushed tones. Soon the kids would be back on the streets, running the rounds, delivering their small plastic packs of heroin and cocaine. They got no pay for their labour, just food, the hint that one day they could have a future within the System and the most valuable thing of all, respect from their peers.

'You want some wine? I think maybe I'm gonna take a glass of red.' Donatello poured himself some.

He was twenty-seven and looked like a young Al Pacino with a beard.

'Not me.' Ivetta put his palm over his glass. 'I think I'll go to the gym.' He rolled up the sleeve of his black T-shirt and a tattooed male angel in chains grew in stature as he ostentatiously flexed his biceps. On the opposite arm was one of St Michael slaying a demon. Ivetta's body bore another twenty, all forms of angels and demons, ink-on-skin illustrations of his own mental struggles.

It had been a good morning. The boys had done well. Their deliveries had grossed a cool three thousand euros. Not a fortune, but the day was only half done and the kids were only one group of the six that Donatello and Ivetta ran. The boys pulled in an average of 5k per day per gang – 30k in total – and they worked six days a week. All in all, it added up to a chunky 180k a week, just short of three-quarters of a million per month. And, if the two Camorristi pushed the kids a little, they should gross almost ten mill for the year.

Running smack and charlie through a pipeline of juveniles was smart practice. If the kids got caught, they landed tiny sentences, maybe even just court warnings. But if any of the adult clan members were arrested, then they were looking at lock-ups north of five, sometimes ten years.

A waitress with blonde hair and dyed black ends cleared plates and handed out dessert cards to the boys. They were barely able to read the menus but the pictures lit up their eyes. They were still pointing and deciding when Ivetta suddenly snatched the cards from their hands and told them to get back to work.

The kids made no complaints. They grabbed their Nike rucksacks and headed for the door. The youngest doubled back to take a final gulp of his cherry Coke.

'You should have let them finish,' said the tall, dark-haired man joining them. 'I'm sure we all remember from prison that a well-fed workforce is much more willing.'

The two henchmen, aware that they were merely older versions of the boys they'd just sent away, ordered more coffees and settled back to hear Bruno Valsi's plans.

# 33

***Campeggio Castellani, Pompeii***

Franco took Rosa's sack to the pit.

It was long and deep and located in a field at the back of the campsite, more than a kilometre away from the last of the caravans. Grandpa Toni had been rich once and had had big plans for the land. Plans which, like most things in Grandpa Toni's life, had never materialized.

Only Franco came to the pit. Paolo would help him tour the shops and restaurants, collecting the trash in their old white van. But back at the site, only Franco would drive through the fields, dump the bags and spend hours burning the garbage. He loved nothing more than his fires. The flames soothed him. They broke chains in his mind and let his thoughts fly free.

Rosa's bag in hand, he slithered down the steep banking, his feet skating in wet mud that had been scorched black. Birds and rats scuttled and flapped, loath to leave the scraps they were feeding on. He put the sack down for a moment and dug beneath his anorak for Grandpa's pistol. The old man had several guns, including a hunting rifle, but the old Glock was perfect for the rats. A fat one spun towards the outside of the pit, running around the circumference like a furry grey ball on a clay roulette wheel. He watched it scarper anti-clockwise, took aim in front of it and squeezed. Boom! *Perfetto!* Franco felt a surge of adrenaline as blood and skin sprayed into the mud banking. But no sooner was the animal dead than it was forgotten. He'd not come to kill. Not this time.

The centre of the pit was where he normally built his fires and the far left-hand corner was where he hid his trophies. He sat there now, perched on a giant wooden bobbin that had once been wound with heavy-duty cable. He plucked at the black skin of the bag until it came away. Milk cartons, cereal packaging and tea bags tumbled out. He put them to one side. A cigarette with lipstick on the filter, a teenage fashion magazine, cotton wool with make-up on – he made a separate pile for those. Gradually, he built up a stack of anything he thought might have come from Rosa. Things *touched* by Rosa. Having items she'd owned made him feel as though he was part of her life. Even if it was only part of what she didn't want any more.

He unfolded a tissue. It was lightly perfumed and bore the pink outline of her lipstick. He lifted it so the dull daylight illuminated the place where her lips had been. Then he put his mouth against the imprint and closed his eyes.

Inhaled her perfume. Tasted her kiss. Slowly the tissue paper dissolved in his mouth. He ran his tongue over his teeth and swallowed. A trace of her inside him. *Heavenly. Like Holy Communion.* A micro-particle of the body and blood of Rosa Novello.

Franco took more than an hour caressing and sorting Rosa's garbage. He hid his trinkets in the bottom drawer of an old wooden bedside cabinet that he kept in a corner of the pit, beneath a makeshift shelter of boarding and clear plastic sheeting. His den. His sanctuary.

Finally, he gathered the rest of the garbage from the sack and put it in the centre of the pit. He balled up the pages of an old newspaper and set them on fire. As the flames rose and the smoke spiralled skywards he put his finger to his lips and thought once more of Rosa and how sweet she must taste.

# 34

***Grand Hotel Parker's, Napoli***

Jack finished dinner in his hotel room and waited for Sylvia to collect him. He wanted to see the crime scene at night. See it in the same way he guessed the killer had visited it and left it.

They met in reception and he saw how, despite her naturally pretty face, the strain of the inquiry was starting to show.

She came straight to the point. 'The ME's notes are in. You were right. The burning was ante-mortem. Francesca was set on fire while she was alive.'

Jack soaked it up. 'It takes a special type of monster to kill someone like that.'

'*Special?* Is that what you call them?' Sylvia led the way to the garage at the back of the hotel. It was hewn out of a giant hillside, high above the city.

Jack saw her point. 'I should have said the *worst* kind of monster. Organized. Sadistic. Relentless.'

She knew what he meant. 'The kind that doesn't stop unless they're caught. The kind that's probably killed before.'

'That's exactly the kind.'

Sylvia lit a cigarette as they waited for the valet to find her car. 'You're not a smoker, I can tell. I'm afraid I'm an addict. I know it's bad. And the more people tell me to stop, the more I have to continue.'

'Says a lot about your personality.'

She smiled. 'All Neapolitans are like that.'

'How so?'

'*Grazie mille*,' she tipped the valet as they got into her Alfa. 'We don't like being told what to do.' She stubbed the cigarette out in the tray on the dashboard and sparked up the engine. 'Take seat belts, for example. Hardly anyone in Naples wears one. Even though it's illegal not to. When it became law, the best-selling fashion accessory was a white T-shirt with a fastened seat belt painted on it. When you wore it, it looked like you had your belt on, even when you hadn't. People who had been fastening seat belts for years stopped doing so when it became law.'

'Shouldn't you know better? Set a good example?' asked Jack, lightly.

'I *do* know better. And I'll never wear a seat belt again. Two carabinieri friends of mine were shot dead in their cars by the Camorra. They still had their belts on. The restriction probably stopped them even drawing their weapons.'

'I'm sorry to hear it.'

'One of them almost lived. The ambulance turned

up really quickly – in fact, too quickly. The killer must have seen the paramedics set to work as they stretchered him away. After one block of lights the ambulance was ambushed. The assassin climbed into the back and finished the job.'

Jack noticed she'd jammed her army issue Beretta between her legs. Clearly she wouldn't be caught off-guard in an ambush. 'Creed mentioned the Camorra. You think they could be involved in all this?'

'Could be. They're like water. They're invisible, spread everywhere and hard to avoid.' The Alfa didn't so much join the traffic flow in front of the hotel as rocket into it. Horns blared and moped riders swerved, but Sylvia was unfazed.

Jack put a hand on the dashboard to brace himself. 'Man, I thought New York was dangerous, but it's Disneyland compared to here.'

Sylvia smiled. 'The secret of driving in Naples is not to care about what others are doing.' A moped zipped in front of their bumper. 'If you show any weakness or hesitation, then they will take advantage of you. Drive as though you are the only person on the road and you will be fine.'

From the city they took the A3 autostrada out towards Salerno. Jack continued to ask about the Camorra. 'If the mob are into everything, then how does that affect the way you investigate murders and missing persons?'

'It's a wall of silence,' explained Sylvia. 'If a Camorrista is involved then none of the clan will talk. Worse than that, if someone from the System is involved then you can bet no one in the city will talk either.'

After fifteen minutes of congestion-free traffic they began a steep spiralling climb. 'Not far from here, over at Sant'Anastasia, one of the biggest Camorra arms caches was discovered. They'd hidden everything from Uzis to AKs, enough to equip a small army. In fact several armies. The System imports weapons for use here in Campania and also to supply much of the rest of the world.'

'You have regular contact with your anti-mob squads?'

'Of course. And we'll reach out to them about this case – when the time is right. They're very busy right now and very difficult to deal with. We need to have more to go on before we knock on their door.' Sylvia spun the wheel expertly into sharp left- and right-hand bends that zigzagged towards the top of Vesuvius. 'During the day tourist coaches rule these roads. When they descend, everyone scatters so they don't get crushed by them.'

'Is this route used only by tourists?' Jack peered through the darkness at signs advertising cheap restaurants and hotels.

'No, not exclusively. There are houses, bars and businesses that locals frequent. Some of the workers in the park, or in the restaurants and snack bars, live around here.'

'Workers on Vesuvius?'

'Yes, on the volcano. Also in the national park where Francesca's remains were found. And further down in Pompeii and Herculaneum too. Work is hard to find and good housing even harder. If you get either, then you stick with it as long as you can. Nothing lasts forever. In Naples, nothing lasts very long.'

It took five more minutes for them to reach a lay-by where Sylvia pulled over. They got out and she produced two high-powered military flashlights from the trunk. Jack had expected a big entrance to the park but instead they took a worn path that wound uphill through a cluster of trees.

'Is this the main way in?'

'There are several routes, but this is the closest one you can take if you come here by car. This is the way that the man who found Francesca had taken.'

'The guy with the dog?'

'Yes.'

'So it's not necessarily the killer's route?'

'No, not necessarily.'

They walked in silence for a while, both wondering exactly who they were hunting. Jack thought of Creed. Had he been here with Francesca? Had he followed her out here? Perhaps approached her and been rebuffed? Had he killed her and returned her bones to the place where she'd rejected him? Or was Creed what he claimed to be – public-spirited and the only person so far to spot that a missing person was a murder victim? Had he not been so obnoxious – so sexually obsessed and twisted – it would have been easier to have believed him. Maybe one of the workers Sylvia had just mentioned was the killer? A tourist guide, bus driver or restaurant worker? They had local knowledge and, given how remote this place was, local knowledge was obviously a factor. Or could there be more than just an organic link to the Camorra, the evil and untouchable shadow that seemingly fell over everyone and everything in Campania?

'Here we are!' Sylvia's flashlight picked out an area still fenced and taped off but unguarded. 'When I first heard of the bones, I didn't think it would be murder.'

'Why's that?'

'Well, recently we've had a spate of discoveries. Bones have been found, not around here but across other parts of Naples.'

Jack looked confused.

'The city's cemeteries are as overcrowded as its slums. To make way for new burials – and the cash that accompanies them – the Camorra exhume graves then re-bury the bones in the countryside. Eventually the dearly departed work their way to the surface. Over at Santa Maria Capua Vetere so many bones were coming through in the fields that locals would cross themselves as they walked past.'

'Is nothing sacred any more?'

'Doesn't seem so. Some of my colleagues in public health discovered that the kids over there were pulling skulls out of the earth, cleaning them up and selling them in street markets.'

'So you thought that might have been the case here? Another field of Golgotha?'

'Right up until we confirmed the burning and breaking of the bones. That changed things a little.'

Sylvia waved her torch at the crime scene. 'This isn't the kind of place many people would come at night. I don't see our guy killing his victims out here, do you?'

Jack shook his head. It was really off the beaten track. Secluded. Miles from anywhere. 'I agree. This isn't the kind of place you can build a pyre, tie someone to a stake and set them alight. Too risky. Too open.'

'And anyway, I guess it'd be too awkward to bring her up here, control her and kill her in that kind of way?'

'Absolutely. He had somewhere else. Somewhere private. Some place no one could see the fire. Or if anyone did see it, then they would never think anything sinister was happening.'

Jack pictured Francesca being burned alive. Imagined her killer standing back and watching her die. *Was he smiling? Laughing? Masturbating?* He turned slowly. The bleached white beam of his flashlight played over the bushes and into the trees. *If he killed her some place else, then why bury her here? Why not drop the bones down some distant drains? Scatter them in far-off garbage sites. Dump them in the nearby bay. What was the significance of this place?* 'We seem to have stopped climbing. Am I right?' Jack queried.

'Well, if you'd have come in daylight,' she teased, 'then yes, you would instantly have noticed that this area is flat – or, at least, flatter than most of the land.' She pointed her beam of light into the distance and it flashed like a *Star Wars* light sabre. 'The ground climbs just a little over there. I wish you could see clearly because there's a wonderful view of Vesuvius from here – in the daylight, that is.'

Jack looked troubled. 'The volcano, this parkland, they have a special meaning for the killer, or his victims. Do any of the women have any ties to this area, any links that I should know of?'

Sylvia shook her head. 'None that we know of. We've only just started looking at the cases, but certainly Francesca didn't have any real links to this place.'

'Then it's the killer. The place holds some special significance for him.'

Sylvia turned in the dark towards the black peak of Vesuvius. 'What significance? I guess it's too early to hope you have any idea?'

Jack gazed into the distance. Tried to fish a

connection out of the darkness. 'That's the mystery we have to solve. And we have to do it quickly. Like we said, this is the worst kind of killer. And the worst kind not only kills again, it always happens sooner than you expect.'

# 35

***Campeggio Castellani, Pompeii***

Rosa Novello snuggled up to her boyfriend's arm as Filippo Valdrano drove his father's barely roadworthy old Fiat to the back of the campsite. He had the perfect spot in mind. A place where they could be alone. Away from the prying eyes of their parents.

The two families had been holidaying together for years, and since he and Rosa had become engaged their parents' attention had been suffocating. It was a relief to be on their own.

'Here's okay. Don't you think?' He drew to a halt and pulled up the handbrake. 'It's near the woods we walked in the other day.'

'It's just fine.' She leaned over and kissed him as he turned the engine off.

Filippo swooned, slipped down the straps of her pink top and nuzzled her neck.

'Wait!' she said playfully. 'Let's at least put the radio on. Get romantic. We don't have to rush.'

'Oh, baby. You don't know how wrong you are. I *need* to rush. I *really need* to rush!'

She pushed him away and twirled the dial, her heartbeat as loud as the crackling FM static.

Filippo pulled his T-shirt over his head and she instantly gave up on the music. God, he was hot! Muscled shoulders, rippling abs, not a pinch of flab. She pushed her mouth against his again and felt her breath escaping.

He pulled away. 'Wait! Hold on, wait!' He was teasing now, pulling away from her.

She stared at him. 'Oh, you really want to wait, do you?'

He tried to look disinterested as she slowly peeled off her top and then slowly released her pale-yellow, front-fastening bra.

All his coolness disappeared.

He lunged forward to put his mouth to her breasts.

'Oh, no, no, no!' She pressed the flat of her palm against his forehead and held him back. 'You said *wait*, so you can wait.'

Christ, he wanted her, ached for her. 'Let's push these seats forward and get in the back.'

'Now, that's the best idea you've had,' grinned Rosa. She kicked off her gold pumps, unzipped her white jeans and wriggled out of them. She arched her back to slip off her pale-yellow panties and, as she did, he kissed the flat of her stomach. She smelled of coconut body lotion. He cupped her buttocks with his hands and kissed and licked the inside of her thighs.

Rosa wriggled free, laughing as she climbed into the

back. Filippo tugged off his shoes and pants. The heat from their bodies was already steaming up the car. 'I'll open the window a little,' he said. He rolled down the passenger side and felt her hand gently rubbing his balls. Her fingers slipped inside his Calvin's and he gasped as she held him.

'Jesus, let me get back there!' Filippo caught a foot on the handbrake as he climbed over but he was beyond feeling pain. Right now there was nothing in the world that could keep him from his woman's body. Or so he thought.

# 36

***Campeggio Castellani, Pompeii***

A shrill scream scythed through the woods. It flew, unseen, like a bat in the blackness of the winter night. Then it thudded to its death against the misted windows of Filippo's father's car.

'*Ma che cazzo è?* What the fuck was that?' Rosa pushed Filippo away.

They froze. Stared silently at each other. Afraid to move. Then another chilling cry ripped the night apart.

'It's a woman screa–'

Filippo never finished. The next noise was even more distinct and terrifying.

It was a bullet.

Gunfire.

Filippo slid naked into the driver's seat and turned on the engine and the lights. Whatever was going down was happening close, real close. Too close.

The car's wheels spun on the soft wet grass. There was no traction. Mud sprayed as the old Fiat lurched forward. The wheels wallowed in the earth as he tried to make a full U-turn. Tried desperately to head back the way they'd come. The car carried on drifting. He straightened her up and turned the beams on full.

Right ahead he could see something. A light of some sort. Safety!

Another gunshot rang out.

A God-awful loud bark. So loud it seemed to bite a lump out of the sky.

It had come from near the light, now less than twenty metres ahead of them.

Filippo slammed on the brakes. The car went into an uncontrollable slide.

'*Fuuck!*' shouted Rosa as she was thrown against the back of the driver's seat.

He wanted to reach out and help, but he couldn't. The car was skidding towards a deep dip in the field. Sliding into a pit filled with fire.

Filippo jerked the handbrake up as hard as he could. Rosa crashed into a rear window. He twisted the steering wheel as far as it would go. The skid seemed to last an eternity.

Finally, the old car rocked to a stop. They were less than a metre from the edge of the pit.

'You okay?' He put his hand on his girlfriend's naked shoulder.

Rosa rubbed her head. She'd have an ugly lump there in the morning. 'Yeah, yeah, I'm fine. Let's get out of here. I'm scared.'

Filippo nodded. The car had stalled. He jammed it into neutral and quickly turned the key. The engine chugged but didn't catch. 'Flooded. I'll try again.' Clutch in, foot flat on the accelerator. He did everything he'd seen his father do. Turned the key again and prayed.

The roar was loud. Rosa thought the engine had exploded. Must have been a backfire.

Then she saw the blood. Filippo's blood. All over the passenger seat and the window.

And then she saw *him*.

His face in the broken window.

The gun in his hand.

That look in his eyes.

And he saw her too. Saw her beauty and her vulnerability.

Rosa was terrified.

She felt transparent, like a puddle that someone was about to stamp in.

'*Buon sonno*,' he said politely.

'Don't hurt me. Please, don't hurt me.' She covered her naked breasts with her arms and pressed her knees together.

His eyes vacuumed her skin. *Hurt*. A wonderful word. So short, yet covering a multitude of possibilities.

Rosa saw his teeth flash. He was smiling.

She could see the gun even more clearly now. See it and even *smell* it. It had the acrid stink of death. Filippo's. She glanced at his slumped body, blood pouring down his side, half of his beautiful face torn away by the bullet.

Fear choked her as she tried to speak again.

She started to cry. '*Please*, don't. Oh, God no, please, don't.' She pulled her knees up in a foetal position.

He watched her for a second, thrilled by her growing fear, excited by her suffering. Then he levelled his gun at her forehead.

'Oh, God. No, no, no!'

'BANG!' he shouted.

Rosa screamed.

He laughed. 'BANG! BANG!'

This time she didn't move. The warped trick no longer worked.

She stared straight into his eyes.

Cold.

Cold as ice.

He pulled the trigger.

He knew what the shot would do. Knew it would spread her face and brains all over the inside of the car. He didn't want to be covered in the mess. He stepped back just before the hammer fell.

*Live and learn,* he told himself. *Less mess means less trouble.*

He looked back into the car.

The windows were streaked in a fatty grey and cherry red.

The top of the girl's skull was gone.

There was no need for a second bullet.

# 37

***Grand Hotel Parker's, Napoli***

Jack was tired but didn't go to bed after Sylvia had dropped him at the hotel. It was still too early, and anyway his jet-lagged mind was still buzzing like a wasp in a jam jar. Instead, he persuaded a receptionist to give him some privacy and unlimited access to their latest dual-processor computer. As he fired it up, he remembered an old Quantico lesson: '*How* plus *why* equals *who*.'

He opened a search engine and a blank Word document. Then he opened his own stream of consciousness. A complete download of his thoughts.

**How?** – *burning, chopping, moving, burying.*

**Why?** – *sex, sadism, control, power, inadequacy.*

**Who?** – *stranger, lover, family, friend.*

Slowly but surely he covered all the key factors – the type of weapon used, the killing scene, disposal site, offender's risks, likely methods of controlling the victims. He thought long and hard about the personality of the killer, the geography of the area, whether the crime indicated any kind of compulsive or impulsive behaviour – the fire was certainly indicative of the former. He considered the ritualistic aspects. Wondered whether the killer would have taken trophies, and what kind. But he dwelled the longest on the burning. The burning was linked to gratification and that made it the killer's behavioural signature.

The pages soon filled up. So did his mind. To the point of overload.

Jack stopped and sipped at some coffee that he'd ordered ages ago and had ignored when it eventually arrived. Now it was cold, but he drank it anyway.

He Googled Vesuvius. Much of it he knew. Some of it he didn't.

> **Known** – *major eruption in 79@c, still live and continuous eruptions this century. Last blew in 1944. Officially rated as one of the most dangerous volcanoes in the world.*
>
> **Unknown** – *three million people live within close proximity of it. Thought by the Greeks and Romans to be sacred to Hercules, the son of Zeus, and named in his honour.*

He finished the last of the coffee and Googled Hercules. The guy came out as pure alpha male. Warrior, sex god, inspiration to warlords like Mark Antony. That he knew too. He read on. Death and sex ran throughout the storyline. Ran through the whole region. He spent some moments looking at a painting – Hercules and the Lernaean Hydra. He vaguely remembered the story. A snake with dozens of heads, and every time one was chopped off another one grew. From what he'd heard, it sounded like the Camorra. From what he knew, it also reminded him of the worst of the serial killers he'd hunted – always a fresh body, always a new horror.

Jack did another search.

*Hercules triumphed over his enemy by the use of fire.*

He *burned* the hydra to death. Then he *buried* it beneath rocks.

Burning and burial so close to a site held sacred to Hercules. Coincidence or connection? Rational or rubbish? He was almost too tired to tell.

Was someone killing their own demons by burning and burying people? Did the killer have a specific enemy that he'd declared a one-man war on?

Jack stretched and yawned. His eyes stung from jet lag and his body cried for sleep. But not yet. There were more questions to answer.

Did the insignificant and inadequate Creed see himself as some kind of Hercules? Or was Jack making connections that simply didn't exist? Sometimes people don't kill for deep psychological reasons; they do it just because they like it. Because it turns them on.

Tiredness kicked in and his thoughts wandered. Images of home. Nancy, Zack and Casa Strada in the rolling Tuscan countryside. Sunshine and laughter.

Long hot days in the Val d'Orcia. Cool nights in the hotel gardens perfumed by lavender and roses. And then he thought of Nancy. Making slow love to her in the morning. Lying close together afterwards, her head on his chest. Her breathing making him sleepy.

Jack's eyelids grew heavy. The warm room and the toll of the day made him drowsy. Within seconds he was asleep at the computer. But there was no sweetness in his dreams. No room – or time – to think about the good things in life. Thoughts of serial murder seeped from his subconscious. Bubbled up like toxic waste from the barrels the Camorra dumped on the ocean's floor.

Relentless killings. Horrendous burnings. A cold-blooded killer on the loose and poised to strike again. It was a wonder he could sleep at all.

Jack's mind continued the struggle to make sense of it all. To understand the links between the murders, the legends of Hercules, the local crime gangs and the strange young man who'd crossed continents to get him involved in all this.

Deep down – way down among all that waste and poison – was the answer. And he knew he'd find it. Whatever it took. Whatever it cost him.

# 38

***Campeggio Castellani, Pompeii***

Franco wondered whether anyone would come. He hung back in the bushes. Cradled his grandfather's Glock. Wait. Part of him wanted to run. Part wanted to be with Rosa. Dead Rosa. *Naked* Rosa.

It was cold and he was shivering. Rain fell noisily through the trees and bushes. Spiky hawthorn branches dug into his face and neck as he hid among them.

*Naked Rosa.* The pull was too strong.

He opened the car door, barely looking at Filippo's corpse. The harsh interior light made Rosa's flesh look bleached white. Or was it death? Did death take your colour so quickly?

Franco didn't notice her blood and brains sprayed all around the interior. His eyes focused only on her nakedness. Her vagina was shaved, like ones he'd seen on the websites he'd visited. Fascinating. Exciting. He reached over Filippo, careful not to get his blood on his clothes, and touched her thighs.

Cold.

Cold, but also *smooth*. And beautiful.

He leaned further into the car so he could run his hand between her legs.

Warm. Still warm.

The intimacy exhilarated him. He stood mesmerized, his hand glued between her thighs. Afraid to let go. Afraid to end the experience.

Reluctantly, he withdrew. Tried not to touch anything as he left. He knew the dangers of doing that.

Poor Rosa.

Poor dead Rosa.

He stopped at the door of the car and looked back inside. A thought struck him. A way of keeping her with him *alive* forever.

Paolo was asleep in his bunk when Franco got to the van. He was still excited by what he'd just done. Rosa had changed everything. Things were going to be different. He just knew it. His body was filled with mutant genes and he could feel them now, moving around inside him, distorting his DNA, making him do things he shouldn't. 'Paolo,' he called lightly, squinting into the darkness.

Unless he was mistaken his eyesight was going too. His doctors had warned him that would happen. Cataracts, they'd said.

'Paolo!' he called again, this time in a pitch somewhere between normal and shouting. His cousin was out for the count. That was good. Franco didn't want him to wake. He just wanted to be *really* sure that he was asleep.

He knelt down by his own bed. Not so he could pray, but so he could go to heaven. Tucked into the springs of the mattress he found what he was looking for. He unwrapped an old cotton flannel. Inside was a small sachet of heroin, the bottom of an old Coke can and a syringe that he'd found in a waste bin at the hospital where he went for his check-ups. He looked at the slightly bent and dirty needle and smiled. He knew the risks that went with second-hand spikes, but hell, compared to all the other shit in his life, why should he care?

He used the spike to suck fifty units of water from a bottle he had. He squirted it in the can and fired up his lighter to dissolve the heroin. He paused and checked that Paolo was still sleeping. Better than that. He was now snoring. He stabbed the spike into one of the blue veins in his left forearm. As he squeezed in the heroin he realized that he'd also pumped in about a quarter of an inch – ten units – of air. Others might have been worried. Franco didn't give a fuck. He thumbed in the rest of the H. Rolled back on to the bed. Waited for it to kick in.

It did.

First a little dizziness. Then nausea. Finally a warm mellowness. A gentle calm. A soft summer breeze flowing through his body.

His *beautiful* young body. The way it should be.

The way Rosa would have liked it.

# THREE

# 39

***Santa Lucia, Napoli***

The early morning sun burned gold on the balconies of the rich and famous along the Santa Lucia seafront. In a fit of pique, Bernardo Sorrentino slammed his morning newspaper on to the glass breakfast table. The exclusive he'd given *Il Giornale di Napoli* hadn't even made the front page. The days when murder had been a forty-eight-point bold-font lead in Naples were long gone. Worse than that, the photograph they'd used on page sixteen was terrible. He was bending in undergrowth and looked like he had a double chin and a fat stomach. What was the point of a hundred sit-ups a day, if the media made a fool of you like this?

He paced uncomfortably by the apartment window and stared east across the bay. Dark rain clouds gathered in the distance like a flotilla of grey ships readying themselves for battle with the weak winter sun. There would be only one winner. He returned to his paper and read the story again. Six paragraphs, that was all he'd got. And he suspected that if Francesca Di Lauro hadn't been pregnant then he might not have got any at all. *Merda!* He poured himself orange juice while his ego feasted on the few words that praised him – *The scientific expert had reconstructed skull fragments to make up Francesca's lower jaw and enable identification from dental records. Sorrentino's painstaking labours are making him a law enforcement legend.*

Legend. He liked that bit. Okay, so these days murder was no longer big news, but *Il Grande Leone* was a legend and still warranted newsprint. He was starting to feel much better when his gold-plated cellphone rang – a ringtone of music that he'd personally composed. He looked at the caller display and grimaced. '*Buon giorno, Capitano.* I have been trying to call you.'

On the other end, Sylvia Tomms erupted. Her language would have shamed a Neapolitan docker.

Sorrentino protested the best he could. 'Sylvia, it wasn't me! It was a leak. Truly, a dreadful leak.'

Sylvia's swearing continued to scorch the phone and Sorrentino had to wait for the abuse to die down before adding, 'My assistant Ruben was responsible for it. I have fired him. He's cleared out his desk and gone back to his precious Catalan friends in Barcelona. Treacherous snake! I am so angry and so embarrassed. I tried to call you as soon as I found out but I was told you were unavailable. And as you know, you refused to give me your private cellphone number when I asked for it.'

Sylvia Tomms felt furious and sickened. His comment about her private number reminded her of the awful day when Sorrentino had hit on her. He'd told her how exciting she would find it to spend an evening – and maybe a night – with him. The memory stoked her anger and she imagined what a good punchbag he'd make if only she were near him and had a spare half-hour to let off steam.

'I really am very sorry about this leak, and I do hope it doesn't personally cause you too much trouble.' Sorrentino made little effort to sound sincere.

Finally she hung up on him and he allowed himself a smile. He was happy there had been no need to tell her what else he'd discovered. What vital information he'd held back from the press, and from her. Something far more significant than Francesca being pregnant. Something that would teach her not to treat him as though he weren't good enough for her. Something that might even make the front page.

# 40

***Campeggio Castellani, Pompeii***

Martina Novello snorted contemptuously at the bed her daughter had *clearly* not slept in. 'Idiot.' Surely she could have waited. No, of course not. Rosa was never one for waiting. No waiting to have sex. No waiting to spend the night with a man who wasn't fit to clean her shoes. *That girl – she'd been born early and been impatient ever since.*

The sheets on Rosa's small bunk were pulled tight and tidy, just as Martina had made them, but she still couldn't help freshening them up, turning back the top sheet and re-creasing it. She smiled as she moved Benni, a tiny teddy bear, given to Rosa at birth and now losing his fur in several places.

Cristiano, her lump of a husband, lumbered into the caravan's awful chemical toilet, clutching yesterday's newspaper. *Damned paper.* These days he spent more time looking at newsprint than he did at her. When had that all changed? More memories tumbled in – Cristiano back in his twenties, with the body of a boxer, a twinkle in his eye and a permanent hard-on. So long ago, and yet still so vivid.

Martina wriggled her feet into blue slippers and padded outside to the neighbouring caravan. She'd give them hell for letting her daughter sleep over with that no-good Filippo. She rapped her knuckles on the cold thin metal of the Valdrano camper and a thought hit her. Rosa had *never* stayed out before, not all night, so why now? Martina could hear voices, mumblings inside, the scraping of furniture and the patter of feet on the thin floor of the cheap van.

'*Buon giorno.*' Filippo's mother had bags under her eyes and no make-up. Her cream dressing gown was pulled tight to reveal a pale neck and fatty legs.

'Claretta, is Rosa here? Is she with Filippo?'

The boy's mother sensed worry rather than anger in her friend's voice. 'No, I don't think so.' She walked towards the back of the van, slid open a wooden door. The empty bed told its own story. 'He's not there, Martina.' Fear creased her face as she stated the obvious. 'He's not at yours – not with Rosa?'

Martina shook her head. 'Your car's gone. Did you know that?'

Claretta stuck her head out into the wind and saw the empty space. 'Oh, God. Come in and shut the door. I'll wake Nico.'

And she did. But her husband had no idea either. Not about the kids. Not about the car. Nor did Cristiano when Martina called him over.

Claretta made coffee while they discussed the possibilities: an accident, an elopement, or something less dramatic and romantic – as Nico speculated. Maybe they'd parked somewhere and fallen asleep, run out of petrol, found a party and stayed but hadn't rung because it had been late. None of them spoke of anything worse. But they all thought it.

Two hours later Cristiano rang the police.

# 41

***Grand Hotel Parker's, Napoli***

Jack was still asleep at the hotel's computer terminal when his cellphone rang. It flashed Howie's number. He mumbled hello and checked his watch. Nine a.m. in Naples, three in New York. 'You up early or going home late?'

'Just got in,' growled Howie.

The big guy sounded dreadful, no doubt plastered again. 'What happened? You get lost trying to find your way around the whisky bottle?'

Howie let out a low grunt. 'No. I was doing fine for sobriety. Then some robbing little punk in an alleyway knifed me in the ass. I've spent all night in the ER, having nurses stare at my butt and stitch up the wound.'

'In the ass? Man, I'm sorry. You okay?'

'Fine and dandy. I tell you, buddy, some little fucko nearly speared me right up the ring-hole. The nurse said if he'd put the knife train any deeper into the big dark tunnel then I would have bled to death.'

Jack screwed up his face in sympathy.

'If you're laughing, I'll never talk to you again.'

Then Howie couldn't help but laugh himself. 'Okay, so I admit it's funny. But listen, I think it'll be a friggin' year before I can sit down again, and Christ knows how much it's gonna hurt when I take a shit.'

'Too much detail. But, hey. I really am sorry.'

'Sure. Anyways, despite my personal tragedy – which you see fit to smirk at – I still done good with regards to your man Creed.'

Jack raised an eyebrow. 'Above and beyond the call of.'

'Yeah, and don't you forget it. So here you go . . .' Howie growled again as he repositioned himself. 'Let's start at the hotel. No guests, no minibar consumption beyond some water, Pringles and two bottles of beer. Room-service dinner – only for one – and breakfast in his room too. Some photocopying and newspapers. You following me?'

'Right alongside. Boring as hell.'

'Sure is, but it gets a might more interesting in a few lines' time. Remember the hotel receptionist you flirted with?'

'Kind of.'

'Polish woman, Brenda Libowicz, at the Lester. Anyways, she remembers you. I took her for that coffee you didn't have time for and it paid off a little. Brenda let me go through everything and it seems your friend Creed pretty much had the porn channel on full-time.'

'Old news. I thought I'd told you that?'

'Not that I recall. But there's more. Movie porn

wasn't his only turn-on. He also spent a lot of time on the Internet.'

'You get browser data?'

'Did Clinton get a blow job?' Howie pulled over a computer printout that was lying on the table next to his notebook. 'Creed did several searches on BDSM and watched some real hard-core adult sites. Get this; he specifically searched for dark-haired women who were between seventeen and thirty. He spent an hour on Court TV's crime library reading stories about killers who buried bodies. He went through all our old friends including John Wayne Gacy and Gary Ridgeway, spent a whole lot of time on the Cleveland Torso murders and then ended up reading everything that was ever written about the Sunday Morning Slasher.'

Jack stopped him. His mind was hopelessly trying to make connections. It felt like wiring a plug in the dark. 'That's ringing all kinds of bells. The Slasher is the Coral Watts case, isn't it?'

'The one and only,' said Howie. 'Coral Eugene *Sonofabitch* Watts. Killed several young women. Drowned them, strangled them, cut their throats or knifed them dozens of times. And the bastard claimed to have murdered dozens more that the cops never found.'

Jack finally made his mental connection. 'Watts buried his victims and that's why they weren't found for years and he was able to carry on killing. On top of that, he used to ceremonially burn trophies he took from the bodies.'

'Yep, so you have some clear comparisons there – the missing women, the burials, even some burning.'

'Thanks, buddy, I'd just about joined those dots on my own.'

'Well done. There's another thing,' he said, his voice growing flat and worried. 'Turns out that Creed *has* had and still *does* have access to FBI files.'

'Say again.' Jack hoped he'd misheard.

'One of the Internet cookies I traced was Creed's log-in to the FBI's Virtual Academy. Seems that he's been enlisted as a *student* of the VA.'

The Virtual Academy was a global distance-learning site, jammed with information and famed for helping to hone profiling techniques. Access was restricted to the law enforcement world.

The breach rendered Jack silent.

'You hear me?' asked Howie.

'I hear you. Only now the dots make a picture that I really don't like. The thought of a possible offender being deep inside our corridors of knowledge fills me with dread. We need to find out everything this sonofabitch has read or written, and whoever he's spoken to. And we need to do it fast.'

# 42

***Campeggio Castellani, Pompeii***

For a split second Franco Castellani couldn't work out the cause of the sharp slapping sensation inside his head. Still slow and wasted from the heroin, he gradually realized that the pain was coming from his grandfather's hand rather than from the after-effects of the drug.

'What in God's name do you think you are doing? You crazy crazy, child!'

Franco covered his face. Not that the slaps carried much weight. *Rosa.* His fingers still smelled of Rosa.

'Sit up! Sit up and tell me that this is *not* what I think it is. Not what I *know* it is.'

Antonio backed off to give him room. Franco forced his eyes open wide enough to see the syringe and the empty plastic packet being dangled above him. The air was hot and stale. Flies buzzed around a dirty plate near his cousin's bed. Franco finally commanded his legs to move and raised himself into a sitting position. The door jerked open and blinding white light flooded in. Paolo stopped in his tracks, fresh bread and milk in a carrier bag swinging in his hand.

'Get out!' shouted Antonio.

Paolo turned on his heels.

Franco noticed his cousin had been dressed in work clothes. He guessed he'd overslept and his grandfather had come looking for him. 'It's heroin,' he admitted, shielding the light from his face. 'If you were me, you'd be taking it too. Lots of it.'

His grandfather slapped him again. 'Don't give me this self-pity shit. Be *proud* of who you are, *what* you are.'

Franco put his hands back to his face; this time the blows had stung. '*What* I am? I'm *the living dead*, that's what I am.'

Antonio hit him again. Slapped hard at the boy's stubborn head. Tried to knock some sense into his thick skull. Then he grabbed him. Shook him and held him. And felt his own tears stream down his face. 'Franco, you shame yourself with this stuff. You disrespect yourself and your family. We are not junkies. We are not cowards. Whatever life throws at us we raise our heads above it and show the world we are proud to be ourselves.'

'But *I'm* not, Grandpa. I'm not proud.' His voice was shaky and his eyes watery. 'I hate myself and everything that's happening to me.'

Antonio held his grandson by the arms. His brown, liver-spotted fingers dug into the thin white forearms snaked with needle tracks. 'Don't do this, Franco. Be a man. Come on; find your self-respect.'

Franco Castellani searched deep inside himself.

There was no trace of self-respect. Only a stinking sump-oil residue of painful memories. His jailbird father, his runaway mother and his current flea-pit, hand-to-mouth existence. Finding respect was impossible.

'I'm sorry,' he said and kissed the top of his grandfather's head. 'I know I disappoint you. *Mi dispiace.*'

Before Antonio could reassure him, Franco had pulled away from his grandfather and was gone. Leaving the wind to slam shut the rusty old door of the van.

# 43

*Napoli Capodichino*

Salvatore Giacomo's knees cracked as he bent to pick up the morning mail behind his apartment door.

It was his fiftieth birthday. Not many people knew that. Even fewer cared.

The mail included several free newspapers, an electricity bill, but no cards. He sat alone in the kitchen of his one-bedroomed rental. Although he was a couple of blocks back from the busy A56 he could still feel the steady rumble of traffic. He breakfasted on instant coffee and old cheese slices. As he ate, he thought about his half-century on earth. What did it amount to? A little cash in a number of false bank accounts. Run-for-the-hills money. Start-all-over-again dough. He'd never use it. Never spent much, anyway. He didn't drink, didn't smoke, didn't have friends. He just worked and came home. What money the Don gave him went on rent, cheap food and the savings he'd never need. Don Fredo had said to put something away every month, so he'd done that. He'd always done whatever the Don had said.

Sal guessed he saw Fredo as a father figure.

A replacement for his old man. He'd been nine years old when his parents had split up. He still remembered the fearful row; his father slapping his mother's face and calling her a cheating slut, then storming off. A father one minute. A memory the next. Then strange men came to stay at the apartment, men who looked at him with spiteful eyes. He hated his mother for letting them in. Into the house. Into his father's bed. It wasn't long before he ran away. Stayed with friends on the other side of Herculaneum or, in summer, camped out in the parkland around Vesuvius, killing wood pigeons and foxes. Then in his teens his mother disappeared and he pretty much made his own way in life. His brains and his fists helped him survive and stay one step ahead of the law.

The distinctive horn of the Mercedes sounding in the street shook him from his thoughts. Valsi had arrived and was waiting.

Sal pulled on the jacket of a navy-blue suit, adjusted his tie in the old tarnished mirror by the front door and, before leaving, checked just one more thing. His weaponry. Sal never opened a door without being ready to deal with anything that was on the other side. It was that level of caution that had got him through the first fifty years of his life, and he hoped would get him through many more years. For that reason, Sal didn't carry just one gun, he carried two. Matching Glock 19s, snugly concealed in a double shoulder holster. The pair gave him a minimum of thirty rounds of 9mm ammunition. What's more, if one jammed or got dropped, then that was no shit, he just pulled the other one. If he was caught in a firefight, he could also throw the spare to whoever was with him. The horn sounded again. *Capo* or no *Capo*, the fucker could wait. He took a leak, locked up and left the building.

'Sal, you're slower than a snail,' shouted Dino Pennestri from the driver's seat as he approached the car. 'We should call you Sal the Snail.'

Giacomo said nothing. He slipped in the back, alongside Bruno Valsi, who greeted him with a curt '*Buon giorno.*'

They drove in silence for about a minute. Valsi shifted in his seat so he was half facing Sal. He wore an open-necked black and blue striped shirt and had a cream suit jacket across his lap. 'I've got a little surprise for you,' he deadpanned.

Sal waited. Valsi tilted his eyes down to the jacket on his lap. Between the folds of cream cloth something smooth and shiny caught Sal's eye. Unmistakably, it was the barrel of a pistol.

'Given that it's your birthday, I'd thought I'd do something truly memorable.' Valsi flicked away the sleeve of the jacket and Sal could see that his right hand was wrapped around the pistol, his index finger already inside the guard and across the trigger.

For a moment all sound seemed to have been sucked out of the air inside the car. No one dared breathe.

Then the laughter in the Mercedes nearly tore the roof off.

Sal the Snake was the only one not splitting his sides.

'It's yours, you old fool,' said Valsi. He spun the pistol round so Sal could take it off him. 'It's a present. A limited edition Ultimate Vaquero. It's been in the family for years.'

Up front, Tonino Farina and Dino Pennestri were roaring so loudly that Pennestri had to pull over so he didn't crash the car.

'Happy birthday, Sal.' Valsi leaned over and embraced him. In the brief clinch, he smelled the older man's fear. A victory in itself. 'It's a point-thirty calibre, a little more unusual and special than the forty-five. The grip is made of white pearl and you'll see the barrel and trigger are bejewelled. Go to a dealer, you won't get change out of three thousand euros.'

'*Grazie mille.* It is *bellissimo.*' Sal checked the chamber. He was glad to find it empty.

'It's a gift from my wife and me,' said Valsi. 'She gave me a card to give you too.'

Sal watched as he slid a beige envelope out of the inside of his folded jacket. The envelope and the card were the type that only a woman would buy. Thick, expensive card. A simple artistic picture of a beautiful Fall sunset on the front and no printed message inside, so she could write her own. In a beautiful hand she had written quite simply: *Happy Birthday 'Uncle Sal', may your own Fall and Winter be the most beautiful seasons of your life. Love and best wishes, Gina x.*

Valsi could see that for the first time his wife had signed only her own name. He was just the delivery boy. Fucking bitch. 'I'm not one for sentiment,' he explained with disdain, 'but I am one for pleasure. So, my very old *friend*, we're taking you to Bar Luca for a celebratory lunch.' He produced a thick wad of fifty-euro bills from his pants pocket. 'Today, I'm gonna pay for all the champagne you can drink. All the food you can eat. And all the whores you can fuck. That is, presuming you can still drink and fuck at your age.'

'I don't drink,' said the Snake.

'Then you can watch us. We'll celebrate for you!' Valsi slapped his shoulder.

Farina and Pennestri broke up again. Sal made an effort to smile. Deep down he was thinking about how dangerously close he'd come to killing Valsi when the snot-nosed little punk had pulled the piece on him.

# 44

***Stazione dei carabinieri, Castello di Cisterna***

Sorrentino's minor splash in the newspapers provided the murder squad with a surprising opportunity. Somehow the story was attracting growing national interest. Maybe the nation had a heart after all. Anyway, Sylvia Tomms saw it as a clear chance to keep the case in the public eye and maybe flush out more information. Perhaps, even, the killer himself. With this in mind she scheduled a press conference for the end of the day and hoped to persuade Francesca's parents to attend and make a public statement.

The inquiry was gathering pace and she needed a brief pause to gather her thoughts. She skipped lunch and took a short walk into the small town of Castello di Cisterna. *Missing women, a burned corpse, a dead foetus, no witnesses, an untrustworthy ego-bloated scientist and a murder squad that was exhausted before it had even started.*

It was like trying to catch cats.

Once she got an investigative focus on one or two aspects, the others escaped her attention and started causing problems.

Was she out of her depth? There were certainly male colleagues who hoped she was. But she didn't think so. This plainly wasn't going to be the run of the mill inquiry everyone had first thought. Better than that, it was going to be a real challenge. A test of wits as well as techniques. She could raise her game. She was good at not being frightened. Good at facing up to big problems and nibbling away at them until she found bite-sized solutions. And she had Jack. He seemed smart enough to come up with a break for them. Experienced enough to pull her through the unfamiliar quicksands of what she feared may well turn into a serial murder inquiry. Her bosses had scoffed when she'd asked for the profiler, but she knew he'd be of value.

It was raining again by the time she walked the last half-mile back to the barracks, but she was so focused she didn't even notice. By early afternoon she had the inquiry team fired up again and locked into the drudgery of sifting statements and checking information. Patience and precision were Sylvia's key tools. Never rush. Never miss anything.

Jack arrived for the three p.m. briefing and afterwards retreated to a spare office to make his daily call home. No matter where he was, or what he was doing, Jack always broke from events to phone home and speak to his wife and son. Last year's ordeal with the Black River Killer had been a stark personal reminder of how precious his family was, and how much the young boy needed regular contact with his father.

'How you doing, big guy? You been having fun with Gramps and Grandma?'

Zack's voice was full of excitement. 'Guess what? Gramps took me to play baseball. He says Santa might bring me a real pitcher's glove and real bat for Christmas. D'you think he will, Daddy? Do you?'

Jack told him there was a *real* good chance that Santa would do that. He flexed his left hand as they talked and felt an ache run from the palm to the elbow. Nerve damage that still hadn't healed properly. Another souvenir from his hunt for the Black River Killer. A twinge that always returned whenever he was tired and stretched. 'Has Mommy been good, or has she been spending money again?'

'She's been spending. And she and Grandma have been drinking wine too.'

Jack laughed and thanked his small snitch for the inside info before asking for the phone to be given back to his mom.

'So, how are you holding up?' asked Nancy. 'You sound tired.'

*You sound tired.* His wife's diplomatic way of delicately reminding him of the burn-out that had once almost killed him.

'I'm okay, honey; just things are a bit more complicated than I thought.'

'They always are, Jack,' she replied tersely. 'You going to make it back sometime soon?'

He flinched. 'Not *so* soon. I'm sorry. I think I'm going to have to be here a few more days yet.'

Silence fell. Then she drew a deep breath and let fly. 'Jack, you said four days tops. Please don't mess us all around on this. I've got Christmas coming up, your son is bursting to see you, and my mom and dad were expecting to share a little time with you as well.'

The telling-off lasted several more minutes before he invented a white lie that there was a car downstairs waiting for him and he had to go. 'Love you, sweetheart. Kiss Zack for me.'

'I will. We love you too.' She meant it, but her voice was strained, not only with annoyance and disapproval but also with worry.

Jack tried to banish the loneliness creeping up on him. Zack had sounded so beautiful. So young. So pure. *Pure.*

The word cannoned around inside him. He'd become so obsessed with Vesuvius and Hercules and the geography of the place, he'd forgotten the deep importance of fire. It made things pure. In religious rites, pagan rites and all magical rites since time began, fire was always a way of cleansing impurity.

But what impurity?

What had the women done?

What was their crime against the killer?

# 45

***Bar Luca, Napoli***

They ate steaks and salads for Sal's birthday lunch. From a distance it looked like they were all having a ball. But everyone around the table knew that soon – maybe sooner than even they thought – either Salvatore Giacomo would kill Bruno Valsi, or vice versa.

As far as Pennestri and Farina were concerned, they would try to avoid picking sides right up until the very last moment. Fredo Finelli was their ultimate boss and for now it was far too early to bank on the ballsy young Bruno being able to topple the Don. If anything, they would bet against it. But the two men had been Camorristi long enough to know you should never say never.

Bar Luca was a basement haunt in the city centre. Recently refurbished, it pumped out ice-cold air conditioning and the kind of atmosphere that made every minute feel like a Friday night. Sitting at a dark wood table, not far from a pole around which a half-naked girl posed and pouted, they'd finished their food and the drink was flowing.

'Fifty years old – half a fucking century, Sal, it's a

wonder you have the strength to haul yourself out of bed in the morning. I salute you.' Valsi raised another cold one to his lips.

'*Salute!* Although, to be honest, I've never felt stronger or fitter than I do now.' Sal raised his own glass of Cola Lite.

'Maybe you should look for a new job, something softer, a bit easier on the old bones?' chided Pennestri.

Sal forced a smile. 'You know, old bones or not, I'm stronger and tougher than anyone around this table. You'd all do well to remember it.'

'Even your boss?' said Valsi. There was a hint of steely challenge in his voice. 'You think you're stronger than me?'

Sal smiled again, but this time he didn't have to force it.

'Bruno, I *know* I'm stronger than you.'

'Okay, birthday boy.' Valsi stripped off his jacket and rolled up a sleeve. 'Arm wrestle me.'

Pennestri and Farina exchanged glances. This was going to be good.

Valsi had wrestled plenty in prison, and had never lost. 'Guys, clear the table. Make room for me and Grandpa.'

Looking across the table, now sticky with beer, he saw no fear in Salvatore Giacomo's eyes. Pennestri and Farina moved plates and glasses from the surface.

'Break a glass,' insisted Valsi. 'Put half of it on one

side, half on the other.' He grinned at Sal. 'Let's make it more interesting.'

Pennestri rolled a beer glass in two napkins and dropped it on the floor. Sal watched with amusement as he sprinkled slivers and shards at opposite ends of the table. 'I'm going for a piss, Bruno. While I'm away, take time to think about whether you really want to do this.' He started to rise from his chair but Valsi grabbed him by the forearm. 'You leave the table when I tell you, and you don't piss until I tell you. Now wrestle.'

Sal laughed at him. 'Don't be such a child. I work for your father-in-law, not you. The Don told me to keep you out of trouble, not cut you up.' He pulled his arm free.

'Just wrestle, you fucking coward,' insisted Valsi. 'Don Fredo would expect you to be a man not a chicken.'

Sal's smile dropped. He'd been pushed too far. 'Okay. Let's do as you say.' Jacket still on, he angled his elbow and opened his hand so Bruno could grip it.

'You call it, Tonino,' Valsi ordered. He moulded his fingers into Sal's grip. Tried to gain the first advantage.

Farina looked at the men's faces, then counted a beat. 'Go!'

Valsi's biceps tensed and bulged. Blue veins rippled down his arm. He powered all his superior weight into Sal's arm.

The Snake rocked for a moment. His opponent's

speed and sudden force made his whole body quake. His elbow slid and almost buckled. He felt his wrist being stretched and strained. Each opponent's arm shook under the effort. Valsi slowly began to inch his way to victory. 'Birthday, or no fucking birthday, I'm going to teach you a lesson, motherfucker.'

Sal looked at the broken glass, ominously positioned exactly where his hand would be crushed back. His arm was now almost at a forty-five-degree angle, but his face still showed no fear. Slowly and very deliberately he began *squeezing* Valsi's hand.

It took Valsi several seconds to work out what was happening. Sal's arm wasn't going back any further. It wasn't going down. But a vice-like grip was gradually crushing his fingers.

Sal's eyes registered no emotion. He carried on crushing. He could feel the bones in Valsi's fingers grinding against each other. He kept squeezing.

The pain started to show on Valsi's face. Pennestri and Farina could see it too.

Sal hunched forward a little. 'Would you like to stop?' he whispered across the table.

Valsi said nothing. He tried to use the pain to summon a second surge of strength. He channelled all his efforts into ramming Sal's hand down on to the jagged glass. But he couldn't.

The Snake's iron grip tightened another notch.

Then another.

And another.

Valsi hung his head low. The pain was unbearable.

He wanted to scream. Yell his head off like a teenage girl at a horror movie. He ground his teeth and ate up the agony. Swallowed the fear, and the shame that came with it. But he knew he didn't have much longer. Soon the bastard would break his hand. Crush his fingers like day-old breadsticks.

'We can stop whenever you want.' said Sal, in a humiliating matter-of-fact tone. 'Just say it.'

Valsi's eyes blazed. Defiance. One last effort.

But he didn't have anything to give.

Sal swung Valsi's crushed hand and drained arm up into the vertical, then, like a felled tree, down towards the spikes of shining glass.

Valsi shut his eyes. Readied himself for the pain. And the humiliation.

And it came. But not in the way he expected. Much worse.

Sal let go.

Just a centimetre from victory, the Snake opened his fingers and slipped his arm away. 'Enough,' he said, as though bored with a naughty child. 'I'm going to take that piss now.'

# 46

***Stazione dei carabinieri, Castello di Cisterna***

In a grey anteroom to hell – a waiting room inside the carabinieri barracks – the parents of Francesca Di Lauro wept in each other's arms. It was the first time they'd touched since divorcing more than ten years ago.

The Di Lauros had thought they could never feel sadder than the moment when they'd learned of their daughter's murder. But the news that she'd also been pregnant had ratcheted them deeper into the depths of despair.

Bernadetta Di Lauro raised her head from her ex-husband's tear-soaked shoulder. She looked sadly into the eyes that she knew had once adored her. 'I'm sorry. I just can't make sense of this.'

He patted her hand gently. 'I know. I don't believe it either. It all seems so unreal.'

She found a handkerchief in her purse, next to a small photograph of Francesca graduating from university. She blew her nose and dabbed her eyes. Dreaded to think what she looked like.

Genarro Di Lauro blinked back the last of his

own tears. He was still in shock. He'd never got over the trauma of learning that his daughter had gone missing. Now he could barely cope with the news that the police had identified the remains of her body. *Remains.* That's what they'd called them – *remains* – what an awful word. The leftovers. The discarded bits. The final dregs of life that couldn't be better hidden. The remains.

'Genarro!'

Bernadetta's raised voice made him realize that he'd been miles away. Lost again in the uniquely depressive fog that engulfs parents of murdered children. 'What?'

She smiled at him and nodded towards a young carabinieri officer. The policeman was about the same age as Francesca would have been. He looked smart in his full uniform. No doubt his parents' pride and joy. 'The *Capitano* is ready to see you now.' His voice was soft and respectful. His eyes suggested he understood their pain. But, of course, he didn't. Couldn't. Not until he was much older and a father himself.

Sylvia Tomms had met them before. She made them as comfortable as possible. Not in her broom cupboard of an office but in a special room reserved for breaking bad news. The furnishings were less harsh but still businesslike. Brown cotton sofas were grouped around a low wooden table littered with plastic cups of coffee left by previous grievers. She cursed the fact that they hadn't been cleared and hastily palmed them into a steel bin.

'Do you have any idea who may have been the father of my daughter's child?' asked Genarro.

Sylvia winced. 'I'd hoped that was something you or your wife might be able to help us with.'

'Ex-wife,' corrected Bernadetta and in the same breath wished she hadn't. She felt her husband – ex-husband – squeeze her hand and somehow the reassurance made her feel like crying again.

'Before she went missing, was she seeing anyone regularly?'

Francesca's parents looked at Sylvia and then at themselves. Predictably, it was her mother who tried to fill in the gaps. 'Francesca didn't say much to me about her love life. Sometimes there'd be a twinkle in her eye, occasionally she'd share a boy's name with me and mention where they were going, but in the main she was a very private person.'

Genarro was looking off into the distance. Francesca was five years old again. Her thick dark hair in plaits with yellow bows that she kept playing with. Her gorgeous eyes sparkled with innocence as he hid a coin up his sleeve and magically produced it out of her ear. He was lost in the mists of time – an age before womanhood, before pregnancy and long before murder.

'Anything?' pushed Sylvia, catching his attention. 'A remark, a name, a period where she seemed odd, behaved differently?'

'I only saw my daughter about once a month,' confessed Genarro. 'When she'd lived with Bernadetta,

I'd seen more of her, but when she went to University and got her own apartment, then she had a new life, new friends and not so much time to see me.' His face showed all the regrets of a parent who wished he could turn back time.

'She loved you very much,' said Bernadetta, looking at him with the soft blue-green eyes that she'd passed down to her daughter. 'She was always saying *Papà* this, *Papà* that.'

'*Mamma*'s girl,' he countered and then looked surprised that he'd said it rather than just thought it. 'She was just like you – looks and temperament. Just like you.'

Sad memories flowed between them. The moment sagged from the weight of emotion. Sylvia tried to give them space. Let them feel their way around their grief. Finally they looked across at her. Two thin smiles. A cue to continue. And she did, with the hardest questions of all. 'You've seen the newspapers today; you know they have now reported the fact that your daughter was pregnant?'

Francesca's parents nodded. They looked uncertain and uncomfortable about where the conversation was heading.

'I know this is awful for you, but we have to do everything we can to keep this story in the newspapers.' Her heart went out to them. 'Murder is now so common here in Campania that it is hard to get people to pay any attention, let alone come forward with information that might help us catch your daughter's killer.' She could see pain welling in their eyes. 'Your daughter's pregnancy gives us a chance to do that. It touches people and, as horrible as it sounds, we have to take advantage of that. We're holding a press conference tonight and I'd like you to be there, to say something about what Francesca was like as a person.'

Sylvia's statement was met with silence. They were in no-man's-land – their grief was private, their horror so great they didn't even want to face the daylight let alone the press – but they did want to do whatever they could to catch their daughter's killer.

Sylvia smiled a serious smile – an expertly crafted friendly but serious smile – the type that only police officers can manage when they want you to *do the right thing* no matter how painful it is for you. 'We've been advised by one of the world's top psychological profilers that it's vital we make the public understand Francesca was a *person*, not just a murder *statistic.* If we can get them to feel your loss, then maybe we can persuade someone who knows the killer to come forward. Would you appear at the news conference? Make that appeal for people to contact us with any information that they think might help?'

Genarro squeezed his ex-wife's hand and she squeezed back. In the split second before he answered he wondered if they should get back together again. Fall in love again. Help each other over this hole in their lives. 'Yes. Yes, if you think it will help, then we'll do that.'

'Good. Thank you.' Sylvia's relief was visible. 'I'm afraid I still have a few questions I need to ask you. Are you all right for me to do that now?'

They both said they were and Sylvia found herself momentarily disarmed by their dignity.

'*Signora*, in the last months before Francesca disappeared, did you have any unusual discussions with her?'

Bernadetta sighed but said nothing. She'd spent years cudgelling herself over questions like this. Had there been something she'd said or done that had upset her daughter? Or, maybe even something she hadn't said or done? She'd tortured herself but had come up with nothing.

Sylvia pressed for an answer. 'Maybe a particular argument? Something that surprised you and caused you to fall out?'

Bernadetta finally shook her head.

'No mother–daughter talk about something awkward? Perhaps men, marriage? Anything like that?'

Bernadetta's mind felt like it was bound with razor wire. It hurt to think. But then something stirred.

At the centre of the ball of grief there was an ugly five-year-old memory struggling to get out. She put her fingers to her temples and closed her eyes. The pain was too great.

*There was something. What? What was it?*

Bernadetta shook her head. 'No. There is nothing special I can remember.'

And then she looked away and hoped the policewoman couldn't tell she was lying, couldn't guess the dark secret she was hiding.

# 47

***Parco Nazionale del Vesuvio***

The forest was sodden and smelled of rotting leaves and swampy earth. Franco Castellani didn't mind. Not one bit. Lying flat on his growling, hungry stomach he steadied his outstretched arms and then, with all the patience of a trained assassin, gently squeezed the trigger of the old Glock.

Fifty metres away a small red deer jolted backwards. It crumpled on its spindly legs and collapsed beside the spidery lower branches of a giant fir. Franco was up and running before the gunshot had finished rolling off the distant hillsides.

The headshot was perfect.

The fawn, along with twenty other deer, had only been introduced into the park in the summer as part of a new wildlife expansion programme. He stood over it. It looked like it had three little black eyes instead of two. It twitched and went into spasm as he touched its head. Franco considered shooting it again, but didn't want to risk any further noise, and he wanted to save the bullets for what he had planned for later. He slipped out his hunting knife, the one he used for fishing, carving and odd jobs at the campsite. He lifted its chin, exposing the soft fur and thin flesh at the neck.

One of the fawn's back legs kicked again. He wondered how long the animal would take to die if he just left it. Its eyes were glazed and vacant. Blood started to trickle from its mouth and nose, but amazingly it still seemed to cling to life. He lowered the chin and rested its head on his knee. Shuffled round so his back was against the giant trunk of a spruce. Settled back to watch it die.

It took several minutes for the animal to stop breathing and, when it did, Franco felt disappointed. Not sad, most definitely not sad, but disappointed.

Even though the fawn was quite small, he found it was too big for him to carry. He picked up the knife again and began the bloody task of cutting meat. He wished he had one of his axes. With one of those he'd glide through the bone. Whoomph, and it would be in pieces. But the knife was too small to sever the head. He sliced skin away, then tried to break the neck bone over the top of a rock. He stomped hard. But everything was wrong. The head got in the way – the ground was too soft – the bone slipped off the rock. Franco found himself just standing there, dribbling sweat and staring at the young dead animal's head.

*Young. Dead.*

The words touched him. Mirrored his own fate. Cut down in his prime. One moment happy and free

– oblivious to the savageries of the world – then killed by a bullet from out of the blue. He felt a rage building. A terrible rage against the unfairness of life. The unfairness of everything. Franco fell to his knees.

Knife gripped tight, he plunged it. Not once, or twice, but dozens of times into the body of the fawn. Only when he was exhausted did he stop.

Only when he was really sure that the rage was spent, did he finish.

Then he collapsed. Wrapped his arm round the dead, mutilated animal and cried.

Wept like he hadn't wept since he was a child.

# 48

***Stazione dei carabinieri, Castello di Cisterna***

Sylvia Tomms took a deep breath as the press conference started. Her hands shook a little as she stared into a white wall of light blazing out from above the TV cameras. But she made sure none of her nervousness showed. She was in a stylishly cut black business suit with a long-collared white silk shirt. She knew she looked smart, authoritative and fully in control. She also knew that her performance was vitally important not only for her, but also for the case and for Francesca and her brave and dignified parents. She'd give them all her best.

Photographers shouldered each other for space. Radio journalists held microphones high above their heads, like unlit Olympic torches.

Sylvia, along with Francesca's parents, sat behind a table covered with a white cloth, on a raised rough wooden stage in what was normally the carabinieri's gymnasium. Feedback made everyone jump as a sound engineer adjusted the levels to amplify Sylvia's opening words. '*Buona sera.* I am *Capitano* Sylvia Tomms, the officer in charge of the Francesca Di Lauro inquiry.'

Sylvia cleared her throat. 'I am joined by Francesca's parents, Genarro and Bernadetta, who have a very personal statement that they would like to read to you. Before they do that, for those of you who are new to the case, there is a written handout being circulated. It gives details of how, where and when Francesca's remains were discovered in the National Park of Mount Vesuvius.'

Sylvia paused while an assistant from the Press Office handed out single sheets of white paper. Photographers seized on the spare seconds and launched another volley of camera flashes.

'As some of you have reported, one of our forensic experts, *Professore* Bernardo Sorrentino, has discovered that Francesca may well have been pregnant at the time she was murdered. I say *may well* because we still have to complete matching DNA tests as a formality.'

Jack watched the conference live on Mediaset from a small TV in the corner of the carabinieri canteen. He thought Sylvia was handling herself well. She looked cool, calm and highly professional. But he was worried about Francesca's parents; they weren't media savvy. It was clearly a stressful and emotional ordeal for them.

Genarro Di Lauro stared into the alien lights and bug-eyes of the TV cameras. A pre-written statement shook noisily in his hands. 'My daughter was a very special woman. She was everything to us – everything.' The words stuck in his throat and his grief welled up so quickly that it took several seconds before he could continue. 'Francesca was a beautiful young woman, full of dreams and laughter. She brought us – and everyone who met her – great joy. She was kind and generous and . . .' His mind wandered. A flashback of her as a baby – soft arms around his neck, angel face pressed against his cheek. He wiped tears from the corner of his left eye. 'My daughter had the most amazing laugh. It was the laugh of someone who loved life and who filled it with love, the kind of life that would warm you all the way through to your heart. I – I want to . . .'

He was lost now. Eyes flooded. Memories welled up, so large and vivid that he thought he would suffocate. Birthdays, Christmases, holidays, Sunday mornings, bathtimes, bedtimes, story times – all the sweetness flooded in but burned like acid. He couldn't hold back the pain any more. He covered his face with his hands and sobbed. '*Mi dispiace.* I'm sorry – very sorry.'

Public grief is a rare, exotic animal and the big-game hunters of the national press took every shot they could. The high-tech cameras clicked like machine guns, another trophy head for tomorrow's papers.

Bernadetta put her arm protectively around her ex-husband. Her voice sounded only a sentence away from breaking. 'Our daughter is dead. Our baby is dead.'

The camera flashguns intensified. Lenses zoomed and refocused, elbows jostled for space and angle.

'The police think that somewhere, someone might know something that could help them catch her killer. Please – *please* – if you are that someone, come forward. Help us.'

Bernadetta was done. She buried her face in Genarro's shoulder and sobbed.

Sylvia spoke to someone behind her and a policewoman gently ushered them both offstage.

The journalists almost created a stampede to get their final shots and Sylvia had to virtually shout into the microphone to restore order.

'Bernadetta and Genarro thank you all for your support and help. The printed handouts we gave you have a telephone number for the Murder Incident Room that anyone can ring if they have information. Calls to that number can be anonymous if people wish. Now, are there any further questions?'

A man's hand went up. A TV reporter, late twenties, well groomed, still hoping one day to get his shot at studio anchor. 'Will there be an opportunity to do one-on-one interviews with Francesca's parents?'

'No,' snapped Sylvia, more curtly than she'd intended. 'You saw how painful tonight was for them. Please give them some privacy. No personal interviews. We won't take kindly to anyone who hassles them for interviews. Next question.'

A woman reporter waved her hand and caught Sylvia's eye. 'Can you tell us how Francesca died?'

'Not at the moment. We have detailed forensic

reports that we are following up. Right now it would be inappropriate to comment further.'

A middle-aged man waved a notebook. 'Francesca was pregnant when she died – do you know who the father was?'

Sylvia raised the palm of her hand. 'I can't comment on that at the moment.' She was keen to change the subject and saw someone waving at the back, a face she half recognized. 'Yes, at the back. Your question, please.'

'*Capitano* Tomms, would you say that this killing is connected to the disappearances of Luisa Banotti, Patricia Calvi, Donna Rizzi and Gloria Pirandello – all local women who have gone missing over the last five to eight years?'

The names stopped Sylvia in her tracks.

Inside the carabinieri canteen Jack stood up and immediately left the TV set he'd been watching.

All eyes flitted backwards and forwards between the reporter and the silent carabinieri *Capitano*. Sylvia's mind was running at frantic speed. How had someone made the connection between Francesca and the other missing women? Was there a leak in her inquiry team?

The well-informed journalist pressed for an answer. '*Capitano*, do you deny that all these women are missing and may, like Francesca, have been murdered?'

Sylvia knew she couldn't stall any further. 'I'm sorry. I'm hesitating on my answer because I don't want anyone here to lose focus of the facts – we're hunting for the killer of Francesca Di Lauro, a young woman, a young *mother-to-be*, murdered in the prime of her life. I don't want to speculate on other random cases, I don't want distractions, I want to concentrate on this one woman's death. I and Francesca's parents need your help. Please remember the faces of Genarro and Bernadetta – let's make sure we catch this man and ensure no other parents suffer like they have. Thank you, everyone. This press conference is over.' As she stepped from the stage she finally nailed the identity of the journalist. She motioned frantically towards Pietro Raimondi. Half the press were suddenly in her way. Squashing towards the exits to file their stories.

Sylvia finally reached Pietro on the other side of some security doors. Before she could say anything, Jack arrived. He was breathless but took the words right out of her mouth.

'That was Creed. The man who just asked those questions wasn't a journalist. It's Luciano Creed.'

# 49

***Via Caprese Michelangelo, centro città, Napoli***

At dusk, high-powered halogen security lights fizzled into life, illuminating the six-storey salmon-coloured building that housed the penthouse of Camorra consigliere Ricardo Mazerelli.

The forty-eight-year-old's home off Corso Vittorio Emanuele was located behind tall black railings in a private park, plush with palm trees and pristine lawns. Three armed security guards – Finelli men – patrolled the grounds 24/7.

In keeping with the trend for glass conservatories built over sky-high terraces, Mazerelli's was probably the biggest and longest in the city. Inside, a fountain-fed pond of ghost koi carp was the central feature of a Japanese garden specifically designed for peace and tranquillity. The privileged few who had stood inside, and gawped at the incongruity of the place, could also tell you that the windows were not only bullet-proof, they were strong enough to withstand a mortar attack.

Don Fredo Finelli sat in a wicker chair, a glass of chilled Prosecco on a small stone table at his side. He loosened his tie. He and his consigliere were alone after a routine business meeting in the financial district. Mazerelli looked tense and the Don wanted to know why. 'So, Ricardo, spill your troubles. Tell me what is on your mind.'

The family lawyer leaned forward, elbows on knees, a businesslike look on his face. 'May I speak openly; without fear of causing offence?'

'You know that is your privilege,' said Don Fredo, 'but please don't use it as a licence for disrespect.'

'It is your son-in-law.'

The Don's eyebrows arched. He couldn't help but tense in his seat.

'How do I know this is not going to be good news?'

'I'm afraid you are right.' Mazerelli slid open the top of another stone table and dialled the combination of the safe hidden inside. He pulled out a large Manila envelope and passed it to his employer. 'You need to see these.'

For a moment Don Fredo considered not opening the packet. He was going to deal with Valsi when he was ready. When the time was right. He feared that whatever the photographs showed might enrage him so much it would cloud his judgement.

The consigliere stood behind the Don and explained the stack of prints. 'They are all pictures of child drug dealers, *fornitori* run by Bruno or, at least, by his associates. The youth you're looking at is the *spacciatore*, the pusher; he is dealing wraps of cocaine and heroin.'

'How old is he?' Don Fredo's voice was low and sombre.

'This one is about fourteen. I'm told younger boys and girls are involved. Maybe as young as nine or ten.'

'*Porca Madonna!* This is not what we do.' Don Fredo threw down the photographs.

'In some ways it is clever,' continued Mazerelli. 'Juveniles are not punished as severely by the polizia or the courts. They are often given second chances rather than detention.'

Finelli banged his fist on the arm of the chair. 'Children are not pawns, Ricardo! We offer them jobs when they are old enough to choose, not when they are too young to say no.'

The consigliere paused and let his boss's passion fade before passing over a new print. 'Now we go up the chain, this is the main dealer –'

'You are sure of that?'

'Yes. There are several shots of him. Look at the blow-up and you will see.'

Finelli took another print and screwed up his face. The shot was taken from a high angle, maybe from an apartment building, or a factory rooftop. It very clearly showed bags of cocaine in the trunk of the dealer's Alfa. Digital scales, wire ties, silver foil and latex gloves were visible near a wheel and a jack.

The Don put two prints to one side and tapped one with his right hand. 'Who are these men? Please tell me they are *not* who I think they are.'

'I am afraid they are. Alberto Donatello and Romano Ivetta.'

The Don shook his head, reached for the glass of Prosecco and drained it.

'They're clearly the gang masters. They organize the children every day. Supply them with the packages and take the cash from them.'

'Scum!' Valsi had defied him and it made his blood boil.

Heavy moments passed as Don Fredo examined the other photographs. A long-lens surveillance shot showed Valsi shoulder to shoulder with the other men. All three were laughing. The background confirmed they had been taken on the same day and in the same place where the kids had been dealing. 'Where did you get these from? Did you spy on my son-in-law, without asking me for permission – without my authority?'

'Don Fredo, no!' Mazerelli steepled his hands together, praying for a pause in the rising outburst. 'I did not take these photographs, nor did I commission them.'

Finelli felt apprehension corkscrew down his spine. 'So, where were they taken?' He feared the worst. 'Tell me it was in the east quarter. Or, at least, in one of *our* territories.'

Ricardo Mazerelli glanced at the carp swimming through his roof-garden pool. The water needed changing. He'd do it later. The calm and peace that he savoured were about to be ruined. His eyes returned to his boss. 'They were given to me by the consigliere of the Cicerone Family. They were taken on his Family's ground.'

The old man rubbed his face.

He wasn't prepared for this. Not at all.

His thoughts and planning had been on keeping peace within his own Family. The one thing he hadn't contemplated was a turf war. But it was going to happen.

There was going to be a blood feud.

# 50

***Stazione dei carabinieri, Castello di Cisterna***

Luciano Creed had vanished.

Pietro barked into a walkie-talkie and marshalled police cars from the back of the barracks. With luck Creed wouldn't have got far.

'He'll take the autostrada,' Pietro motioned to Jack. 'There's a junction only a few kilometres from here, we must go now.'

Jack followed the tall lieutenant to an old Lancia parked across the road. The profiler's mind was more troubled about *why* Creed had turned up than whether they had a chance of catching him.

'Motherfucking bastard!' Raimondi swore softly as he sped away from the barracks with a squeal of car tyres.

Jack had guessed that the press conference would provoke a reaction. Maybe a letter from the killer. Maybe a tip-off from someone who'd been touched by Francesca's parents and thought they knew the killer. But he hadn't bargained on this.

The old car lurched round bends and accelerated

down the autostrada slip road. Pietro opened it up and the exhaust rattled.

'There! There!' shouted Jack as they drew level with a Land Rover Freelander.

Passing sodium lights played on and off the windshields as the two cars drove in parallel at approaching 140kph.

Luciano Creed looked across and spotted Jack King peering back at him. He didn't seem frightened. He smiled a jagged yellow-toothed smile, lifted his right hand off the wheel and used his thumb and small finger to illustrate a phone.

'What's he doing?' asked Pietro, wondering whether the old Lancia was strong enough to force the Freelander to stop, or whether it would just get chewed up under the 4x4's big wheels.

'I'm not sure,' said Jack. 'He's making fun of us, I think.'

Suddenly the Freelander veered sharp right. It crossed on to the hard shoulder and careered down the banking.

'Fuck!' shouted Pietro. 'What happened? Has he crashed?'

Jack craned his neck and squinted out of the rear window while the Lancia squealed to a stop. 'I can't see anything.' His eyes scanned the darkness for any sign of flames or lights.

Nothing.

'Christ, where's he gone?' Pietro hit reverse and backed up. 'There was no turn-off there.

You can't get off the autostrada for another five kilometres.'

Creed was nowhere to be seen.

They'd been within touching distance of him. Close enough for Jack to have almost pulled open the car door and slapped cuffs on him. Then the weird little punk had just disappeared.

They looped on and off the autostrada. Blue police lights criss-crossed bridges and slip roads above and below them as they searched high and low. Intense radio chatter filled the airwaves, but no one had news of Creed's whereabouts. After forty-five minutes Jack and Pietro headed back to the barracks.

Sylvia was in her office. A face like thunder. 'Well?'

Pietro threw his hands wide. '*Andato.*' Gone.

Sylvia slapped her desk. 'He made us look like fools. Like stupid, damn idiots. I wish now we'd never held that press conference.'

'Hindsight is a wonderful thing,' said Jack, checking his cellphone, more out of the need for a distraction than any sense of urgency.

'*Affanculo!*' swore Pietro. 'Now the motherfucker is gone and we'll never hear from him again.'

'I wouldn't bet on that.' Jack looked down at the phone in his hand. 'Remember that gesture he made as we passed him? Well, it seems the manipulative little creep was planning to contact us again.' He spun the phone round so they could see the display. 'I've just got a text message from Creed.'

Pietro and Sylvia squinted at it.

I KNOW WHAT YOU'RE THINKING BUT I DIDN'T DO IT. I'M INNOCENT. CREED.

'So, if he's innocent, why all this?' said Sylvia. 'What's all this about?'

Pietro shrugged sympathetically. 'He is messing with us again. He is lying now and was lying right from the start when he met Jack and said he was still working for us and the university.'

'And he lied about being involved with Francesca?' added Sylvia.

'Exactly,' said Pietro. 'Look at it this way. He books out of his hotel early in New York and then he comes back to Naples and won't talk to us. He turns up at the press conference tonight and then he runs away again. These are not the actions of an innocent man.'

'No, they're not,' agreed Sylvia, the message stoking her anger.

Jack wasn't so sure. To him the actions seemed like taunting. More a case of someone proving their point. 'The question that he asked at the press conference, when he listed the names of the missing girls –'

'What about it?' snapped Sylvia.

'If Creed is Francesca's killer, and maybe the murderer of more women, then it was a bold and crazy thing to do. An unnecessary risk. Why put himself so clearly in the frame and chance being caught?' Jack looked across at Pietro and Sylvia and made sure they were following him. 'The more I look at this case, the more I think we're hunting someone who is willing to cope with risk, but doesn't court it.'

'Evil can't always be explained,' said Raimondi.

Jack disagreed, he thought evil *could* always be explained. 'Let's look at the options. Creed was either egotistically trying to point the spotlight at himself as the killer – trying to enjoy the public horror and concern over the crimes he's committed – or else, he was being public-spirited and was attempting to focus attention on the missing girls and force you to put more resources into trying to find them. Angel or devil? Which is he?'

'Perhaps both?' said Pietro. 'Perhaps he is a Mr Jecky and Dr Hid?'

Sylvia laughed. 'I think you mean Dr Jekyll and Mr Hyde.' She patted him playfully on the shoulder. 'Good try, Pietro.'

'I mean half of him wants to kill and half of him wants to be stopped,' explained the big lieutenant, not amused at his own faux pas.

*Split personality?* It was something Jack hadn't thought about. But that didn't fit the profile either. 'There's one other possibility,' he said.

'I'm all ears.'

'What if Creed is doing all this as revenge?'

'Revenge? How so?' asked Sylvia.

Jack rolled out his latest thoughts. 'The carabinieri crushed his dream of becoming a psychological profiler. Stopped him being a *hot-shot* working high-profile police cases. The force ended his secondment and complained about him to his university, which also ruined his academic career. So, this could be his idea of payback. And I bet there's a lot worse to come.'

# 51

***Casa di famiglia dei Valsi, Camaldoli***

By the time he got home, Bruno Valsi's hand was hurting even more than his damaged pride. That old thug had maybe broken two of his fingers. He went straight upstairs, showered and changed. If he'd had it his way he wouldn't even have acknowledged that his wife was in the house. But she followed him around, complaining that he was late for dinner and shouting at him. He'd eaten enough for the day and now he was going to go out and have some fun on his own.

Gina dogged him all the way to the hallway, where he finally stopped to adjust his tie in the mirror. 'I can't believe you're going out *again*. Since you've come out of jail, you've spent virtually every night away from me and Enzo.'

'You have a better idea?' he snapped. 'You think I should stay here, so you can shout all night and sit with a sour face? Or maybe instead I should go out and earn some money?'

'*Ma vai!*' Gina waved a hand at him and flounced away. But she couldn't leave it like that. Pride and her fierce spirit stopped her in her tracks. '*Work*, you say? Since when did fucking other women qualify as work?'

Valsi tried to ignore her. He'd had a bad day. That bastard Sal had publicly humiliated him. The last thing he wanted was trouble at home.

'Do you think I'm stupid?' Gina pushed him. 'Do you think I can't smell your whores on you and your clothes? See their scratches on your body? You make me fucking sick.'

'You *are* stupid. And you're talking nonsense. So shut the fuck up.'

A text message bleeped on Valsi's phone beside his wallet on the hall cabinet. Gina picked it up. 'Who's sending you text messages?' She held it behind her back. 'I read the ones you sent to Kristen. Is it her?'

Valsi wheeled round from the mirror. Slapped her hard. 'You never touch my phone. That's my business. Right!'

Gina held her cheek. It burned. 'You piece of shit. You cheating piece of shit.' She hurled the phone at his head.

Valsi dodged. It hit the wall and then the floor, smashing into several pieces.

The look on his face told Gina she was in for a beating.

She made a run for it.

'Come here, bitch!'

Valsi slipped to her left and blocked the corridor into the main body of the house.

Gina doubled back. One foot slipped on the tiling, twisting her ankle. She kept her balance. Ignored the stab of pain.

'Leave me alone! Bruno, just leave me!'

She headed towards the conservatory. If she made it through to the pool house she could lock herself in.

But she never got there.

Valsi grabbed her left shoulder and spun her round. His face was like stone.

Gina was scared. She jerked her right knee up between his legs. It never made impact.

His hands were quicker than a crocodile's jaws. His instincts still prison-quick. Fast enough to dodge a cell-made knife, let alone a clumsy woman's knee. He held her leg off the ground and slapped her face. She put her hand up to the burning skin and lost her balance. Her head struck the wall. He held on tight and kept her upright.

'Bruno, please don't. *Please.*'

Valsi could see the fear in her face. *Wonderful.* He felt powerful. Made him forget all about Sal the Snake and the humiliation he'd experienced.

He pulled her leg higher. Stretched her hamstring until it burned.

Gina had to hold his shoulders to stay upright. He flipped the door open behind her, backed her into the sitting room and dragged the door closed with his foot.

He could smell the fear on her now. See it in the

sweat on her brow. Feel it as her heart pounded against his chest. It was exhilarating. It was the first time she had made him *hard* since he'd come out of prison.

He jammed her against the wall. Forced his mouth against hers.

She tried to bite him.

His hand grabbed her throat. Strong fingers on her windpipe. She wouldn't do that again. He could feel her heart banging against his chest. So fast. So afraid.

Gina closed her eyes. She didn't want him to see her cry. Didn't want him to see the disgust she felt as he fumbled between her legs.

And when he finished, when he'd fucked away the last of the love she had for him and had walked off, laughing, somehow she still held back the tears. Still kept the tiniest shred of her dignity. Just enough to build a new life with.

# 52

*Capo di Posillipo, La Baia di Napoli*

Salvatore Giacomo was always nervous meeting the great Don Fredo Finelli. Always had been, always would be.

Although they'd known each other for more than two decades, Sal still felt intimidated by his employer. And in a strange way, he liked that feeling. Liked to work for someone who was better, richer and cleverer than him.

As Sal was shown through the hallway to the office in the Don's home he found himself more nervous than usual. Two things were making him anxious. Fear that the Don knew about the incident in Bar Luca with his son-in-law. And the fact that there had been no card on his doormat from his boss. Don Fredo had never forgotten before. Never. But this time – and this was a landmark birthday too – there had been nothing. He was afraid he might say something. Might forget his position.

Fredo Finelli instantly rose from behind his fine desk when the bodyguard showed Sal into the study. '*Ciao*, Salvatore, come here, my friend!'

Finelli embraced him warmly, patted his back and gripped his shoulders. 'Let me look at you. My, you don't look bad at all for a man of fifty. You feeling good?'

Sal straightened his jacket and nodded. '*Sì*, Don Fredo. I think I am as fit and healthy as I have always been.' For a moment Sal feared the old man was about to pension him off, put him out to grass and bring in some young gun to fill his place. It was in his nature to always fear the worst.

'Sit down, Sal.' He pointed to the leather sofas. 'I have to get something from my desk.'

Sal sat and waited. His eyes took in the wood panelling, the photographs of the Finelli family. He liked it here. Liked to feel part of it all.

'I have a little gift for you. Something small to say "Happy birthday", and also "Thank you" for everything that you've ever done for me.'

Sal's face didn't show it, but he was as excited as a kid. The Don handed over a small square box wrapped in gold paper, topped with a gold ribbon and bow. Thirty years ago Sal had dated a girl called Giovanna. She'd kept every bow and ribbon from every present she'd ever been given and had stuck them on her bedroom wall. He remembered it now as his big clumsy hands fumbled to open the gift.

'It's nice,' he said, finally getting through all the wrapping. 'Thank you, Don Fredo, it is nice.'

Finelli smiled. Most people would have managed more than *nice* if they'd been given a €15,000 watch, but he was all too familiar with Sal's ways. The manner in which he kept himself to himself. His emotions always tight and under control. *Nice* was about the best he could have hoped for.

'It's a special watch, Sal. Do you know why?'

Sal turned the gold Rolex over and over in his hands. He concentrated hard on the question. He looked relieved, and proud, when the answer came to him. 'It's like yours, Don Fredo. It's just like yours.'

Finelli shook his head. 'No, it isn't. It's not *like* mine at all. It *is* mine.'

Sal was shocked. 'Then, Don Fredo, I must not take it. It is too much.' He stretched his hands out and offered his boss the watch.

The Don waved him away. 'No, I want you to have it. It's a Cosmograph Daytona. Eighteen carat gold, with a diamond dot dial. I hope it serves you well.'

The Don paused for a reply, but Sal remained speechless.

'Salvatore, I hope it proves as reliable and trustworthy to you as you have been to me. It's supposed to be the most dependable watch in the world. It is always good to have at hand something or, better still, someone you can rely on.'

Sal didn't look up as he slid the bracelet awkwardly on to his left wrist, pocketing his old Sekonda with its cracked glass and frayed leather strap that stank of his sweat. He couldn't find the words to express himself but he fully understood the compliment he was being paid.

'I can always rely upon you, Sal, can't I?'

Now Salvatore's eyes lifted from his gift. He knew his boss's ways, just as well as his boss knew his. He was going to be asked something important. Something that needed his full attention. 'Yes, Don Fredo. Of course you can. I hope you know that of me?'

Fredo nodded. 'Of course I do, Sal. I need to talk to you about my son-in-law, Bruno. What I am about to say to you must never leave this room. You must never discuss it with anyone else, do you understand?'

Sal understood. He always understood this kind of chat. He was going to be given the best birthday present of all. The chance to kill Bruno Valsi.

# 53

***San Giorgio a Cremano, La Baia di Napoli***

That night, Creed came to Sylvia in her nightmares. In the fitful two hours that she slept, his yellow-toothed mouth spat out the question again: '*Would you say that this killing is connected to the disappearances of Luisa Banotti, Patricia Calvi, Donna Rizzi and Gloria Pirandello?*'

*Well? Would you, Sylvia? Would you?*

Calm – he'd been so damn calm – and arrogant. Creed was still on her mind when she woke. And he stayed there as she showered, dressed, skipped breakfast and drove to work. She was so preoccupied she didn't notice her lieutenant walking in behind her.

'*Buon giorno.* Are you okay, boss?' asked Raimondi.

'Yes, yes I'm fine, Pietro. I've been thinking of what Jack said about Creed. What do you think? Is he innocent or guilty?'

'Well . . .'

'No wells! No painfully long answers! This man is driving me mad. Just tell me; what do you think? Innocent or guilty?'

'I don't know,' he shrugged. 'I really don't know.'

And neither did Sylvia. There was no real evidence

– certainly no forensic evidence – but his behaviour was so odd, his character so unpleasant, that it made it hard to even connect the word *innocent* to him. 'I know we've run checks on him having any links or relationships with these women, but please run them again. Shake the whole thing down once more. See if we can sieve something out.'

Pietro's reply was halted by a knock on her office door. A woman clerk stuck her head round it, '*Scusi, Capitano*, but your phone, it is off the hook.'

Sylvia peered through the rubbish on her desk, found the receiver and slapped it back on its cradle. '*Grazie*.'

'Downstairs there is a *Professore* Sorrentino, asking to see you. May I bring him up?'

Pietro laughed. Sylvia dropped her head into her hands. 'No, you may not! God save me from this. Sorrentino is the last person I want to see.'

'Shall I send him away, *Capitano*?' The clerk seemed confused.

Sylvia turned to Pietro and looked flirtatiously at him. The look was a little jaded, but still did the trick.

'Okay. *I* will see him.' He followed the clerk to reception.

The door banged shut behind them and Sylvia stared down at the mass of paperwork, growing like bacteria on her desk. If the Francesca Di Lauro case had been the only one she was overseeing then things might not have been too bad. But to her left were witness statements, forensic evidence and psychiatric evaluations on a teenager from Portici who had raped five elderly women. And to her right was a reminder from her chief that a week ago he'd requested her Quarterly Crime Analysis Reports. She settled down in the middle of the paper maze and tried to find her way out.

Minutes later, the door reopened and Pietro entered with Sorrentino.

Sylvia's heart sank. She'd hoped Pietro would have got rid of him.

'I thought you had better hear this yourself,' he explained.

Sorrentino flashed his perfect white teeth. She could see that he'd dyed his hair again. This was a man who would go to his grave denying he'd ever had a grey hair on his head.

'*Professore*, good to see you,' she pretended. 'To what do we owe the enormous pleasure of your company?'

Sorrentino killed her sarcasm in mid-air, swatted it like a pesky fly.

'There are more bodies.' He tossed a file on to her desk. 'Some of the human bones recovered from the park don't belong to Francesca Di Lauro. They belong to someone else.'

Sylvia was open-mouthed. 'You're sure? You're certain they are not Francesca's?'

Sorrentino enjoyed his moment. 'I wouldn't be here if I wasn't certain.' He reached across her desk and flipped open the file he'd dropped in front of her.

'Here in this picture you see the skeleton of Francesca Di Lauro. Okay, maybe we've missed some bones, here and there, but it is a good reconstruction.'

*Horrible*, not good – that was the word Sylvia would have chosen. She looked at the photograph and couldn't suppress a shiver of sisterly sympathy.

Sorrentino slid the black and white blow-up to one side. 'This photograph shows sixteen separate fragments of bone, also burned and blackened, and as you can seen I have assembled them. They're clearly from the left tibia and right femur of another woman.' He paused and went back on himself to make sure Sylvia fully understood. 'Bones not from Francesca, but from another woman. This one is aged somewhere between nineteen and thirty, probably about one-and-a-half metres tall.'

'*O porca puttana!*' Sylvia looked across at Pietro. He seemed as shocked as she was.

What a setback. One murder like this was a drain on resources, two sucked you dry.

'How do you know it's a woman?' Pietro gestured towards the photograph. 'And all that about age and size? How do you know her age?'

Sorrentino was glad to explain. 'Generally, female bones are thinner and shorter than male ones. The biggest clue, though, is in the femur.'

'The *thigh* bone?' checked Pietro.

'Yes. Femur is Latin for thigh.' He looked at Pietro as though he were a stupid child. 'It is the largest and strongest bone in the body. After reassembling the whole of the femur, it's a simple calculation to project the size of the individual.'

'And the sex and age?'

Sorrentino sighed wearily. 'Size and shape of the bone. To determine sex we look at the length and diameter plus the way it joins the hip bone. Age – well, we know the head of the femur is fully developed when a woman is about eighteen or nineteen – and in this case, it was.'

Sylvia stared at the photographs and felt as drained as a dead car battery. She handled the scattered images on her desk and absorbed the reality of what she now accepted was probably another murdered woman. *Were these broken and burned bones really all that were left of some lost soul like Luisa Banotti, Patricia Calvi, Donna Rizzi or Gloria Pirandello?* The thought angered her. It dropped like a match into a pool of gasoline and sparked her into action.

'Pietro, I want search teams, exhibit officers, scientists, photographers and every other goddamned overworked person we can find back out in the fields. Dig the whole fucking park up if necessary. We have to see exactly what's there.'

Sorrentino smirked at her. 'I'll tell you exactly what's there.' His tone was *sotto voce*; he waited a beat, then dropped the bomb. 'A necropolis. That's what's there, *Capitano*. You have stumbled into a serial killer's secret graveyard and you are about to open up your very own necropolis.'

# FOUR

# 54

***Via Caprese Michelangelo, centro città, Napoli***

There had never been any love lost between Bruno Valsi and Ricardo Mazerelli. Each had always been fully aware of the other's ambitions and powers.

Valsi threw his jacket down on one chair and made himself comfortable in another. He hated Mazerelli's superior tones and condescending looks. Hated his *stupid* penthouse. 'What's with this place? You some kind of Jap lover, Ricardo? All these weird plants and fish.' Valsi spat into the stream that gently flowed near his feet and tapped the tattoo close to his heart. 'Vipers have no love for water.' He turned to his side and contemptuously flicked his fingers at a wooden board with a bowl of black and white playing pieces. 'And what is this shit? Jap chess, or something?'

The consigliere smiled; he liked it when the anger and hatred were out in the open. It was those with the strength to conceal their emotions that he feared the most. 'It's Japanese, yes. But what it is won't really interest you –'

Valsi took the bait, hook straight into the soft, pink flesh. 'Don't treat me like a schmuck. I asked you what the fuck it was; now do me the decency of giving an answer.'

'It is a game called Go.'

'Go?'

'Yes. Go.' Mazerelli had the upper hand and was making the most of it. 'Fifty million people in the Far East play the game.' He smoothed a finger over the wooden base board. 'Actually, it probably started in China – not Japan – invented by generals who used the stones to map out positions and strategies of attack. The Chinese call it *Weiqi* – The Surrounding Game.'

'War games.' Valsi clapped his hands, 'Now you're talking! This is something I'm good at.'

Mazerelli drummed two fingers on the board, then swivelled it round to face his visitor. 'This is called a *goban*; it's made from a tree that is more than seven hundred years old. The stones are called *goishi*; the white ones in front of you are made from clamshells, these black ones are cut from slate.'

Valsi scratched his nose. 'What do we do?'

Mazerelli disdainfully dropped a single black stone on to a square. 'You have to surround my stone with your stones. You have to claim your territory and out-think your opponent. Do you understand?'

'Course I understand. It's like a gang war. Here *you* are . . .' Valsi pointed at the black piece, then poured a handful of his white pieces around it in a circle. 'And here *I* am. All over your head, your ass, your fucking heart and your weak lawyer balls. Game over!' He swept his hand across the board and sent the expensive pieces clattering noisily on to the hard floor.

Several lay chipped and broken.

Valsi didn't apologize. He didn't even look to see where they'd fallen. His eyes stayed locked, challengingly, on Mazerelli's.

The consigliere didn't blink. His face showed no trace of anger or even disappointment at what had happened. 'You're right. If crude and ugly moves like that were allowed, then yes, you'd have won hands down. But there are *rules* to the game.' He bent down and began gathering the *goishi* from near Valsi's feet.

'Not for me,' said the *Capo*. 'I've never played by the rules. Maybe you best remember that.'

'I'll be sure to.'

'What? You think great generals play by the rules? You think the Brits and Yanks, the Russians and your beloved fucking Japs do it all by the rule book? Don't be so fucking naive.' He glanced around the room, the argument was over for him. 'You got any water, or anything to drink?'

Mazerelli slowly finished gathering the pieces and put them away in subtle stone bowls next to the *goban*. He walked back into the galley kitchen, poured a tumbler of fresh water from a dispenser on the fridge and shouted, 'You want ice?'

'Yeah, plenty of it.'

The consigliere handed over the glass and wondered what Gina had ever seen in the mannerless brute. 'Your father-in-law has asked me to speak to you.'

Valsi sipped the water. 'Then speak.'

Mazerelli rubbed his hands thoughtfully. He considered how exactly to phrase things. 'Apparently, you have been indulging in some activities which are beyond your scope and beyond our territory.'

Valsi put his water down. '*Non capisco.* Try again. Maybe this time use a language I might understand.'

'Okay.' The lawyer lifted an envelope off the top of a rosewood cabinet in the corner of the room. 'Take a look at these. There are no difficult words, just pictures – you might be able to keep up with the conversation now.'

Valsi fingered open the flap and shook out a set of black and white prints. He felt his pulse race as he fanned through the shots of his team of dealers, pushers and gang leaders plying their trade.

Mazerelli lifted Valsi's glass and put a bamboo coaster beneath it. 'Good, aren't they?'

'I don't know these people. Why are you showing them to me?'

'I didn't take them, a Cicerone took them. And you *do* know these people. They work for Ivetta, Donatello – and for you. Turn to the back and you'll see some very revealing shots of the three of you. The Fun Boy Three. Only the Don doesn't think you're that much fun.'

Valsi was shrewd enough to say nothing. He stared at Mazerelli as if he'd suddenly grown bored. 'So, why am I here? You got a message to deliver – then deliver it.'

'Ah, see – you *do* understand that games have rules. Good. Yes, I *do* have a message to give you.'

Valsi sat forward a little and scratched his back.

'You won't need *that*.' Mazerelli recognized the move as a cover to check a gun tucked in the back of his belt.

Valsi pulled out the pistol anyway. The conversation had taken a turn for the worse and if it got any uglier – maybe with some armed knuckleheads materializing out of nowhere – then he'd rather have the piece in his hands. 'So, get on with your message. What's the word?'

'Whatever money you made from the dealing, you give to me –'

'The fuck I will.'

'Let me finish.'

Valsi glared at him, then waved a hand. 'Go on.'

'Whatever money you made from the dealing, you give to me. *All* of it. *Plus* one hundred thousand euros. I will pass this to the Cicerone consigliere and cement a peace between us.'

'Bullshit!' Valsi stood up, shook the creases out of his trousers and tucked the pistol in his belt. 'I'm leaving.'

Mazerelli stepped to one side and waved him to the door. 'Then go. But if you do not do this, you disrespect Don Fredo. And he may not be able to give you the protection of the Family.'

Valsi slapped Mazerelli between the legs. Grabbed his balls and squeezed hard. 'Now you listen to me, you bollockless, fancy-worded fucker. You dare talk to me about disrespect and protection? Who the fuck do you think you are?' Valsi swished his leg in a fast curl behind the lawyer's knees. Dropped him to the floor with the ease of a father play-fighting a young son. 'I'm paying *nothing*. If the Don wants to wad-off the Cicerone Family himself, then fine, let the old man do that. If he chooses to encourage a Cicerone goon to try to whack me, then also fine. Good luck to him. Let them try. It would be good to have the war we should have had years ago. So, now I have a message for you, my dear consigliere. Tell my father-in-law not to disrespect *me*. Tell him that if he's got a problem, he raises it with me *personally*, he doesn't send his monkey.' Valsi stepped away from the lawyer, held out his hand and helped him stand. 'Oh, and tell the consigliere of the Cicerone that if they move against me, I will personally rip their Don's heart out of his body, make calzone out of it and feed it to his whores.'

Valsi brushed dust off Mazerelli's shoulders. 'Now, I'll leave you to your work. Seems like you've suddenly become a very busy messenger boy.'

# 55

***Parco Nazionale del Vesuvio***

Pale pink sunlight streamed through the rain clouds, making patches of broken ground in the National Park look like rare-cooked steak. On the safe side of the crime-scene tape, Sylvia Tomms slouched against the broad trunk of an evergreen and wondered how many women's bodies had been buried in the earth that her team was now digging and sifting.

*Necropolis.*

Sorrentino's word rolled noisily over her thoughts, like a primed hand grenade.

Inside the cordoned-off search area, young carabinieri soldiers ignored the rain and dug hard volcanic earth. Each crack of a shovel made Sylvia wonder whether they'd hit centuries-old lava, or recently buried bone.

'*Caffè!*' announced Pietro, handing over a plastic cup that was so thin Sylvia couldn't hold it.

'*Che caldo*, that's hot!' She hurriedly put it down, at the foot of the tree.

'It is the boiling water that makes it like that,' joked her lieutenant.

Sylvia was too tired to laugh. Every volt of her brain power, every watt of her energy, was spent on the investigation. 'You check with the overnight team? Any news? Any sign of Creed?'

'I checked. Nothing. I have two details canvassing houses near where Jack and I saw him pull off the autostrada. Local patrols are still searching for the car. It's his own, not stolen.'

'Good. I want this man sitting in a cell – as soon as possible.' Her eyes scanned the scarred, rugged parkland, settling on the soldiers as they dug for bones. 'How many, Pietro? How many bodies do you think might be out here?'

The big Italian gazed over the fluttering tape. 'Depends. Maybe we'll find only one more.'

*What an optimist! Only one more?* Somehow Sylvia didn't think so.

*Necropolis.*

She retrieved her coffee from the foot of the tree and warmed her hands around the cup.

*A serial killer's secret graveyard.*

The rain stopped and the sun's warmth created an eerie mist around the soldiers as they dug. A much larger area had now been measured out in a grid. One team was still deployed on the inner squares of the old excavation zone – the area that had yielded the remains of Francesca Di Lauro. Another group worked intensely on the neighbouring site – the one that, according to Sorrentino, had produced the second victim. Four other groups, one for each point of the compass, dug outwards into new ground. It was hit and miss whether they would find anything. Sylvia hoped they wouldn't.

Sorrentino was back in the thick of the action, his hands darting this way and that, as expressive as an orchestra conductor. His staff bobbed from dig to dig and checked when the topsoil had been removed and lower layers of earth had been sieved. Meanwhile, a pace back from them all, a crime-scene photographer alternated between snapping away with a digital camera and filming video footage with a hand-held recorder. It was hard, laborious work, and it had to be done meticulously.

'Do you think we'll read about all this in the newspapers tomorrow?' asked Pietro.

Sylvia threw the dregs of her coffee on the ground. 'I hope not.' She crumpled the empty plastic coffee cup and shoved it in the pocket of her blue wool coat. 'I really hope Sorrentino now understands that this kind of exercise is best done without the public knowing.' Her thoughts turned to the families of the missing women. She knew they'd be reading every column inch of every paper, praying every day for news that would end their doubts and suffering.

The sun was soon high enough to show the brooding outline of Vesuvius and to start casting shadows on the hard ground near where the teams toiled. Armed carabinieri ringed the excavation area and brusquely turned away a few early morning dog walkers and an old, breathless jogger. Sylvia had seen enough. 'Come on, let's go back to the office. This place has all the atmosphere of a funeral. We can't do anything more here.'

Pietro nodded and fell in behind her. She was right, the depressive solemnity of the dig was tangible, no one even talked as they dug.

And amid the silence, no one noticed *him*.

Watching.

Silently cursing.

Damning them all for the sacrilege they were carrying out on his hallowed ground.

His eyes bored into Sylvia. She was nothing much. He was good at first impressions. *Not a threat.* Not nearly intelligent enough to worry him.

His gaze slipped across to Sorrentino.

The anthropologist's face was easy to recognize. It was plastered all over the press. *Il Grande Leone.* Now he could be a threat. A serious one.

*Why was he here again? What had he found now?*

Another victim. That would be it. That would explain all the activity.

The so-called *genius* was about to make more discoveries. He was pointing and people were running. He was creating excitement. Not the kind of excitement that was wanted. Not the kind that was helpful.

*Kill him and you stop the inquiry in its tracks. Slow them down. Screw them up. Burn them out.*

Sylvia caught his eye again as she walked back to her car.

Come to think of it, there *was* something about her. Not drop-dead beautiful – he liked that phrase, *drop-dead* – but she had a certain style. A certain *way* about her. She was – he struggled to describe her – *challenging*.

Yes, that's it. She was *challenging*. Well, he was always up for a challenge.

Sylvia Tomms walked out of his view, but not out of his mind.

*She'd look good naked. The stupid policewoman heading the inquiry would look great dressed in flames.*

*But first, there was some lion-taming to be done.*

# 56

***Stazione dei carabinieri, Castello di Cisterna***

Back at her desk, Sylvia mainlined on more coffee and nicotine. Creed's picture stared up at her from an open file and begged a bunch of questions. Was he the type to kill because he felt inadequate? The type to crash a press conference to flaunt his power? Or, was he the proverbial fly in the ointment? One of those weird interlopers who bog you down and bleed you of resources?

The last thing she needed right now was another twist in the already tangled tale of murder and missing women. But that's exactly what she got. It came in the form of the man hastily ushered in to see her. A fresh-faced detective from the local homicide division of the polizia. He'd arrived unannounced and had insisted on seeing her straight away.

'*Capitano*, my name is Mario Dal Santo.' He was in his early thirties, maybe even late twenties. Sylvia noticed the trousers of his smart grey suit were splashed with mud, as were the soles and heels of his highly polished shoes. 'Please, sit down.'

'I saw you on the news yesterday – the Di Lauro

killing. Everyone at the station house is talking about that press conference.'

*Great, a surprise dose of public humiliation. Get used to it, girl, you're going to hear that a lot.* 'And that's why you're here?'

He managed a sympathetic look. 'No. Not at all. We're investigating the shooting of a young courting couple, not far from here – teenagers . . .'

'Wait a second,' Sylvia cut him off. She picked up the overnight area crime report from her in-tray. 'This must be really fresh. I've no cross-force intel.'

'We're still at the scene. The ME isn't even there yet. My boss sent me because he remembered a *confidential* you'd circulated, asking to be alerted if anyone came across a homicide in which a woman was killed by fire.'

Sylvia frowned. 'But you said two *shootings*, didn't you?'

'I did,' he smiled. Perfect teeth and puppy-dog eyes. 'But I hadn't finished telling you the full story. Two teenagers were killed in the car belonging to one of their parents. A third body was also discovered, a woman's, and this one *was* burned as well as shot.'

'How? Where?'

'In a pit near where the kids were killed. It's some kind of garbage dump for a campsite. Maybe local rubbish is torched there as well.'

'You said burned – *how* was she burned? Completely burned, partly burned? I mean, forensically is there anything left of her?'

'There's almost nothing left. Well, there didn't seem much to me. Like I said, the scene is still active. You want to come and see for yourself?'

'Mister, the last thing I *want* to do is go and see another burned body, but I think I'd better.' She grabbed her lighter and cigarettes and slugged back the now cold coffee, knowing it might be her last for a while. 'Give me a second to update my team. If this incident is connected, I want jurisdiction, understood? No disrespect, but I think we're better equipped to deal with this incident. Agreed?'

'Agreed. I'll have to double-check with my boss but we've got so much on, I reckon he'll be glad to dump the paperwork on your desk.' Dal Santo glanced down at the mess. 'Providing you promise not to lose it in there.'

# 57

***Crime scene 1, Campeggio Castellani, Pompeii***

A carabinieri driver sped Jack to the new crime scene. From what Sylvia had told him on the phone, the fresh killings might provide a breakthrough. The scene was rich in forensic evidence that hadn't been corrupted by five years of burial, and – Jack guessed – probably just as rich in psychological evidence as well. The new deaths were only a few kilometres from where the graves of Francesca Di Lauro and the second victim had just been found. Given the burning of the bodies, it seemed probable they were connected. This might – just might – be the scene where both women had been killed.

The driver flicked on an indicator. 'We're here. I just have to turn in about a hundred metres,' said the driver, looking at a satnav screen. The car veered right into the campsite. There was so much crime-scene tape fluttering in the wind that it looked as though the area had been marked off for marathon runners. Soldiers swarmed around the vehicle and chatted to the driver in Italian. Then they waved them on; down the driveway, past static caravans, a run-down children's play area, some decrepit wooden chalets that needed refurbishing, a shabby shower block, a screen that hid overflowing waste bins and then more static vans. They stopped alongside a parking area on soft ground. As he got out, Jack recognized the big shape of Lieutenant Pietro Raimondi.

'*Ciao*, Jack. Sylvia, she is down at the other scene.' They shook hands and Pietro motioned them forwards. 'Sorry we have to walk, but the forensic teams they are still examining the grass for vehicle marks.'

'No problem, I need the exercise. Sylvia said the polizia were first on the scene. Is there a jurisdiction problem?'

'No. The parents of the teenagers they called the polizia, but we cooperate very well and they say we can run the case.'

They trudged briskly into a gathering wind and were slightly breathless by the time they reached the crime scene.

The pit itself resembled a crater that had been made by the impact of a giant meteorite. Inside it, everyone wore white Tyvek coveralls with protective masks and gloves. They looked like spacemen. Jack paused to take it all in. The excavation was deep at the centre, maybe as much as two metres. The pit was more rectangle than square. In its centre was a patch of heavily blackened ground, with mounds of burned rubbish and a white forensic tent.

'What was this used for?'

Pietro shrugged. 'I don't know. Looks like a building excavation. I think a house was going to be made. My uncle was a builder and he had digs like this.'

'But there's crap everywhere.' Jack pointed to old, burned cans and shrivelled plastic lying between the duckboards that the forensic teams had put down.

'They've been burning trash here. We have a problem with garbage in Naples. The authorities don't collect properly, so many people with land make money burning garbage, or burying it.'

The top of the pit was marked off with crime-scene tape and guarded by officers logging in anyone with authority to access the area. Pietro pointed to it. 'Sylvia is down there, with the ME. You want to join them?'

'In a minute.' Jack's gaze moved on to another tented area. It was obviously where the car was being examined. Where the young couple had been murdered.

'That shooting looks routine, they are almost done there.' Pietro pointed to the middle of the pit. 'The other site is – how you say? Far more complex.'

In Jack's mind there was no such thing as a *routine* shooting. Every killing had its own peculiarities – the signature marks of the murderer. He walked across the boards to the tent and came out at the driver's side of the car. The vehicle's metalwork had already been dusted with fingerprint powder. 'Pietro, can you talk me through what went on here?'

'Sure. The boyfriend was in the driver's seat when

he was shot. We know this from the blood and angle of the bullet. The girl, she was in the back and –'

'Why?'

'*Scusi?*'

'Why was the boyfriend in the front while she was in the back?'

Pietro smiled. 'He was naked except for his socks. She – she was naked too. So I think he *had* been in the back, kneeling or sitting. It is possible that they heard or saw something that frightened them, so he got in the driver's seat and drove off.'

'Towards the pit?'

'We think so.'

'So he drove *towards* where the other woman was killed?'

'*Sì.*'

Jack puzzled it out. *The couple must have been killed* after *the woman in the pit. Perhaps they heard her scream and thought they could help. Poor kids. They obviously hadn't recognized the true nature of what was happening or they'd have driven in the opposite direction. Unless, of course, it had been so dark that they hadn't really known in which direction they were travelling. Or, so close that they'd* had *to drive this way to be able to turn the vehicle around.*

Pietro seemed to read his thoughts. 'They were parked not far from here. If you look where I'm pointing, there are tyre marks over there. Seems they skidded when they tried to turn round and ended up here.'

'And we think *here* is where they were shot?'

'*Sì.*'

'Angle of gunfire?'

Pietro made a pistol out of two fingers and crouched at window level. 'About this height. *Scusi* . . .' he shuffled Jack to one side, 'and about from here.'

Jack's mind turned to the killer. *He would have been in the pit with the burning girl. After she screamed, he would have shot her. Then no doubt he heard the car start up and thought he was going to be discovered. He'd have rushed out of the pit, seen the headlights of the vehicle, then moved in to wipe out any witnesses.* Jack pointed to the pit. 'At the edge – the one nearest to where we are now – you may find finger indentations, trace evidence, footprints, marks from the front of the killer's footwear. There'll be elbow marks on the clay banking – all that evidence could have been left as he climbed out in a hurry.'

'We know,' said Pietro. 'We are not the FBI, but these things we know to look for.'

'Sorry,' said Jack. 'I was just thinking out loud.' Both bodies had just been removed from the scene. He'd want to see the photographs later. Hopefully they'd been stripped of the few remaining clothes before being bagged. The reason was simple. Inside the zipped bag, they would bleed through their wounds as soon as they were moved. By the time they got to the morgue, any clothes left on them would be soaked in blood. Any fibre, skin or hair evidence left by the offender would be lost in the blood flow.

'The dead teenagers. There's no way you're looking

at them for the murder in the pit?' Jack couldn't see *how*, but he wanted to check anyway.

'No, we are not thinking so. The families are decent families. It looks like the boy and the girl they were just out having some fun.'

'May I look inside?'

Pietro spoke to a technician who was squatting in a tiny protected space in the vehicle, and he climbed out. Jack asked for gloves. He snapped them on and was careful not to brush against anything as he leaned inside.

The vehicle stank of blood, forensic swabs and a new pine air freshener that was still hanging from the cigarette lighter beneath the plastic dashboard. 'The girl was in the back, her head on the right side, behind the passenger seat?'

'*Sì*, that is right.'

Jack ran sequences through his head. *He shoots the boyfriend, blowing out the window, then opens the door and leans into the vehicle. The girl's frightened so she moves as far away as she can from him. It's a two-door, so there's no exit from the back. He has to have got his face inside to see her, maybe even talk to her. Then he shoots her.* 'Have Ballistics already been all over the vehicle?'

Pietro nodded. 'Been and gone. That's what you say, yes?'

Jack smiled. 'Yep, that's what we say. There'll be gunshot residue all over this car. Massive amounts of it. And, of course, all over our killer's hand and clothing.'

'They have taken the GSR tests.'

'Good. You find the cartridges?'

'Two.'

'I guess one was outside, near the back of the front tyre, that would be the first shot. The other, the second – well, the second one would be inside, in the footwell beneath the driver's seat?'

Pietro looked surprised. 'How did you know?'

'All handguns – well, at least, all the handguns I've ever heard of – eject cartridges only to the right. So given where the bodies were, the discovery sites are pretty obvious.'

Pietro made a mental note to remember this.

Jack's head was once more inside the car. His mind was back at the moment of the murders. 'Our shooter will have pushed the dead boyfriend out of the way and the girl would have been screaming or pleading for her life. If the girl screamed, then he probably shot her immediately. If she pleaded for her life, then he would have dragged it out. Enjoyed it more. A man who likes to see women burn to death doesn't like to kill quickly, unless he has to. So, let's guess that he tried to calm her down. He would have made her believe she could live – he'd have liked that – then he'd have killed her.'

'*Ritardato!*'

Jack ignored the obscenity. He slowly reversed out of the vehicle, sucking in fresh air to clear his lungs and his head. *He'd have tried to calm her down.* The thought stuck to him like hot tar.

'Shall we go down to the other scene now?' asked Pietro.

*Made her believe she could live, then killed her.* 'I think our killer may have made a critical mistake. Right here. And it may tell us exactly who he is.'

Pietro frowned. 'Where?'

Jack leaned into the car again. 'He'll have been very careful when he shoved the boy out of the way, anxious not to snag a cuff or leave fibres. The victims' bodies will be clean of any trace of him. But I bet he's missed something.'

'What?'

'Somewhere here.' Jack pointed around the back of the driver's seat and the window area. 'This is where you'll find it. Test all around here. The fabric of the roof lining, the plastic back of the seat, even the inside of the window, and you'll find it.'

Pietro was still confused. 'What? What will we find?'

'DNA,' said Jack. 'That old Gene Jeanie might just do his magic for us. Our killer will have spoken to the girl. Maybe even shouted at her to control her. When you speak, even though you can't see it, you spray saliva. Not huge amounts, just a small mist, invisible to the naked eye. But it'll be there. A microscopic dot will be there.' Jack pointed closely to the metal frame of the car door and window. 'Good scientists will find DNA, replicate it, and they'll get this guy's genetic fingerprint. And you never know, our boy just might have a criminal record to match it to.'

As Jack finished his sentence he realized it was a long shot. Many serial killers didn't have previous convictions. But if they did find DNA, at least it was a beginning, something to build on. A match waiting to be made.

Jack hung back while Pietro thanked the technician and passed on orders for the DNA testing. There was another thought that he kept to himself. One too alarming to share.

The killer had been disturbed.

He'd been forced to abandon his fire – and abandon his prize.

That meant he was dissatisfied.

Tense. Angry. Pent-up.

It also meant he'd need to kill again.

And he'd need to do it very soon.

# 58

***Crime scene 2, Campeggio Castellani, Pompeii***

Sylvia Tomms and Medical Examiner Boris Stern stood beside the burned corpse of the dead woman beneath a forensic tent in the centre of the pit. The sun, rarely spotted in Naples for the last week, had cruelly broken cover and was cooking the plastic ceiling above them, increasing the stench of burned flesh and decomposing rubbish.

Stern, a small, white-haired man with Einstein-like glasses and moustache, was Munich born and bred. At social gatherings Sylvia enjoyed speaking German with him and discussing places and events she'd shared with her father. Now, though, their common language was that of death and they spoke Italian for the benefit of those around them.

'She's been shot through the head.' Stern pointed at the blackened, fleshless skull. 'A very precise shot from the front, probably two metres away. The entry wound looks like a nine millimetre. That's the most likely cause of death.'

'Not the burning?' asked Sylvia.

'No, no. Absolutely not. Though she was burned

– or, at least, partially burned – before she was shot.'

Sylvia grimaced. 'You're sure of that?' She glanced at the corpse. It was charred beyond recognition. Skin around the skull was missing. All her clothing destroyed. Only the fatty tissue around her thighs seemed to remain.

'No question about it. The burning is consistent with her being upright and fighting to get free from some wire around her wrists. You'll notice, as in all burnings, that the thinnest parts go first – the joints, elbows, knees. The fatty parts – the muscles and biceps – they hold out longer.'

Sylvia had seen floaters and frenzied knife killings, bullet-riddled bodies and strangulations, but never anything like this. It was grotesque.

'What chances of identification, Prof?'

'Oh, good. Very good.' He stretched out his foot in its rubber boot and carefully stepped on to a clear spot of earth. 'Look at her fingers.'

'You mean, what's left of them?' Sylvia gingerly followed his lead.

Stern put his double-gloved finger across the blackened remains of the woman's right hand. 'You can see that she's made a fist, like she's just about to punch someone. We call this Pugilistic Posture. It's happened because the fire caused contractions in her arm. But bend a little closer and look.'

Sylvia stooped so her eyes were barely six inches from the blackened hand.

'The skin around the inside of her middle two fingers on this hand is intact. The fire has blackened it and dried it considerably. We can rehydrate those areas and probably get prints. We've been lucky. The skin on the other hand is almost totally destroyed. The fire was probably hotter there.'

The *Professore* straightened up, put the back of his left hand against his spine and stretched. 'A touch of rheumatism, I think. Besides the fingerprints, there's plenty of bone left to get good DNA samples from. And there are enough teeth left for us to age her accurately, and maybe even identify her too.'

They stepped back and studied the burned remains. Their thoughts were in sync. Both wondered who the victim was? What awful twist of fate had led her to this dreadful end?

Sylvia put her hand on her old friend's shoulder and broke the silence. 'I need you to lie to me. Tell me that the gases from the fire will have knocked her out and she never felt a thing.'

Stern patted her hand. 'You know that's not true. I'm afraid this will have been a slow death until the moment he shot her.'

'How long?'

'I can't tell you that until I get her back to the mortuary and examine her more closely. It will certainly have taken minutes for all her skin to have burned off. After that, mercifully, she would have been pain free.'

'Why so? Because the brain blocks the agony?'

'No, not at all. Quite simply because all our nerve

endings are in our skin. Once the skin has burned away, then there is no feeling.'

*What an awful way to go.* Sylvia wondered what kind of person would want to actually watch someone suffer like that.

Stern removed his glasses and used his arm to blot sweat from his brow. 'When your fire experts arrive they will be able to tell you much more about her last moments. But looking at the skeleton, and particularly the skull, I would say the murderer started the fire at the top of her body.'

'Why?'

Stern replaced his glasses. 'Come around this side. I'll try to explain.'

They picked their way into a position closer to the victim's head.

'See down there, around the tops of her legs?' He pointed out the area. 'While there is no skin left, there is still some tissue and burned muscle. Now look here; the upper skin that should be around her neck and skull is completely missing, front and back.'

Sylvia caught his drift. 'Fire rises; so if the blaze had been set at her feet then you'd expect most damage down there, rather than at the top of the body?'

'Absolutely right.'

'So you'd say he doused her in petrol and set her head alight?'

'That might be what *you* would say, my dear. I don't think so. I think your killer was a little more precise in his practices. Look at the skull. There is incredible damage around the mouth. I think he may have forced a rag, probably soaked in some accelerant, into her mouth, pushed it deep into the back of her throat, and then set it alight.'

*Like a garden lamp*, thought Sylvia. Her killer used a petrol-soaked rag like a wick in an outside lamp.

'There is also extensive burning on the chest. He probably threw accelerant over her once she was ablaze.' Stern lowered his mask so it was below his nose and sniffed. 'Paraffin, I think, not petrol; but I could be wrong. These days my nose is better suited to sniffing a good Barolo than anything else. Again, the fire team will know for certain.'

Sylvia had seen enough. 'Excuse me for a moment, *Professore*. I just need to go outside for a while. I'll leave you to get on with your work.'

He smiled knowingly at her. 'See you shortly.'

Sylvia was keen to escape from the charred corpse and get to the other side of the crime scene. She was desperate for a smoke.

Jack and Pietro caught Sylvia as she ducked out of the forensic tent. A packet of cigarettes was already in her hand. Before the two men had reached her a voice stopped her in her tracks.

'*Capitano!*'

Sylvia turned to see a young male Exhibits Officer beside her. 'You need to come to the other side of the pit.'

'Why? What is it?'

'We've found some things in the far corner, in an old chest of drawers.'

'Things?'

Jack and Pietro followed, a pace behind.

'Underwear. Tissues used by women, smeared with make-up, old lipstick – those kinds of things.'

When they reached the corner of the pit, Jack stepped back and tuned out the fast-spoken Italian comments being exchanged. Old planks and plastic sheeting had been arranged to form a sort of shelter and forensic teams were now erecting their own protection around this area as well. A rusty oil drum lay on its side in the treacly mud and there were footprints everywhere. It looked like investigators had rushed into the scene and probably compromised it. There were some forensic walkways, but not enough. He was saddened to think of what might have been lost. A crime-scene photographer flashed his camera at something being shown to Sylvia. Jack was in no hurry to see it. He was still trying to decode the importance of what was in front of him.

The pit was at its deepest at this point. The place with the planks and the oil drum was most sheltered from the elements. It had been carefully chosen. *This was his place to linger. He sat here to savour the blaze. Wanted to be alone with his thoughts. The drum was his seat. The drawers now being rifled by Forensics were his treasure chest. He was a regular – no, more than that, he was a routine visitor.* Jack looked again at the makeshift shelter. It really wasn't very big, and certainly not sophisticated.

Some old wooden doors – one a front door of a house with splintered panels that looked as though it had been staved in during a drugs raid – formed the sides of the shelter. A small trench, about six or eight inches deep, had been dug in the ground so the doors would slot in. Planks of wood – rough flooring timbers and pieces of cheap plywood – had been crudely layered on top and nailed down. Old plastic sheeting had been fed and trapped beneath them to form some kind of waterproof membrane. Whoever had done this wasn't tall; the height and poor design of the roof showed he'd struggled to arrange things with any real neatness or competence. More than anything there was a real sense, though, that he'd spent a lot of time here – he'd come with a spade and tools and had collected the right combination of wood and sheeting to make the shelter. This undoubtedly was *his* place.

'Jack. Look at these.'

He responded slowly to Sylvia's voice, carefully stepping on to a short walkway that had just been put down. It took him to the heart of the group.

The young Exhibits Officer held a long drawer across his arms and a camera whirred and flashed from somewhere to the side.

In the left side of the drawer were maybe six or seven pairs of panties. From their size and style they looked as though they'd been worn by slim – probably young – women. Next to them was a pile of used cosmetics. Lipsticks, eyeliners, blusher, powder, even some hairspray aerosols. In the right side of the drawer was a strange mix of papers – tissues that had yellowed but still bore marks of lipstick or make-up, old letters that had been crumpled up and then straightened out, torn photographs of girls' faces that had been Sellotaped together again.

'You recognize any of these girls?' asked Jack.

'Not yet,' answered Sylvia, 'but I wouldn't be surprised if at least some of them turn out to be our missing women.'

'These are trophies?' said Pietro. He pointed to the tent that covered the place where the last woman had been burned. 'He kills his women there, then he collects here what he wants to keep from them.'

'Maybe,' said Jack, his attention caught by two forensic officers struggling to move heavy cans in an adjacent corner. 'What have they got there?'

Pietro interrupted the search. He lifted one of the cans, his face beaming with an ear-to-ear smile. '*Paraffina!* Looks like we've found your paraffin.'

# 59

***Campeggio Castellani, Pompeii***

Antonio Castellani was on the toilet cursing his haemorrhoids when the carabinieri rushed his caravan. By the time he'd come out, frightened and still hurting, his grandson Paolo was flat on the floor with his hands cuffed behind his back.

They were both read their rights and told they were being taken to the carabinieri barracks for questioning in connection with three murders. The arresting officers noted they looked genuinely shocked. They also noted that another Castellani – Franco – was missing. His grandfather made frantic protests about needing to stay to run his business but his words fell on deaf ears. Confused campers crushed around the two separate police cars that flashed their blue lights and sped away.

Search teams poured into the old man's van and the one that Paolo and Franco shared. They found nothing in Antonio's office, except accounts, scrapbooks of his younger years, old clothes, a cupboard full of cans and dried foods, some letters from his wife and enough medicines to stock a *farmacia*.

Things were different in the other caravan.

Forensics were having a ball.

Mud from the pit was all over the place, but especially close to one of the stinking bunks. There were specks of heroin all over the floor. They stripped the bed sheets and sent them off to be tested for other substances – specifically gunshot residue. The pillow cover was pulled off and bagged. Something soft tumbled lightly on to the floor.

Alberto Morani, a veteran forensic investigator, felt his heart thump. 'Stop! Don't touch it until you've photographed it.'

His assistant, newcomer Giulietta Sielli, pulled back her hand. She flicked round the camera she was holding and took several pictures of what even she knew could be hugely significant.

Lying on the floor by Franco Castellani's bed was a pair of tiny yellow panties. The type that undoubtedly matched the yellow bra that had been worn by Rosa Novello.

# 60

*Stazione dei carabinieri, Castello di Cisterna*

Within seconds of seeing Antonio Castellani being interviewed in the holding cell, Jack knew he had nothing to do with the triple murder on his land. The old man's body language showed he was completely confused by the whole affair. His brow was furrowed, his eyes startled, but there was no indicator of guilt, only genuine bewilderment.

Sylvia was gentle but firm with him. First she explored his relationship with his grandchildren and the absence of their parents. Then she moved on to his business and the kind of activities that happened at the site. From the viewing window in the adjoining room Jack listened to the man's strange Neapolitan dialect. It was nothing like the Italian he'd learned. What was clear, though, was how arthritis had stiffened the old guy's joints, how old age had bent his spine and slowed his responses. Antonio Castellani would have trouble swatting a fly in his filthy caravan, let alone hunting and killing humans.

On the other side of the viewing room, Pietro Raimondi was in another interview area using completely different tactics on Paolo Falconi. He was leaning half across the thin grey table that separated them; his broad neck bulged with bloated veins and stretched muscles, his eyes piercing and provocative. 'Don't mess with us, Paolo. You know something about what went down, now tell us.'

'I told you. I don't know a thing.'

'Rosa Novello. You had the hots for her, right? You've been sniffing around her like a big bad street dog just waiting for the chance to grind up against her leg.'

Paolo shifted in his chair. 'No!'

'No?'

'Yes – no! How many times do I have to tell you? I don't *even* know who you're fucking talking about.'

'Hey, watch your filthy little mouth.'

Paolo backed up in his seat and looked away from the big lieutenant. He was staring straight off into space, right at Jack, but couldn't see him through the one-way glass.

The profiler studied him. Paolo was stressed to the hilt, anxious, aggressive and panicky under pressure. But was he really clever enough, mature enough and controlled enough to carry out a triple murder? Not on his own. Certainly not on his own. Did he have a killer instinct? They were about to find out.

Pietro undid his pistol from its holster and slid it across the table. 'Pick it up. Cock it. Aim it at me.'

'What?'

'You heard me. Do it! Now!'

Paolo fumbled with the Beretta. He picked it up and swapped it between hands. He ignored the safety and raised it. Pointed it, not at Pietro – but off into space, well wide of his left shoulder. His finger wasn't even inside the guard.

Jack had seen enough. The stunt with the gun – unloaded, of course – had been his idea. He could see that Paolo had no affinity with the weapon. He was cautious, clumsy and almost scared when he handled it. The real killer would be *more* than comfortable with a firearm. Even if he'd tried to disguise his familiarity with a gun, there would have been telltale traits in the lifting, levelling, sighting and gripping. Even the putting down of the weapon would have betrayed him.

Pietro holstered his gun and stared into Paolo's eyes. It was a look of controlled violence. A visual threat that stuck needles in the brain of anyone on the receiving end. 'A pair of girl's panties were found in your caravan. What were you doing with them?'

'I don't know what you mean.'

'You don't know what panties are?'

'Yes, of course I do. But I don't know about any in my van.'

'Well, they were found in there. Nice yellow ones, G-string type. You know, the type that Rosa would have looked really sexy in.'

Paolo looked angry. 'I told you – I don't know any Rosa and I don't know anything about her underwear!'

Pietro slammed a hand on the table and Paolo jumped back. 'Let me jog your memory. Rosa is the dead girl we found not far from your van. She's the pretty kid who was staying at your camp and whose brains were blown all over the inside of a car. The girl who, according to her mother, owned yellow panties, just like the ones we found in your caravan. So, I think you *do* know Rosa. And I think you'd better start talking to me now, before I charge you with her murder.'

Jack could see sweat rolling down Paolo's cheek. Seconds passed while Pietro's words sank in. Paolo rubbed away the salty drizzle from his forehead. 'Franco, my cousin. I think he must have had the panties.'

'Explain.'

Paolo sweated some more. Finally he gave up what he was holding back, 'I've seen him with women's underwear before.'

Pietro read his face – it was full of secrets. 'What else, Paolo? You're not telling me everything. What else about Franco?'

Paolo sucked in air. All the pressure in the world seemed to be on him. 'Look, he's my best friend. Franco and I are like brothers. I'm not saying anything else.'

'As you like. But then you both end up in jail. We *will* find him, Paolo. It's only a matter of time. You know that, don't you?'

Paolo looked away. Stared at the wall. Stared at his hands on the table. Looked anywhere in the room except into the face of the cop who looked like he wanted to tear his head off.

'Paolo, look at me. Pay attention. This is for your own good.'

He turned his head slowly towards the big policeman. Did his best to stare him down.

'From what I know, your cousin's not well. He's sick and he's in trouble. Unless you tell me what you're holding back, things are only going to get worse for him – and for you.'

Paolo held his silence. Looked into the dark-brown eyes that were boring into him.

'Paolo!' Pietro slammed his hand on the desk again. 'You want us to make a mistake? To chase after him and shoot him down in an alleyway? You want to risk all that?'

Paolo swallowed. Looked around. Fought the doubt in his mind. 'He's got a gun. My grandfather lets him use one of his guns to kill rats on the site. I looked yesterday, and it's missing.'

# 61

***Stazione dei carabinieri, Castello di Cisterna***

Twenty minutes after Paolo's interview, the photograph of Franco that his grandfather kept in his wallet had been copied and wired to every carabinieri patrol in Naples.

Sylvia and Pietro sat with Jack and compared interview notes. Soon, life at the Castellani campsite became clearer. The two grandsons collected garbage and burned it in the pit. It was Franco's job to do the incineration, a job he guarded closely, one he liked so much he wouldn't let anyone else do it. Paolo merely helped drive the van and load up. Old man Castellani wasn't capable of even helping with the heavy garbage sacks, so they all agreed that he could safely be ruled out as a murder suspect. When it came to the night of the murders, Paolo had said he'd been asleep in his bunk – no real alibi. Nevertheless, it seemed to tally with his grandfather's version of events. What's more, none of the team felt Paolo alone had the potential to be a killer. He was too passive, too nervous. And then came the more obvious pointers. Franco was missing. What looked like Rosa's panties had been found beneath what was now established as his pillow. Other items of underwear and female 'trophies' had been discovered in the pit where only he went. On top of all that, his grandfather had admitted finding Franco using heroin. Finally, Paolo had confessed that his grandfather's old Glock was missing.

Pietro was convinced Franco was their man. Sylvia and Jack were more cautious. They could both see the clear links connecting Franco to the triple murders at the site, but struggled to see any connection between those three murders and the killing of Francesca Di Lauro. And what really troubled Jack was that he was sure the triple murders *were* linked to the Di Lauro case. He was certain because he couldn't believe that two separate killers would both choose to use fire as a means to murder a victim. Such an MO was highly uncommon. It was impossible to think that two such killers would spring up at the same time in the same area.

As Sylvia and Pietro went in for a team briefing, Jack sat alone and tried to make sense of it all. If what they were beginning to think was right, then Luciano Creed was entirely innocent. He could live with that. The guy was creepy as hell, but maybe that's all he was – creepy as hell. Whoever said the world of psychological profiling didn't have its fair share of sex-obsessed perverts?

*So, what about Franco Castellani?*

News was now in from search teams that shoes recovered from Franco's caravan looked as though they matched prints at the murder scene. Analysis of soil samples from clothing was already underway to further test the link. For Jack it was another *so what?* Given that Franco regularly went to the pit, they were bound to be able to forensically place him there. It was all a hell of a puzzle.

Jack looked down at the photograph of Franco. The kid's face was a mess. Beaked nose, horribly wrinkled skin. He looked like a shrivelled sparrow. Mother Nature sure had fucked up. Sylvia had said he was suffering from Werner Syndrome. Jack knew little of it. He hit Google on the office computer in front of him and soon got lost in a mass of medical extracts. The snippets he pulled were disturbing. It was an awful disease. It kicked in around puberty and aggressively got worse until you died at an all too young age. He noted the facts:

**Cause** – *mutations of the WRN gene. Passed on by parents, each of them showing no symptoms but both having copies of the defective gene.*

**Frequency** – *higher incidents in Japan than USA and Europe. Medical estimates vary from a frequency of 1 in a million to as high as 1 in 200,000.*

**Life expectancy** – *death usually occurs between 30 and 50 through atherosclerosis or malignant tumours.*

Poor bastard.

Life could be awfully cruel and unfair.

The facts prompted Jack to think of a whole new batch of questions.

*Had the disease stopped him having normal sexual relationships?*

For sure it had.

*Would it screw you up to the extent that you might torture women who are repulsed by you and reject you?*

It certainly might.

*Could rejection by a mother and father at an early age, and a hard underprivileged upbringing, worsen your feelings of alienation and unfairness?*

Absolutely.

Jack felt sad and worried. The psychological motivations were all there. Had Franco Castellani been born *normal*, had he been blessed with healthy cells, then his whole life could have been amazingly different. But this kid? This kid had been damned from birth. Scrub that – it's even worse. He'd been damned before he'd even been born.

# 62

***Bar Luca, Napoli***

Bar Luca had recently become Bruno Valsi's home from home. In the past few years the Camorra had steadily increased its stake in the business – 10, 25, 40 per cent – and it hadn't taken Bruno long to push it to 51. The two young owners, Giorgio and Marco, were smart enough to realize that 49 per cent of one of the city's hottest night spots was better than a shallow grave somewhere.

Valsi sat in their office, feet up on their desk, watching a bank of surveillance monitors that followed the action in the bar and pole-dancing areas. Sitting opposite him were his new trusted lieutenants, Romano Ivetta and Alberto Donatello. There was no longer any point hiding them.

Romano couldn't ever have been named anything other than Romano. His long broken nose, strong dark eyes and gladiatorial size made him look like he'd come straight from Hollywood casting. Donatello was totally different. Small and wiry with a shaven head, permanent five o'clock shadow and hollow cheekbones, he resembled an undernourished prisoner of war.

'The way I see it,' said Valsi, his eyes still watching the dancers on the screens, 'we face aggression on two fronts – the Cicerone and my own Family. The big question is . . .' he cued a finger at Donatello, 'do we wait for them to come for us? Or do we take them by surprise?'

'We take them by surprise,' answered the little man.

'Correct.' Valsi took his feet off the desk and peered at the monitor. One girl was upside down now. The pole gripped by one serpent-like leg curled around the shiny steel, the other spread out like the blade of opened scissors. 'Is it me, or is that the most fuckable woman in all of Italy?'

Ivetta and Donatello laughed.

The *Capo* grabbed the phone and hit an internal speed dial. 'Giorgio, it's Bruno. The girl on pole two, she has the face of a sainted angel. She looks like she was sent from heaven just for me to fuck. Tell her to stay behind when she's finished. And make sure I don't have any trouble getting what I want.' He dropped the phone back on its cradle. 'So, we move first. You both agree?'

'Absolutely. No question,' said Ivetta, 'but *who* first? Which one do you want us to tackle?'

'Good question. And I've been thinking about it. My father-in-law is planning to kill me. I'm certain of that. And I'm fairly sure that he's already told Salvatore to take care of it.'

'Sal the Snake?' checked Donatello, waggling his hand like a sidewinder.

'*Sì.*'

'Pheeeew!' whistled Ivetta. 'That's some tough motherfucker –'

'Well, who the fuck do you think he would send?' interrupted Valsi. 'Mary Poppins?'

The three of them laughed, then Valsi added, 'But the Don will not order the hit until he is sure he has everyone's support. It is his style to want the *guaglioni* to know that the hit was necessary because of my dealings with the Cicerone crew. He'll want it to look like I had put the whole Family in danger.'

Ivetta and Donatello could see where the conversation was leading. 'So, we hit the Cicerone boys first,' said Ivetta. 'We hurt them bad, and then we kill Don Fredo.'

Valsi waved a headmasterly finger at them. 'Too fast. You're going too quickly. We wipe out the Cicerone *leadership*. Then, we pause a little. We let the Finelli diehards see our strength. If we are vicious enough, then the ambitious ones among them will weed out the weak.'

'Brilliant,' said Donatello. 'The young bucks will kill the old guard for us.'

Valsi winked at him. 'Now you're learning. What we need, though, is a plan to hit at the heart of the Cicerone. It may be bloody. How many men, good men, can you put on the streets?'

'If the price is right?' Ivetta held his hands open.

'Of course.'

‘However many we need. One, two dozen – maybe more.’

‘Wait,’ said Valsi, a thin smile bisecting his handsome face. ‘I have an idea that may require fewer men. In fact, only one man and one very beautiful woman.’ He turned to the club monitors. ‘One with the face of a sainted angel.’

# 63

***Stazione dei carabinieri, Castello di Cisterna***

By nightfall, Jack, Sylvia and Pietro were consumed with the werewolf hunger that hits most murder squads at the end of a high-adrenaline shift. The antidote was a case of cold beer along with several boxes of locally made pizzas.

Sylvia shook a warm strand of dangling mozzarella from her fingers. 'We've let old man Castellani go home. He's no value to us here and he was worrying himself sick about his campsite business.'

'And worrying about his grandsons?' asked Jack.

'Especially Franco,' said Pietro, his mouth full. 'He didn't say much about Paolo, except that he's a good boy and we should treat him properly.'

'Then Franco's *not* a good boy? Is that his implication?' Jack took a wedge of garlic bread.

'Franco's probably a murdering little bastard,' added Pietro. 'But all his grandfather will say is that life has been unkind to him and we shouldn't misjudge him.'

'An understatement.' The garlic bread made Jack's stomach growl. 'Life has been *wickedly* cruel to young Franco. Has he got any form?'

Sylvia nodded and hurriedly tried to finish chewing. 'Violence. A suspended sentence about five years ago for a very bad beating he gave someone stupid enough to make fun of him.'

'How bad?'

'Put the guy in hospital.'

Jack wiped his fingers and sipped a beer. 'Nothing connected to arson, or involving fire?'

'Not that we can find. We're rerunning our checks and seeing if there are any psych reports as well.'

'And Paolo – anything on him?'

'Nothing.' Sylvia thought for a minute. 'I'm just trying to remember what Paolo said. He told us Franco wasn't there when he went to sleep, then when he woke he was crashed out in bed. There's heroin and a spike on the floor. The old man sees it, goes *pazzo* and then slaps him about.'

Jack sealed his fate with another garlic-loaded slice. 'You mean Paolo has no alibi, and we're ignoring his potential role in all this because the forensics are pointing the big finger at Franco?'

'Just a thought.'

'And a good one.'

Jack put the bread back. 'Franco and Paolo, I was just wondering how they compared to Bianchi and Buono.'

Pietro was lost. *'Scusi?'*

'Ken Bianchi and Angelo Buono. They were both cousins, grew up together, hung out together, played games of rape and murder together.'

Sylvia took the bread Jack had put back. 'The Hillside Strangler case?'

'The same. California, late seventies. Ten-plus victims. Cops had it down as the work of one guy. The press dubbed the perp the Hillside Strangler. Anyway, turned out the killings were done by two cousins.'

'They even sound Italian,' noted Pietro.

'Half of America does,' joked Jack. 'And probably the good half.'

Sylvia took one final bite and dropped the bread. She scrunched her napkin into a ball and dumped it on the paper plate. 'My eyes are bigger than my belly. You think maybe Paolo and Franco might be the same? Like Bianchi and Buono? Maybe Paolo's as guilty as hell but is now trying to shift all the blame on to his cousin?'

'That's possible,' said Jack. 'These cousins are – what? Twenty-four, twenty-five?'

Pietro searched his memory. 'Both twenty-four. Franco is twenty-five in a couple of months.'

Jack took another slug of cold beer. 'Agewise they're on the edge of the profile that I'm thinking of. If these missing women are all connected, they stretch back eight years or so, which puts these cousins around sixteen. It's kind of tender for this sort of sadism, but not unheard of.'

Sylvia was following his drift. 'I get what you mean. The sexual component in this case puts the offenders north of the puberty line. But what about the element of control used? Surely the offender, even back in the days of his first clumsy kills, must be much older than sixteen?'

'Agreed,' said Jack, 'but two offenders working together can distort things. They cover for each other, make fewer mistakes. A combination of two young offenders can give the impression of one more mature single perpetrator.'

Glumness hung in the air as they all pictured the possibility of the two cousins working in concert, picking off the women together, maybe one providing a distraction, the other delivering a disabling blow from behind. 'To be truthful,' said Jack, 'I think we're at that stage where we can't rule anything out. It's worth keeping in mind, though, that Bianchi and Buono were not a one-off. The eighties threw up Dave Gore and Fred Waterfield. When the curtain came down they pinned six rape murders on Gore and two on Waterfield. Though some old-timers say they might have killed as many as fifty. And, in fact, the first real recorded case of serial murder was the Harpe case.'

Sylvia uncapped another bottle of Peroni. 'Harpe? We didn't do that at the academy. How long we going back?'

Jack played with his beer. 'Way, way back, to the eighteenth century – late 1700s, I think. Micajah and Wiley Harpe were wild kids, rode with outlaws and renegade Indians. Murdered some men and boys, but it's thought they killed about forty women between them. Maybe more. They kidnapped, raped and murdered their way across frontierland. Used to ride into farms, rustle livestock, rape the women and then burn down the buildings and leave them to die inside. The crimes bound them together.'

'Burned them to death?' asked Pietro.

'So the reports say. Fire has been an age-old method of covering tracks. And sociopaths who kill for fun and profit are not a modern-day phenomenon.'

Sylvia looked down at the notes she'd made on the back of the pizza box. She scrunched up the waste and binned it. 'Time to go, I think. Let's get some sleep. Pietro, I have a job for you. Early doors, crack of dawn. And tomorrow I'll have another session with Franco's cousin and see if he really is hiding anything.'

# 64

***Campeggio Castellani, Pompeii***

Pietro Raimondi was cursing both Jack and Sylvia as he prised himself away from the warmth of his naked fiancée and rolled out of bed. Sylvia's last instruction of the night was for him to pay an early morning visit to old man Castellani.

The recent spate of long days and long nights meant he was spending too little time with his fiancée Eliana, and he didn't like it. It was straining their relationship. Pietro didn't mind working for a living, but he wasn't one of those cops who made the mistake of living solely for his work. Far from it. He lived for Eliana – for money to spend on them both – for the chance to have a better home than their one-bed studio in a flea-pit tenement building. He lived for better than this. He mulled everything over as he drove out to the Castellani place.

Mussolini, the Castellani's mongrel dog, ran at his old Lancia, barking at its tyres as he pulled to a stop. He decided to wait a beat until it backed off.

A caravan door clunked open. Castellani creaked down the short metal stairs and recognized him. He tied the dog up and walked back inside. Left the door open for Pietro to follow. The younger man climbed the steps and was still shutting it when Antonio asked, 'When are you letting my Paolo come home?'

'*Buon giorno!* Just as soon as he helps us find Franco.'

The old man headed to the kitchen sink. 'You want *caffè*?'

'*Sì*. Please.'

The van was roasting hot and stank of stale sweat. It must have been years since it'd been cleaned. If, indeed, it ever had been.

The two men sat either side of a cheap, narrow table that flapped down off the wall.

It almost broke as Pietro leaned his big heavy arms on it. 'Antonio, you are too old and, I suspect, too wise to play games with us.' There was a glint of menace in the lieutenant's dark-brown eyes. 'We have found three people murdered on your land. One of your grandsons is in custody and the other is on the run. You've had time to reflect since yesterday. Now I need answers from you. I need to be able to clear up these crimes.' Pietro flipped open a pocket-sized spiral pad and tapped a pen on the blank page.

Antonio rubbed his bald brown head. Dry skin fell like snow in the grey air of the caravan. 'I don't know where Franco is. If I did, I'd tell you. He is ill and I want him to be safe – even if that means he has to be safe with you.'

'Does Paolo know where he is? Did they hang out anywhere special together?'

'He could do. Though they never went anywhere *special*. They have no money. Times are tough. Maybe you noticed?'

'I noticed. I grew up around here. As you see, I'm no Roman millionaire.'

The old man shuffled back to the kitchen area. Poured the coffee that had been brewing.

Pietro came straight to the point. 'Are they capable of murder? Could your boys do that?'

He studied the old man for his reaction.

Antonio looked away. He'd been floored by so many big moments in his time. So many body blows, kidney punches, surprise knockdowns. Anything was possible. But surely not this? 'Not Paolo. He's gentle. I've never seen him hurt anyone.'

'But Franco?'

'Franco has a temper. He hates how he is. You can understand that, can't you?'

Pietro nodded. 'The way he is would give me a temper too. But could he kill?'

Antonio remembered his missing gun and shells. 'He could kill. You know he has my gun. He fires it in the pit. I don't know if he hits anything – he says he aims at rats – but he fires it. And he has this temper. But I don't think so. No, I don't think so.'

Pietro's eyes gave away his thoughts – parents never considered their kids to be capable of murder.

Antonio held the officer's gaze. 'Please go gentle

on him. Do whatever you can to bring him in safely.'

The police cell was cold and Paolo Falconi hadn't been given the second blanket he'd asked for. He was tired and his body ached as they marched him to the interview room. They showed no interest in his complaints about last night or his requests for something to eat or drink.

Sylvia Tomms, however, was well rested and raring to go. She got the formalities out of the way as they settled themselves at a small table. Once more Paolo said he didn't want a lawyer. Insisted he had nothing to hide. She opened a case file and slid over pictures of the dead bodies of Rosa Novello, Filippo Valdrano and the still unidentified female corpse found in the Castellani pit.

'I hope these people came to you in your dreams last night, Paolo.'

You could hear a pin drop in the interview room as her words sank in.

'Did they? Can you live with their deaths? With what was done to them?'

The pictures turned his stomach. Now he was glad they hadn't given him breakfast.

'Nothing to say, Paolo?'

'Nothing new. I told you everything yesterday. How's my *nonno*? Can I see him? He's really old and –'

'We let your grandfather go home. He's fine.'

Paolo looked relieved.

Sylvia touched Rosa's picture. 'This girl can't go home, though. She used to be pretty – not now. Look at her.'

He glanced at the picture, took in the missing part of the girl's skull. Her milky eyes. His face showed both shock and sympathy. Right from the start Sylvia had been having trouble seeing him as a killer, but the conversation last night with Jack had raised doubts in her mind. 'Do you like girls, Paolo, or are boys your thing?'

He frowned at her. 'You think I'm *finocchio*.'

'So, you have a girlfriend?'

He didn't answer.

'I said, do you have a girlfriend?'

'I heard what you said. No, I don't – but that doesn't make me anything. I just don't have a girl.'

Sylvia pushed all three photographs nearer to him. 'I'm not bothered if you're straight, or if you're gay. I'm bothered whether *you* – and your runaway cousin – had a motive to kill any of these people.'

He glared at her.

'Well? Did you?'

'You're crazy. You're all fucking crazy. I told that lieutenant yesterday everything I knew.'

'What about the panties, Paolo? The yellow panties?'

'I told him about them too.'

'You told him nothing. Just that sometimes you'd seen Franco with women's underwear.'

Paolo scowled at her. 'That's it. That's all I know. I told that big guy.'

Sylvia stood up and sighed. '*Va bene*. You want to be stupid. Fine. We've got other leads to chase up. I have a job to do, and I have to do it before anyone else gets hurt. You think I give a damn whether you rot in here for another month?'

They stared at each other.

Paolo scratched the back of his head.

Sylvia gave him a make-your-mind-up look.

He let out a sigh and looked down at the floor. 'Franco sometimes stole underwear and stuff from the campers' vans.'

'Go on.' She stayed standing.

'He'd see a young girl walking around and he'd talk about wanting to fuck her. But he knew that was never going to happen.'

'Because of the way he looks?'

'What do you think?'

Sylvia sat back down. 'So, he would steal their things – the girls' things – then what?'

'I don't know.'

'You don't know?'

Paolo looked embarrassed. 'He did things in the dark, or in the bathroom with them – on his own.'

'So how did you know he had them?'

'Sometimes he'd show me. He'd point out a girl, then show me her panties. It was like he was somehow connected to her. I told him it was sick.'

'And what did he say to that?'

'Told me to fuck off. He used to keep their stuff in the van – our van. He'd hold them, sort of cuddle them and sleep with them. But after I told him it was sick he stopped doing it, or he kept them somewhere else.'

'Like the pit.'

'Guess so.'

Sylvia picked up Rosa's picture and held the dead girl's face in front of his. 'So you're telling me that he stole *this* girl's underwear from her on the very night that she got murdered? Hell of a coincidence, isn't it?'

Paolo shrugged. 'Coincidences happen.'

'Did he ever approach the girls – do anything to them?'

'You're joking. He was too chicken-shit scared to approach them. He'd shout things if I was with him, but he was frightened to death of women. He wanted one – wanted one really bad – but he was terrified of being alone with them. Scared of them saying anything about how he looked.'

'Did that happen?'

'Sometimes. A while ago – before he looked anything near as bad as he does now – he tried to hit on some girls, but they were horrible to him.'

'Like how?'

'They'd put their fingers in their throats to show he made them feel like throwing up.'

Sylvia felt a pang of sympathy for Franco. But at the same time she knew that such humiliation could easily engender thoughts of murder. The interview lasted another hour. By the end she was as sure as she could be that he'd been telling her the truth. 'Do you know where he is, Paolo? He's not well, and we have to find him. We have to help him and we have to make sure he hasn't got anything to do with these deaths.'

Paolo didn't hesitate. 'He didn't. I know Franco better than anyone and I know he didn't kill anybody.'

'You might be right. But we have to talk to him ourselves. You know we have to do that. Where could he be, Paolo?'

There was a long silence, then he shifted awkwardly on the hard interview chair. 'I don't know. I'd tell you if I did, but I really don't know.'

Paolo shut his eyes and covered his face with his hands. He wanted to go home. Wanted to check his grandfather was okay. Wanted this nightmare to end. But more than anything, he wanted to clear his mind of the images of where Franco might be and what he might do with his grandfather's Glock.

# 65

*Grand Hotel Parker's, Napoli*

A few too many beers and far too little sleep conspired to give Jack an early morning headache. He'd been hoping for a gentle start to the day. A little low-volume news on the TV, then a longer than normal soak under a hot shower. But after being awake for less than ten minutes he was already compelled to run yesterday's events through his head. What was still bugging him was the link between the killings at the pit and the murder of Francesca Di Lauro. He was still far from certain any of them were the work of the runaway Franco Castellani.

Jack used the bathroom, then padded over to the desk in the corner of his room and emptied out his thoughts. In that blurry moment when the killer at the pit had been disturbed, he'd shown that instinctively his weapon of choice was not fire, but a firearm. Fire was his fantasy, his pleasure, his turn-on. But when it came to split-second survival, then it was a gun that he turned to.

A shooter.

That's what he was.

When the chips were down and he had to *react* rather than *plan*, when he had to get down to *business* rather than indulge his *fantasy*, he was a shooter.

And shooters were cold and deadly. Remote, unemotional and detached.

They had to focus their hunt on finding a man who regularly handled a gun. Someone who was a proficient shot, felt confident and comfortable enough to kill strangers without hesitation.

Was that really Franco Castellani? Could you get that sort of proficiency from shooting rats in a pit?

Sadly, today's video game generation was proving to be among the world's deadliest and youngest shooters. Pennsylvania State, Columbine, Iowa, Omaha, Virginia Tech, Dawson, the list went on and on. Stats showed that around a dozen kids a day died in the States from gunshot wounds – kids these days were made to leave their innocence at the school gates.

Maybe psychology was going to have to bow to forensics. If the Castellani kid was guilty, then his DNA would be inside the young couple's car. His fingerprints would be on the bodywork and his trace evidence would be somewhere on the girl or on her clothing. Forensics could make an impressive prosecution case and Jack knew it would take more than his niggling doubts to dismantle it.

He took a pen and paper from the desk and totted up the ten major things that he believed he now knew about the offender.

1. He kills his victims and – with the exception of the murders at the pit, where he was disturbed – disposes of them in separate places.

2. He uses a gun to control his victims and take them to where he wants.

3. He is turned on by power and control. That turn-on is of a sadistic nature. More than anything he enjoys witnessing the suffering.

4. He has a vehicle, something big enough in which to conceal and move a victim, no doubt bound and gagged.

5. He has excellent local knowledge and the burial site is so well known to him it probably has a significant memory for him.

6. He is fit and strong enough to climb mountain paths and get in and out of deep pits in a hurry.

7. He is sexually active but is probably not in a relationship, so he is sexually frustrated.

8. He is noticeably cruel, perhaps even violent, and is probably known to be dangerous.

9. He is able to come and go of his own free will. He is not accountable to a close partner or scrupulous boss who might question his movements at odd times.

10. The use of fire is indicative of massive internal

> stress and frustration, which is only relieved when the flames roar and someone else suffers.

*Suffers externally like he suffers internally* – could that be it? This last thought hovered in his mind.

Jack reviewed the ten points. Franco Castellani ticked some of the boxes, but not all. One thing for sure – this kid undoubtedly knew all about suffering. Perhaps he felt compelled to *share* suffering around.

Inflict it on others.

Get others to feel the agony that was slowly killing him.

Given the age, race and gender of the victims, Jack summarized the profile.

- White male/s
- Has experience and knows how to control violence, probably aged thirties to fifties (maybe younger if two people involved)
- Single or divorced – a loner
- Born and lives locally
- Has special local connections to National Park area where victims' remains found. Also connections to holiday campsite in Pompeii where murder scene discovered
- Holds driving licence. Owns – or has access to – vehicle big enough to move victims around in

- Comfortable with a gun – possibly law enforcement officer (or works with such officers), ex-military, rifle-club member, sports shooter, prison officer. Perhaps a career criminal. A Camorrista with a history of violence?

- Sexually active with fetishist/paraphilic tendencies

- Sadistic – has a need to see others suffering

Once more the fit wasn't perfect. He trawled the list again. On reflection, he really didn't feel this was a two-person crime. And if you ruled out a second person then Franco really didn't seem to have the maturity and cunning to fit the profile.

Jack scanned the rest of the outline. He also didn't think the profession was right. There was a difference between shooting vermin every day and taking human lives. Unless Franco saw those really pretty women – the ones who rejected him and ridiculed him – as vermin. That would make sense. That would make perfect sense.

He was still caught in the tangle of contradictory thoughts when his cellphone rang.

'Jack, it's Sylvia. I just got a call from Sorrentino. One of his excavation teams has just found another body. The third. And it's another woman.'

# 66

***Campeggio Castellani, Pompeii***

It took Antonio Castellani two more pots of coffee to tell Pietro everything about Franco, Paolo and his hugely dysfunctional extended family.

The more he heard, the more Pietro was convinced that Paolo Falconi was no gunman and no serial killer. But his cousin Franco stayed top of the list of key suspects.

He was about to wind up and leave when Antonio stopped him in his tracks. 'There is something that I didn't tell you yesterday. A secret I thought I would take to the grave.' He opened his hands expansively, a sign of surrender. 'With *all this* happening, I think I should talk about it.'

Pietro couldn't help but glance at his watch. His business was done and whatever secret Antonio had, he was sure it wasn't going to help his case.

'For years now I have been paying debts to the Camorra, to the Finelli clan.'

Pietro nodded sympathetically. 'You and many others. I have colleagues who may be able to help you. I'll write . . .'

'Shush, let me finish. This is not about the *pizzu*. I don't mind a little tax here and there. This is something more.'

'I'm sorry. Please go ahead.'

'Finelli sent his yobs, his guys, to frighten me away from my home. I have a debt from decades ago – fifty years in fact – now they want to foreclose, shut me down and build on the land. I'll have nothing.'

Pietro was worried. This was a messy secret. Messy secrets meant a lot of social work and wasted time, something he couldn't afford right now. 'You won't lose your home. These days we have special units that can protect you. People can intervene and –'

The old man cut him off again. 'You young are so impatient. Let me have my say. It will not be the waste of time you fear.'

And so Pietro sat back and gritted his teeth. Slowly the story of the gambling debt and the crude and cruel threats of the hired muscle unfolded. His sympathy went out to the old man. Life had certainly dealt him the proverbial losing hand. He was about to try – for the third time – to give him a contact name and number in the anti-Camorra unit, when Antonio Castellani shuffled to the back of the caravan and returned with half a dozen scrapbooks and photo albums.

'*Signor* Castellani, *please*. I really must go now.' Pietro rose and began to pull on his coat.

The old man ignored him. 'When your team searched the other day they only glanced at these.

They should have looked closer. They should not have rushed – like you are doing now.'

Pietro's eyes fell on the faded newsprint and old black and white pictures stuck in a cheap cardboard binder that was thick with dust and smelled like stale bread.

'These books go back half a century,' said Antonio proudly. 'They are records of every payment I've made. Every meeting I've ever had with the Camorra. They start with the late Luigi Finelli and then go on to his son, Fredo.' He turned a wad of crinkly pages and stopped at a news cutting that showed Bruno Valsi going to prison. 'And then they finish with Fredo's son-in-law, this little bastard. I'm sure you recognize him.'

Pietro certainly did. He took the book in his hands. The pages at the front and back were decoys. They were filled with boring family memorabilia – marriage certificates, birthday cards and school reports. But sandwiched between them was a layer of dynamite. Antonio Castellani's scrapbooks were personal logs of all the dealings he'd had over the years with the Finelli clan. He'd kept an account of all his payments, taken notes of all his conversations with them, jotted down every rumour and half-truth he'd ever heard about how they operated. And he'd listed every name and associate he'd heard mentioned. Antonio explained that his dearly departed wife, God bless her soul, had even secretly taken photographs of protection money being paid and countless henchmen coming and going in a variety of cars.

The biggest prize of all, though, were the photographs and corresponding notes and maps relating to weapons that Fredo Finelli had demanded Antonio hold for him. It had been an old gangster trick. Wipe a gun clean of your own prints and then have it held – and in doing so, printed – by someone indebted to you. If it was ever discovered by the cops, then the holder was expected to take the fall. Certainly they'd never dare divulge the true owner's identity. The consequences would be fatal.

Antonio had clearly kept all the stuff as an insurance payment, and now – with Valsi and his thugs threatening to evict him – it was time to cash it in. Pietro stared in silence at the documents. They were Camorra treasure maps. Find the guns, match the documents and, with Antonio as a witness, it would be a prosecution gold rush.

Antonio nodded at the undivided attention he was now getting. 'I'll make more *caffè*,' he said. 'I think it will take you a while to get through all that.'

And it did.

It was dark when Pietro left the caravan and walked back to his battered and rusty Lancia. He sat inside with the engine off and let it all sink in.

The futures of Bruno Valsi and Fredo Finelli – the two biggest names in Camorra circles – lay solely in his hands.

Suddenly, finding Franco Castellani really didn't seem to matter as much as deciding how he handled the information that he knew could change his career forever.

# 67

***Capo di Posillipo, La Baia di Napoli***

Fredo Finelli was in his garden when his daughter found him. The rain had stopped, the air was fresh and he was meandering around the borders, trees and shrubs, lost in his own world.

'Needs more colour,' said Gina.

He was surprised to see her. Then happy. He kissed her and hugged her. 'I think you're right. I've had tulip bulbs planted for the spring; they should look wonderful.'

'*Mamma*'s favourite.' Gina felt a pang of sadness.

Her father felt it too. 'The gardeners have planted them like she used to.'

'You mean all the colours laid out separately, rather than mixed together?'

He smiled. 'Yes, you know how she loved symmetry. Everything had to have its place. Have a balance. Your mother was so fond of ensuring order.'

Gina put her arm around her father's waist, hugged him and then rested her head on his left shoulder. 'I still miss her too, you know.'

'I know you do, sweetheart.' He kissed the top of

her head. 'All these years, and the loss still hurts like it was yesterday.' He moved half a pace away from Gina and took her hand. 'Anyway, let's not be sad. We have happy memories and happy things to look forward to.' He lightly patted her tummy. 'Any more grandchildren for me?'

Gina was horrified and her father couldn't help but notice it. '*Papà*, I don't want to have another child. I know you expect Bruno and me –'

He cut her off by raising his hand. 'Then don't.'

She tried to calm herself. 'You're not mad?'

'No, my sweet, not at all.' He smiled at her. 'Come and walk with me. It's going to rain soon, let's make the most of the dry weather.'

The garden was nearly an acre. In summer the orchard was lush with apples, cherries and pears, but now the dark leafless trees looked as sad and sombre as Fredo's daughter. 'I know things are not good between you and Bruno, haven't been good since he came out of prison.' He stopped and turned to face her. 'But tell me honestly, Gina, just how bad are they?'

She felt ashamed. Personal failure was something she hated. 'He doesn't love me, *Papà*.'

'You're sure?'

'I'm sure. He's told me as much.'

Don Fredo flinched at his daughter's pain.

'He says I am fat and ugly and he will take his *pleasures* elsewhere. The marriage is a sham, Papà.'

Finelli pulled her close to him. 'Oh, baby. My poor

baby.' He held her and felt anger boiling inside him. 'This man is not good enough for you. We have our customs, but this cannot be tolerated. You and Enzo must come and live here with me, while we sort this out.'

Gina felt tears welling in her eyes. Tears of relief. Tears of shame. 'The other day, in the house, he beat me. And then – then, he raped me.'

Fredo Finelli clenched his fists so tightly his knuckles turned white. He spoke softly but there was a hardness in his words. 'I will kill him, Gina. For this alone, I will kill him.'

Gina was silent for a second. She hung on to her father, just as she'd done as a child when she was hurt and worried. 'I hope so, *Papà*. I really hope so.'

And then she shut her eyes and prayed to God that she'd done the right thing.

# 68

*Parco Nazionale del Vesuvio*

Jack felt he was getting to know the park's 130 square kilometres better than most locals. As well as his visits, he'd studied maps and websites in every spare moment he'd had. He'd memorized its nine main footpaths and how they lifted people to more than 1,200 metres above sea level. He'd studied its flora, fauna and geology. Soon – very soon – he hoped he'd know the area as well as the man he was hunting.

'*Buon giorno!*' shouted Sylvia, as he completed the last bit of the climb after the carabinieri car had dropped him. 'Sorrentino, the big guy over there, was called by his team. They've found more fragments of bone. As I said on the phone, they're sure it's another body.'

Jack looked across the site as they walked together. The unearthed graves of Francesca Di Lauro, the still unidentified second victim and now the third and newest victim were all so close together that there was a danger of the scenes being cross-contaminated. Access planks and grid lines only went so far in protecting multiple-victim scenes, and Jack could see workers struggling not to step into each other's territory. Sorrentino was now on his knees in the third site, sifting soil, shouting and pointing at people.

'Let me introduce you to him.' Sylvia wiped strands of wind-blown hair from off her face. 'His English is good and lately he's been behaving himself.'

'No leaks to the press?'

'None. Maybe *the Great Lion* is tamed.'

'Good.' Jack noticed she was missing her trusted sidekick. 'Where's Pietro?'

'He's still interviewing Antonio Castellani. He might join us out here if he finishes in time.'

'Any news on the grandson – Franco?'

'No. We've still got cars out searching. He has no wheels, so he can't be far.'

'And his cousin?'

'Paolo. There's news on him. Forensics don't put him at the pit. Or near the car in which Rosa and Filippo were killed, or in contact with the underwear or trophies we found. We'll take DNA for further comparison tests, hold him until nightfall, then have someone re-interview him before we let him go.'

They gingerly made their way along the last narrow plank to the newest site.

'Bernardo, this is Jack King, an American psychological profiler who is helping us with our case.'

Jack held out his hand but Sorrentino didn't take it immediately. His brain had to absorb the fact that there was someone around who *might*, just *might*, be more interesting than himself. 'Bernardo Sorrentino, *Professore* Sorrentino.' He stressed his title as he finally took the profiler's hand.

Jack nodded at the hunched figures toiling in the dirt. 'Looks like a major job. You got any pattern yet?'

Sorrentino unveiled his most patronizing of looks. 'Aah, I wish it was that easy. This is not a structural burial. There are no rooms, no underground chambers, and no buildings of any kind that can provide us with the type of design that would make discovery easy.'

'Rough time frame?'

'Francesca we dated around five years. The second is more like six. And I'd say the third is the same – maybe even a little older.'

Jack's mind wandered to the killer. How had he carried the victims' remains here? *Sacks, bags, buckets?* What had he used to get his bearings? *A compass or just strong memories?* Why had he buried them apart – *was it by accident, or out of respect?* Did he have some twisted, fractured but still prevailing sense of decency deep inside him? Or did he want them to have separate graves for other reasons?

Sylvia and Sorrentino were talking Italian now. She was asking whether the new bones would yield DNA and Sorrentino was hopeful. She was pushing him for dates on when it would be done – when she could expect results. As he wandered away, Jack smiled at the hard time she was giving Sorrentino. He liked women with ambition, dedication and determination. Liked them professionally, liked them personally.

The profiler stopped and banged a heel into the ground. The earth was as stony as hell. The killer wouldn't have been able to dig *exactly* where he liked, so he would have had to have chosen softer ground. He eyed the bushes, the brambles, the patches of overgrown grass and the trees, the circle of pines and cypresses that stretched out their roots like tentacles. Jack had soon walked a full twenty metres away from the others and was now entering a copse of trees south of where Sylvia and Sorrentino stood. From here he looked back on the steel poles that had been driven into the ground. They were labelled UNO, DUO and TRE – like the numbers of a clock.

*Like a clock face.*

Of course. It all seemed so obvious now.

So simple.

Jack hurried back and interrupted Sylvia and Sorrentino. 'I think our killer's been burying the bodies in a circle. Look back at the poles on the graves of what you've called Victims One, Two and Three. You can see the start of an arc, like the circumference of a clock.'

Soft rain fell as their gaze moved over the site. The curve soon became apparent. Sylvia was the first to grasp the full significance. 'If you're right – if he has buried them following the numbers on a clock face – then it would be logical that his first victim was buried as due north as he could guess at.'

Jack looked again at the steel poles jutting out of the ground. 'Which is nowhere near where you found Francesca, the area you've marked as Victim One.'

'That fits with our science,' added Sorrentino. 'Timewise she looks like at least the third victim in the sequence that we've already identified. If we discover more bodies – earlier victims – then chronologically she moves further down.'

Jack nodded. He could already tell that Francesca's burial site wasn't due north, nor was Victim Three.

Sylvia screwed up her face. Paced restlessly between the poles. 'If we're to hit on any other graves we have to get the curve right, follow exactly the same arc that our killer had in his mind when he returned to the scene and buried each victim. Bernardo, what about a radar sweep?'

The Great Lion flicked a paw dismissively through the air. 'I hate radar. With electronics you find only what you think you are looking for. As a consequence you miss so much more. Let's think of it as a last resort.'

Sylvia let it slide. Sorrentino was in charge of the excavation and his record spoke for itself. 'Let me get this right,' she said. 'Victims Two and Three are found to the left of Victim One, and they were both buried earlier. So if we keep going west, then we should keep finding earlier victims until we hit north?'

'That's if my theory is right,' said Jack. 'And it presumes that he buried his first victim as due north as he could guess at.'

Sorrentino nodded. 'Due north representing twelve o'clock?'

'Exactly.'

They looked across the land. There was a lot of west to go. Lots of room for more bodies.

'We need a compass.' Sylvia looked to Sorrentino. He huffed and strode away from them. Walked the planks between the victims. 'I admire precision, but sometimes you should also go with instinct.' He moved almost two metres north-west of the third victim, lifted a spade and sliced it into the muddy ground. 'We've already photographed the hell out of this site, so we should get on with it and see if your theory holds up.'

Jack and Sylvia watched as Sorrentino worked away.

She produced a small, telescopic umbrella from her coat and held it over them as the anthropologist slowly toiled in the freshly falling rain. 'I forgot to ask, any news from your friend Howie? He come up with anything on Creed?'

'A little,' said Jack. 'I left a message on Pietro's phone. Howie showed Creed's mug around some diners and bars. Seems he kept pretty much to himself, but it appears he may have visited a street girl.'

'Any ID on her?'

'Afraid not. It also seems he was logged on to our Virtual Academy. He named someone in the carabinieri for accreditation.'

Sylvia frowned. She knew enough about the VA to understand it had restricted access. 'You know the name of who vouched for him?'

'Nope, but it was probably faked.'

'The more things develop, the less I like Creed.' Sylvia fought more hair from her face and vowed to get it cut. 'Still not sure he stands up as a serious suspect for serial murder, though.'

'You're right to feel that way. But I think Creed is partly a monster of your own making.'

'How do you mean?' She sounded surprised.

'Given all the details on these missing girls, and what we've recently discovered, then maybe someone should get a roasting for ignoring Creed's earlier claims that the cases warranted looking at.'

'I've asked about that. It's not quite the way Creed told you. Seems he did inform several people about the links, but he refused to share all his data unless he was given a full-time job. He was holding info back in order to serve his own ends.'

'That would figure.'

Despite Sorrentino's remark about enough photographs and records having been done, Sylvia still called a crime-scene snapper to take more shots. He arrived wet and cold. She directed him to the new dig. Kristoff Sibilski, a soil analysis expert from the carabinieri's science labs, and Luella Grazzioli, Sorrentino's new Number Two, had rolled up and were now at work as well. Their expert fingers dug in the wet mud and grit. They pulled out stones, filled buckets, sifted soil through metal meshes and removed twigs and glass. Finally, they tagged and bagged samples that meant nothing to either Jack or

Sylvia but seemed attractive to Sorrentino. 'Trowel!' he shouted to Luella, akin to the way a surgeon calls for a scalpel.

She slapped it into the palm of Sorrentino's rubber-gloved hand and within seconds he was back on his knees, operating at close quarters, making incisive cuts at precision speed.

Jack watched the rain pour over his long, matted black hair and found himself admiring the man's passion and skill.

Without speaking, Sorrentino delicately lifted something from the earth. He rose slowly to his feet, one hand cupped beneath the trowel, and turned to face them.

Everyone stared at what he held.

'Bone,' he said decisively. 'Human bone.'

In a patch two metres west of the last grave, in a near perfect arc, they'd found Victim Number Four.

# 69

***Parco Nazionale del Vesuvio***

*A fourth victim.*

Was it a setback or a breakthrough? Sylvia rang her superiors from the site and they were in no doubt – it was *una catastrofe, un disastro, una tragedia* – and they told her so in ways that made it seem as though it was her fault. News about a serial killer was not good for tourism. Not good for the city's image. And certainly not good for votes. Sorrentino, meanwhile – well, he was as happy as a pig in shit. He could barely wait to get back to his laboratory and get the newly discovered bones under his microscope.

Sylvia made several calls as she drove away from Vesuvius. She spoke to Pietro, who said he'd drawn a blank with old man Castellani and was going home early because he thought he had the start of flu. Then she spoke to another of her lieutenants who'd re-interviewed Paolo Falconi and had also come up with nothing new. How she needed a break! She ordered Paolo's release and asked for surveillance to be put on him, in case he contacted Franco.

Jack had gone back to the hotel to change his soaked clothes. She'd promised to ring him after her trip to the labs to see how the forensic evidence was progressing.

The carabinieri's *Raggruppamento Investigazioni Scientifiche* was housed in a building that Sylvia thought belonged more in Rome than in Naples. The grand five-storey terraced building was salmon pink with dark-green shutters. Potted rose trees stood sentry either side of a lavish slab of marble doorstep.

On the third floor she pushed open the doors to the lab of Marianna Della Fratte and found her old friend, white-coated and hunched over a stack of paperwork. Marianna was thirty-five, single and had the smart and easy sense of humour that made Sylvia wish they both had enough free time to become even closer than they were.

'Can you search your stack and see if you've got a one-pager that solves my case so I can go on a long, long holiday?'

Marianna took off her stylish black square-framed reading glasses and smiled. '*Ciao*, Sylvia. I would if I could. But I'm pretty sure if that was possible, I'd have sent it already. How are you?'

'*Sto bene.* I'd be better if I could have two weeks on a beach – with George Clooney to bring me drinks, rub on some lotion and be my sex slave.'

'Clooney's booked. Brad Pitt and Matt Damon might still be free. You want me to ring for you?' She picked up a phone and waited for the command.

'Nah, it's George or nothing.'

'Then I'll order *caffè* instead. Why don't you take a seat?' Marianna dialled for a lab secretary to bring some. 'I do have some tests back for you. No holiday with a hunk but we got DNA from the Jane Doe burned and shot in the pit. Mother of Christ, what kind of monster are you hunting this time?'

Sylvia shrugged. 'Your guess is as good as mine. Whatever happened to the days when we thought weird and kinky just meant a strangling with a fishnet stocking?'

'Long gone. The profile has just been sent over to your team. It was quite good, so I'm sure you'll get an ID from it.'

'Anything on the car and other bodies?'

'Rosa Novello and Filippo Valdrano?'

'The very same.'

Marianna shuffled files and found the notes. 'We've discovered a lot of loose hair and trace samples inside the car and we're eliminating the two victims and members of the family. His mother and father used the car as well, so it's quite a compromised site. We've singled out some very distinct samples – arm hair, we believe. It was found on a rubber door buffer. It looks like it may have been scraped off by someone leaning to get into the back of the car.'

Sylvia's hopes rose. 'It's not Filippo's?'

Marianna smiled. 'Definitely not. And before you ask, no, we haven't yet had time to compare it with the other DNA samples you had brought in.'

Sylvia had ordered all Franco Castellani's belongings to be confiscated and sent for testing. 'When will you be able to tell me if there are matches?'

'Forty-eight hours – earlier, if I can.'

Sylvia rested her head on one hand and tried to rub the tiredness from her eyes. She always seemed to be waiting for things to happen, things she couldn't speed up, couldn't control.

'Sorry, Syl. That really is as fast as we can get them to you.'

'Sure. I know. Thanks.' She hauled herself out of her chair, mainly because she feared that if she stayed there much longer she'd simply fall asleep.

'I'm going to skip the *caffè* and hit the sack. Hope you don't mind?'

'Of course not. But before you go, I want to mention something else to you.'

'Go ahead.'

Marianna searched a scaffold of desk trays. Some papers were in folders, some were in plastic covers, others were marked with yellow Post-it notes and covered in black pen scribblings. 'A carabinieri desk sergeant in Scampia had a human tongue thrown at him by a young child.'

'Yuuck! *Che scivo!*' Sylvia screwed up her face. 'They ran out of stones and bottles in Scampia?'

'This gets worse. We've just completed tests for

the division. The tongue was cut from the body of a woman called Alberta Tortoricci – that name mean anything to you?'

'Rings a bell, but I'm not sure why.'

'Tortoricci was the prime witness in a Camorra prosecution. She testified against a mobster called Bruno Valsi, the son-in-law of –'

'Fredo Finelli. I remember it all now. Valsi is just out of Poggioreale. I saw pictures of his release in the papers. Handsome bastard.'

'Brutally handsome, with emphasis on the brutal. Tortoricci testified against him five years ago. A couple of days after his release she disappeared from protective custody.'

Sylvia raised her eyes in irony. 'A pure coincidence, of course?'

'Of course. As was the fact that she turned up dead in the grounds of an old factory complex with her tongue cut out.'

'Typical Camorra revenge attack.'

'Then, someone burned her body. Crisped her up like the last of the chicken on a barbecue grill.'

Sylvia scratched at her hair. 'I didn't read anything on the internal bulletins, or in the news. Did the Anti-Camorra Unit go dark on this?'

'Very dark. Since the last attacks on their staff, the unit is keeping everything close to its chest. I had to ask Lorenzo Pisano if I could share this with you.'

Sylvia let out a sigh. 'I've put two calls in to his

office recently, just to fix up a meeting and see if we had any common ground.'

'You know Pisano, his feet never touch. Anyway, they've got Valsi in the frame for the Tortoricci hit. Though I hear no one will go within a kilometre of him until they've got a warehouse full of evidence and three armed units to back them up.'

'Seems the right tactics.'

'Her body's at the morgue if you want to go and see. Seems she was stripped and doused in paraffin and then set alight.'

Sylvia raised an eyebrow.

'Before you ask, the answer's no – I don't yet know whether the paraffin matches the stuff recovered from the Castellani site.'

Sylvia crossed her fingers and held them up for her friend to see.

'Anyway, when they were done they rolled her in an old carpet and dumped her among rubble on an old industrial site.'

'You got the name of the ME?'

'I certainly have. Dimitri Faggiani. You know Dimitri?'

'Nope. I've heard of him, but we've never met.'

'Well, for once you got lucky. He's upstairs now, on the fifth floor. There's a case meeting – not Tortoricci – some child who died of neglect. If you're quick, you might just catch him.'

* * *

Sylvia was quick.

Dimitri Faggiani was just coming out of the men's room when she caught him.

'*Buona sera. Capitano* Sylvia Tomms.' She stuck out her hand.

The ME hesitated to shake it. 'No towels. I'm afraid my hands are still wet.'

'Oh, I'm sorry.' She laughed and let her arm drop. He was thin and studious with dark brows and a bush of black curly hair that looked as if he visited a topiarist rather than a hairdresser. 'I've just been with Marianna Della Fratte, she told me you examined the body of Alberta Tortoricci. Is that right?'

He looked puzzled. 'Do you work for Lorenzo Pisano?'

'No, no, I don't. But . . .'

'Then I'm afraid without his permission, I can't discuss this file with you.'

'I understand. I've called Lorenzo several times. You know how busy he is.'

The ME smiled. 'No permission, no information. Sorry.' He wiped his still damp hands on his black trousers.

'I'm working the murders at Pompeii – the Francesca Di Lauro case.'

Faggiani knew of it. 'My sympathies, I think you too are very busy.'

Sylvia gave him a shy look, a crafted flash of vulnerability, calculated to elicit male help. 'I am. And I *really* need your help. Marianna told me that

Alberta Tortoricci was badly burned. As you may know, Francesca's corpse was also burned. We have another woman's body in a rubbish pit and, again, she was burned.'

His dark brows furrowed. 'I'm sorry; this is not a good time. I need to get back to my meeting.'

'*Professore*, I'm pushed for time as well – I'm trying to catch a serial killer.' She paused to let her point sink in. 'Please, just tell me one thing. Alberta – was she burned ante- or post-mortem.'

Faggiani cracked. 'Post. This woman had been tortured – crudely electrocuted – and then she was set on fire.'

'Not tortured by being set on fire?'

The ME's face gave away the fact that he'd said enough. Said more than he'd intended. 'No. The body was definitely burned post-mortem.' He held up the palms of his hands. 'Now that's it.'

'*Grazie*. You've helped a lot. I'll talk to Lorenzo and maybe come back to you – if you don't mind?'

'Not at all. *Arrivederci*.' He opened a door just a few strides away and was gone.

Sylvia stood and let the information sink in. Was the Tortoricci case really connected to hers, or not? Was she grasping at straws? Post-mortem burning was very different to ante-mortem burning. And if the cases were connected, then what about the electrocution? Was that simply another sadistic pastime in this particular serial killer's repertoire of murder? Then there was another thing. Maybe significant.

Maybe not. There was a clear gap of at least five years between the recent murders and the dates the other women went missing. Could it really be only a coincidence that Bruno Valsi had been locked away for exactly that same half-decade?

# 70

***Grand Hotel Parker's, Napoli***

The downpour at the burial site had caught Jack without a coat. Back at the hotel he showered, changed and sent his soaked clothes to the laundry. His trousers were so drenched they looked like they'd been made out of crêpe paper. Sylvia had called and said she was heading off to the morgue and would see him in the morning, so he settled on the bed and tried to unwind a notch or two.

This case now had the makings of a long one and he couldn't afford to get trapped in it. That meant getting out sooner rather than later – and *sooner* seemed round about now. The few days he'd promised Nancy it would take had already gone. Christmas was looming. His thoughts turned to his son – still at that incredible age when he believed a fat man in a red suit could land a sleigh pulled by flying reindeer on the roof of a house and then slip down a chimney so narrow you couldn't post a supermodel down it. How beautiful!

*Grilled salmon or meatballs and spaghetti?* Jack was torn. He'd just about eaten his way through everything room service could offer. He was leaning towards the meatballs when his cellphone rang. He hoped it was Nancy.

'*Pronto*,' said Jack, rolling his 'r' in his best possible accent, then waiting as usual for his wife to laugh at him.

'Mr King, I'm in reception. Perhaps we could meet downstairs and talk?'

Jack's spine tingled.

Luciano Creed.

*Downstairs?*

You bet they could talk.

Jack didn't bother answering – or waiting for the lift. He hit the stairs two at a time. Covered four floors faster than an Olympic sprinter on steroids.

Creed was standing near the front desk, wet and stinking. Even if he made a run for it now, Jack could catch him.

'Nice to see you, Jack.' He cracked a yellow-toothed smile and swung out a bony hand.

Jack grabbed it. Not out of friendship, but just to have a firm grip on him. 'Come over here, Luciano. Sit down.' He effectively manoeuvred Creed into a plush wing-backed chair in the reception area. 'Stay still.' He flipped open his phone and dialled. 'Sylvia, it's Jack. I have Creed with me at my hotel. Send a car; I'll bring him to the station.'

His stomach growled. The meatballs would have to wait.

* * *

Jack said little to Luciano Creed as they waited at the hotel, and even less in the carabinieri car that whisked them back to the barracks.

Creed rattled on about his innocence. Said he'd known they would suspect him because he knew so much about the missing women and because he was unusual, outspoken and honest. They weren't the words that Jack would have used to describe him. He did his best to tune out Creed's monologue. There would be a time to talk – and plenty of it – but not now. He wanted tape machines turning, witnesses present and a proper interview strategy. Another thing was on his mind too, and he needed to call Howie urgently to fix it.

Sylvia met Jack in her office as Creed was shown through to an interview room. Technically, he wasn't under arrest; no charges had been laid and he could walk away at any moment. Or, at least, he could try. If pushed, they'd probably come up with something – perverting the course of justice, suspicion of involvement in an indictable offence – they'd find a sticky label somewhere.

Sylvia crossed her arms and rubbed her hands up and down them. She was tired and cold and needed desperately to warm up and wake up. 'Why now? Why the hell had he turned himself in at this very moment?'

'Timing. He said he'd achieved what he wanted at the press conference. Brought attention to the cases you folks had ignored. And he figured that by now we'd all have worked out that he was a brilliant profiler – his words, not mine – and not a suspect.'

Sylvia snorted a laugh. 'Everything about this guy is *suspect*.'

'Sure, but – as we both know – *suspect* doesn't mean guilty. There's a way to finally settle whether he's telling the truth or not. Do you know about LVA?'

She frowned. '*El Vee-ay*. Arabic?'

'No. LVA – Layered Voice Analysis. It's voice-sensitive stress-detection software. Developed by Israeli whizz-kids, used by Mossad and security forces in many countries.'

'We have nothing like that. Polygraphs, yes, but even their use is very limited and controlled.'

'My buddy Howie has a laptop rigged with LVA monitoring equipment that's been beefed up to be a near-perfect lie detector. He's the king of this stuff. He's used it everywhere. If I can get hold of him – and that's a big "if" these days – then he can run it from NYC while we interview Creed.'

Sylvia frowned. 'Doesn't Creed have to be attached to it somehow?'

'Nope. It works on voice patterns. It's so sensitive that it can detect even the slightest hesitation, a variance or stress. If we open up a phone line in the interview room and just get Creed to talk normally – discuss things he wouldn't lie about – then we can have a baseline reading to calibrate from and Howie can give us real-time readings and results.'

'So throughout the interview he can tell us whether Creed is lying or not?'

'Exactly.'

'And this is how accurate?'

'Ninety-eight per cent. Beats the pants off the poly.'

'Let's do it.' Sylvia looked pleased. 'Great thing is, because the test is being run outside Italy, I don't even need permission.'

Jack phoned Howie. He was in luck. It was now ten p.m. in Italy, four p.m. in NYC.

It turned out that apart from a couple of Buds with his corn dog lunch, Howie hadn't touched a drop. Sylvia grabbed some files she needed, then headed to IT to fix the connections.

Howie had his Dell up and running before Jack's ass hit the seat opposite Creed. The profiler wore a small, covert, Bluetooth earbud receiver linked to his cellphone that was on an open line to Howie's phone.

Sylvia reminded Creed that the interview was being recorded on tape – but she didn't mention the LVA. She got him to state his full name, age, current address, and asked him again if he wanted a lawyer. He waved her away. 'I'm here to help. I've always been trying to help. I don't need a lawyer.'

*Got the baseline and the guy's already lying,* Howie whispered in Jack's ear.

'That's not quite right, Luciano, is it?'

Creed stared at Jack. He was shocked to be pulled

up so quickly. He reflected. 'You mean the press conference? I suppose you're right. I wasn't trying to help there; I was trying to embarrass you. I hope I succeeded.'

'Why would you want to do that?' asked Sylvia.

'Because for more than a year now I've been trying to get the constipated minds of the carabinieri to look into these cases. But, oh no, you people keep telling me, "*Shut up, Luciano. They're not linked, they're not murders, they're just missing people.*" Well, now you know the truth. You fucked up. They're murders – they're *dead* people, not missing people –'

'Okay, we get the picture,' interjected Jack. 'You want to help – great. Let's start at the beginning.'

Creed glared across the table. 'Fine. The beginning.'

'Did you have any connection to these women? Other than the research work you did for the carabinieri during your secondment from the university?'

'None at all.'

*True*, Howie whispered in Jack's ear. *He's telling you the truth.*

'You never dated any of these women – weren't *personally* involved with them or had any sexual connection to them?'

'No. None. I never knew any of them.'

*LVA reading shows uncertainty – strong hesitation*, said Howie.

Jack went back over the same ground. 'What was the sexual link, Luciano? There was something sexual between you and at least one of these girls. What was it?'

Creed looked away and let out a *huuh*. 'The last one, Francesca, the hot one. I used to jerk off to her pictures. There were some swimsuit shots in the police file – I photocopied them and used to look at them when the urge took me.'

Sylvia looked away so Creed couldn't see her disgust. Jack showed no emotion. 'Back in New York, I found some drawings that you'd made. Sketches you'd done while staying at the Lester. Can you remember them?'

Creed shuffled in his chair. 'Not really. I doodle all the time. I have a creative mind. Why are they of interest?'

*He remembers them*, prompted Howie.

Sylvia opened one of the files she'd brought and slid across the table the drawing Jack had retrieved and pieced together.

'Not bad,' said Creed looking at the pencil scribblings of vaginas and breasts. He swung it round to get a closer look and smiled. 'Some of my better work actually.'

'And you had some photographs too. Sylvia, perhaps you could remind Luciano of them?'

Her hand slid into the file again and produced more pieced-together pornography. This was a shot of a naked woman cuffed to a metal pole, being whipped and branded with hot irons.

'That kind of stuff turn you on?' asked Jack.

Creed smiled. 'Yeah, it does. Naked women with tight asses and big tits – it hits all the spots.'

*Very true*, whispered Howie. *LVA shows exceptionally high level of arousal and excitement.*

'It does for most men,' said Jack, 'but you know that's not what I mean. I mean the violence. You get turned on by the idea of women being tortured?'

Creed's bravado buckled a little. 'Not so much the violence. I – err, I like to see them vulnerable. Women on their knees, women under threat. It's not that unusual.' He read Sylvia's face. She looked an inch away from punching him. 'Hey, you know men like me get knocked back all the time by women like you. How come it's a surprise I might like to see you not looking so smug?'

Jack turned back to Creed. 'You ever indulge these fantasies further than masturbation? Ever deliberately hurt a woman, or have a woman hurt for your own gratification?'

'Listen, I came here to help. Not to answer twenty questions about what turns me on.'

*Anxietywise, he's off the score right now*, said Howie.

Jack held his gaze. A single look that seemed to turn silence into guilt.

'Okay. Sometimes I pay hookers to whip each other, while I watch. They fake being hurt and I like that. I like it a lot.'

*Altar boy's telling it straight.*

'So, how can you help? What have you got to offer, Luciano?'

Creed slouched forward on his elbows. Jack leaned back as he caught a draught of sour breath. 'You should be looking at these cousins. I saw the stuff in the papers. You should be grilling them like steak. You know how close cousins can be. I reckon –'

Jack cut him off. 'Is that the best you've got to offer, Luciano? We should follow up on stuff that's already made the news stands? Is that how *brilliant* a profiler you are?'

'I know these cases better than either of you.' Creed reddened. He turned to Sylvia. 'Better than anyone on your team. I've studied every detail for months on end. I know the clubs they went to, the taxi firms they used, the bars they visited, even where they shopped for their clothes. I can save you time and help you narrow down leads. Let me work up a profile with you –'

Jack cut him off again. 'What were you doing on the VA website?'

'You mean the Virtual Academy?'

'Aha.'

'Learning. That's what it's for, isn't it? I was being tutored. Check my grades. Check the hours I logged in. I bet there are not many global students who put in as much time as I did and got scores as good as mine. You and me, Jack, we can be a team.'

Jack had already checked. Creed had made the top ten per cent of students, even though he'd had no right to be there in the first place.

'You shouldn't have been on the site, Luciano,' said Sylvia. 'You told them you were employed full-time by us as a law enforcement officer. You faked references and you routed material through our servers so it would look authentic.'

'So, arrest me for it.'

Sylvia was tempted. Instead, she closed the interview. She and Jack took a break outside while coffee was sent in for Creed. They stood together in the corridor and Sylvia searched for her cigarettes.

'What a creep. I'm really itching to charge him, but what good would it do?'

'Paperwork – and bad publicity. It would create lots of both.'

'Exactly.' She shook the last cigarette out of her packet.

'So, you think he's of any value to your inquiry team?'

'Only dead. I can't, Jack. I know he knows the cases, but I just can't stomach the idea of him being anywhere near me.'

'Then you'll have to let him go.'

'I know.' She lit up and inhaled deeply.

Jack waved away the smoke. 'And warn him.'

'Sorry. I'm going to kick this damned habit when all this is over. To stay away, you mean?'

'Absolutely. This guy crossed a continent to get me involved in this case, and now that I am, he wants to ride shotgun and share the glory. That's what this is all about. He's inadequate and insignificant. Being seen as a champion has made him feel important. He's not going to give that up without a fight.'

Sylvia thought about it as she finished the cigarette and walked back to the room. 'I just want him out of here, Jack. I couldn't integrate him into our inquiry team, you know that. Right now I just want that stinking sonofabitch off my suspect list and out of my interview room.'

Minutes later it was done.

Luciano Creed told them they were making a big mistake. And he'd prove it to them. He'd humiliated them once when they'd ignored him, and he was determined to humiliate them again.

He stomped across the courtyard of the police headquarters out into the narrow streets of the small town of Castello di Cisterna. That stupid female *Capitano* had looked at him like he was dirt and then had virtually thrown him out, rather than accept his offer of help. Crazy bitch. Like she knew what she was doing.

It was no wonder they couldn't solve this case. Fucking amateurs. They couldn't catch a cold, let alone a killer. And King, well, what a disappointment he was turning out to be. Emasculated and impotent. He just went along with whatever that dumb cow of a *Capitano* wanted. Maybe he was fucking her? Yeah, that would be it. That was the only decent explanation why someone with his kind of pedigree could have lost his senses. Call himself a profiler? A joke. That's what he should call himself. A big fucking joke.

Creed kicked a stone as hard as he could and turned

down a rough back street that led towards the town centre. He was without transport. It was late and he was starving hungry. The slops they'd offered him in there hadn't been fit to fatten pigs. He would find an all-night bar in town and eat. First thing in the morning he'd call his contact at the newspaper and then they'd set to work.

With or *without* carabinieri permission he was going to be involved in this inquiry. They'd been foolish – damned foolish – to choose *without*.

# 71

*Centro città, Napoli*

Romano Ivetta and Alberto Donatello had been drinking all night. They started at Bar Luca and, after Valsi disappeared with some unfortunate woman, they spent an hour at a casino before ending up in a two-bit club not far from the prison they'd recently called home.

'You sure we're doing the right thing. Absolutely sure?' asked Donatello, easily the more drunk of the two of them.

'Second thoughts, Alberto?' Ivetta picked peanuts from a bowl on the small high table they were at. He didn't want them but took them anyway. That was his nature.

'I don't think so. But maybe last-minute nerves.' Donatello clinked his bottle against his friend's. 'Guess it's natural?'

'It's natural,' Ivetta reassured him.

The booze helped fog Donatello's worries. Small of stature and poor of pocket he'd had to use his fists, and sometimes a knife, for most of his life. Bully or be bullied, that was the choice you were forced to make on the streets of Naples. But he'd never fired a gun and had never been shot at. Just the thought of it turned his bowels to water. 'You think maybe this can be settled without a firefight?'

'No.' Ivetta smiled and signalled to the barman to bring more beers. Everyone else got served at the counter but he'd been coming here since he was too young to drink and his Camorra connections meant he got special treatment, including never paying. 'Alberto, grow some balls. There's going to be bloodshed. Be brave or be blown away.' He pinched his small friend's shoulder with his giant fingers. 'We have the advantage, my friend. We will strike first. First and fast. It is always the best way.'

The beers came and went. So did Donatello's fears. An hour later the two men slapped backs on the pavement outside, then went their separate ways in the cold drizzle of the early hours.

By the time Alberto Donatello got back to his rented studio apartment in the Spanish Quarter he'd grown the balls that Ivetta had demanded of him. He would do his bit. He would not be found wanting. He was so drunk he struggled to put his key into the lock of the front door. Fuck, he was pissed.

Really pissed. Finally the key slid into the lock. He'd made it. Home sweet home.

He didn't see the figure in the shadows by the basement steps.

Didn't hear the steely swish of the metal chain.

Didn't feel much at all, as Sal the Snake slowly strangled the life out of him.

# 72

*Parco Nazionale del Vesuvio*

At first light, under the supervision of the carabinieri – most of whom were more interested in *her* than the task she was about to undertake – anthropologist Luella Grazzioli and her team shipped in the latest Ground Penetrating Radar System.

Under pressure, Sorrentino had finally decided that it was worth giving GPRS a go and had given strict instructions for every inch of the gridded area to be meticulously swept. 'Go over it like you are brushing your beautiful teeth. Then when I arrive you can show me something that will make my smile as wonderful as yours,' he'd told her. Typical Sorrentino.

Luella walked the safe corridor that had been established to protect evidence gained from the old excavation site and headed into a new section of the grid. Carabinieri officer Dino Gallo, two of his colleagues and two of hers followed. They brought with them the GPR system and also a set of state-of-the-art airspades.

'Last year, I dug up a body near Ischia,' Gallo confided as they walked. He was thin and suntanned;

Luella thought he'd look better if he put on a little weight.

'Complicated?' she asked, happy to make small talk.

'No. We had all the right equipment, all the things you requested today, but we never needed it.'

'Sounds like you were lucky.'

'In some ways yes, in some ways no. The body was buried in a shallow grave.' Dino Gallo was keen to make an impression on the pretty anthropologist. 'As you probably know, in cases when the corpse is only about eighteen inches below the surface, you can usually start smelling the body after around seventeen days.'

Luella paused and took a check on where she wanted to start the sweep. 'You're right. The smell comes from dozens of different gas compounds released during decomposition.' She looked mischievously at him. 'Your expert carabinieri nose will no doubt have picked up on some of them.'

Gallo had a smile that broke hearts. 'My nose would rather smell roses over a dinner table, with you sitting on the other side.'

'I'm sure it would,' laughed Luella, well used to flattery, 'but for now I would like it sniffing over those boxes as we unpack them. Any chance?'

'Your wish is my command.' He added a perfect, military-trained bow.

Luella's colleague Giulietta was fitted into the harness containing the antenna and got ready to start her pre-mapped walk of the grid. Gallo finished wiring the monitor and the rest of the rig.

'One minute!' shouted Luella, doing a final systems check before giving her colleague the cue to start walking. 'Okay, off you go.'

Every hour, Giulietta switched with her other colleague, Emilio. Every two hours they took a break and talked. Every half-hour it rained. Every three-quarters of an hour Dino Gallo suggested different restaurants, clubs, parks and places he would like to take Luella to. After six hours she was on the verge of giving in and consenting to dinner.

Then the call came.

Luella took off her rubber gloves, grateful for the cool air on her hands. She pulled the cellphone out of the pocket of her overalls.

The voice on the other end – the coordinator from her office – said she was being put through to *Capitano* Tomms, who was at Sorrentino's home.

Luella listened carefully but couldn't believe what she'd been told.

Bernardo was dead.

# 73

***Santa Lucia, Napoli***

Sorrentino had been found by his housekeeper.

Dead in the middle of his waterbed.

Blood and water all over the place.

Bella Di Lazio had taken her weekly money off the worktop, rung the cops and gone home.

She wouldn't weep for him. He'd been mean and arrogant. Hadn't given her a pay rise or a tip in the two years she'd worked for him. Good riddance.

Less than two hours after Bella had gone, the ME had already completed his visit.

Sylvia Tomms arrived with her brain still reeling from all the other developments – Creed; the Tortoricci murder; the killings at the Castellani camp; and of course Franco, the runaway cousin.

Lieutenant Marco Vassopolus – known by all who couldn't remember how to say or spell his surname as Marco V – showed her around the scene. 'Housekeeper found him like this. Bullet wound to the skull. Silencer. No forced entry.'

'ME give you time of death?'

Marco shook his head. 'Still fixing it. He did a

partial on the body, said by the cooling he reckoned it might be ten to twelve hours ago.'

Sylvia checked her watch. 'Late night, early morning by the sound of it.' She walked the protective transparent sheets around the deflated, blood-soaked waterbed where the corpse still lay. It looked like Sorrentino had fallen into the mouth of a giant man-eating plant. Something straight out of *Beetlejuice*.

'The guy was a skunk, but he didn't deserve this.' She bent over the body. 'When will the van be here to move him?'

'Next thirty minutes. Morgue said they'll ring when it's on its way.'

Sylvia peered at Sorrentino's waxy face. His jet-black hair was now plastered in the crimson gel of his own blood. 'Hard to think that he was such a playboy. Tried it on with everything in a dress. Even me. Guess dying on his bed is somehow appropriate.'

'Exhibits team said they found a lot of – you know – erotica, around the place.'

'Erotica?' Sylvia laughed. 'Any chance of being more precise?'

He coloured a little. 'Lubricants, lotions, velvet handcuffs –'

'Velvet, eh? Imagine if we had those as standard issue. Any letters or diaries?'

'No letters. We found some address books. Not one black book, but two – well, actually they were red and green address books.'

'Let me guess, one for work, one for pleasure?'

'Both pleasure. The green one was for women he'd slept with – complete with ratings out of ten – the red one was for those he was still hunting.'

'Yeah, well, I guess all of us reds can heave a sigh of relief.' Sylvia grimaced as she looked closer at Sorrentino's empty eyes and pale-blue lips.

'The bed's blown out but he wasn't popped on the mattress,' said Marco. 'Look near the edge and you can see where the perp slit it with something after he dropped the vic there.'

Marco always talked in American cop jargon and it irritated the hell out of her. She'd have picked another lieutenant if there had been any others to pick. Some of her homicide squad were currently working more cases than she was, and to top it all Pietro had called in sick.

'Where exactly was he when he got shot?' asked Sylvia, noticing no powder burn marks on Sorrentino's face. 'From the size and shape of the flesh wound it looks as though he was more than a metre away. Am I right?'

'Doc said the same – though he didn't stay long. He had another case to get to. Said he'd do his notes on this one when he got back to the lab.'

'Who was it?'

'Larusso.'

Sylvia slapped her forehead. 'Was he sober?'

Marco V shrugged. It was about as diplomatic as he could manage.

Sylvia said what they were both thinking. 'That

man's a disgrace. He should run a wine cellar not a Medical Examiner's desk. What else did he say?'

Marco motioned his boss around the circular bed towards the doorway. 'See the spatter up the wall? Larusso thinks the shooter took Sorrentino out just after he entered the bedroom. Light switch is interior left side of the door. *Il Grande Leone* comes in the darkened room, pops on the switch, takes a few paces forward and then, *blam!* That's the way he thinks it went down.'

Sylvia studied the spatter marks. She wasn't so sure. Sorrentino was a tall guy. Six foot, maybe six-one. The blood had sprayed vertically, not horizontally. 'Look at the cornice and the ceiling,' she said. 'We've got spray up there and . . .' she looked closer, wrinkled her face and added, 'what also looks like part of his once great brain. See the grey matter, clinging to the bottom of the cornice?'

Marco cringed. 'I see it.'

Sylvia paced around again; her feet in slip-ons, similar to the plastic clogs surgeons wear. 'Get the techies to send me the first reports when they've run a laser trajectory kit over it.' She pulled up beneath the blood spray and examined the area at her feet. 'This carpet's all fucked up with blood, but look at the wall. This brown spot here around waist height looks like something else, maybe a trace of faeces. Did the great La-fucking-Russo sniff this one out?'

Marco shook his head.

Sylvia took in the room from the killer's perspective.

Walked it through. 'Sorrentino was made to stand here by the shooter. Then – well, then he literally had the shit frightened out of him before he was killed. He'd pressed himself against the wall, scared to move.' She pointed to the dead scientist. 'When you move him, you'll see he messed himself. Our ME should have seen that. And if he had been sober and not aching to run for his next drink, then maybe he would have done.' Something else was wrong. A shot from close up should have blown a bigger hole in the wall, not to mention a bigger hole in Sorrentino's head. 'Forget what the Prof said. Bernardo wasn't killed straight away. It wasn't that kind of killing.' Her eyes roamed across the room. 'Even more interesting is the question of where our shooter had been standing.'

Marco was still staring at the stains of blood, brains and shit. 'Why? Why does it matter that much where he was? Someone blew Sorrentino's brains out and dumped him on his bed.'

Sylvia wagged a finger. 'It certainly *does* matter. For a start it tells us the killer is a man, not a woman. Look at the carpet pile and the blood flow. There are no drag marks across the carpet. Someone picked up a six-foot-tall, dead man, carried him several metres and dumped him on the bed. Not many women can do that.'

'I've dated a couple,' he joked. 'Not that that's anything to brag about.'

'As may be, Romeo. But I doubt any of them could

put a bullet in your brain from across the bedroom with one single shot.'

Marco started to get the picture. 'The killer was a pro?'

Sylvia wondered how Marco had made lieutenant. 'Another thing; given most of the blood is on and around the bed, leaking out towards the wall, our man may well have got himself covered in it. You can bet someone's burning old clothes tonight, if they haven't done so already.'

Marco V started making notes. He'd have street dumpsters, house garbage sacks, garden fires and local drains checked straight away.

Sylvia walked and talked from the doorway to the corpse. 'I think our killer was waiting in the dark. I'd say he stuck his gun to Sorrentino's head when the light came on. Then he moved him over here.' She stepped gingerly to the spot where the carpet was stained the heaviest. 'While Sorrentino stood here, the gun still on him, the shooter stepped back and made himself comfortable on the bed. I think for a minute or so he just sat there and enjoyed scaring the living crap out of him.'

'Forensics said they'd come back to the bed, they're still dusting other parts of the apartment.'

Sylvia moved back to the corpse and examined it once more. 'Then, after he'd had his moment of fun, he shot him. Just the once. Dead centre in the forehead from nearly three metres away. Hence the blood and brain sprayed up there on the wall and ceiling.'

'So, I'm right. It certainly sounds like a pro job.'

'You're an annoying little shit, but yes, you are right.' Sylvia pointed up at the wall in front of her. 'Now, when forensics dig the bullet out of that wall, I want to know its entire ballistic history and I want to know it in Ferrari-fast time. I'm betting that for once it's Sorrentino's *work* and not his *play* that got him into trouble. And I also bet that slug matches those from the victims at the Castellani campsite.'

Sylvia had seen enough. She stepped out of the crime scene and shuffled off her gloves and changed shoes. On the way to the car she checked her phone and picked up a message from Susanna Martinelli, a coordinator in the Incident Room. They finally had an ID on the second victim found buried near Vesuvius.

It was nineteen-year-old Gloria Pirandello.

She'd been missing for six years and was another one of the names on Creed's list.

# 74

***Stazione dei carabinieri, Castello di Cisterna***

The briefing that afternoon turned out to be one of the longest Jack had attended. During it, he literally found himself reading the writing on the wall.

Creed's picture had been removed from the Priority Board. He was no longer a suspect.

Franco Castellani's photograph was ringed in red marker – the search for him had drawn a blank but was ongoing. Surveillance was still on his cousin Paolo, and there were reports that someone fitting Franco's description had been seen boarding a train to Rome. Security cameras were being checked.

Sorrentino's famous face and crime-scene pictures from his apartment filled a new Evidence Board and a separate but linked team was working that line of inquiry and dealing with the press. Sorrentino was certainly going to make front-page news. Few people doubted that it was the handiwork of the man who had killed the missing women. Taking out Sorrentino would certainly slow down their progress on identifying victims at the dig.

The crimes at the Castellani campsite had their

own board and Jack couldn't help but feel saddened by looking again at the young faces of Rosa Novello and Filippo Valdrano.

The Jane Doe burned in the pit still hadn't been identified. The body shots of her were so graphic that some of the team struggled to look at them.

Sylvia finished handing out the actions, then turned to what Jack found the most intriguing board of all. The one dedicated to the murder of Alberta Tortoricci. 'What I say to you all now is in confidence and doesn't leave this room. No gossip in the canteen, no chatting to your friends outside.' She pointed to a portrait shot of Alberta Tortoricci taken almost ten years ago, a time when her hair was much longer and her face was free of the worry of having met and testified against the mob. 'This thirty-eight-year-old woman was the prime witness in the trial of Bruno Valsi, the son-in-law of Camorra *Capo* Fredo Finelli. Here's the timeline – Valsi comes out of Poggioreale after a five stretch and within five days Alberta turns up dead. But this lady isn't just killed. She's tortured, mutilated and then, after death, her body is set on fire. I hope no one is struggling to see the connections.'

The room filled with mutterings. Sylvia let them die down before she continued. 'They found her body in Scampia, rolled in an old carpet and dumped in rubble near a disused factory. They'd electrocuted her. Broken more than twenty of her teeth, then sliced off thirteen centimetres of her tongue.'

The audience, hardened though they were, audibly registered their disgust.

'Finally, after all that, they'd doused her in paraffin and burned her to the bone.'

A small man near the front raised his hand, 'Was she alive when they set her on fire?'

'No. I met the ME – and earlier this morning I spoke briefly to Lorenzo Pisano, who's heading the inquiry. They tell me she died of "*asphyxiation, caused by the cessation of breathing and heart activity*". Maybe some small mercy in that.'

There were more murmurings. Pisano was carabinieri top brass. One of the few public figures brave enough not only to spearhead the battle against the Camorra, but to be *seen* to spearhead it.

'At the end of this meeting, Major Pisano has prepared a special briefing and some of you will be asked to attend that. There is a possibility – nothing more, nothing less at this stage – that the Tortoricci death may be linked to our case.'

Questions and comments flew thick and fast. *How could a mob revenge-killing be linked to their serial killer? Was there any significance in the fact that no women disappeared, or were tortured and burned, during Bruno Valsi's five years in prison?* Opinions were divided. During that time frame there'd been several unsolved murders and missing women that they'd not even considered. Many saw the hand of the Camorra everywhere but nobody could point to anything amounting to forensic or circumstantial evidence to connect Valsi to any of the murders, except that of Tortoricci.

Jack was also in two minds. The use of torture on Alberta Tortoricci was consistent with his profile of a serial sadistic murderer, but the post-mortem burning of the corpse threatened to be a red herring. Then again – take it away, and would they even be connecting the cases?

Jack was still answering the question as he, Sylvia and two of her team made their way across the city to the briefing with anti-Camorra supremo, Major Lorenzo Pisano. Maybe he could answer the most worrying question of all. How do you hunt down a serial killer when he's surrounded by a mob of other killers?

# 75

*Parco Nazionale del Vesuvio*

Flies buzzed hungrily around the remains of the slain fawn, their grey wings tipped with blood. Franco Castellani watched with fascination as they disappeared into its wounds and gorged themselves on meat and plasma.

He'd hacked off chunks of the animal, cooked them on a camp fire and eaten them. Now he felt sick. He guessed the flames hadn't been hot enough to roast the meat properly.

Worse than anything, his throat felt as though he'd swallowed a ball of fibreglass. His head ached and pounded. He was desperately thirsty and was out of water. The big irony was that it was now raining again. Absolutely pouring down.

There were shops a few kilometres from where he was hiding. He knew them well. He'd stolen from them as a kid – biscuits and sweets – and he was fully prepared to steal from them again.

His feet squished in mud as he trudged through the sodden undergrowth. He soon felt drained and faint. He settled on a rock beneath the shelter of a cluster of pines and giant old maples. His stomach growled and then twisted itself in painful knots. Franco got to his feet and threw up. He felt better for a second and then hurled again. For the next ten minutes he retched continuously. Afterwards, he slumped in the undergrowth near the piles of vomit and passed out.

Visions came in his state of delirium. Images of Rosa, lying naked in the back of the car. Her eyes as big as saucers. Her mouth open in a perfect O. He wished he'd touched her mouth; put his fingers on those lips – plump and red against her china-white skin. He reached out in his mind and it was his mother, not Rosa, who reached back. He was a toddler now, waking in bed. Mother's hand brushed his perfect baby face and she told him how beautiful he was. His father called – a deep voice full of gravel and grit – and mother's hand vanished. A flash of blue jeans and an open white shirt. The smell of cigarettes and cologne. Then everything went dark. Too dark. No touch – no contact. A child's cry filled the darkness. Voices faded. Franco strained to remember their faces – their eyes, hair colour, the shape of their mouths – but he couldn't. He had nothing. He was alone again.

The rain touched his lips and reminded him of his thirst. He got to his knees and felt the sodden earth soaking through his jeans. He was covered in vomit and mud. He stood and the world swirled. His heart drummed a deep bass warning through his chest.

Slowly he weaved his way across the parkland, Vesuvius boiling silently behind him, rain clouds stretching their grey spectral arms from above him.

There were voices nearby, he could hear them clearly. Police voices, carabinieri. He'd heard them several times, even seen the troops on a couple of occasions. They were working in the taped-off area where the bodies had been found. They looked stupid, digging – like they were planting potatoes.

Franco put his hand to the back of his jeans and pulled out the old Glock.

It was fully loaded and the safeties off.

He'd kill them if he had to.

In fact, it'd be his pleasure.

# 76

***Raggruppamento Operativo Speciale (ROS)***
***Quartiere Generale***
***(Anti-Camorra Unit), Napoli***

Major Lorenzo Pisano had headed the carabinieri's Anti-Camorra Unit for close on half a decade. A small, slim, bespectacled man in his early forties, he had floppy greying hair that was combed back with a centre parting. Unless you knew that he wore a Kevlar vest, doubly reinforced over his heart, you could easily mistake him for a sociology lecturer rather than a gang-buster.

He shook hands with a surprisingly firm grip and, after brief introductions, showed Jack, Sylvia and two junior members of her team through to a small briefing room. It was dimly lit, a white projector screen was already rolled down, and a machine hummed somewhere at the back of the room.

'Please, sit down.' He motioned to black plastic chairs facing the screen. 'What's the latest on the Sorrentino murder? I only just heard about it.'

Sylvia filled him in. 'Professional hit. Bullet through the head. Killer dumped him on his own waterbed and then disappeared.' She glanced at her watch, 'Ballistics are digging the slug out, right about now.'

Lorenzo picked up a remote clicker for the projector. 'You think your serial killer might have done this as well?'

'You mind if I smoke?'

Lorenzo shook his head.

Sylvia dug out her cigarettes while she answered him. 'It's possible. Sorrentino was the public face of the inquiry. He was all over the press – certainly much more visible than me. Any breakthroughs we had were credited to him.'

'We talked a bit about this on the way over,' added Jack. 'While it's very unusual for a serial killer to attack a member of an inquiry team, it's not unheard of. Normally, they like to watch from a safe distance and be ready to flee. If it is the same guy, then he really has some balls.'

'There are a lot of those kind of guys in the slide show I'm about to give you.' Lorenzo hit the clicker. 'This is Alberta Tortoricci – killed in Scampia. Sylvia and I have spoken about her.' A colour shot of the corpse filled the wall. It looked like a half-blackened candle. Flesh was melted, blackened and dotted with tufts and strands of the old carpet that she'd been wrapped in. 'Alberta was the main witness in the trial that sent local Camorra gang member Bruno Valsi down for a big five. Now he's got balls. *Coglioni* bigger than cantaloupes.' The slide changed to a close-up of her face. 'Our brave lady turned up dead. I saw the body myself. She'd been electrocuted, had her tongue cut out. I guess you know the rest.'

'Heading over here, I picked up a message from the labs,' interrupted Sylvia. 'Seems the accelerant used on your victim was gasoline not paraffin. We were hoping it matched the fuel used on our victim over at the Castellani site.'

Lorenzo shrugged; he wasn't deep enough into their case to offer a valid comment.

'The type of accelerant used isn't nearly as important as the fact that he used one,' explained Jack. 'Given this crime wasn't in the same location as the Castellani killing, it's reasonable to think he used petrol from a can in his vehicle.' He turned to Lorenzo, 'In the Tortoricci case, you have no doubt about the order of events? You're sure the burning came after the electrocution?'

'No doubt. The ME said the brain had hardened and shrunk, almost like it had been baked. Apparently, that's consistent with sustained electrocution.'

Jack pictured toasted walnuts – a treat his grandmother made. 'How'd they do it?'

'They fixed something around her neck. The doc said there was blistering of the skin on both sides – like electrodes had been placed there.'

'Joule burns,' explained Jack, 'the entry and exit points of the electricity. I've come across them before. They usually leave some burning and bruising that gives away the shape of whatever was used to electrocute the victim.'

Lorenzo nodded. 'Sounds right. Faggiani – that's the Medical Examiner – said the marks looked like some metal collar had been clamped to her neck.'

Jack tried to imagine what had gone down. Payback time. A *wise guy* cashing his revenge cheque. And he sure as hell got his money's worth. 'The body was set on fire afterwards. Is that also part of Camorra rituals?'

Pisano screwed up his face. 'No. The severing of the tongue and gouging of a cross on to her lips were ritualistic – they are done to show people what happens if you don't have the sense to look the other way and, instead, you speak about things you shouldn't. But the burning wasn't. That was just tidying up.'

'And do the Camorra regularly *tidy up* with fires?'

Lorenzo gave him one of those looks that said the profiler had much to learn about his homeland. 'Fire is a tool of the poor. The System is staffed by the poor and it burns everything people want to get rid of – waste, dead animals, stolen vehicles and sometimes human bodies. So much burning goes on in the Giugliano-Villaricca-Qualiano triangle that it's known as the Land of Fires.'

Jack's face registered a new level of interest.

'Don't see too many images in the flames, Jack, everyone around here has a match in their hands.'

'Point taken.'

Lorenzo pointed the clicker at the screen. The slide

changed. The head and shoulders of a strong-jawed, dark-haired young man, complete with prison number across his chest, stared down at them. 'This is Valsi. The shot was taken some five years ago, at the time of his conviction for witness intimidation. He's just come out and this is what he looks like now.' A series of new slides showed him getting out of a car and walking towards a building. He looked crisp and cool, like a male model on a photo shoot. 'As lean and mean as they come. Prison was good to him.'

'You said *witness intimidation*. Was that of people due to testify against him for something?' asked Jack.

'No, against his father-in-law. Valsi's dirty work meant we had to bin the fruits of several years of undercover surveillance on the Don.' Lorenzo clicked again. 'This elegant-looking pillar of the community is Fredo Finelli, or Don Fredo as he prefers to be known. Don isn't a term the Camorra use much, but Fredo adopted it. He's old school, very much into respect and values.'

Sylvia scoffed. 'Sadly, those values don't stop short of killing and torturing people.'

'Indeed,' said Lorenzo. 'We had good stuff on Finelli, enough to maybe put him away for five to ten, and then the witnesses started recanting. A plague of Alzheimer's broke out, courtesy of Valsi and his thugs.'

Jack got the picture. He'd seen similar trials collapse back home in Little Italy. 'So, the Tortoricci woman testified that Valsi had threatened her?'

'You got it. Unfortunately, all the evidence she

would have given us in the Finelli trial was destroyed by her bosses, so the best we could do was charge Valsi.'

'Then as soon as he comes out, he whacks her?'

'Pretty much.'

'You're right, he's got balls. He obviously feels that no one *dares* testify against him any more. Have you got his records?'

'Not to hand, but we'll pull them for you. Lots of previous.'

'Arson among them?'

Lorenzo shook his head. 'Not from memory. Could be wrong. Certainly he was in big trouble as a kid, ran drugs just as soon as he was able to walk or run himself. Stacks of violence, illegal possession of weapons, usual stuff.'

'Would be good to know the type of weapons he had handled,' said Sylvia. 'As well as Sorrentino, we're looking for a shooter in connection with a triple-victim kill.'

'I know – the killings at the Castellani site.'

For a second Sylvia wondered *how* he knew. Then she realized, people like Lorenzo Pisano probably knew just about everything there was to know about anything worth knowing.

'This next slide gives you an overview of the Finelli clan and best-known associates. Valsi you're familiar with. Word on the street is that he was promoted and given his own zone when he was released from Poggioreale, but there are three other playmates as well. The Finelli territory is divided into north, south, east and west. Valsi runs the eastern sector; he took over from Pepe Capucci, an old-timer who died of a heart attack.'

'How very convenient,' quipped Jack.

'Actually, it was. We had MEs all over the body and this goon really did die of natural causes.'

'So there is a God after all,' added Sylvia.

'I hope so.' Lorenzo blessed himself and then clicked on. 'This is Angelico d'Arezzo, he runs the north. He's in his late fifties, past his prime, growing fat on his restaurant businesses. We expect him to be replaced in the near future.'

The slide changed to show another man in his late fifties with a long horse-like face, no hair but thick black eyebrows. 'This good-looking specimen is Giotto Fiorentino. He runs the south, specializes in smuggling tobacco and, well, pretty much anything else that can be smuggled.'

'Is violence business or pleasure to those guys?' asked Jack.

'Strictly business. Angelico's done his share of rough stuff, but not recently. Giotto's probably never thrown a punch in his life. He's a wily old fox, but not one for getting blood on his own hands.'

The slide clicked to another middle-aged man. He had slicked-back hair that was white at the temples, making him look like a hooked-nose badger. 'Ambrogio Rotoletti. The west is his area, and he's a gambling man. He did a ten stretch about fifteen years ago. Came out early, as many of them do, and the Don gave him back his full rights as *Capo Zona*.' Jack was about to ask what for, when Lorenzo answered for him. 'He was implicated in the murder of a politician. Since his release he's not been connected with anything heavy.'

'All old-timers, except for Valsi,' observed Sylvia. 'These three *wise guys* are, what – twice his age?'

'And some,' confirmed Lorenzo. 'We're expecting a bloodbath any day soon. Way we read it, Valsi has to take out Finelli, or vice versa.'

'The young buck will make first play,' said Jack. 'That's the way it always goes down.'

Lorenzo shrugged. 'I'm no profiler, but I'll tell you this. Most Camorra bosses are dead within five years of sitting at the top of the tree. Fredo Finelli has been squatting up there for close on twenty. My money is on the old man.'

Silence hit the room like a slap in the stomach, as Pisano clicked to a giant blow-up of the Finelli gang tattoo.

'This is really unusual. While crime Families like the Sicilian Mafia and the Japanese Yakuza favour identity tattoos, it's uncommon in Camorra circles.'

'Honour, loyalty and vengeance,' said Jack, translating from the screen. 'What's the meaning of the serpent and the knife?'

Lorenzo sat on the edge of a desk as he answered. 'It's a viper. I'm no expert, but I'm told they have hidden fangs and giant hinge-like jaws that allow them to lock on to something and then grind it to death or swallow it whole.'

'Highly appropriate then,' said Jack.

'Some vipers also keep the eggs of their babies in their mouth,' added Sylvia. 'And there are many different types of viper. I dated a herpetologist once and he bored me to death with stories of snakes and reptiles.'

'Talking of reptiles, take a look at this.' Lorenzo flashed up an organization chart of the most important members of the Finelli clan.

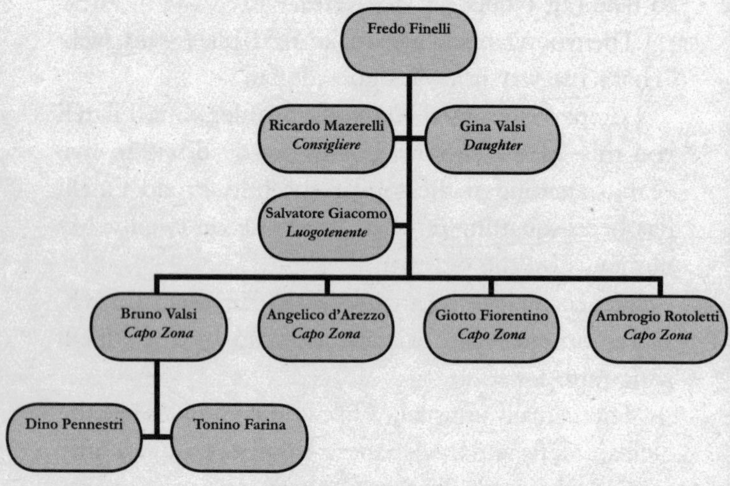


'It's far from complete, but it deals with the main players, especially those connected to Valsi.' A shot of a pretty-faced, dark-haired young woman appeared. 'This is Gina Valsi, Bruno's wife, Fredo Finelli's daughter. Don't be taken in by that butter-wouldn't-melt look. Gina's quite a lady, a power in her own right. She runs several garment factories and counterfeit fashion houses. Probably makes as much money as any of the *Capi*.'

He clicked on. 'And this is their consigliere, Ricardo Mazerelli. He's understood to have an increasing say in the Family business, and not just on the legal front. He manages a lot of the old man's business portfolio as well. These days, most Families have two consiglieri, but Finelli has only ever used this guy.'

Jack sat in silence in the semi-darkness, studying the dynasty. 'Who are these other two – Pennestri and Farina? You see them in the bottom left on the chart.'

'I don't have their mug shots here. They're new recruits, members of Valsi's crew. He's starting to put together his own Family-in-waiting.'

'And the guy in the box beneath Mazerelli – the bodyguard?'

'Salvatore Giacomo.' Lorenzo pulled up a grainy head-and-shoulders surveillance shot of a grey-faced man wearing big, old-fashioned sunglasses. 'He's Finelli's personal *luogotenente*, his minder, nothing to do with Valsi. Old muscle, old school, he stays glued to the Don and makes sure Finelli doesn't fall down the stairs or catch a cold.'

Jack rubbed his chin. 'How many kills between them all?'

Lorenzo snorted and walked into the light so he could read all the name boxes and do the maths. 'Finger in the air, just guessing?'

'Sure.'

'These guys cover thirty, forty years of Camorra activity between them. All of them have *made their bones*. The old-timers will have planted between five and ten apiece, the younger bucks two to five. So – in direct personal kills – I'd guess at a minimum of fifty, though they'll have been involved in plenty more. In the past thirty years, countrywide, we connect the Camorra to close on four thousand kills. These guys will have done their quota.'

The projector whirred noisily as they all weighed up the death toll. Jack voiced what was on their minds. 'You know this clan; you understand its values, norms and rules. If they discovered they had a serial murderer in their midst, one who killed just for kicks, and targeted innocent civilians, would they give him up?'

Lorenzo laughed. 'Not a hope. And, for the record, they don't have any values – except get rich quick and kill anything that gets in the way.'

'I agree,' said Sylvia. 'If they found such a person, then they'd probably kill him. They don't like undue publicity so they'd get rid of him. But their contempt for us is so profound they would bury the body rather than give him up.'

Jack pointed at the organization chart. 'Bruno Valsi – from what you know of him, do you think he was personally involved in the torture and murder of Alberta Tortoricci?'

Lorenzo didn't hesitate. 'No doubt about it. If he

didn't do it himself, then you can be sure he had a front-row seat, a bag of popcorn and a giant Pepsi. All the intel on him says he's a Grade A sadist, and a clever one too.'

'And he was jailed five years ago, and just got out?'

Lorenzo nodded.

Sylvia completed the picture. 'And most of our women went missing five or more years ago. We've dug around and can't find anyone linking Valsi and the women. Would be good to get to speak to the man himself – and his father-in-law?'

'I've got numbers for their lawyer, Mazerelli. You want me to give him a ring?'

'Thanks, that would be good.' Sylvia let out an ironic laugh. 'I'm just thinking about Franco Castellani. Until the Sorrentino killing he looked good for the murders. Now, if you compare him to Valsi and this mob, he doesn't fit. He's like a frightened kid.'

'Maybe that's exactly what he is,' said Jack. 'That'd explain why he's run away. Everything in life just got too much for him.'

'He's a frightened kid with a gun, though,' said Lorenzo. 'That still makes him dangerous. Maybe even deadly.'

'True,' agreed Sylvia. For a second she wondered how Lorenzo knew about Franco having a gun. Then she realized it had probably been on the APB she'd sent out.

The room lights buzzed into life as Lorenzo killed the projector. 'I'll phone Mazerelli,' he said, heading for the door.

'Hang on,' called Jack, worrying about how long they could get dicked about by a mob lawyer. 'I think I might have a better suggestion.'

# 77

***Capo di Posillipo, La Baia di Napoli***

Three carabinieri Fiats sped Jack, Sylvia and Lorenzo through the slow evening traffic and across the Bay of Naples. 'Not exactly good for our global footprint, but impressive nevertheless,' observed Jack as they travelled together in the middle car. He figured a surprise visit to the Finelli home – the Viper's Nest – was more likely to get results than a polite request to their smart-arse lawyer. 'Always better to apologize than ask permission,' he said as they wound their way out towards Capo di Posillipo.

Most of the case got discussed en route, including the post-mortem burning of Alberta Tortoricci and the ante-mortem burning of the still unidentified woman in the pit at the Castellani campsite. 'It's probably a form of pyrophilia,' explained the profiler. 'It's a relatively uncommon deviancy in which the offender derives gratification from starting and watching fires.'

'Firebugs?' said Lorenzo from the front passenger seat.

'Yep, but the worst kind. Not your normal crazies

who listen to scanners and chase 911 calls. These guys are twenty-four-carat sadists seeking extreme thrills.'

'What *makes* them like that?' asked Sylvia.

Jack gave the textbook answer. 'Pyrophilic offenders have feelings of loneliness and sadness, followed by rage. There's always great tension or arousal prior to the act and massive gratification when it is over.'

'That seems to fit all our suspects,' said Sylvia. 'Valsi is straight out of prison, Franco Castellani has been an outcast for much of his life. Even Creed is a loner. They all seem a whole galaxy beyond normal to me.'

'It's more than them just being loners,' corrected Jack. 'In watching the flames they feel a relief of their stress. This condition is rare – much rarer than loneliness – and it's fuelled by the need and the gratification attached to watching objects or, in this case, victims burn.'

'How rare?' asked Lorenzo.

'This form of pyrophilia is extremely uncommon. It's really an impulse control problem.'

'That mainly a male problem?' asked Lorenzo.

'Course it is,' joked Sylvia. 'All males have impulse control problems.'

'Pyros are not all male, but this one undoubtedly is. He may even be in the criminal records system for fire-related offences. That's partly why I asked about Valsi's record. Our man may also have convictions for violence. He may have been institutionalized at a very early age and he will certainly have relationship problems that stretch way back.'

'We'll have the records for you tomorrow,' said Lorenzo.

Sylvia's cellphone rang. '*Pronto. Sì.*'

Jack and Lorenzo fell silent as her face betrayed the fact that it wasn't good news. She flipped the phone shut and looked totally dejected. 'That was Sorrentino's Number Two, Luella Grazzioli. They've been following your clock-face theory and doing a radar sweep along projected lines before and after the graves we've already exhumed. They've found more burials.'

'How many?' asked Jack.

'She's not completely sure. But she's guessing it could be as many as seven. Seven new bodies. And they've still not hit true north.'

# 78

***Parco Nazionale del Vesuvio***

News of the fresh body sites spread like a bushfire across the excavation site. Franco Castellani didn't know it, but this was the reason why he was able to slip, unseen, past the carabinieri and down the steep Vesuvian hillside.

As the rugged parkland gave way to the winding, potholed road that took busloads of tourists to the summit, he jammed the old Glock back into the waistband of his jeans. The retching had stopped but his head was still pounding and he remained desperately thirsty.

On the road below, filled with noise and crowds of people, he felt strangely alien again. Alone in the woods he'd enjoyed not being stared at or whispered about. Now that luxury was gone.

The old horrors were back.

A middle-aged man stepped from a Mercedes and frowned when he saw him; a woman crossing the road turned her head to check what she'd seen; a mother, bending down to fasten her toddler's coat, shielded the child's eyes when she spotted him. All standard stuff. All layers of humdrum humiliation that were regularly piled on top of him. But today Franco felt more vulnerable than ever. Today he felt bad enough to shoot them all.

Every fucking one of them.

The Glock could end their prejudice, wipe it all out in just a single, sweet burst of ear-splitting gunfire. His blood fizzed at the thought of it.

Umberto Leopardi kept an old *supermercato* on a road off the junction with the A3. He also kept bottled water in stacked trays just inside the door. Two litres of Ferrarelle, fresh from the nearby Val D'Assano, vanished before Umberto had even looked up from the counter. Near the front window of neighbouring Buscaglia's was a rack of stacked snacks. Two fat packs of *patatine fritte* disappeared with the same deftness as had the water.

Franco took his meagre hoard to one of the places he and Paolo frequented near the visitors' entrance of Pompeii. The rain started again as he sat behind the street hoardings near the railway line and hurriedly fumbled the bottled water to his mouth. From his shelter he watched families and couples passing on the street. The feelings of loneliness and isolation multiplied inside him – bred like the mutant cells that were silently murdering him.

Exiled.

An outsider. That's what he was. Sitting with the sodden rubbish behind the hoardings, he'd never felt as low as he did right now. His fumbling, claw-like hand found the Glock.

Soon he would use it.

Soon they would understand the true depths of his pain.

# 79

***Capo di Posillipo, La Baia di Napoli***

Armed officers flanked Sylvia, Jack and Lorenzo as they walked towards the tall wooden gates of the Finelli mansion.

'Cameras just about *everywhere.*' Jack's head swivelled from one to another.

Sylvia pressed a bell and waited. 'I hope they catch my good side.' She shot him a flirtatious smile and tucked her hair behind her right ear. Static stung the air – a tinny male voice trickled from the entry phone, asking who they were and what they wanted.

'I'm *Capitano* Sylvia Tomms.' She stood on tiptoes to speak into a small grille. 'I'm here with my colleague, Lorenzo Pisano, and an American psychological profiler, Jack King. I do not have a search warrant or an arrest warrant. It is a matter of public importance that brings us here and we really would be most grateful for *Signor* Finelli's assistance.'

There was another sizzle of static, then the intercom went dead. Several minutes later there was a clunk and the big automatic gates swung slowly open.

Jack caught himself saying, 'Wow!'

The view was breathtaking.

Manicured lawns and magnificent marble statues gave way to a grand old palazzo complete with castellated frontage, shuttered casement windows and gutter-height Boston ivy.

Lorenzo nodded. 'Yeah, *big* wow. Who was the jerk who said crime doesn't pay?'

Rich, golden light spilled from an open door across the gravelled courtyard. The small, trim form of Fredo Finelli appeared. He was alone and looked relaxed in navy-blue striped suit trousers and an open-necked white shirt.

'*Buona sera*,' said the Don, extending his hand and a smile to all of them. 'Please come inside, it will be much easier for us to talk.'

Jack scanned the area as they walked. There were no guards to be seen, but they were there. He could feel invisible eyes on his back as he passed into the warmth of the house. Jack was the only one to slip his shoes off at the front step.

'No, no, there's no need for that,' said Finelli, touched by the courtesy.

'It's the way my wife trained me,' joked Jack.

They were shown through to one of the lounges on the side of the house, overlooking a floodlit lake. Servants materialized to take coats and attend to drinks with all the speed and subtlety of a top hotel.

Finelli settled his surprise *guests* in a plush, wide curve of bespoke light-brown settees covered in a mix of cotton and silk. 'Lorenzo Pisano, I don't think I've seen you since my son-in-law's trial?' He smiled fondly, as if he were talking to an old friend. 'How are your parents? I understand your father, Benito, spent a little time in hospital with a hip problem?'

If Lorenzo was bothered by the intimate knowledge, he didn't let it show. 'They're perfectly well, thank you. Both my mother and father are very carefully looked after, as I'm sure you know.'

'Glad to hear it.' Finelli then turned to Jack and spoke in perfect English. 'I'm so sorry, I'm being very rude. We will continue in English, so you can follow us. Major Pisano and I were merely exchanging pleasantries.'

'That's kind of you.' Jack didn't mention that his Italian was good enough to have understood everything being said.

'So,' continued Finelli, sitting back in his armchair. 'How exactly can I help you?'

Sylvia outlined the three murders on the Castellani campsite, stressing the deaths of the two young teenagers and touching lightly on the death of the Jane Doe, who'd been found burned to death in the rubbish pit.

'My dear God, how perfectly terrible. What is the world coming to?' Finelli made a passable attempt at sincerity. 'And please, do forgive me – I just realized that I recognize your face. Aren't you also heading the inquiry into the murder of that young woman – what was her name?'

'Francesca Di Lauro.'

'That's right. I saw the press conference.' He let out a playful chuckle. 'I'm sorry, I shouldn't laugh. I was just remembering that journalist who threw you with a question about all those other missing women. Seemed a difficult moment for you. Are those cases all connected, as he said?'

Sylvia felt her temper rising, but she kept it in check, even managed an unconcerned smile for the old goat. 'We have to keep an open mind. And, as I'm sure you appreciate, a press conference isn't the best place to divulge our private thinking.'

Finelli nodded. 'Quite so.' There was a noise outside. 'Wait a moment, please.' He rose and left the room. Through the crack of the door Jack recognized the face of Finelli's daughter. Gina looked fatter than in Pisano's picture of her. His eyes dipped. She was holding the hand of a young child, probably her son. The boy lifted his face and opened his arms for Grandpa to kiss him. A touching moment and one that reminded Jack of how deceptive crime dynasties can be when you see them masked in middle-class normality.

A minute later, Finelli returned with a pad and a black Montblanc fountain pen. 'The young lovers, what were their names?'

'Rosa Novello, she was eighteen.' Sylvia gave him time to write. 'She was with nineteen-year-old Filippo Valdrano. Their parents expected them to get married shortly.'

'I have influence in this community; I will ask for you. And the other victim, you have a name?'

'We don't. Not yet. *Signor* Finelli, we are wondering if these deaths are connected to that of a woman called Alberta Tortoricci. I'm sure you know *her* name. She was recently found dead in Scampia. Her body had also been burned –'

Finelli cut her off. 'The whole of Italy knows I am aware of the woman you mentioned, and the ridiculous accusations she made about me. But I have no knowledge of her unfortunate demise.'

Lorenzo butted in. 'We're not seeking to hurt you on this. We're merely trying to share with you the information that we believe the man who killed Alberta Tortoricci may be the same person who killed the people on the Castellani campsite.'

'Excuse me,' interrupted Jack, 'do you mind if I use one of your washrooms? I'm afraid I really need to go.'

Sylvia and Lorenzo shot daggers at him. Finelli was on the rack. It was a crazy time to interrupt their flow.

'I'm sorry, I have some stomach problems.' Jack looked embarrassed.

The all-round discomfort seemed to amuse Finelli. He chewed back a wry smile. 'Certainly. I'll show you.' He walked his troubled guest to the double doors of the lounge and pointed across the marble hallway.

Jack waited until he heard the doors click shut behind him, then confidently strode up the stairs.

If he was stopped he would just say the bathroom downstairs was occupied or he was confused about directions.

As he hoped, Finelli's guards were kept out of the private quarters. Windows, doors, exits and driveways are the places you mostly find mob muscle. Seldom are they allowed near master bedrooms. As he strode up the steps, he could hear Gina and the child playing in a room near the front of the house. On the top landing he opened doors quickly – and took in the facts even faster. Finelli's room – neat, tidy, black suit on a hanger, silk-sheeted bed already made. Guest room – no one in it, no fresh flowers, no water jug or glasses by the bed, the room smelled of damp. Another guest room – windows partly open, a woman's shoes on the floor, make-up and jewellery on an antique dresser, designer bags on the floor. This was where Finelli's daughter was staying. He stepped in. The soft toys on the bed and a Lego spaceship seemed evidence of an early morning visit from her son, a mother and child's moments of play before starting the day. Jack opened the door to the en suite. Shampoo, conditioner, tampons, toothpaste, one adult toothbrush. He'd seen all he needed. Within ten seconds he was out of the room. He quickly checked next door. This was the child's room. Toys everywhere, books on the floor, clothes turned inside out and not yet put into the laundry basket by the maid. He shut it and headed downstairs. Quickly he found the toilet, flushed it, splashed cold water on his face and didn't towel it dry. By the time he re-entered the lounge he knew the water would make his face red and give the appearance of the sweats. 'My apologies,' he said. 'I think I've got some bad kind of stomach bug.'

'Probably the change of diet, good food can be a shock to the system.' Finelli did his best to sound understanding. 'When did you get in from the United States?'

'You could be right,' said Jack. 'I've been here a while but probably not made the full adjustment yet.'

A tray of coffee and water arrived, courtesy of a young woman in a black dress that fell modestly to below her knees. She never spoke, except for the obligatory *prego* as they took their drinks and thanked her. She left without having looked directly at anyone. The air was thick with discretion. The kind of well-practised, silver-service discretion that always prevailed in the homes of the monstrously corrupt.

'This is an incredible house,' said Sylvia, balancing an espresso on her lap. 'You live here alone, or with the whole family?'

'My wife died some years ago, but I still live here. As you said, it is our family home, and I cannot see myself living anywhere else.'

'And your daughter, Gina, she lives here too?' added Jack.

Finelli read the depth of the question. He answered cautiously. 'At the moment, yes. She and her family come to stay sometimes. It is nice for us all to be together.'

The bedrooms Jack had just looked in had told a fuller story. Bruno Valsi was certainly not staying in the house. There was clearly a rift in the family. But was it between Gina and her husband, or between her husband and her father?

'Why do you ask?' the Don added, defensively.

Jack put on half a smile. 'Guess I'm missing my wife and child. Seeing your daughter and grandson here made me think of my own family.'

Finelli looked across at the door and worked out how Jack might have spotted them. 'Forgive me, but I am quite busy tonight. Is there anything more I can help you with?' He put his coffee cup down and gave out all the signals that he wanted them to leave.

They rose and Finelli shook hands with Sylvia, Lorenzo and finally Jack. 'I hope you feel better very soon.'

'Thank you, I think I already do. Before we go, I'm interested to know how you get on with your son-in-law?'

Finelli smiled. '*Signore*, I've been very generous in my hospitality, please don't abuse it.' He motioned an open hand to the doorway.

Jack stood his ground. He leaned towards Finelli and spoke in a confidential tone. 'From what little I know of Bruno Valsi, he is not the type of man I would want *my* daughter sharing her life with. And not the kind of man I would consider good for my own health.'

Finelli looked amused. 'Thank you for your opinion. Now, it really is time for you to go.'

A gym monster in a black suit appeared from nowhere. Jack guessed he was six-two, late thirties and no doubt tooled up. Nothing would have delighted him more than demonstrating how quickly he could disarm a monkey that big, but he didn't have to. Lorenzo stepped forward and quietly said something in Italian that stopped the guy in his tracks. It gave Jack a final chance to speak to Finelli. '*Signore*, your charm doesn't disguise the fact that you're a very worried man – and you have a right to be. If there is anything you can tell us about your son-in-law, then you may well be helping yourself and your daughter and grandchild as much as you help us.'

The Don said nothing but, just before he walked away and left them, the look on his face told Jack, Lorenzo and Sylvia that he'd probably rather die than offer them any help.

# 80

***Campeggio Castellani, Pompeii***

Antonio Castellani had become desperately worried about Franco. So much so, that he was actually pleased to get a knock on the door from two new carabinieri officers who wanted to go over everything again with him.

Once more the old man faithfully retold it all – leaving out only the private arrangement he'd made with the big lieutenant. Antonio was old enough and smart enough to know that you only told such important secrets to one person. Apart from that, he did as they asked. He went right back to the very beginning. Started from the moment the people on Lot 45 had reported their daughter and her boyfriend missing. Went right up to his recent brushes with the Camorra and the order from the Finelli clan that he leave his home and surrender his business.

The woman seemed genuinely moved, sympathetic and kind. The male officer apparently didn't care that much. They were quite a pair. Chalk and cheese, he thought. The man, Mario or Marco something, he couldn't remember the name, was intense and wiry, maybe even a little rude and disrespectful, while she – Cassie – was beautiful, polite and intelligent. He even liked her name. She was everything that he'd hoped his own daughter would have turned out to be. Cassie was one of those bright girls who would go far, he could tell. For a start she'd written everything down, had been careful not to miss anything. Her male partner had seemed happy just to fire off the questions. In fact, he'd only really become interested when Antonio had mentioned that Franco was missing. He still believed the police were the best hope of finding him. His grandson wasn't well. Sometimes he got really sick, they had to find him, look after him, bring him back home. She said they would. *She promised* they would. Good girl, that Cassie, you could tell. She even took away some pictures of Franco. Promised again she'd find him.

Antonio settled down in his chair and knew he'd fall asleep. He was tired of it all. These days just living exhausted him. If he'd known that the two carabinieri officers he'd spent so much time with were actually Luciano Creed and a female journalist called Cassandra Morrietti, then it may well have been the death of him.

# 81

***Via Caprese Michelangelo, centro città, Napoli***

Ricardo Mazerelli's visitor parked more than two blocks away and insisted that at the end of their meeting he was given the footage from the surveillance cameras that he was sure would be running.

Lieutenant Pietro Raimondi settled down in a chair in the penthouse conservatory, overlooking the streaming firefly lights of cars heading along the Bay of Naples. Ice tinkled in the two highball glasses of vodka and Coke that Mazerelli placed on a stone-topped coffee table beside the trickling waters of the Japanese garden. 'So, what have you got that is so valuable you wish to see me at such short notice and under such unusual conditions?'

Raimondi told him. And he told him his price for ensuring that the information never crossed another investigator's desk. 'I have Antonio Castellani's dossier, with its diary entries and photographs. I also have details of where *Signor* Castellani stashed weapons given to him by Fredo Finelli and his Family members. And, I have detailed accounts of money extorted from Antonio Castellani over more than a decade.'

Mazerelli picked up his drink and looked unperturbed. 'Ramblings of an old man. Not enough to raise a warrant, let alone bring a case to trial. And even if you got that far, you would be gambling that *Signor* Castellani's health held out. He is, after all, quite aged and could die at any moment.'

'I also have video-taped testimony – made by myself – of *Signor* Castellani. Should it ever be needed,' he lied.

Mazerelli swirled the ice in his glass. 'And for this you want one million euros in untraceable cash?'

'I do.'

The two men studied each other. Mazerelli wondered whether the cop was wired and it was all a trap. Raimondi wondered whether he had stepped out of his depth and made a mistake that would get him killed.

'I think our meeting is over,' said the lawyer.

Raimondi was shocked. This wasn't at all what he'd planned. He stalled for time. 'I haven't finished my drink yet.'

The consigliere rose from his chair and gestured to the door. 'Take it with you. I have plenty of glasses.'

The policeman put the drink down. 'You promised me the surveillance tapes. I'd like them now.'

'Lieutenant, you come in here making preposterous suggestions about my employer, most of which constitute defamation of his good character, then you demand a million euros for worthless rubbish. You're lucky to be leaving without a lawsuit, let alone with testimony of your offensive visit.'

Raimondi stood up, shook the creases out of his suit trousers and in one swift movement grabbed Mazerelli by the throat. He banged the consigliere against the wall. Knocked the breath out of him. 'Now listen, you sweet-mouthed motherfucker, the price has just gone up to two million. And, unless you give me the recordings, I'm going to pull your balls off, stick them in your mouth and make you swallow a whole lot more than your pride.' Raimondi thumped him against the wall one more time, then let him go. 'Don't piss me around. This is a serious offer, so take it seriously.'

Mazerelli doubled up, red-faced and coughing for air. He was still wheezing when he reached the cupboard in the hallway and ejected the disc from the surveillance unit's recorder.

'Thanks,' said Raimondi as Mazerelli handed it over. '*Two* million. *One* month. Give your boss the message. And tell him not to even think about trying to *get* at me. If he does, then everything I told you about will be in my boss's hands within an hour of such foolishness.' He opened the front door and was halfway through it when he turned back. 'One final thing; Antonio Castellani and his family get to stay where they are. No evictions and no further intimidation.'

# 82

***San Giorgio a Cremano, La Baia di Napoli***

Freshly showered, smelling of apple and swaddled in a white towelling robe, Sylvia Tomms relaxed at her dressing table and dried her hair before going to bed. She'd always had a brutally honest streak and, as she glanced in the mirror, she had to concede she wasn't looking her best these days.

'You are a pig! Look at yourself! How did this happen?' She squinted at the lines beneath her eyes, then painfully tweezed hairs from a brow that she thought horses might have trouble jumping over.

Having chastised herself for going to seed, she determined to get as much beauty sleep as possible.

Unmade and unwashed for almost a month, her bed had never looked so good. She crawled in and curled up. Pulled the duvet tight so she created the illusion she was being held. Sleep came quickly.

It engulfed her. Wrapped itself around her like the warm musky arm of a man who'd just made love to her. She floated. Drifted far, far away. Floated back to when she was seven years old and with her father in his boat. It was her first sailing trip and she remembered almost crying when he made her wear that ugly orange life jacket. They were on Lake Starnberg. The Wetterstein Alps towered up in the background. Water, distilled from Ice Age glaciers, shone crystal blue beneath a high midday sun. A soft breeze stroked her face. Her father's hands guided hers up and down the ropes as the sail swung and the craft flew across the lake. She missed him. Missed him so much that she often dreamt that he was still alive. Just a phone call away.

And then the phone rang.

Her heart banged and her eyes blinked open.

Within two rings she answered, '*Pronto!*'

It was eight a.m. The precious night's rest had already gone.

'Sylvia, it's Marianna. You'd better come by the labs as soon as you can. I have those ballistics and forensics reports you wanted – and I'm afraid they don't make easy reading.'

# 83

***ROS Quartiere Generale, Napoli***

Unlike Sylvia, Jack had not slept well. He was still yawning when the driver dropped him outside Lorenzo Pisano's office. Armed guards patrolled the outside of the carabinieri building and questioned him at length before he was let into reception, let alone escorted to the anti-Camorra unit.

The major had already been in for more than an hour. A childless marriage in his late twenties had ended in divorce in his early forties. Now work was all he had left.

They made little small talk and got straight down to business – Bruno Valsi's criminal record and his family history.

'Take a look at these.' Lorenzo dropped the rap sheet and briefing notes in front of Jack. 'Valsi was a real problem kid in a real problem area. You want *caffè*?'

'Sure – whatever you've got. Espresso, if possible, please.'

Lorenzo fired up an ancient Gaggia in the corner of his office. 'Valsi's father died in some industrial accident, when he was a baby. His mother brought him up on her own.'

'Anything more on his father's death?'

'Not much. I can dig around and find the full details. I know a boiler blew. One of those decrepit gas and oil combination jobs. It exploded and old man Valsi and two of his workmates died in a fire at the back of the factory.'

Jack digested the facts. *Could such a tragedy become a future trigger for offending? He certainly couldn't rule it out. Was there a tenuous link there with fire and suffering?*

Lorenzo shovelled freshly ground Arabica into the machine and sniffed at the last teaspoon before closing the container. 'Valsi lived most of his life in Scampia, an area that's been a Camorra stronghold for as long as I can remember. It's the kind of place that brands you, inks a tattoo on your soul. Tortoricci's body was found less than a kilometre from where Valsi was born.'

'Stupid question, but Forensics didn't find anything to link Valsi to the woman or the body?'

'Not a thing. I had the labs run comparison tests with Valsi's fingerprints, his DNA profile and all the trace evidence. I've also asked for his dabs and DNA to be checked against all the trace evidence in the Castellani campsite murders. So far, nothing.'

Jack wasn't surprised. Thugs as brutal as Valsi were usually careful thugs. He flicked through more of the rap sheet. 'Back in his early childhood, he was arrested several times but never charged. We talking routine stop and search, or was he lawyered-up even then?'

Lorenzo laughed. 'Camorra do that. For the good kids, they treat them good, get them top briefs. Other kids, the ones they don't want, they disown, let them get wasted. The cream of the crop are looked after, though. They make them feel protected and have them back on the streets before *Sesame Street* has finished. Valsi was cream – crème de la crème. He ran "errands" and pushed drugs before he even pushed a bike. But prior to the big witness intimidation case that put him away, we never got a mark against him.'

'A boy soldier?'

'*Sì, piciotto.* The Camorra has armies of them across Campania. They rope in kids like Valsi and soon they're willing to kill in return for a new Vespa. Children are the cheapest contract killers you can hire.'

Jack read the sheet again. *Assault against a male – charges dropped. Assault against three other men – charges dropped.* 'These aborted charges – we talking fists or weapons?'

'Early ones were fists. Street fights, bar fights. Polizia did catch him with a weapon once. A semi-automatic. Beretta, I think. They even got as far as charging him.'

'And?'

Lorenzo smiled. 'The gun disappeared before the ink had even dried on the crime sheet. No evidence, no case. They never even got it in front of a magistrate.'

'I understand. We've got our share of bent cops back home.'

'Hasn't everyone?' He tapped the rap sheet. 'Gets even more interesting as he gets older. In his late teens, he wounded a guy. It was the father of a girl he was dating. Old man had had a few drinks and told Valsi he should stay away from his daughter, said she deserved better than drug-dealing scum like him. Valsi beat him senseless and then left him on a kitchen seat with a knife through his pants and a testicle pinned to the chair.'

Jack couldn't help but grimace.

'Sliced him up so bad that the guy had to have one of his balls removed.'

Jack flicked through the rest of the notes. There were police black and whites buried in there of Valsi as a kid and as a teenager. He looked young and innocent. No hint of the evil within. Jack had seen dozens of pictures of apple-fresh kids who their mothers worshipped. Perfect sons. They'd all grown up to become monsters far worse than Valsi.

'Have you got anything against him for attacks on women, or was it all macho shit?'

'Some of both.' Lorenzo drew breath as he recalled his next story. 'Same girl. When she did finally come to her senses and dumped him, was kidnapped and taken to an old school building.

There, six of Valsi's goons sat on her arms, legs and chest while he personally sewed up her vagina.'

'Christ! And you couldn't put him away for that?'

Lorenzo shrugged. 'Wish we could've. Kid didn't even come to us. We heard it on the street. Local doctor who treated her even denied he'd seen her for as much as a cold. We guessed Valsi had threatened to do much worse to anyone who said anything.'

Jack looked down at the photographs again. Strong face, good teeth, most women would probably say he had nice eyes. All proof that you shouldn't judge a book by its cover. 'How old was he at this time?'

'I think the coffee's about there.' Lorenzo headed back to the Gaggia. 'He was eighteen, maybe nineteen. Not long after that he hooked up with Gina Finelli.'

'Don Fredo's daughter?'

'The very same. Not that she had much of a calming influence on him. Sometimes marriage and babies settle a guy down. Not Bruno. His reputation for meanness and cruelty just kept growing. We all heaved a sigh of relief when we took him down. Now the bastard is back out there, the air is poisoned again. You want sugar?'

'No, thanks. Thick and black's fine.' Jack searched for more pictures. 'You got surveillance on him at the moment?'

'Best we can. But he's savvy. And we don't have

unlimited funds. Plus, there aren't many officers keen for that kind of chore.'

Jack found a couple of long-range telephoto pics at the back of the briefing pack. They were all similar. Smart suit jacket dangling over his right shoulder, crisp expensive shirt partly opened, sunglasses on, head turned to the side. The guy sure took a good shot.

'Here you go.' Lorenzo handed over a small off-white espresso cup.

'Thanks.'

Thoughts as thick and dark as the coffee brewed inside the profiler's head. Bruno Valsi was clearly an egotist, confident and sure of his power. He was also a brutal sadist, devoid of emotion. Worse than all that, he was clever and charismatic enough to command others to follow him. The Tortoricci case was proof that he was the kind of man who could torture and kill a woman. The cold, efficient and breathtakingly arrogant murder of Sorrentino was also very much his style. All in all, he was a formidable package of trouble.

'You're thinking that you want to interview this guy?' asked Lorenzo.

Jack looked up from the photographs and sipped the espresso. It was hot, sharp and good. 'No, not at all. I'm thinking I want to interview his wife.'

'His wife?'

'Valsi won't tell us anything more than his records already do, or his father-in-law already did. But get me half an hour with his wife and I promise you we'll have everything we need on him.'

'Finish your coffee, and we'll fix it. I know exactly where she's going to be this morning.'

# 84

***RIS, Raggruppamento Carabinieri per la Investigazioni Scientifiche, Napoli***

Sylvia couldn't believe what she'd heard. She pushed the files back across the table to her friend and looked dismayed.

'All results are progress. Think of the positives,' said Marianna Della Fratte.

Sylvia flipped open a notebook and rubbed the ballpoint up and down on the page to get it to write. 'Go through it again – the good news and bad news. Maybe second time around it comes out better.'

'Gladly. Which do you want first?'

'The good.'

'The ammunition in both the Sorrentino case and the Pompeii shootings is the same.'

Sylvia scribbled. 'Fine – same ammo, so maybe the same offender. The two cases are linked.'

'So it would seem.'

'Now it turns bad. Give me the small print again.'

'The slug dug out of the ceiling at Sorrentino's apartment is a Remington nine-millimetre JHP.'

'Jacketed Hollow Point, right? The nasty kind where the nose of the bullet flares out and makes a mess on penetration.'

'The very same. Ballistics think it came from a Glock. It matches the rounds that killed your couple in the car.'

Sylvia scribbled in silence for a moment, then asked, 'To be clear, this means it's the same shooter?'

Marianna's half-smile said it wasn't going to be that simple. 'This is where it loses shape. The bullets that killed the woman in the pit – and the two lovers, Novello and Valdrano – were the same ammunition that killed Sorrentino, *but*, and it's a *big but*, the bullet that killed Sorrentino was *not* fired from the same gun. The same *type* of gun, yes. But most definitely not the same gun.'

Sylvia put her pen down. 'So, same ammo at both crime scenes, but two entirely different guns?'

Marianna frowned. 'Not *entirely* different. Ballistics say all the bullets were fired from Glocks – they can tell from the rifling – but . . .'

'But different Glocks?'

'But different Glocks.'

Sylvia made some more notes. Then pushed on with her questions. 'How different? I mean, just what are we talking about here?'

'Same make. All the bullets came from a Glock 19 – or, to be precise, two 19s. You know the model?'

Sylvia nodded hesitantly. 'Enough to pick it out in a crowd, but I've never fired one. We're all Berettas.'

'They're standard issue in Israel and the US, particularly loved by the NYPD and Shabak. USAF is also fond of them. It's a serious piece of kit.'

'The attraction being?'

'Size. It may be the only time men brag about having something small. It's especially good for concealed use.'

'So it's a weapon of choice for an assassin as well as a cop?'

'You got it.'

Sylvia drummed her pen on her notebook. 'Right now, what you're telling me is pointing – no, let me correct myself – is *jabbing* a huge finger of accusation at Bruno Valsi, a sadistic young Camorrista who's blipped on to our radar.'

'That would make sense. Camorra links with the US are good, and they've always had a penchant for foreign weapons.'

'Okay, so let's go on to the DNA and trace-evidence reports.' Sylvia turned a fresh page and braced herself to hear the findings again.

Marianna shuffled files and spread out three separate sheets. 'Easy one first. Paolo Falconi. He comes up clean everywhere. No DNA or fingerprint matches with any of the victims or crime scenes.'

Sylvia allowed herself a slight smile. It was good to at least eliminate someone.

Marianna picked up another sheet of her report. 'Now then, Franco Castellani. This is a different story.

We got clear DNA profiles from his bed sheets. The things were so crawling with evidence they could have walked to the scopes themselves.'

Sylvia pretended to hurl.

'Franco's DNA is all over the car where Rosa Novello and Filippo Valdrano were killed, and all over the pit where the woman was burned. But there wasn't a trace of him at Sorrentino's apartment.'

Sylvia weighed up the two out of three strikes against Franco. On what she'd just heard, a court would probably convict him of the killings of Novello, Valdrano and the Jane Doe in the pit, but wouldn't entertain a case against him for Sorrentino. Yet she and Jack were both sure that whoever had killed the first three also killed Sorrentino. She was full of questions. 'Our profiler mentioned that he thought there might also be DNA on the door frame. He had some theory about the killer taunting Rosa while she was in the back of the car.'

'I don't know about the taunting, but he was certainly right about the DNA.' Marianna ran a finger down the columns and paragraphs. 'We found genomic DNA on the window and door frame in dried saliva spittle. It was fresh enough to obtain a good amplified profile.'

'And?'

Marianna read Sylvia's mind. 'It's not Franco Castellani's DNA. And so far, our databases have drawn a blank on any match with a convicted offender.'

Sylvia scraped her fingers through her hair. That

cut was certainly long overdue. 'So Franco was in that car – beyond a doubt?'

'Beyond a shadow of a doubt.'

'But someone else was also at the car. Someone who stood exactly where the profiler said the killer must have stood, precisely at the point from where the fatal gunshot was fired?'

Marianna nodded. 'Spot on. Exactly the same point. I'd say whoever left the geno is your man.'

'And that DNA doesn't match any convicted felons?'

'Not one.'

'Not even Bruno Valsi – you're sure of that?'

Marianna pressed her lips into a thin smile. 'We're sure of it. Lorenzo Pisano asked the same question. We've double-checked. It's not a match.'

Sylvia sat in silence and tried to unpick the tangle of clues and knockbacks. Forensics didn't seem to be able to put any of her prime suspects at the right scene with the right evidence. Franco Castellani had one gun – his grandfather's Glock – but not two. She'd have to check whether the old man had forgotten there had been two. Franco was undoubtedly connected to all the murders at the pit, but not to Sorrentino. Two killers? Could there really be two killers? Franco and Valsi? An impossible pairing? Nothing was impossible, but this was very close. Then again, there seemed absolutely no forensic evidence to link Valsi to anything. 'Can we get a cross-check between all our DNA samples and the Tortoricci woman?'

Marianna shook her head. 'Again, already done.'

'Lorenzo?' That man always seemed to be a step ahead of her.

'Aha. There's no match there either. To be truthful, the trace evidence from the Tortoricci kill was incredibly poor quality and seemed to come from dozens of different sources, no doubt going back years. We found some hair and flaked skin particles, but it's going to take us centuries to clean it up, replicate it and check the databases.'

Sylvia needed space and time to work it all out. A cold, impossible thought hit her.

Creed.

They had no DNA sample on Creed. He had been their only other suspect. Had they been wrong to write him off?

She rubbed her tired face with both hands. She was grasping at straws and she knew it. 'God, Marianna, I really need a break here. You think I'm hunting one killer with two guns? Or two killers with two separate but similar guns who work together? Or two completely separate killers with almost identical weapons? Or – most likely option of all – do you think I'm just going stark raving mad?'

Marianna laughed. 'No doubt about it – last on your list – you *are* going mad.' She tapped a big stack of files in front of her. 'Now, I need you to take your madness away. I've got my own piling up in front of me.'

# 85

***Fuorigrotta, Napoli***

Gina Valsi's friend Tatiana had been right – the answer to all her problems was to find another man. Not an affair, though. What she wanted was a permanent new man in her life. She prayed to God that her father would kill her vicious bastard of a husband as quickly as possible. She'd grieve for a while. Be supportive towards Enzo. But then she'd start again. Slim down, shape up. Find herself someone who was sensitive. The kind of guy who couldn't kill a spider in a bathtub, but would pick it up and put it out of the window. A guy like that could change your life.

Her love for Bruno was dead. Finally gone. It was a relief.

She felt as if someone she knew were suffering from a fatal cancer. It would be merciful for them to die quickly. Get it over with.

Gina was still mentally rebuilding as she parked her silver BMW X5 outside her factory. She employed more than a hundred *macchiniste* who ran up counterfeit designer garments and made more than a million euros a year for the Family. Some of the clothing even got exported to her father's friends in Russia, Spain and France. The rest went straight into the shops her Family owned in Naples, Milan and Rome.

'*Signora* Valsi,' shouted a voice from a pace or two behind her.

Gina turned and saw two men. One was small and thin with geeky glasses, the other tall and clearly not Italian. His clothes, his face, everything about him told her straight away that he was a foreigner – probably British or American.

'*Signora*, I'm Lorenzo Pisano from the carabinieri. This is Jack King, an American colleague of mine.' Lorenzo held out his wallet ID. 'We'd like to talk to you about your husband.'

Gina was no stranger to men with badges or warrants in their hands and she knew immediately that something wasn't right. Why hadn't they called at her home, her father's home or contacted her through Mazerelli?

'Gina, this is an off-the-record chat,' said Jack, reading her silence. 'It'll take twenty minutes of your time and then we'll be gone.'

Gina bagged her car keys and high-heeled past them. 'Guys, if you don't have any paperwork that says I have to see you, then I don't see you.' They were pushing their luck and she knew it.

'Your husband, Bruno, I'm betting that you're sorry he ever came out of prison?' Jack knew he had to hook her quickly. 'We don't want you to testify or give evidence against him in any way. I just need you to tell me what he's like as a person, what he's capable of.'

Gina screwed up her face in disgust. 'My husband's an animal – a pig – but at least he's not a filthy carabinieri pig like you two.'

Jack could see beyond the words. They barely hid her fear. He stepped forward a pace and blocked her. 'I'm not carabinieri. And neither of us is a pig. We're trying to protect people. Just doing our best to stop women like you getting hurt.' He'd touched a sensitive point. 'You know what I mean, don't you, Gina? He's hurt you in the past – hurt others – hasn't he?'

She moved away from him. He made her edgy. 'I don't know what you're talking about.'

'Where did you meet him, Gina? What was your first date?'

'What?' The question threw her. But it did everything it was designed to. It stopped her panicking, stopped her walking away. 'You want to know what? Where I first dated him?'

Jack smiled at her. 'Yep, that's all. Where and when did he ask you out?'

She relaxed a little. Hands on hips, Gucci bag over shoulder. She slipped back in time. 'He worked for my father. Drove me home from a nightclub after the birthday party of a friend. Asked me if I'd like to go out sometime, and I said yes. Simple as that.'

'Why did you agree to the date?'

'You kidding? Take a look at Bruno, there's not a woman in Naples who would say no to him. What is this? The carabinieri runs some marriage guidance service now?'

'Please, *Signora* Valsi,' pleaded Lorenzo.

She jerked her shoulders. 'He was a good-looking guy, I was a young girl and wanted a boyfriend. Goes on all the time. You guys should get out more; this kind of thing wouldn't be such a mystery to you.'

Jack took the cheek out of her voice. 'He once stabbed the father of a girl he was dating in the testicles, did you know that?'

Gina didn't answer. Nor, noted Jack, did she look shocked or repulsed.

Lorenzo finished off the story. 'And when the girl dumped him, he and his gang attacked her. They held her down and mutilated her.' He put a hand between his legs. 'Just to teach her a lesson.'

'These are sick lies you're making up. If they were true then Bruno would have been arrested. Listen, I'm very busy and have to go.' Gina turned away from them and headed towards the factory entrance.

Jack walked alongside her. 'One last question – I saw you at your father's house the other night. We were in the downstairs lounge and you and your son had just come in.'

'Lucky you. Must have been a treat for you.'

She had thirty metres to go, then she'd be rid of these guys.

'What made you leave your husband? Was it because he was violent towards you? What did he do, Gina?'

She tried to look away from him. But in her mind Bruno was up against her again. Holding her back. Hand to throat. Eyes wide and dark. Ramming himself inside her. Hurting her. Laughing at her. Degrading her.

The door was five metres away.

Jack stepped in front of her again. 'What did he do to you that still frightens you so much?'

Three metres to go.

Jack touched her shoulder. He just let his fingers rest there to stop her moving and to see if he'd get the reaction he expected.

Gina jerked her body away. She stood her ground. Face blazing defiance. She looked ready to fight. Ready to kick and scratch and scream the sky down. 'Don't you *dare* touch me. Don't you *ever* fucking touch me again!'

Now Jack could see it. The full story. As clear as if she'd given a written statement that he had brutalized and raped her. Her own husband scared her so much that she'd fight him. Fight anyone. Fight to the death to protect herself and her child. It was a chilling and, for the profiler, an invaluable insight into what Valsi was capable of.

Gina was crimson by the time she reached the factory entrance. She tried to hide the shake in her voice. 'Leave me alone, or I'll call my lawyer.'

Jack and Lorenzo saw the flash of pure hatred on her face. The door banged and Gina was gone.

# FIVE

# 86

***Il Giardino di Zeus, Napoli***

Mazerelli met Pietro Raimondi twice more within twenty-four hours of their first get-together. But not at his home. Instead, it was in the one place that he was sure would be safe – his private health spa, the Garden of Zeus.

Stripped to their Speedos, sitting in the bubbling water and watched only by marble statues of Greek gods, the consigliere had made certain the officer hadn't been taping anything. They'd spoken openly. And, on Finelli's instructions, Mazerelli had demanded proof of Raimondi's claims. Proof the officer had promised to supply.

Now, Raimondi was literally in hot water. It was delivery time. After tonight there'd be no more talking. He was sure he'd either get his money, or get a bullet in the back.

Between the meetings, Mazerelli had run checks on the lieutenant with other carabinieri on the Family payroll. He was clean as a whistle. No hint of scandal or corruption. But that meant nothing. In Hollywood movies, cops only go bad when they're blackmailed;

maybe a member of their family is threatened with violence or faced with ruin. In real life, the truth is simpler. Cops go bad because it's a short cut to easy money. Double money. Pay from the police and tax-free pay from the other side.

Mazerelli and Raimondi stepped out of the hot tub and dripped water through to the pine-benched changing room.

'So, I will be hearing from you?' The lieutenant changed, then ran a comb through his still-wet, slicked-back hair while bending slightly in front of the mirror on a locker door.

'Let's hope so,' said the lawyer. '*Ciao.*'

Raimondi left. Empty-handed. The way it was supposed to be.

Mazerelli, still with only a towel around his waist, waited a full five minutes on the slatted bench and wondered how all this was going to end. Not good. He had that feeling. And he was seldom wrong.

Red-faced and sweating, Salvatore Giacomo entered from the sauna.

'*Buona sera,*' he said, as though they'd never met before. He took a yellow band off his ankle and used the key to open a stainless-steel locker next to Mazerelli's. The consigliere dressed and left without saying another word.

Five minutes later, Sal the Snake swung open the long, thin metal door of the locker that Pietro Raimondi had just used. He pulled out the blue and white Adidas holdall that had been left in there and didn't even bother to look inside.

If Raimondi was telling the truth, it contained the gun Finelli had used almost twenty years ago to murder a prominent gang member. Proof beyond doubt that the cop really was on the take and had enough ammunition to bring down the whole of the Finelli Family.

# 87

***Stazione dei carabinieri, Castello di Cisterna***

Jack and Sylvia sat in her office updating each other. He recounted his meeting with Gina and his growing suspicions about Bruno Valsi and the Finelli clan. She painstakingly laid out the latest forensic evidence and how it heavily implicated Franco Castellani in all the deaths near the campsite, but not in the Sorrentino murder. And how it didn't put Valsi into any of the murder frames. It seemed they had taken one step forward and two steps back.

'I think Franco's a red herring,' said Jack.

'What exactly does that mean?' queried Sylvia. 'I mean, I know what it means – a sort of false clue – but why the mention of fish, red or otherwise?'

Jack laughed. 'It's an old expression. It means something that's drawing our attention away from what we should be looking at. Herrings are not naturally red but they turn red when they're smoked.'

Sylvia cocked her head in acknowledgement of his explanation.

'I think DNA has smoked Franco Castellani guilty of murder, but he isn't.'

'I'm not so sure. What about his trace evidence being all over the pit, all over the car, and Rosa's underwear being in his bunk?'

'Exactly,' stressed Jack.

'*Exactly?*'

'The panties are the real clue. Franco's a sick kid. His disease has alienated him from society, and especially from women. Like all young men he has urges – probably very strong ones – for female contact . . .'

'And maybe huge hatred and resentment towards those women for rejecting him and his *urges*?'

'Maybe. But let me finish. You and I probably both resent a lot of people for a lot of things, but we don't go around killing them.'

Sylvia jumped in again. 'But – and these are your own words – the two most crucial pieces of evidence we have are the panties, and the DNA on the car door at the spot where the killer stood when he talked to Rosa before he shot her.'

'They are crucial. But I'm starting to believe they're not connected.'

'Meaning?'

'They're contra-indicators. Stolen panties point to a different kind of individual than someone who taunts a victim seconds before he blows her head off with a nine millimetre.'

Sylvia still wasn't done. 'But you're guessing that the killer did that. You don't *know* that for sure.'

Jack's head fizzed with images. Gun raised, girl cowering in the back, boyfriend already dead. 'Believe me, Sylvia, I'm not guessing. I'm sure. Our killer spoke to Rosa before he shot her. That DNA is our killer's and that killer's not Franco Castellani.'

She knew where he was heading. 'And it's not Bruno Valsi's either. The labs say that. They've run comparisons on all known offenders and it's not your boy. I specifically asked about Valsi, and his profile is different.'

Jack stared off into space. Could he be wrong? Could the DNA comparison be wrong? Then he remembered his conversation with Pisano. 'What if it's not Valsi's DNA on file?'

Sylvia frowned. 'I don't understand.'

'Lorenzo said the Camorra once sprang Valsi from a gun rap by having the weapon disappear from the evidence store. What if they got to his DNA profile and switched it?'

Sylvia's stomach flipped. 'You mean the Camorra paid off someone in the Records Office?'

Jack raised a brow. 'Maybe not only Valsi's. Could be that the Camorra do a routine switch on all their top boys. Once their DNA is on file, they pay a mole to switch it. Would be a nice earner for someone.'

Sylvia couldn't bear thinking about it. And if the Camorra had done that with DNA, then they'd have done it with fingerprints too. And blood samples. If the whole of the Records Office had been corrupted, then law and order in Naples was about to fall apart.

Jack moved on. 'You have to get a fresh sample

from Valsi and see if it matches what's on file. And if they're not the same, then see if the new sample matches the DNA on the car door at the crime scene.'

Sylvia felt exasperated. 'We can't just ask Valsi for a sample. He'd laugh in our faces.'

'Sure he would. But maybe his wife would help. Him going back to prison would be a blessing for her.'

'Worth a shot.' Sylvia glanced at her watch. '*Cazzo!* We're late for the briefing.'

They hurried to the Incident Room. The air was already buzzing with voices, the smell of wet clothing and freshly made coffee. Sorrentino's number two, Luella Grazzioli, was standing at the front, fastening diagrams and photographs to a giant whiteboard with coloured magnets. She had long, layered, shaggy brown hair that had once been blonde but now was dark at the roots and full of dried earth and frizzy ends. When all this was over she'd treat herself to a good cut, a fabulous manicure and enough mellow Pinot Grigio to make her lose the power of speech. But, as she put the last of the pictures on the board, she knew those moments of indulgence were still a long way off. She pointed to a grainy aerial shot marked with red crosses, showing opened graves and the spots the radar had pinpointed as most likely to contain more bones.

'Here you can see the five distinct female recovery sites that we've already opened up, including those of the first victim we discovered, Francesca Di Lauro, and the second female, recently identified as Gloria Pirandello.'

Luella paused to let everyone scan the pictures and get their bearings. 'As you can see, these *female* graves radiate in a semi-circle. I have teams working with your crews to complete the other half of the circle, and if you're right,' looking at Jack, 'then we're likely to find more burial sites.' Her phraseology made Jack uncomfortable but he didn't interrupt and hoped his instincts were wrong.

'If you look down from the arc – that clock face, as I know some of you now call it – you can see two more graves. These are roughly twenty metres away from those of Francesca and Gloria. On the way over I got a call from the lab and I can now confirm that these are, in fact, *male* graves.'

It was like a bomb had gone off. First silence as the news stunned everyone. Then an eruption of murmurings.

'Quiet!' shouted Sylvia. '*Male?* You're sure they're male?'

The look on Luella's face said she was sure. 'The sex is confirmed. One hundred per cent certain.'

'And not in the circle,' said Jack, more as an observation than a question.

'No. As I said, they're about twenty metres further away.'

And the photographs on the board spelled it out.

Two dark radar blobs, nowhere near the female graves, and not that near to each other either.

'What made you dig there, out of pattern?' asked Sylvia.

There was a blink of sadness in Luella's eyes. 'Sorrentino had made notes saying where he thought there could be other bodies – outside the circle. I guess he was looking at the lie of the land and working on his own instincts rather than yours. Anyway, when I swept the GPRS over it, these sites looked hot.'

'How long have the males been buried?' pressed Sylvia.

'Can't yet tell you that. Years, not months. At least as old as the females. The lab says most likely older.'

'Any ages?' asked Jack.

'Again, they're working on it. The bones were those of fully grown, fully nourished adults. We can say at least mid twenties. Probably older.'

Jack stared at the markings of where the two male graves were. They made no sense. Didn't fit his clock-face pattern at all. They weren't side by side, not aligned – just dumped, sort of randomly south of where the women had been found.

Luella continued with the lecture but Jack didn't really hear any more of it. He kept studying the seven sites, trying to work out their chronology and their relationships. As soon as the briefing finished he strode over to where Sylvia and Luella were standing.

'I know,' said Sylvia, 'you want to go straight back to the site. Me too.'

'Somehow I thought you might,' said Luella, realizing instantly that her date with that Pinot Grigio had been put back even further.

# 88

***Capo di Posillipo, La Baia di Napoli***

At home, waiting with Ricardo Mazerelli for Sal to arrive with the bag from Raimondi, Fredo Finelli nervously paced his office. 'He should be here by now. He was, what? Only five to ten minutes behind you?'

'The traffic was bad. Don't worry. Whatever all of this is, we can deal with it.'

The sound of tyres crunching on gravel and the burble of guards through the intercom told them the wait was over.

'*Ringrazi il Dio* – thank God,' said the Don. 'As I grow older I become less patient. I like everything planned, Ricardo. Unplanned is unprofessional. Unprofessional is lethal in our business.'

He poured brandies for himself and Mazerelli, and water for Sal. House guards opened up and ushered the *Luogotenente* through to the office.

There were no courteous hellos; Finelli cut straight to the chase. 'Have you looked what's in the bag?'

Sal looked offended. 'No, Don Fredo. *Signor* Mazerelli told me not to, just to bring it straight here. That's wha–'

'Fine. Give it to me.'

Sal placed the bag on the big wooden desk. Finelli snatched it and unzipped it. It seemed to contain nothing but wet trunks and a towel. The Don grabbed the towel and felt his heart pound. There was very obviously something inside. He lifted it out and placed it on the expensive desktop. He felt short of breath as he unfolded the cheap powder-blue towel. In the middle was a soil-stained, old white plastic carrier bag. Finelli ripped it open.

An old Beretta 951 slid out on to the towel.

The Don's face registered shock. Without realizing it, he stepped back, away from the gun.

'Wait!' shouted Mazerelli. He held a finger to his lips. He looked around the outside of the bag, then the inside. He examined the side pockets, straps, logos, floor studs and lining. From his pocket he produced a slim electronic device the size of a credit card and swept it up and down the bag and then all over the gun. 'It's clean. No bugs.' Despite the electronic sweep he still took the holdall outside and placed it further down the corridor.

Don Fredo stood and stared. Twenty years ago he'd held the 9mm weapon. He hadn't seen it since. 'I told Pepe to get rid of the damned gun himself, but he insisted on using that old worm, Castellani. Said we owned his soul and was sure Castellani would dispose of it wisely.'

'Seems he did,' observed Mazerelli. 'Wisely for him.'

Finelli slugged back one of the brandies and poured himself another. 'So, we must take what this carabinieri lieutenant says seriously?'

Mazerelli nodded. 'He's made quite a demand. Two million euros, in return for all the documents, records and . . .' he pointed towards the Beretta, 'other memorabilia.'

Sal caught their attention. 'I can have him and the old man dead and buried by daylight tomorrow.'

'He's thought of that,' countered Mazerelli. 'This cop might be greedy; but he's no fool. He has video-taped testimony from the old man. On top of that, he very clearly knows where other weapons are.'

There was silence. Don Fredo bit at a thumbnail and tried to think.

'There's another demand too,' added Mazerelli. 'He says he wants the eviction order to be lifted on old man Castellani. He and his family are to be allowed to live at the site without any more pressure or threats.'

The Don stopped biting. 'Eviction notice? What are you talking about?'

'Presumably Bruno is intent on forcing them out,' explained the lawyer.

'Christ give me strength.' Finelli looked towards Sal. 'We really are going to have to deal with my son-in-law sooner rather than later.' He turned back to Mazerelli. 'But what about this weasel cop? What can we do about him?'

The consigliere picked up his brandy and swirled

the liquid in the crystal glass while he pondered. 'Two million is a joke. An opening negotiation. I think we can pay him much less. Maybe two hundred thousand. He will argue for more but he'll take the money. We need to secretly record the handover – this is easy enough to do – then we shift the balance of power. He can keep the 200k and we tell him there may be more. But only if he agrees to work for us when we need him, or else we expose him as a bent cop.'

Finelli wasn't convinced. 'And what if he decides 200k is not enough? Or, what if he takes it and still turns everything over to his bosses and then disappears with our money?'

'Point taken,' conceded Mazerelli. 'Then we promise him more money, but in defined stage payments. One million spread over five years in instalments of 200k. He can be a millionaire within half a decade. That is worth hanging around and keeping your mouth shut for.'

Finelli liked it. 'Also buys us time. Time to intimidate the old man. Time to get at the cop from another direction.' He turned again to Sal. 'Find out who both Raimondi and the old man care most about in their sorry little lives – family, girlfriends, boyfriends, I don't care – and then let me know how soon you could make them disappear.'

# 89

*Parco Nazionale del Vesuvio*

It was no longer a colourful clearing in the woods. No longer a wildlife habitat overgrown with trees, bushes and endangered plants.

It was a graveyard.

And it was as silent as a graveyard too.

Exhumations were underway and on the rare occasions when people did speak, they did so in depressingly quiet and reverential tones.

Luella showed Jack and Sylvia where the male graves had been found. They were exactly as shown on the photographs, radar printouts and sketches, but somehow the real thing seemed different. Bleaker. Even more out-of-pattern. The partial circle of female graves was orderly and deliberate. No doubt about that. This had been done with thought. But the other two, the male graves, well, they looked like bodies had simply been dropped out of a helicopter and had landed randomly. Jack mentally completed the circle. One of the men would be inside the female victim circle, the other would be outside. That made even less sense.

Small portable bridges between the graves had been built, with boardwalks carrying excavation and forensic teams from one grave to another. The walks spread outwardly towards the mobile Incident Room vans that stood near the circumference of the circle. Sylvia sloped off and slipped inside the main control van to see some of her team. Luella tagged behind Jack, guessing his thoughts. She'd never worked murders before. Maybe never would again. She wondered how the hell he'd done it all his life and how it hadn't screwed him up.

The whole taped-off area was now about fifty metres in radius, a hundred in diameter. Jack took it all in as he walked to a spot near the centre of the circle. It was about fifteen metres away from one male victim and forty metres away from the other. 'Luella, can you explain the geology for me? What went on with the lava flow around here?'

The question surprised her, but she did her best. 'We're on lower ground, nestled between two small hills. The summit of Vesuvius is north and above us.' She picked areas out with her hands. 'This part here wasn't where the densest flow or fall of lava was. That hillside and this part of the park won't have caught nearly as much of the main pyroclastic flow as Herculaneum and Pompeii did, but you can still see some dense settlements of lava.' She moved closer to where Jack was. 'Remember that when Vesuvius erupted, the air was filled with lava. The spattering was like a huge arterial blood spurt. Some flows were formed when the spatters landed, others came in rivers that oozed in cascades from the brim of the volcano.'

'So you think these were from the spatters?'

'Yes, I think so. Why do you ask?'

Jack put his foot up on the bottom of a mound of volcanic rock. It was virtually at the centre of their gridded-off area. 'This big hill of rocks, for example, was formed by spattering?'

Luella sized it up. 'Not all of it. Some of that lava will have been there since seconds after the eruption. Other lumps, the smaller ones, have come later. I suspect they probably rolled off the eroding hillside to the side of us. No doubt came down as the ground shifted and subsided over the centuries.'

Jack felt drawn to the rocky area and he couldn't quite work out why. Maybe it was because it was the closest to the male bodies? He forced himself to forget the female sites. Imagine he was dealing only with the two male deaths. Now the rock mound started to make sense. One male body was east of it, one west of it. Not quite equidistant, but it certainly looked as though the killer may have used it to get his bearings. A male graveyard and a female one? Could be. Especially if the male graves were older. If he'd *made his bones* killing men, then later on found his fun in killing women. That would make some kind of sense. It would also explain why the female burials were special and the male ones just functional. He hadn't cared much about where he'd concealed the first corpses, but the others – well, the others meant something to him.

'Jack!' The look on Sylvia's face said she'd been talking to him and he'd been ignoring her. In fact, he hadn't even noticed that she'd rejoined them.

'I'm sorry. Give me a minute.'

'Sure.' She fingered her wind-blown fringe from her face and waited patiently. She could see him working out all the pieces of the puzzle, wondering which fitted where.

'Okay,' he said. 'I think I've been too obsessed with thinking about what's *beneath* the ground and haven't given enough attention to what's above it.' He crouched down so he could put both his hands around one of the big chunks of lava. 'This is the only place where several big, broken pieces of the lava are gathered together. All around us we see patches of the stuff, but they are singular patches, with perhaps a crack or two in them. But these little beauties here, well they've been put here. Someone's gathered them from around this clearing and deliberately put them here.'

Luella joined him in a crouch and examined the chunks of rock. 'Looking at this, yes, I would say you're right. These pieces of lava don't come from the same single piece, they are all jagged, and different shapes.'

Sylvia sized up the position of the rocky mound in relation to the circle of female graves. 'This is the centre of his circle of death, isn't it? The middle of his burial clock, maybe even his starting point.'

Jack nodded. 'Yes, I think it is. This is the point that

he got all his bearings from. Every time he returned he would look for this centre and then work out his burial lines. The position of the trees – his marks around the circle – I think they only relate to the female victims. Again, it was his way of differentiating.'

Sylvia pointed outside the arc to the other male grave. 'But what about that other male body? Why is it over there?'

Jack looked at her – he knew that if he gave her a second she'd come up with the answer herself.

'Because it didn't matter?' she suggested. 'Because it meant nothing to him. It was just something he had to do, rather than something of any significance.'

'You've got it.' He turned now to Luella and pointed again at the rocky mound. 'Have your people dig beneath here. If what comes up is a male body, then I'm right and we'll discover a crucial link between our killer and his first victim, *Numero Uno*, his earliest kill.'

'And if you're wrong?' asked Sylvia.

Jack smiled. 'Well, if there's nothing there – or if it's a female body – then theory-wise, I'm blown, and everything I've just said is bullshit.'

# 90

***Centro città, Napoli***

Camorra *Capo* Carmine 'The Dog' Cicerone was a cube of a man with the face of a bulldog. He also had the business brain of a stockbroker. Every day he went to morning Mass and left a soul-saving fifty euros in the wooden collection bowl of the Santa Maria Eliana church. Every night he ate a dinner at *Ristorante Corte dei Leoni* that was large enough to feed Africa. In between, he consulted an astrologist, had a personal daily horoscope compiled for him and carried out his own numerological calculations. Carmine was forty-five, single and obsessively superstitious. Friday the thirteenth was avoided at all costs, as were black cats, walking under ladders and being in the company of lesbians. Lesbians, in Carmine's mind, were devils and witches. Satan had sent them to earth in the form of women and, if you slept with them, then they stole your soul. People had been badly hurt trying to explain the many flaws in his crazy theory, starting with the simple fact that lesbians didn't sleep with men, but Carmine was not open to argument. He knew their tricks. He just prayed that his Church contributions and nightly rosary would protect him.

Carmine would probably have been a laughing stock rather than a crime lord, if he hadn't been a financial genius. He ran legitimate property and investment portfolios through established legal companies and was a millionaire long before he crossed the line into criminality. Legitimate business was what he called the *light* side of his life. While on the *dark* side, he was *Capo* of one of Italy's most powerful crime Families. The Dog was clever enough to realize that to stay rich in Naples, you either had to pay the Camorra, or *be* the Camorra. He'd chosen the latter. He'd infiltrated their world with the same guile and cunning that most businessmen would use to build a global empire. Furthermore, he enjoyed it. Loved it. It was where he got his kicks. There, and in the company of a few select women who, he was absolutely certain, were not lesbians.

In his office, just windows away from the carabinieri's city-centre headquarters, Cicerone held one of his more unusual Management Meetings. In this case it was a grand name for the weekly get-together of the ragged circle of villains who ran his criminal undertakings.

'Profits up and problems down, that's what I want to hear today, gentlemen.' He sounded jovial as he took his position at the top of the table.

The Cicerone crew put up with his eccentricities because year after year Carmine the Dog made them all richer. Privately, Vito Ambrossio summed up their loyalty in one perfect phrase: 'We all like putting our snouts in Dog's bowl because Carmine still has the biggest bowl in town.'

Ambrossio was the Family's main triggerman. When everyone else's nerves snapped and people ran for the hills, he was the guy who would step forward and do the dirty work. He killed a priest in Scampia after the Father publicly spoke out against the Family's drugs activities. And he pulled out a politician's tongue, then chewed off his fingers with bolt cutters after the fool went on television calling for a clampdown on local authority corruption.

Around a long rectangular table of polished mahogany, Ambrossio and five unsmiling men in their late thirties listened to their crime boss and his plans for expansion. Few spoke during the hour-long meeting, and none took notes, mainly because most of them couldn't read or write. But as they disbanded, they all fully understood what the Dog had meant. Unless an accommodation could be reached with the Finelli clan, they would be *going to the mattresses*. The first turf war in years. And Ambrossio for one couldn't wait for it to happen.

Cicerone beckoned Vito to follow him back into his office. They settled around an opulent glass and metal desk in front of a giant picture window overlooking the city's newest skyscrapers.

'What's the latest on the consiglieri? Have Emile and the Finelli man met?'

Ambrossio said they had. He'd spoken to their own lawyer, Emile Courbit, just before the meeting. 'It's taken place. Emile has met him. The photographs have been delivered and Mazerelli said he would come back to Emile within a matter of days. I suspect the bomb has already gone off within their clan.'

Cicerone savoured the thought. 'This is sure to have Valsi and Finelli at each other's throats. Hopefully sooner rather than later.'

'It will be sooner. My information is that Valsi and Finelli are no longer even on speaking terms. The Don has made it known to Valsi that he is not welcome in his house any more.'

'Indeed?' Cicerone's jowly face glowed with pleasure. 'And Valsi's wife and child?'

'Gina and the young boy, Enzo, have moved back in with her father. Meanwhile, Valsi fucks anything female with a pulse.'

The Dog smirked. 'And the men on the ground, what's their mood?'

'As you guessed, they are nervous and are starting to split.'

Cicerone corrected him. 'I didn't guess. I saw it in the stars. An eclipse of Mars; the timing is perfect.'

Ambrossio bit back the urge to tell the Dog that he was barking mad. 'The *white hairs* are with Finelli, they think he is in control and knows how to play Valsi.'

'And the young and hungry ones are with Valsi,'

grinned Cicerone. 'It is always the way. Brutal ambition is forever in the blood of the young and the bold.'

Ambrossio nodded. It was true. And no one was bolder and more brutal than he was.

# 91

***Parco Nazionale del Vesuvio***

The clay was stained and smelled like the sweat of a skunk in summer. After ninety minutes of rock shifting and another sixty of digging, Luella's team called her over. They'd shovelled out a big trench and had found something.

Jack and Sylvia stood way beyond the excavation, outside the crime-scene area, in the safe zone. She could see them talking intensely. Serious faces, sombre moods moulded by death. It was something she still had to get used to. She sent one of the carabinieri soldiers over to get them. They needed to see this.

Luella clambered into the trench and stood at the end of it. Her team had cleared the ground around something bulky, bound in grey-black plastic sheeting. She tried to imagine it was anything other than what it obviously was. A body wrapped and buried in plastic sheeting. A crime-scene photographer hovered above her. He'd already snapped twenty minutes' worth of frames. The pale light dimmed further as Sylvia and Jack appeared at the edge of the dig and peered down. Their faces were full of expectancy and sadness.

'I'm just about to open it,' she said.

Sylvia nodded. Luella dipped her head and hands to the earthy plastic and heard the camera click. It took a while to find the edge of the sheeting. It had been wrapped several times around whatever was in it. 'I'm going to need help. Can you call one of my assistants over?'

Sylvia shouted to the rest of the team. A well-muscled guy called Gelsone slipped into the hole and helped Luella. She directed his hands beneath the sheeted lump and he took the weight as she carefully unfolded the wrapping. It was an awkward job, like getting a king-sized quilt into its cover, only here you couldn't shake anything.

Luella stopped. 'Get a photographer down here.'

The snapper slid into the pit.

'Careful!' shouted Sylvia.

Luella finished pulling back the sheeting. The camera clicked again. The image of the rotted skull burned into everyone's mind.

Body Number One, Jack was sure of it. *Numero Uno.*

But which sex?

And then another revelation rocked them.

The bones were dark, creamy yellow. Unburned.

# 92

***Pompeii***

Paolo Falconi searched in vain. He'd been as far north as Sant'Anastasia, as far east as San Giovanni a Teduccio, as far west as Monterusciello and as far southeast as Santa Maria la Carità. He'd figured Franco would follow the train lines circling the Parco Nazionale, stealing rides in mail wagons, thieving snacks from shops and scavenging slops from restaurant bins. Everyone he'd spoken to knew his cousin was a wanted man. No one had expressed anything that would remotely pass as sympathy. In a town dependent on tourism, Franco wasn't popular.

Paolo drove the family's old white van back to his grandfather's campsite, fully aware of the carabinieri tail that followed him. The old green Skoda Octavia usually stayed three, maybe four, cars back, but sometimes it got confused or careless and ended up just a car behind. Then he would slow down and let a few vehicles pass to give himself cover. That killed Paolo. Only one type of vehicle in Naples *wanted* to get overtaken, so he might as well have strapped a flashing neon sign to the roof saying *Carabinieri Sorveglianza – Police Surveillance.*

Back at the campsite Paolo checked on his grandfather. Antonio was asleep in his chair, looking older and more vulnerable than he'd ever seen him. He kissed his mottled head, grabbed a chunk of bread off a wooden chopping board and went out again.

The Skoda was parked in Via Plinio, cop noses pointing towards the west of the city. Paolo dropped back inside the camp and worked his way east along the fencing for more than a kilometre. He climbed back on to the road just where it met the railway line and Plinio became Viale Giuseppe Mazzini.

The street was wet and dark. Tourists were either gone or were heading back to their hotels for hot pasta and red wine. Paolo felt sure he was unwatched as he zigzagged across Via Colle San Bartolomeo. He skirted round the hospital, Casa di Cura Maria Rosario, then slipped into the southern part of the Pompeii ruins.

Unlike Franco, Paolo hated the place after dark. It gave him the creeps. And tonight, the biting December wind and pale moonlight did nothing to improve things. He'd looked here before in the daylight, but now, after searching everywhere else, he reckoned it had to be worth another try.

An hour later he found Franco. His cousin was sitting alone in the necropolis. Milky light played on the side of his face. Most of his body was hidden in the darkness of night. He was throwing sticks for a wild dog that was so thin you could see every rib in its body.

'*Ciao*, Franco.' His tone was as casual as if it had been only a few hours since he'd last seen him.

Franco looked up. '*Ciao,* Paolo. You got the cops with you?' He sounded croaky. It was the first time he'd spoken in days.

'Like I'm that stupid.'

'You *are* that stupid.' Franco slowly got to his feet and the two cousins embraced.

'*Come stai?*'

'Not so good. I've been puking my guts out. I had some water, though, and a little food. But my stomach still hurts like fuck.'

Paolo held his arms. 'Cops had me and Grandpa in. They've got your face plastered up in windows, mail offices, every-fucking-where. They think you killed some people on the site.'

Franco pulled away. 'Well, I didn't. They can think what they want.'

They talked in hushed voices, their backs turned against the wind, their conversation constantly interrupted by the feral dog that wanted its stick throwing. Paolo told the whole story about him and his grandfather being arrested. Franco told everything – well, almost everything – about Rosa Novello, her boyfriend, and what was left of another woman in his fire pit.

The dog returned and Franco wrestled the stick in its mouth, pulling the mutt backwards and forwards. The two cousins chatted for nearly an hour before

Paolo left. It had felt like old times. Batting the breeze. Talking about something or nothing. There weren't many people in life either of them felt that easy with.

Paolo climbed back out of the ruins and trudged home, lost in his own thoughts.

If he'd been more attentive, he may have seen the grey-faced man hiding in the slim shadow of a doorway opposite the campsite entrance.

The Don had asked Sal to find leverage with old man Castellani. The veteran Camorrista reckoned he'd done just that.

# 93

*Parco Nazionale del Vesuvio*

The bones were almost entirely intact. The hands seemed to be the only parts that had been dismembered. And to make matters even easier, the victim had been buried in his suit and shoes. No doubt about it, stiff number eight was male. And by the cut of his clothes, he'd been buried several fashion generations ago.

Luella Grazzioli hadn't even needed to go back to the laboratory to make a skeletal assembly. The plastic sheeting that he'd been buried in had been lifted out of the grave and laid alongside the mound of lava rocks. Jack and Sylvia watched the scene, illuminated by arc lights, as Luella unpeeled the full horror of the sheet's contents. All manner of creatures had fed on the flesh, fat and ligaments but the plastic had preserved much of the clothing. Jack thought it ironic that many years ago the sheeting had probably been used to *prevent* evidence being left at the murder scene, and now here it was, hopefully *presenting* them with their clearest clues to date.

The skull was a little broken up, but still held together. There was a glaring hole in the right cheekbone and another through the forehead. Everyone guessed they were bullet wounds. The skull showed bigger but corresponding holes in the temporal and occipital bones. The rotted remains of a grey jacket and a shirt were opened up.

The guy's ribcage had been caved in.

'Is that the work of the ground, or his killer?' asked Jack.

'Most likely the ground,' said Luella. 'He wasn't lying flat in the hole. He was all scrunched up. Almost foetal. I expect the weight of the earth and rocks heaped on top of him would have broken his ribcage.'

'What about that?' Sylvia pointed at the left side of the chest, close to the heart. 'Is that rounded nick at the bottom of that rib consistent with a bullet wound?'

Luella looked up from her work. 'I'm sorry, you know that I'm really new to this. I helped Bernardo with the archaeology and the assembly, not the forensics. I'm really not qualified to tell you that kind of thing.'

'But it could be?' Sylvia pressed.

Luella let out a light sigh. She repositioned the skeleton and pulled up the tail of the tattered grey jacket. She looked closely at the back of the ribcage. 'I can't exactly line them up, but there's corresponding damage at the back.'

'The bullet's exit point?' asked Jack.

Luella smiled. 'I'm really, *really* not qualified to –'

'Don't worry, you're not in court and we won't quote you,' said Sylvia.

Luella hesitated. 'Okay. Yes, it looks like an exit wound.'

It all added up for Jack. This was most definitely *Numero Uno*. The first kill. Not nearly as professional as the later ones. He walked around the skeleton. The chest wound would have come from the killer's first shot. Probably aimed for the heart and missed. The victim would have just looked stunned, dropped to his knees, mouth open, hands to his wound. The killer would have panicked and rushed to finish him off. Hence the second shot to the cheekbone. Also not good. Finally the trigger-man would have got his shit together. Probably walked up close and finished the job with a bullet to the brain. Determined but messy. The work of a beginner.

The crime team didn't rush anything. Numerous photographs were taken. Dozens of items were bagged and tagged. Most were mundane and useless. Some were pure treasure. The hands had been hacked off, an old-fashioned way of stopping fingerprint identification, but the skull was good enough to get a very accurate facial reconstruction from. They'd get DNA as well.

There had been nothing in the pockets of the jacket or trousers but there was a label in the waistband, naming the tailor as *Tombolini, Napoli*.

Luella said she'd send bone samples to specialists in Rome for isotopic examination. It would take more than a month to get the results but she was confident they'd confirm her suspicion that the body had been buried for at least ten to fifteen years.

Aside from the forensic clues, there was a big psychological one too. The body hadn't been violated. It hadn't been stripped, let alone burned. It was almost as though there had been respect between killer and victim.

*Respect.*

Jack hung on to the word.

Maybe the kind of respect the Camorra would show to someone?

# 94

***Centro città, Napoli***

Cicerone consigliere Emile Courbit was the son of a French immigrant who'd died of bronchitis in a Neapolitan slum before his fortieth birthday. Emile vowed he'd never suffer the same fate as his father. As a consequence, he worked harder and longer than anyone Carmine the Dog had ever known. The two met just before midnight, the late hour not being a problem for either of them.

'*Ciao*, Emile, you like espresso?'

The lawyer nodded.

The Dog called his PA, also well used to burning the midnight oil, and ordered coffees and water. There was only one thing on the agenda – a meeting earlier that evening with Finelli's consigliere.

'Did he show?' asked the *Capo*, his lush leather chair creaking as he craned forward over the desk.

'*Sì,* Mazerelli came. He said they understood our position, respected our rights. They will pay restoration for their actions.'

'Hmmm,' grunted Dog. 'He say how much exactly, and when?'

Courbit shook his well-groomed head. 'No, not how much. Mazerelli has spoken to his boss and to Valsi. I cannot distinguish whether payment will be made by Finelli or by his son-in-law. But he did promise we would have it within forty-eight hours.'

'If Fredo has any sense he will beat it out of the young blood's hide and make him bring it here on his knees, the money in his mouth like a whipped dog.'

'Amusing thought. But I don't see Valsi backing down. Not if our information on him is correct,' said Courbit. 'It's possible Finelli may pay, even if Valsi doesn't, and then he'll settle the dispute internally. As we know from Vito, all is not well in the Family.'

'I don't care. I just want my money and their undertaking that they will never again trespass into our territory and our businesses.'

'I understand. If they *do* pay, then the question is, what will you see as acceptable and what will you consider an insult?'

Cicerone waved a hesitant hand in the air. 'If Finelli pays, he will be generous. I think maybe half a million. If he leaves it to Valsi, then the stack will be short. Less than two fifty would be unacceptable. Less than six figures would be insulting.'

The tray of coffees arrived, brought in by a young J-Lo shaped Russian girl called Agata. They both fell silent until she'd gone. Then Courbit continued, with a wry smile, 'Do you want these troubles with Finelli to go away, or do you want to try to take advantage of them?'

Cicerone bobbed his big heavy head from side to side as he weighed up his answer. Instinct urged him to wait. Play the long game. But the cards pressed a different case. Today's Tarot had told him to be brave and opportunistic, to be strong when others were weak, to lead and not to follow. 'What would *you* advise, consigliere?'

There was no hesitation in Courbit's voice. 'I would not wait any longer. If you do not kill both Valsi and Finelli in the next twenty-four hours, then one day Bruno Valsi will control our neighbour's clan and you can be sure that he will make it a priority to try to kill you.'

'Twenty-four hours?' The Dog looked amused. Haste was seldom wise in business.

'Yes. Strike now, *before* the payment is made. You will have a story on the streets. Wait until *after* Finelli pays, then you will look unfair. Untrustworthy. After a war, we then have to win the loyalty of the beaten soldiers, we have to become one Family.'

Cicerone liked the idea. But secretly he was frightened. It was one thing to order someone to be beaten up or even killed, but an all-out firefight was something completely different. Something he had no experience of. As usual, he erred on the side of caution. 'Consult with Vito; you will find him in some bar somewhere in the city. Finalize the plans we have spoken of and be ready to explain how they will be executed. I will sleep on your notion and we'll talk before morning Mass.'

Cicerone looked at Courbit and could see that the young man didn't understand his reasoning, his reluctance to draw first blood. Nor should he. At his age, the Dog had known little about the combined powers of God and the Supernatural. But he'd learned his lessons. And so too would Emile. After a brief sleep he'd cleanse his soul, consult the Tarot and then decide whether to fill the gutters of Naples with the bodies of his rivals.

# SIX

# December 22nd

# 95

*3.45 a.m.*
***Stazione dei carabinieri, Castello di Cisterna***

They'd drawn straws – literally drawn straws from the carabinieri canteen – and Claudio Mancini had picked the short one. He dialled the emergency number on the Incident Room wall and waited for *Capitano* Sylvia Tomms to answer the phone.

It was the dead of night and she was going to kill him.

Most of the Murder Squad's graveyard shift watched with amusement as he braced himself for a nuclear blast to the ear.

'What? What is it?' slurred Sylvia. She was coming out of a deep sleep. Brain grinding to find first gear.

'*Capitano*, it's Mancini from the Murder Squad. I am sorry but it is urgent, that's why I'm calling you.'

'What? What's urgent?' She frowned at the bedside clock. Eyes too blurry to read. The digits just red snakes.

'*Capitano*, you left instructions that whatever time it was you wanted to be informed as soon as we had an ID on the Jane Doe in the pit.'

'Yes, I did. Is that what you're calling with?'

Mancini thought he detected a sense of understanding in her voice. Maybe he would be okay. 'Yes. We got DNA back from the lab very late last night and we've been working on an ID ever since. Missing Persons didn't come up with anything but we checked the blood banks and hospitals and . . .'

'Mancini, cut the how, just tell me the *who*.' Sylvia dragged herself upright and propped pillows behind her back.

'Kristen Petrov, twenty-four years old, born in Prague, emigrated when she was nineteen, has been in Naples for three years.'

She was awake now. Wide awake. 'Who the hell is she? Does she have any connections to our suspects?'

Mancini glanced across at a whiteboard. 'She worked as a call handler in a sex centre that the Finelli clan has run for the past decade. You know, they advertise on late-night TV, you can telephone and . . .'

'I know what phone sex is, Mancini. *Un momento* . . .' Sylvia used her phone-free hand to rub an itch from her eyes. 'Get this information to Lorenzo Pisano's office – you know who he is?'

'Yes.'

'Good. Mark it urgent. I'll call him as soon as he gets in. Get round to this woman's apartment and strip the place bare. I want calendars off walls, diaries out of drawers, unwashed underwear, receipts; absolutely *everything* that can tell us *anything* about who she is, who she knows and who she's ever slept with. Got it?'

'Got it,' said Mancini.

The phone went dead and the young officer realized just how short the straw was. His night shift was about to go on for a whole lot longer than he'd expected.

***6.30 a.m.***
***Casa di famiglia dei Valsi, Camaldoli***

The angel-faced lap dancer from Luca's Bar was proving a much better fuck than Bruno Valsi had dared imagine she would be. In his mind, beautiful women usually turned out to be a big disappointment between the sheets. The plain ones usually tried harder. But this babe, well she was an exception. Just how exceptional, Valsi would never know.

Stephanie Muller was a lesbian. She'd slept with him several times and worked hard to pleasure him all night because she needed the money. Especially the big money he was offering for the job she'd do for him later today.

Most of Stephanie's recent life had been a fake. She just switched off and sailed through whatever shit life had thrown at her. The first dollop of brown stuff came her way when she was a stripper in Hamburg. While working the city's Sinful Mile, the infamous Reeperbahn, she fell head-over-heels in love with an Italian businesswoman. She trusted her heart rather than her brain and moved to Naples. Predictably her new Latin lover turned out to have several other Latin lovers and Steph got dumped within the month. Life was a bitch. Penniless and hungry she'd done anything she had to in order to feed herself. And the latest offer that Valsi had made her would keep her fed for a long time.

'I gotta go,' said the twenty-six-year-old, wriggling out from beneath his muscled arm.

'Not yet. I'm not finished with you.'

Steph glanced at the plastic Swatch on her wrist. 'It's six thirty; you know everything I have to do today.' She sat up on the edge of the bed and felt raw and sore. The sheets were marked with blood from the rough anal sex that he'd made her endure. She felt too dizzy to stand. In a second she'd be okay. She looked across the room to find where her clothes had been thrown.

Valsi grabbed a clump of the thick black hair that hung in little-girl curls down her slim pale back and pulled her towards him.

'Ow! Hey!'

'You got time.' He forced her head towards his groin.

There was no point complaining. No point inviting a beating. Steph switched off. Let her attention drift as she did his bidding. The room was pink and green with the kind of carpets, bedding and curtains that she knew she could never afford. The furniture looked antique. Chairs with curved backs and big dark wood wardrobes with matching chests of drawers. A dressing table full of perfumes and a matching full-length mirror. She had no idea what it was worth but she'd love to have stuff like that.

Valsi finished grunting and rolled away from her. 'Okay, get the fuck out of here.'

Steph struggled painfully to her feet. She walked naked to the bathroom and spat his semen in the sink. He'd told her not to use his toothbrush, or his wife's or child's. Both still stood unashamedly in a glass on a shelf, like two abandoned soldiers. She squirted toothpaste on her finger and scrubbed as best she could.

'There's money on the dresser,' Valsi shouted from the bed as she appeared from the shower, recovered her clothes and dressed.

Steph took the five hundred euros he'd placed next to a photograph of two people she guessed were the owners of the untouchable toothbrushes. With any luck this would be the last time she'd be brutalized by him. He'd promised her ten thousand euros for the job she'd do in two hours' time. Ten grand for a morning's work. Not a fortune, but enough to change your life. Rome, Milan or even Florence were good places to start over if you had that kind of cushion in your purse.

She let herself out without saying goodbye. Lit a cigarette as she walked along the driveway to the iron gates that protected Valsi's house. Usually a man emerged from a wooden security hut to flirt with her and let her through, but today no one came.

'Hello!' she shouted, craning her neck around some large laurels that hid the small hut. 'Hello, could someone let me out, please?'

Steph was about to knock on the window but stopped with her hand in mid-air. '*Madonna Santa!* Oh, my sweet God!'

The guard had been shot dead. His blood and brains were sprayed up the wooden back panel of the shed. The man was still seated, his automatic rifle cradled in the crook of his left arm.

Steph froze with fright.

Should she run back to the house and tell Bruno? Or should she just get the fuck out of there as quickly as possible?

She chose the latter.

Shaking. Close to tears. Careful not to look again at the near headless body, she slowly snaked her hand inside the wooden hut and pressed the button that electronically opened the iron gates.

They clanked into life.

She was through them just as soon as the gap was wide enough.

Gone long before they'd finished opening.

***7.30 a.m.***

***Casa di famiglia dei Valsi, Camaldoli***

Bruno Valsi was still in bed when two armed men crept cautiously into his house.

He'd heard them at the front door.

Listened to their hushed voices and creaking feet on the staircase.

Known what to expect.

He grabbed the gun from beneath his pillow, rolled off the far side of the mattress and opened fire.

'Boss, boss! It's us!' The shout came from one of two men who'd just turned up for security duty and found their colleague dead in his hut. 'It's Alfonso and Gerardo.'

Valsi had blasted holes in the bedroom door. 'What the fuck are you doing?' he shouted as they cowered outside the room. 'Get the fuck in here!'

Alfonso, thirty-two years old, entered first; he was white-faced from shock. Gerardo, a young man of just twenty, followed, even more afraid.

Valsi was naked. Kneeling behind the bed. His arms were stretched across the mattress and he gripped a pistol in a shooting stance. 'Put your hands up. Let me see them.'

Their hands went up.

'Walk to the centre of the room.'

They knew the drill. Knew they should never have entered the house without permission.

'So, what the fuck is this about?' he demanded.

'Beppe's dead,' explained Alfonso. 'Someone shot him in his hut and the house intercom is dead as well.'

'What?'

'Bullet in the face. His head is spread everywhere.'

Alfonso looked towards Gerardo. 'Tell *Signor* Valsi what you found.'

Gerardo was so scared he had trouble speaking. 'L-like Alfonso said, he was dead. He *is* d-d-dead, *Signor* Valsi.'

'Calm down.' Valsi waved his gun at the other man. 'Alfonso, throw me those trousers, by the chair.' They looked away as he pulled them on. 'Let's go.' Valsi whipped a used white shirt off the back of the chair, walked barefoot downstairs, through the house and out to the guard hut.

He didn't even blink when he saw Beppe Basso's bloody body. Beppe the Short – that was his nickname – now he really was short.

To be precise, he was about four inches shorter than he used to be.

Valsi bent down inside the hut and found the missing inches, spread across the inside of the roof and the back panel of the guard shelter. 'Fuck and damn!' He banged his fist against the door frame.

He jammed the pistol into the waistband of his pants and turned to Alfonso. 'Call Pennestri and Farina for me. I want them here as soon as possible.'

Valsi headed back to the house. The war was on. This was just the start of it.

He avoided the landline and used an untraceable cellphone to call the Family consigliere.

Ricardo Mazerelli picked up after two rings. *'Pronto.'*

'It's Bruno. I have a dead guard here. Shot in his hut. The cops are going to be all over the joint in minutes.'

Valsi listened closely to Mazerelli's reply. Tried to judge from the tone of his voice how shocked he was. 'Okay, I'll get people round. Have you touched anything?' The lawyer sounded unfazed.

'Not the body, but the hut. Alfonso and some kid were here too. They've trampled the fuck out of the place, probably got their prints and hairs all over the stiff.'

Mazerelli noted that Valsi hadn't even had the decency to give the dead guard a name. The guy was a monster. Nobody mattered but himself. 'Have you called the police, or had anyone ring them?'

'No. Not yet. You want that I do that?'

'No. I'll do it. Put the phone down now and get in a taxi and come straight over to my apartment. Bring with you any clothes you were wearing when you went near the guard. Don't speak to anyone else.'

'Okay.' Valsi clicked off his phone and smiled. He knew Mazerelli would call the cops and make sure there were no loose ends when they came asking questions. Cleaning up was part of his job. After that, he would call his father-in-law and the old man would presume the hit had come from a Cicerone triggerman. The last thing he would suspect was that in the dead of night Valsi had sat laughing and joking with one of his own guards and had then shot him dead. What a turn-on that kill had been. No wonder the little lap dancer could barely walk this morning.

The game had begun. And like he'd told Mazerelli, he wouldn't be playing by any rules.

*7.58 a.m.*
***San Giorgio a Cremano, La Baia di Napoli***

After the call from Mancini, Sylvia Tomms had fallen into a heavy sleep and missed the alarm. Once more she found herself being woken by the bedside phone.

'*Pronto.*' She was alert within a second. It was Pietro Raimondi. Had he not talked so fast, she would have torn him off a strip for taking to his sick bed when so much was happening. Instead, she listened intently as he filled her in on the call he'd just received. There'd been a shooting at Bruno Valsi's home. A security guard had been killed in his gate hut. His lawyer had phoned to report the murder.

'Where's Valsi now?' she asked.

'On his way to the station house, with his lawyer, Mazerelli.'

'*Cazzo!*' Sylvia scrambled to the bathroom. 'I'll be there as soon as I can. Maybe half an hour, forty minutes. Depends on the traffic.'

'Don't worry. I'm only five minutes away. I'm told Major Pisano is en route as well.'

She dropped the phone and ran the shower. Thank God Pietro was back. One thing annoyed her, though. How had he known about Valsi before she had? And how come he knew that Pisano was already on his way?

*8.15 a.m.*
***Centro città, Napoli***

Thunder boomed and rolled. Forked lightning cracked the grey sky and darted across the darkened bay. It looked more like late evening than early morning as Mazerelli's Lexus emerged from a maze of cobbled backstreets and parked at a nightclub the Family owned near the carabinieri's central HQ.

At the front desk, Mazerelli introduced himself in a very deliberate manner. 'I am Ricardo Mazerelli, legal representative of Bruno Valsi. A short time ago I telephoned this station and reported a murder at *Signor* Valsi's home in Camaldoli. It is now a little after eight fifteen a.m. and, as promised during my call, my client and I are here to assist you in any way we can.'

'Who did you talk to?' asked the male desk officer, sounding bored as he ran a chubby finger down a ledger for times and notes.

'Lieutenant Pietro Raimondi.'

The desk jockey scanned a list of extensions pinned to the top of his desk. 'Raimondi is not stationed here.'

'I know,' snapped Mazerelli. 'I called your switchboard and they put me through to him. He'll be arriving here shortly.'

'Then take a seat, over there.'

'First, please make a note of the time of our arrival.' Mazerelli turned his wrist and ostentatiously tapped his watch. 'Eight eighteen.'

The officer glared at the lawyer. 'Your time of arrival is noted. Now, please take a seat.'

'In a moment.' Mazerelli leaned forward over the desk to check the time had been entered in the ledger. 'Fine. Thank you.' He touched Valsi on the shoulder and they settled in some black plastic chairs by a window. Valsi grabbed a magazine from a wobbly-legged table piled high with old reads.

'Raimondi will be here shortly,' said the lawyer. 'With a little luck we'll have all the formalities done within the hour. Then we'll be out of here.'

'No rush,' said Valsi. 'They can take as long as they like.' And for once, he meant it.

Right now, there was nowhere else he'd rather be than in the company of the carabinieri.

***8.20 a.m.***
***Capo di Posillipo, La Baia di Napoli***

Gina Valsi's hair was still a little wet. She and her son Enzo had been swimming in her father's indoor pool when Don Fredo had been told of the guard's murder. Not surprisingly, the Don had chosen not to say anything to his daughter as he breakfasted with her and his grandson in the conservatory.

'You look tense, *Papà*,' observed Gina. 'Work is giving you problems already?'

He laughed dismissively. 'Work is always giving me problems.' He poured coffee from a silver pot. 'You want some more?'

'No, *grazie*. I have to get Enzo ready for the child-minder.' She ruffled the boy's hair as he dabbed a jammy fingertip into a plate full of croissant crumbs. 'Go scrub your teeth. And make sure you do them properly.' She bared her gums and waggled a finger up and down as he escaped to the bathroom. Gina turned back to her father. The top of his head was now all that was visible above a wall of newspaper. 'I'm going to have Leonardo bring my car round. *Papà*, do you want me to call your driver too?'

Finelli didn't hear his daughter; his mind was elsewhere, and not on the newspaper. Cicerone had some balls whacking his son-in-law's guard. If they'd waited twenty-four hours then they'd have got their money in full. A generous amount as well. A pre-emptive strike like this was meant as a warning. Or a challenge. When Mazerelli was finished with Valsi, then he'd call him in. After that he'd ring Cicerone himself and see where they stood. He doubted Carmine the Dog wanted a war. But if he did, then he'd certainly give him one. A war to end all wars. Perhaps the killing was a way of hiking the settlement price up and showing his own clan that he wouldn't be publicly disrespected. If that was the case, he could live with it.

'*Papà*, do you want your car? You're supposed to be at the doctor's in thirty minutes.'

The paper wall crumbled. '*Merda!* I'd forgotten.' Finelli sprang to his feet. '*Grazie*. I'll be there in a minute. God, the traffic will be awful now. I should have left ten minutes ago.'

Gina smiled. Her father was growing increasingly forgetful. She and Enzo had lived with him for only a short time, but already it felt as if she were looking after two children. Yesterday he'd forgotten she was cooking dinner and he'd eaten before coming home. And now today he'd almost missed his monthly check-up and blood tests. His cholesterol had shot up over the past year and the doctor said he was now borderline for type 2 diabetes, hence the checks.

Enzo reappeared, toothpaste all around his mouth. Gina couldn't help but laugh. 'Come here. At least I can see you scrubbed.' She picked up a napkin from the table and he wriggled while she wiped away his white moustache. 'My sweet baby, you're growing up just fine, aren't you?' She straightened his jumper, tucked in his shirt and kissed his head.

Then he hit her with it.

Straight out of the blue.

'*Mamma*, why doesn't *Papà* live with us any more? I miss *Papà* being with us.'

Gina caught her breath. What could she say to her beautiful baby-faced child? How could she explain that when his father wasn't playing soccer with him in the garden he was torturing people and raping his mother? 'He's busy, Enzo. You'll see him again, soon.'

Busy – what a great word to cover his father's multitude of sins. The boy took it at face value and looked disappointed. For a second Gina felt sad that the next time Enzo would see his father would be in a box at a funeral parlour.

But only for a second.

*8.30 a.m.*
*Pompeii*

The Visitors' Centre opened daily at eight thirty, but in winter the coach parties seldom arrived before ten. Franco had been sitting for hours with his back against a wall of the ancient amphitheatre. Cradled in his hands was his grandfather's Glock. Simmering in his mind was the thought of how he'd use it.

After Paolo had gone he'd roamed the ruins. Imagined he was the sole survivor of the eruption of Vesuvius. The strongest of them all. The ruler of all he surveyed. Now the darkness was gone and so was his dream.

The grey light of another drizzly morning brought with it the harsh reality of the impending crowds. Those who would come to stop and stare. Well, today he'd give them something to gawp at.

Franco got to his feet. His bones ached. Blood rushed to his head and pounded hard in his temples. He was short of breath and it took him several minutes of walking before he felt okay.

He could hear voices from a long way off. Workers moving down Via dell'Abbondanza, the long cobbled road that stretches past the Stabian Baths. They were heading into the Forum and then the Basilica and Temple of Apollo.

Soon they would be around him. Their eyes on him. Scorching his skin with scowls and prejudice.

For a moment the December sun dodged a rain cloud and painted the cobbled streets and stone walls in shimmering gold.

Franco hoped Paolo and his grandfather would forgive him. Not only for what he'd done – but, most of all, for what he was about to do.

He put his hand in his pocket. One more shot of heroin. Two more magazines of bullets.

It was enough.

He set off on his walk. His final walk around Pompeii.

***8.45 a.m.***
***Capo di Posillipo, La Baia di Napoli***

The Mercedes Maybach wound its way down the spiralling hillside. The interior temperature, as always, was twenty degrees. Outside it was down to four. And it was foggy too. Fredo Finelli sat in the back reading *La Gazzetta*, trying not to think of the doctor's appointment and how late he was going to be. This was the crunch meeting. If his blood sugar levels hadn't normalized, then they were going to start treating him for diabetes. That's what they'd warned, and he was damned sure that was what was going to happen.

He'd ignored symptoms of raging thirst, dizziness, tiredness and headaches for as long as possible. Now he simply hoped that whatever they decided to do, it wouldn't involve needles. He'd heard somewhere that these days there were tablets that could be taken instead. If a clean bill of health wasn't in the offing, then that's what he wanted.

The 62S was itching to go, keen to get on the autostrada and ignite its V12 engine. Instead, the traffic was getting worse. Soon it was forced to a halt.

'What's wrong?' Fredo called from the back.

Armando Lopapa, a fifty-year-old no-nonsense Neapolitan who'd been his driver for more than a decade, slid down the dividing glass. 'I'm not sure. It's not the car in front. Must be something ahead of that. Looks like a kind of accident.'

'Probably the damned fog. People seem to have forgotten how to drive properly these days.'

The driver behind them honked his horn.

'Go see what it is,' insisted the Don. 'Get them out of the damned way.'

Armando did as he was told. The horn behind him blared again. 'Hey, fuckhole, shut the fuck up,' he shouted, slipping on his chauffeur's cap.

A racing bike lay on the misty blacktop. A teenage boy in yellow cycling Lycra was struggling to sit up. He was holding his face and had badly cut legs. A thirty-something businessman in a blue suit leaned over him. 'He fell. I didn't hit him,' he protested weakly. 'It was an accident, I did nothing.'

Armando wanted to backhand him. He was clearly the kind of asshole who wouldn't slow down for a kid on a bike. Naples was full of them. Maybe later he *would* slap him. 'You okay?' he asked the boy. The youngster was about fourteen, could easily have been his own son. 'Can you stand up?'

The driver behind them blasted his horn once more, got out, banged shut his door and joined them. 'What the fuck's happening? I'm really late for a meeting. Can't we get things going here?'

'Kid fell off his bike,' repeated the coward in the suit.

Armando ignored them both and checked his watch. The Don would be furious if this wasn't sorted quickly.

'My head hurts, I feel really sick,' groaned the kid. He looked shaken, maybe concussed.

'Come on,' said Armando. 'Let's get him to the side of the road. Someone call an ambulance.' He moved round the boy and carefully put his arms under his body. He knew he should really leave him until medical help arrived but there wasn't the time, so he tried his best to keep the kid's head and spine straight.

Traffic was backing up badly. Inside the Merc, Fredo Finelli was growing impatient. He'd give it another five minutes and then call the doctor and rearrange his appointment.

The jerk in the blue suit picked the boy's bike up and wheeled it about twenty metres down the road and rested it against a tree. Meanwhile, horn blaster called for help on his mobile, then muttered more about being late for something and headed back to his car.

Armando quickly settled the kid on the grass verge and checked him again. 'It'll be all right, we'll have a doctor here pronto.' The kid rolled over on to his side and clutched his head, then pulled up his legs. 'You okay? Try to stay still. Don't move about, you might do yourself some more damage.' Maybe that bastard in the car had hit him after all.

But the kid wasn't in pain.

The blood on his legs and face was fake.

He was curled up because he was taking cover.

The car at the front of the Mercedes, and the one at the back, blew up simultaneously.

The Merc's custom-made bulletproof glass and reinforced metalwork could only do so much. The explosion flipped the Maybach like a pancake. It flopped and tumbled over the crash barriers. Slid down the hillside, taking out trees and rolling over boulders.

The noise ruptured Armando's eardrum and the blast threw him to the ground. He scrambled to his feet and ran to the edge. The car had fallen nearly twenty metres on to rocks. The windows were blown out and the roof was mangled. It had dropped on to the road below, broken through the next set of barriers, then careered down another part of the hillside.

Armando turned round.

He was alone.

The boy and everyone else had gone.

It had been a classic hit.

***9.00 a.m.***
***Santa Maria Eliana, centro città, Napoli***

Morning service was a traditional Latin High Mass. As always, Carmine Cicerone settled down to what he knew would be a truly uplifting experience. A spiritual detox.

Thunder rumbled outside but there was still enough daylight to shine sharply through sections of the pristine stained-glass windows that depicted the Stations of the Cross and ran the complete length of the seventeenth-century church. A pepper cloud of dust swirled in multicoloured shafts of light and a small rainbow fell across the white marble of the altar floor. Carmine the Dog loved everything about going to church. The architectural grandeur of the building. The deeply colourful and symbolic costumes. The centuries-old script. Even the smell of frankincense swung by the broody-looking altar boy whose eyebrows met in the middle. It was wonderful. Pure theatre.

Today he placed two hundred euros in the rose-wood collection plate that passed down his pew and he thanked God for making him wise enough to have slept on things. The plan that Vito had put together and shown him just before he'd settled in his pew was crude and shabby. He really wished he could instill a more businesslike approach in the man. Put bluntly, he'd advocated the simultaneous killing of Finelli, Valsi and as many other of their *Capi* and soldiers as they could manage. A day of bloodshed, then a decade of peace, that's what he'd promised. No, thank you. Carmine wasn't buying. He knew it was shrewder to take compensation from Finelli and then let his clan rip itself apart. Once they were weak, then he might consider finishing them off.

The service lasted forty-five minutes. He looked around at the end and was sad to see that the grand old church was virtually empty. Never mind – Father Mario had still put on a stellar performance. Carmine had taken *la sacra Comunione* and, as he filed out behind half a dozen people, he felt positively rejuvenated.

As usual the back of the church was littered with homeless drifters who'd come in off the street to shelter from the weather. He dipped his hand into the holy water, made the sign of the cross facing the altar, and then turned to walk outside into the bright winter sunlight. He was right to have chosen peace, not war. He and Fredo Finelli would talk. They'd find common ground and then they'd both enjoy the rest of their lives.

*9.00 a.m.*
*Capo di Posillipo, La Baia di Napoli*

It took Armando Lopapa almost ten minutes to run from the first broken barrier on the bend of the winding hillside road to the second one. He was breathless by the time he reached the mangled metal and peered over the side at the crushed and crumpled Mercedes. The car had hit all manner of rocks and trees on its deadly drop. He called the emergency services, then hurdled the last barrier and began the final steep climb down the ankle-twisting terrain.

'Please God, let him be alive,' said the loyal chauffeur, his suit patched with sweat and his cap long since lost.

First glance at the $300,000 Mercedes told him that despite layers of armour plating, it was still a write-off.

He replayed the astonishing events as he descended. A double blast. Two cars parked front and back. The car flipped like pizza dough. Someone had clearly known their route. Had been aware of the strict drill that made sure the Don always stayed the other side of the anti-hijack locks and bulletproof glass until he was assured that everything was okay. Some safety drill. It all seemed pointless now. The attackers must have known about that too, and the fact that the Maybach was a tank, so strong it would have stood a chance of surviving one blast. But not two. Especially when they were coordinated and calculated so well that the car would be sent plunging down the rocky hillside. It was an inside job. About as inside as you could get.

Armando put his hand to his mouth. 'Oh, fuck!' He was close enough to see now. Fredo Finelli lay jammed up against the back headrests. Tossed there like a rolled-up umbrella thrown in the back in case of a rainy day.

'Don, Don Fredo!' He didn't expect an answer but hoped beyond hope that he might get one.

He could see blood now. Spread and spattered across the cream trim and matching leather.

The doors had locked and Armando couldn't get in. Shards of glass stuck up like stalagmites from the rubbers on the door frame. Armando took off his jacket, balled it up and knocked them out. Finally, he was in.

The left side of Don Fredo's face was smashed up. His jaw broken and out of line. Teeth had been hammered back. There was so much blood in one eye socket that it seemed the eye was missing too.

Armando felt sick. He put two fingers to the Don's neck and felt for a pulse.

Nothing.

He shuffled his hand around a little to see if he'd missed it.

Still nothing.

The Don had been good to him, always paid him well, always respected him. The sense of loss kicked in. Death is truly awful when you're the first to discover it.

*Thump.*

He couldn't believe it.

*Thump, thump.*

A slow but slight beat between his fingers. My God, the old bastard was actually alive!

He put his face close to the Don's mouth and checked for breath.

Nothing.

*Thump.*

*Thump, thump.*

Outside he could hear voices. Help was close at hand! Thank God.

'Here! In here!' he called.

Armando could see the feet and trousers of the paramedics descending the last rocks. They'd know what to do. They'd save him.

*Thum–* The pulse fell again.

'Quick! Please, come quick, he's dying!'

*Thu–* Fainter.

'Hey, we came as quick as we could,' said a calm male voice.

Armando turned to the side window. His eyes widened just before a bullet smashed into the middle of his face.

Romano Ivetta lowered his weapon and fired two more shots into the still-beating heart of Fredo Finelli.

*9.00 a.m.*
*Napoli*

En route to the Anti-Camorra Unit's HQ, Sylvia pulled over to the side of the road and took another call from the Murder Squad. This time it was one of the coordinators, Susanna Martinelli. 'Boss, Missing Persons have come back with a match on victims three and four.'

Sylvia held her breath. 'And – are they our women?'

'Yes. Yes, they are.'

Sylvia didn't know whether to feel elated or dejected. 'Go on.'

'Victim number three is Patricia Calvi. That's the nineteen-year-old student from Soccavo.'

Sylvia remembered her. Long brown hair, razor-thin eyebrows, pale brown eyes. She'd been missing almost six and a half years. 'And the other?'

Susanna read from her notes. 'Luisa Banotti, the secretary from Santa Lucia. She's been missing seven years and two months.'

Sylvia recalled the photographs. She'd looked much younger than her twenty years. Dark hair – like all the victims – but very fine and barely shoulder-length. Eyes pale blue and beautifully large, like a child's. 'Have we informed the families?'

'Not yet. We've got positive DNA matches, so now we can call them in. Do you want to be there?'

Sylvia wished she could. She hated this kind of news being delegated. 'I can't. Can *you* look after it? Make sure the parents have time to talk about it, don't rush them.'

'Sure. I'll be careful.'

'Thanks.' Sylvia started the engine and was about to ring off.

'Boss, one more thing. Bernadetta Di Lauro just rang. Can you call her back?'

Sylvia turned off the engine and took down the number. What could she want? An update? A complaint? Just someone to talk to?

Francesca's mother answered on the second ring. '*Pronto*. This is Bernadetta.'

'*Signora*, this is *Capitano* Tomms. My office said you just called and asked for me.'

Francesca's mother sounded surprised. 'That's very fast. It's less than ten minutes since I rang.'

'How can I help you?'

'I hope I'm not wasting your time. You said if I remembered anything . . .' for a moment she struggled, 'then I should call you! Well, to be honest, there is something. Something I should have told you last time we met but I couldn't bring myself to say it.'

'*Signora*, whatever you say to me is in complete confidence.'

Bernadetta relaxed a little. The policewoman seemed to understand her desire not to share in public any private thoughts about her daughter.

'*Grazie*. It's a long time ago. And I'm not really sure if it's that important, but –'

'Please let us be the judge of the importance, *Signora*.'

'Okay. I think Francesca *was* seeing someone. A married man.'

Sylvia's investigative senses prickled. 'Do you know who he was?'

Bernadetta let out a sigh. 'No. No, I don't. Not at all. Like I told you at your office, Francesca was a very private person. She didn't talk a lot about the men in her life.'

'So why do you think she was seeing a married man?'

'There was an old film on TV, with Tony Franciosa in it. The one in which he and his wife both have a string of affairs, and I said to Francesca that she should steer clear of married men as they brought nothing but trouble. She laughed and said it was a bit too late for that. I asked her what she meant. She went shy and said she was just joking. But I don't think she was. She looked awkward that she'd said it. I tried to get her to discuss it some more but she grew quite irritated with me.'

'And the reference to *too late*, you now think that was because she was already pregnant?'

Bernadetta paused. 'I don't know. I torture myself by going over every word she ever said to me. Maybe I should have pushed her more. Maybe she was trying to let me in and wanted me to make her talk about it. But I couldn't. She just clammed up. I'm sorry.'

Sylvia told her not to blame herself, but she could tell her words had little effect. She thanked her for the call and drove away.

*A married man and a dead, pregnant woman.*

It was an interesting development. A development that at last might provide them with a motive and a link to someone.

# 96

***9.50 a.m.***
***Pompeii***

Luciano Creed was playing a waiting game. Something that irritated the hell out of freelance journalist Cassandra Morrietti. 'I have deadlines and I have bills,' she glared at him over the bad espresso she'd bought from a tourist bar near the Castellani campsite.

'Patience, Cassandra. Patience.'

Creed was backing a hunch. When he and the hack had posed as cops, old man Castellani had told them that his grandson Franco was missing. He was certain he knew why. Franco was the kidnapper and murderer they were all hunting. The photograph he'd been given by the doting grandfather showed the kid to be hideously deformed. Freaks like that don't get sex. What they do get is the urge to abduct pretty women, fuck them and then kill them because they can't risk letting them go. It was simple stuff and he was amazed King, Tomms and the rest of the carabinieri hadn't been clued up to it. Actually, he wasn't that amazed. They were all a bunch of fools and not bright enough to realize that sometimes the most obvious things were overlooked. Well, that wasn't a mistake he was going to make.

'Trust me,' he told the journalist. 'We follow the freak's cousin and he will lead us straight to the freak killer. Then all your waiting will have been worthwhile.'

Cassandra was about to argue the point, when she had to swallow both her words and the last of her espresso. 'There's our boy!' Creed nodded across the road. Paolo Falconi was heading straight towards them.

***9.50 a.m.***
***Santa Maria Eliana, centro città, Napoli***

The sun seemed to bless Carmine Cicerone as nine a.m. Mass finished and he emerged from the heady smell of burning candles and the calming cool of the church. It was almost as though God had lifted the fog for a moment to show his personal approval of the Dog's decision to choose words rather than war.

God – and a truly great Tarot reading.

According to his daily Internet subscription, Gemini's moon was in conjunction with assertive Mars. A bountiful Sun–Jupiter square was in the offing, as was an imbalanced Venus–Uranus quincunx. Now was plainly not the time for rash and foolish actions.

Halfway down the double flight of stone steps that grandly spread east and west on to the pavement, he narrowly avoided bumping into two preoccupied nuns.

They were in a line, hurrying in for the next service. It was one of those awkward encounters when one person moves left and so does the other, then everyone swings in the other direction at exactly the same time. '*Scusi*,' he smiled politely, then stood still so they could choose whichever direction they wished.

'*Grazie*,' replied the smaller of the sisters at the front. Then she smiled at him. She had a lovely face. Even seemed flirtatious. Carmine had a sinful thought. He chastised himself. Seconds out of church and he was needing confession already.

The pretty nun was still staring at him when the holy sister just behind her stepped forward and shot him. The silenced bullet fizzed from beneath the Bible in her hands. Hands so big they were now clearly not female. The cough of the 45 was swallowed in the jackhammer noise of rush-hour traffic. Not a single head turned on the nearby pavement.

Carmine went down on his knees, like an opera singer centre stage in the final act. He clutched his heart and opened his mouth wide to hit the top note. The death note. His two men, waiting metres away in his limo, would have sprung to his aid, only they were both dead as well.

The holy sisters disappeared down the side of the steps and headed towards the back of the church. Twenty metres further on they slid into the shade of an alleyway, slipped off their grey habits and heavy wooden rosaries. Sister Vito Ambrossio folded everything into two white supermarket shopping bags and handed the gun to Sister Steph Muller. She pushed it deep into the front of her patched jeans and covered it with her shirt and thick jumper.

Stupid idiot, thought Vito, it was good to be finally rid of him. Valsi had promised him his own territory, half the Cicerone turf and a key position in the bigger Family. Fancy Carmine the Dog, Carmine the great business brain, not understanding how takeovers and consolidations worked.

At the end of the alleyway Steph turned left and Vito turned right. Both became invisible in the bustle and business of the rush-hour streets.

They would never meet again. As Vito vanished he started laughing. That old Dog Carmine had been right after all. You just shouldn't trust lesbians.

***9.50 a.m.***
***Pompeii***

Paolo Falconi had already finished most of the chores that usually lasted until lunchtime. Today he needed time on his side, time to spend with Franco. He'd shifted the overnight rubbish from outside the campers' vans and chalets and stacked the bags on a bonfire in a field, far from the campers. Since the incident in the pit, the carabinieri had blocked off their usual burning spot, so he'd had to create a new one. He'd burn everything at nightfall, when everyone was in bed – just as Franco had done.

Chores completed, he followed the first part of the

route he'd taken the night before. He wasn't surprised that there was no sign of the carabinieri Skoda. The cops were probably lazy as well as clumsy. He could see the street clearly and felt confident he wasn't being watched, so he took a more direct route to the ruins. He passed a row of gift shops, cheap cafés and ice-cream bars, then headed up a side street away from the main visitors' entrance. He didn't notice Creed or Morrietti, arm in arm, fifty metres back. Minutes later he was inside the ruins, courtesy of one of several secret routes that he and Franco had used since they were kids.

School kids were already strolling down the narrow streets, shepherded by their teachers. It didn't seem five minutes since he and Franco had been doing the same.

Paolo knew he'd find his cousin in one of three places. He struck out on the first two – the Forum Granary and the Amphitheatre, the last being where he'd seen him last night.

He rounded the south side of the ruins, near the Quadriporticus, and stuck close to the outer walls until he reached the Garden of the Fugitives. There, alongside the huddled plaster figures of the dead, was Franco.

The glass-panelled door that normally held back the viewing public had been broken open. His cousin was sitting cross-legged, leaning against the reconstructed corpse of one of the youngest of Pompeii's doomed youth. He was shoulder to shoulder with the cast of someone who'd died almost two thousand years ago.

Paolo was shocked to see Franco's left sleeve was rolled up and in his lap was a syringe. He'd been unaware he'd had an extra stash of heroin. More disturbingly, in his right hand was his grandfather's old gun.

His finger was wrapped around the trigger.

To Franco, the world felt blurred and smeared, as though it had been wiped by a giant wet hand across the inside of his eyes. Everything was soft and slow. All the edges had gone. All his anger dissipated.

Franco Castellani felt normal.

Wonderfully normal.

How funny. Franco had heard that most people took hard drugs to make them feel great. He was more than happy just feeling *normal*.

Through the smears he could see his cousin moving towards him. His face looked taut and stressed.

*Poor Paolo.*

He wished he had an extra spike to share with him.

Even though the heroin had numbed his senses, Franco clung to the golden thread of his plans. He knew what he had to do. Those people who'd come to stare – to gawp at Pompeii and to scowl at him – would see a sight they'd never forget.

He raised the palm of his left hand in a 'stop' gesture to his cousin. Then he raised his grandfather's gun to his head.

But Paolo Falconi didn't stop. He knew what Franco intended to do, and it wasn't going to happen.

Franco forced a smile and mumbled his final message, 'Love you.' A surge of energy ran from his brain down to his hand and into his trigger finger. Like he was plugged into heaven's own generator.

Franco shut his eyes and pulled.

Paolo threw himself. A desperate, last-second lunge.

The gunshot roared and echoed across the ruins.

# 97

***ROS Quartiere Generale (Anti-Camorra Unit), Napoli***

Ricardo Mazerelli apologized as his cellphone rang in the middle of the carabinieri interview. He turned it off, let the voicemail deal with it and then switched his attention to Pietro Raimondi. 'Lieutenant, I called because I hoped you could deal with today's developments within the framework of our new relationship. Do we have an understanding here?'

'Of course.' Raimondi gave the hint of a smile.

Valsi scowled at his brief, then leaned over towards the officer. 'I want to give a full interview and I want to give it now. That's presuming a piece of shit like you can actually write.'

The lieutenant had never been the type to allow himself to be intimidated. The two men stared at each other. Less than a metre of air separated them. Valsi didn't frighten him. '*Signor* Mazerelli, tell your client to watch his foul and offensive mouth, or he'll need a dentist and will be spending a lot longer in here than he needs to.'

Raimondi heard a voice of calmness in his ear:

'Keep it cool, Pietro.' Not the voice of his inner self, but that of anti-Camorra boss Lorenzo Pisano, whispering through a micro-receiver earpiece.

'We'll take your written statement in good time,' said the lieutenant politely. 'Please be patient, I have just a few more preliminary questions.'

'Very good,' said Lorenzo in his earpiece. Raimondi had gone straight to him after interviewing Antonio Castellani, and the major had pulled his strings ever since. If all went well, Raimondi would be in line for promotion and a big salary rise. He'd probably need a transfer too. He and Lorenzo had put Sylvia in the picture only moments before starting the interview with Valsi.

Standing in the darkness of the monitor room, she watched the interview unfold and told Jack how Pietro had deceived her.

'I understand the need for confidentiality. Of course I do. But damn it, he could have trusted me.'

Jack chose not to comment. Local business was always quicksand and best avoided. 'What's Valsi's game, walking in here all lawyered-up? Why do that? Why not make your guys chase around after him?'

Sylvia cleared her head of Pietro. 'I'm thinking the same. Maybe he was just spooked by someone whacking his guard and thought here was a safe place to be until he could mobilize muscle and ammunition.'

Jack studied the young Cammorista. Spooked was a word that didn't fit. The man exuded violence. It glowed around him like a force field. Nope, he wasn't buying spooked.

'You tempted to ask him about Kristen Petrov? Or maybe drop Francesca Di Lauro's name in his lap and see if he jumps like you spilled hot water on his gonads?'

'Very tempted,' said Sylvia, 'especially as Bernadetta Di Lauro told me this morning that five years ago Francesca may have been having an affair with a married man.'

'Valsi and Francesca?' Jack pondered on it. Fire and ice. A striking couple.

'But I think we should wait. I have no forensics to link him to either woman. Not yet. Things might change in the next few days.'

'If that dead guard is the start of a turf war, then things are going to change mighty fast and Valsi could be pushing up daisies in a few days' time.'

Their attention returned to the TV monitor. Pietro was asking the *Capo Zona* about his movements last night. Who he'd been with? Who could alibi him? Valsi was toying with Raimondi. Promising to show him footage of the woman he'd fucked all night, a woman who wouldn't look twice at a streak of carabinieri piss like him.

Sylvia's phone rang. She moved quickly to the back of the room to take it and then hurried outside. There was someone in reception, directed there by the Incident Room, and it was urgent.

Lorenzo flicked a talkback switch on the control panel. 'Pietro, ask Valsi about Alberta.'

Raimondi did as he was told. '*Signor* Valsi, the body

of the key witness in your trial, Alberta Tortoricci, turned up in Scampia . . .'

'We're leaving,' interjected Ricardo Mazerelli.

'She was found with her tongue cut out . . .'

'My client has no knowledge of, or connection with, the incident you're describing.'

Valsi looked bored. He checked his watch and yawned.

The *Capo* stood up and slowly shook the creases out of his trousers and slid his jacket on.

'She'd been tortured to death. Electrocuted and burned . . .'

'We have no further comment to make.' Mazerelli had to push his client towards the door, otherwise he'd have stood there all day patting his mouth in mockery.

Valsi checked his watch again and bit back a smile. By his reckoning, the Don and the Dog should both already be dead. Murdered at exactly the time he had the world's best cast-iron alibi, courtesy of the carabinieri.

And any moment, many more of his problems would be solved.

# 98

***Pompeii***

Just as Franco Castellani's life had been a terrible fuck up, so too was his death.

Blood and brain spattered the features of Pompeii's famous ashen fugitives.

The two cousins lay in a heap. Arms around each other.

But for the smell of muzzle blast and burned flesh, you could have been forgiven for thinking they were wrestling. A boisterous play fight that had ended in deadlock. *Dead* lock.

Feelings of hopelessness and a hardening addiction to heroin were what had driven Franco Castellani to the brink of despair. The point where suicide seemed a sweeter option than survival.

Paolo Falconi had been too late to stop Franco's finger from pulling the trigger. And he'd been too quick for his own good. The desperate last-minute lunge had been just enough to knock his cousin's gun away and divert the fatal bullet into his own head.

Paolo was dead.

Franco lay on his back. His cousin's brains were

all over his face. His blood ran off him and formed dusty balls in the dirt of the Pompeii ruins.

Franco struggled to move Paolo off him. When he was free, he knelt there, crying and cradling his cousin's corpse. Gradually people crowded around. Strangers' eyes locked on the two youths and the gun in the dirt. They were uncertain whether to help, or to run.

Franco spotted them. And helped them decide.

He picked up the weapon and pointed it towards them. 'Get away! Get the fuck away, or I'll kill you all!'

Most ran. Some stayed frozen to the spot. Franco fired a shot that tore into brick above their heads. Now they screamed. Now they ran.

The Garden of the Fugitives was empty again. Except for the dead. The old dead. And the new dead.

Franco Castellani hugged his cousin and kissed his bloodied head.

And then he put the pistol into his mouth.

And fired.

***Capaccio Scalo, La Baia di Napoli***

Salvatore Giacomo parked up west of Vesuvius at the junction of the SS18 and SP277. From here he was only minutes away from most of the major routes in and out of Naples. Black coffee in the cup-holder on the dashboard, croissant crumbs on his lap, he dialled the numbers again. First the Don. Then Armando.

Next Mazerelli. No replies. Even Valsi was unobtainable. Something was wrong.

Sal guessed it had started. War had broken out. He cursed himself. He should have killed Valsi long ago, killed him first. That son of a bitch would be at the centre of it. The Don had asked him to bide his time, wait until he was ready, and he'd done as he'd been asked. He'd always done as he was asked. And now they were paying the price. He should have followed his instincts, not the old man's orders.

*Gina!*

Was she dead too? His big fingers fumbled and misdialled. He tried again.

*'Pronto.'*

The air whooshed out of him in relief.

'Gina, it's Sal, Uncle Sal. Are you okay?'

She could hear the tension in his voice. 'Sure, what's wrong?'

He didn't want to alarm her. 'Nothing. Where are you?'

'I'm in my car. On my way to work.' Music played from the radio.

'I've been trying to call your father and I can't reach him. Armando's not picking up either.'

Gina turned down the tunes. 'Don't worry. They're probably in the doctor's. He had to go for a check-up this morning and was running late.'

Sal ignored the reassurance. 'Where's Enzo?'

There was an edge in his voice that began to worry her. 'Sal, what's wrong?'

'Where's Enzo?' he repeated, more urgently.

'At the house. He's with his childminder. Probably driving her crazy.'

Sal wasn't sure what to say next. He didn't want to panic her, but he couldn't just say nothing.

Gina picked up on his hesitancy. 'Sal, tell me what's happening. What's going on?'

He searched for a different way to say what was on his mind, but couldn't express himself as he wanted. He knew it was brutal as soon as he said it. 'Gina, I think your father's dead. I think Bruno killed him, and he might now take Enzo from you.'

***(Anti-Camorra Unit), Napoli***

Sylvia took the backstairs from Lorenzo's office, down to the main reception which served the various other units in the carabinieri HQ. The last person she'd expected her urgent visitor to be was Luciano Creed.

At first, she thought he'd turned up to waste her time. To complain or cause more embarrassment. But she revised her opinion as the first images from his journalistic friend's camera card appeared on the computer screen in an office at the back of reception. 'And this was taken when?' she asked.

'Less than an hour ago,' said the woman glued to Creed's shoulder. 'May I politely remind you, *Capitano*, this is my camera, my pictures, my copyright.'

Sylvia couldn't help but laugh. 'My case, my cell

block, my right to charge you with anything my little mind can dream up. *You* remember that. You'll get your story, but not until we're ready.'

Five minutes later Creed and Cassandra Morrietti were giving statements in another room. Sylvia went back upstairs to Jack and Lorenzo.

News had just come through that a car bomb had killed Fredo Finelli, and Carmine Cicerone had been shot dead leaving church.

'Jesus, I only stepped out of the room for half an hour,' said Sylvia. 'What the hell next?'

Lorenzo filled her in. He'd been briefed by his own team and half the Anti-Camorra Unit were already out on the streets trying to make sense of it all. 'Believe me, it's going to get a lot worse. At least we know why that slimy bastard Bruno Valsi was here this morning with his brief. He was getting himself an alibi that no court in the world would reject.'

They were in Lorenzo's office. A techy fired up a PC, loaded Sylvia's pictures and got them on to the monitor.

'Messy,' said Lorenzo, looking at the bloody corpses of Paolo Falconi and Franco Castellani. 'I remember you saying you thought these cousins could be your killers? They still in your frame?'

'Unlikely,' said Jack and Sylvia almost simultaneously.

Sylvia sat behind the computer and worked through the images. She opened shots of the crowd, then a badly out-of-focus zoom, some wide frames of a man approaching the cousins' bodies. Probably the guy who phoned emergency services, thought Sylvia.

'Wait!' shouted Lorenzo. 'That's Salvatore Giacomo.'

Jack remembered the name from the slide show Lorenzo had given. The man had a casualness and calmness about him that was chilling.

The major tapped at the picture. 'Giacomo has been part of the Finelli crew for close on twenty years but we've never been able to link him to anything more than a parking ticket.'

'You said he was the old man's muscle – his *Luogotenente* – that right?'

'Right.' Lorenzo looked bemused. 'What the hell is he doing with these kids?'

'There's more of him a little later.' Sylvia clicked her way through the rest of the images. 'Here. Look, he goes right up to their bodies.'

Jack watched closely. The guy was a pro. All the signs were there. The bodyguard was focused on the gun and Franco's body but his peripheral vision was sweeping the crowd. His jacket was loose. As he walked his hands were up around his waist, ready to grab for a concealed weapon. 'I know all this Camorra mob are killers or potential killers,' said the profiler 'but what about this guy? You've nothing on file to prove he's a triggerman?'

Lorenzo frowned. 'Like I said, nothing record-wise. But he has a nickname, Sal the Snake. Word has it that he once strangled someone with a length of chain. But we never found the body, and we've certainly never seen him with a chain.'

'Urban myth?' asked Sylvia.

'I think so. The snake part is also said to refer to his rather large manhood.' He half laughed. 'In truth we've nothing on that either. These fellas all have nicknames; for all we know his might have come from a game of Snakes and Ladders.'

Jack didn't hear anything else. The images on the computer burned in his brain. Giacomo's eyes were blank and soulless as he unemotionally tried to find the kids' pulses. There wasn't a trace of care or concern about him. Jack watched him wheel away from the dead cousins, like he'd dropped a McDonald's wrapper in a trash can. This was a guy who was so comfortable around death, it didn't even make him blink.

Jacket on the back seat, Gucci shades on, head tilted back against the leather rest in the Lexus, Bruno Valsi gave Mazerelli his orders. 'I don't want to go home. Take me for breakfast. I'm starving.'

The *Capo* was amused to see him hesitate.

'Forget calling your Don. His brains and guts are spread over the hillside of his blessed Posillipo.'

'What?'

'Ricardo, you're not deaf. You heard me. Fredo Finelli is dead. Gone. *Morto.* No more paying your fucking wages or saving your lawyerly ass.'

Mazerelli turned on the radio. If it was true it would be on the news. He twiddled the tuning knob, then stopped. Of course it was true. It wasn't the kind of thing you could make up.

Valsi leaned forward and peered into the consigliere's eyes. 'You *sad*, Ricky boy? Or don't you really give a fuck? Deep down, are you just as mean and ambitious as the rest of us?'

Mazerelli was as nervous as he'd ever been. He chose his words carefully. 'I want to live.'

Valsi laughed and sat back. 'Of course you do. Of course you do. Now, find me somewhere fucking good for breakfast and then you can tell me again about that funny Japanese game of yours and how we all have to follow rules.'

# 99

***Stazione dei carabinieri, Castello di Cisterna***

It was time to pull everything together. So much was happening – and happening so fast – there was a danger they'd miss something.

A major case conference had been convened back at the Murder Squad HQ in Castello di Cisterna.

Sylvia, Lorenzo, Pietro and Jack were joined by Luella Grazzioli, *Professoressa* Marianna Della Fratte, Claudio Mancini and Susanna Martinelli. They settled in a row of chairs facing a projection screen and set of whiteboards. As they waited for the meeting to start their eyes settled on the first board, the one listing all the missing and murdered women.

**Francesca Di Lauro (24) Missing 5 yrs, found dead, location Mount Vesuvius National Park**

**Gloria Pirandello (19) Missing 6 yrs, found dead, location MVNP**

**Patricia Calvi (19) Missing 6.5 yrs, found dead, location MVNP**

**Luisa Banotti (20) Missing 7 years, found dead, location MVNP**

**Donna Rizzi (19) Missing 8 years, body not found**

Sylvia kicked off. 'Thank you all for coming here at short notice. A number of things happened this morning, and are still happening as we speak. One of our prime suspects, Bruno Valsi, is at the centre of the latest developments. Because of this we are joined by members of the Anti-Camorra Unit. Major, could you please share some of your information with us?'

Lorenzo Pisano modestly introduced himself, though everyone in the room was well aware of who he was. 'The Finelli and Cicerone families have operated side by side for more than a decade, but whatever peace they had, it is now over. Earlier today, Fredo Finelli was killed by a car bomb near his home and Carmine Cicerone was gunned down on the steps of the church of Santa Maria Eliana. We had Bruno Valsi, Finelli's son-in-law, in custody at the time of both hits. A security guard had been killed at his home. We had nothing to charge him with and when he was bored with us and satisfied he'd established a good alibi for himself, he just upped and walked.'

Questions flew: Who died first, Finelli or Cicerone? What other casualties were there? Had Valsi orchestrated it all? Lorenzo did his best to fill the gaps. Half an hour later extra intel came in – the body of Valsi's henchman Alberto Donatello had turned up in a skip just metres away from his front door. The war was certainly underway.

Jack tuned in and out of the conversation. It was becoming harder to separate the Camorra killings from the serial murders.

But at the same time, there was still no motive, no obvious links between victims and suspects.

For a while Jack perused the whiteboards. Some listed only the female victims. Some only the bodies found near Vesuvius. One detailed all the killings and all the missing women. Another – the latest – showed only the Camorra murders.

CAMORRA DEATHS

**Fredo Finelli (64) – Finelli Don**

**Armando Lopapa (50) – Finelli Chauffeur**

**Alberto Donatello (27) – Finelli/Valsi Clan member**

**Beppe Basso (30) – Valsi House Guard**

**Carmine Cicerone (45) – Cicerone Don**

At first glance, today's troubles looked like a Cicerone-instigated war; with the death count running three to one in their favour. But Jack felt sure Valsi had drawn first blood. It was what he'd predicted.

He slid his attention to the next board.

**Bernardo Sorrentino (42) – forensic anthropologist – killed at home**

**Kristen Petrov (24) – telephone sex centre worker – Finelli/Valsi business – killed in Castellani rubbish pit**

**Rosa Novello (18) – killed in car at Castellani campsite**

**Filippo Valdrano (19) – killed with Novello in car at Castellani campsite**

**Franco Castellani (24) – suicide at Pompeii – lived on site where bodies of Petrov, Novello and Valdrano found**

**Paolo Falconi (24) – killed by cousin at Pompeii – lived on Castellani campsite**

**Alberta Tortoricci (38) – Valsi trial witness, killed by electrocution – body burned and found in Scampia**

So many deaths. So many links – strong or tenuous – to the Camorra. But, as Jack had learned, in Naples this wasn't uncommon. The Camorra touched everything. He lingered over the list and started to eliminate suspects. If the Castellani cousins were the serial killers, they could now be trimmed from the list. Case solved and then all that was left was a turf war. But surely that was too easy an answer.

Jack considered the alternatives. If the cousins were not serial killers, then Bruno Valsi continued to emerge as the main suspect. Valsi and the cousins had all shared much of the psychological profile he'd drawn up of the murderer. Franco and Paolo had both been manual workers. Neither seemed to have had any steady sexual relationships. Both had access to a van – which would be perfect for abducting victims and disposing of corpses. And they'd even lived and worked on the site where the bodies of Petrov, Novello and Valdrano had been found. But to Jack they didn't seem to possess either the expertise to kill efficiently, or the sadistic streak to want to burn women to death. Valsi on the other hand – well, he seemed to have those *qualities* in spades. Sylvia's voice caught his attention and drew him back to the briefing.

'Mancini. Tell us about Kristen Petrov – what's new on her?'

Claudio Mancini cleared his throat and tried to settle his nerves. He'd never spoken at a briefing in front of senior officers before. 'We've been to the call centre where she works – sorry, worked – and we've spoken to some of the girls on the sex lines. Seems that Bruno Valsi visited the centre with some of his thugs and removed the woman running it, Celia Brabantia. Our girl Kristen replaced her.'

Jack had questions. 'Any suggestions of a sexual relationship between her and Valsi?'

'Err, yes. One of the girls said that Kristen had bragged about seeing Valsi; she said that one day she would end up owning the sex centre.' He looked towards Sylvia.

She took up the story. 'The plan with Valsi is this – if necessary we will detain him for questioning in connection with the murder of Kristen Petrov. I know he'll walk, and probably quickly because we have nothing – I repeat *nothing* – to link him forensically to this killing, or to suggest a motive. But it may buy us time.'

Jack's attention drifted back to the whiteboards. Valsi certainly fitted his profile in the sense of being capable of immense violence, and no doubt enjoying it. The interview with his wife had confirmed Jack's suspicion that he was capable of anything, including murder.

And then there was that intriguing gap of five years. Five years in which no more women disappeared. Five years that Valsi spent in prison. But Jack had trouble believing Valsi had killed Kristen. He might have *had* her killed – that would be more his style – just as he'd had Alberta Tortoricci killed, but he certainly hadn't done it himself. And as for all the other missing women, the endless canvassing of family, friends and neighbours had failed to produce any link between them and Bruno Valsi. Not that many people expected anyone to say anything about one of the country's most notorious Camorristi.

Jack scanned the whiteboards one final time and hoped for inspiration. His mind was fogged by all the names and dates and twists. But the answer lay there in black and white. Valsi was involved *somehow*. He just had to figure out how big the *some* was and exactly what the *how* was.

# 100

***Casonia, Napoli***

A cop on a retainer was the first to ring Finelli *Capo* Giotto Fiorentino, and tell him of the Don's murder. Seconds later, Fiorentino rang Ambrogio Rotoletti, his friend of thirty years, and woke him at his mistress's apartment in Casonia. Ambro took his cellphone and walked out into the corridor in his string vest and baggy white underpants. He was crying by the time he rang the third *Capo*, Angelico d'Arezzo.

'Angelico, it's Ambro. Listen, the shit's started . . .' He never finished his sentence. He took two bullets in the stomach before he even saw the shooter. A third bit a hole out of his heart. Blood spurted through the gaps in the string vest. He sank to his knees, then slumped on to his side.

Vito Ambrossio picked up the phone. 'Don Fredo's dead. So is that fat fuck Rotoletti, and within the hour you will be too.' He tossed the phone away.

The other end of the line was already empty. Angelico d'Arezzo woke his wife. She sat dazed in the marital bed they'd shared for a quarter of a century. Angelico pulled cases from the top of the oak wardrobe his parents had bought them as a wedding present and hurriedly emptied drawers into them. Within ten minutes they'd be gone.

Angelico had a stash of cash in a small villa in Greece. They'd go there and stay there. Maybe forever. Certainly until it had all died down. He was too old for gang battles. Too wise to think this war was winnable.

Meanwhile, Vito Ambrossio stepped over the corpse in the corridor. One *Capo Zona* down. Two more to go.

***Centro città, Napoli***

They breakfasted at Rocco's, the place the Don had been eating at since he was old enough to buy his own food. Just an espresso for Mazerelli. Steak for Valsi. The new head of the Family didn't leave a scrap. Both Rocco, the owner, and Myletti, the chef, visited the table to check everything had been all right. Valsi told them it was shit. Said he wasn't Finelli and warned them he wouldn't eat their crap again unless it improved. He picked up the check. Surprised he'd even been asked to pay. Unaware the Don had always settled in full, plus a generous tip. 'And do you know what, Rocco? To make sure your food gets better I'm going to invest in your business.' He peeled a twenty off a roll. 'This covers the shit you served and gets me fifty per cent of your business. My friend Ricardo will be round with the paperwork.'

Mazerelli couldn't look them in the eye. He'd sat in the restaurant a thousand times with Don Fredo. All the memories were now worthless. Blown away by a murderous bad-mannered oaf. '*Ciao*,' he managed sadly, as the old doorbell clanged on the way out.

Though it was grey outside, verging on fog and rain again, Valsi slipped his shades on as they walked through the Piazza Nazionale and back to the Lexus. 'Now, take me to the Don's tailor. By the time I've been fitted for a new suit, the bloodshed will be over. Then you and I can talk of the future.'

***Capaccio Scalo, La Baia di Napoli***

Salvatore Giacomo sat frozen in his car, his cellphone on his lap. Giotto Fiorentino had just told him the Don was dead. The Cicerone clan was clearly on the rampage. Giotto had been in the process of adding that the Don's driver, Armando, was also dead, when the sound of a door breaking and automatic gunfire completed the story. He was dead as well.

Sal sat and figured things out. Valsi would be in the thick of it. Stirring up bad blood. Serving his own purposes.

He should have killed the young piece of shit, instead of Donatello. If only he'd trusted his instincts instead of doing as the Don had instructed him. But that's what Sal did. He followed orders. Always did as he was told. And now loyalty to the Family was going to get him killed.

Well, not if he could help it. Certainly not without taking some of the bastards down with him.

*What about Gina? What about Enzo?* Valsi wouldn't hurt his kid, not the boy. But he wasn't sure about Gina. He'd seen him with women, seen the violence, seen the brutality in his fists and in his heart.

The Don would want her protected. *Keep an eye on her, Sal. Look after her like she was your own daughter.* That's what the Don had asked him to do in the past. And he had done it. Best he could.

Now there was only one way to truly protect her. And it didn't involve running, or hiding. It involved what Sal did best.

Killing.

# 101

***Stazione dei carabinieri, Castello di Cisterna***

The case conference continued at a slow, methodical pace. Nothing was to be missed. Every link scrupulously examined. A mistake now could prove fatal.

Sylvia was growing tired and short-tempered. 'I asked for checks on Celia Brabantia, the former manager of the Finelli sex centre. Is she dead or alive?'

Claudio Mancini hesitated. 'Alive. We think.'

'You *think*?' queried Sylvia. 'Alive is when you breathe, dead is when you don't. Which is it, Claudio?'

'One of the women said she'd quit and moved home to Sansepolcro. She gave us a number and we spoke to a woman who *said* she was her, but we haven't yet had a chance to physically ID her, so we *think* she is alive but can't be certain.'

'Okay, we get the picture, thanks.' Sylvia rubbed at her hair and paced while she thought. 'Susanna, update us on the body count and body IDs. Where do we stand? Who's linked to whom?'

Susanna Martinelli was a tall, thin confident woman in her late twenties with long black curly hair that shook from side to side as she walked to the front.

She picked up the projector control and began with the slides of the dead cousins, Paolo Falconi and Franco Castellani. 'Their deaths now seem like a single planned suicide by the elder cousin, Franco, a heroin user, that went wrong and ended in a double tragedy. Onlookers say the younger cousin, Paolo, tried to stop him and was accidentally killed.'

Sylvia stepped across the conversation. 'We've been considering these two as suspects in our murder cases. It could be that Franco Castellani had planned to kill himself out of shame or guilt and he bungled the suicide and shot Paolo Falconi as well.'

Susanna continued her narrative. 'I've been asked to put up these slides as well.' She clicked on to several images of the cousins' bodies being examined by a well-built, middle-aged man in a grey suit.

'Salvatore Giacomo, aka Sal the Snake,' explained Lorenzo from the shadows of the room. 'Fredo Finelli's personal muscle. We want to know why he was there. What's his connection with the cousins? Had he been told to threaten them, abduct them or even kill them? We have information – which, unfortunately, I can't go into at this moment – that suggests there was bad blood between Sal's boss, Fredo Finelli, and their grandfather, Antonio Castellani. Was Sal following the cousins on Finelli's instructions?'

Jack's eyes were glued to the frame of Giacomo. This was a man who had slipped under their radar for most of the inquiry. No criminal record. Yet he was a career criminal who was certainly smart and efficient.

He ticked a lot of boxes on Jack's profile. 'Lorenzo, is this Sal a local? Was he born and bred around here?'

Pisano didn't need any notes to help him. He knew the background on the Finelli Family as well as he knew the history of his own family. 'Giacomo is Neapolitan. As local as they come. Born and bred in Herculaneum. Lives alone in a one-bed in Napoli Capodichino. He's been there since we've been keeping tracks on him.'

Jack mentally reran the profile he'd drawn up. *White male, knows how to control violence, probably aged thirties to fifties, single or divorced, born locally, has good local knowledge, holds driving licence, comfortable with a gun, perhaps a career criminal, a Camorrista with a history of violence.* But what the hell was Giacomo's connection to Valsi? The two men seemed more enemies than friends. Sal the Snake was unlikely to kill on Valsi's orders. And there was no way Jack could imagine the two sharing some joint sexual pleasure in sadistically murdering women.

The slide show moved on. They reran the start of the sequence where Sal first appeared on the scene. He walked coolly into frame, checked the cousins' bodies for signs of life and then disappeared again. 'Can you flick through all those shots of him again, please? Maybe magnify by two and jog them back and forth?'

Susanna did as Jack asked. The quality dipped as the picture doubled in size. Sal moved in a near comical, jerky slow motion around the bodies, checking for pulses, wiping his hands.

'Okay, you can stop there.' Jack turned sideways to *Professoressa* Marianna Della Fratte. 'Ballistics say the same ammo was used in the murders of Rosa Novello, Filippo Valdrano, Kristen Petrov and Bernardo Sorrentino. Two different sites, the same ammo, correct?'

Marianna nodded. 'Yes, correct. Jacketed Hollow Point. And before you ask,' she glanced at Sylvia, 'yes, I'm absolutely certain that there were two separate guns. Both Glocks, both the same calibre, but the barrel markings and firing-pin impressions were entirely different. We double-checked.'

Jack held up a hand. 'Okay, can we run those last few slides again, please? I just want to see something, maybe it ties in with what the *Professoressa* just told us.'

Susanna repeated the shuffle and Jack moved close to the projector screen. Bright light caught his face and cast a giant shadow of his head on the screen before he backed off. 'As you can see, Sal is right-handed. Look here, when he checks Franco's neck for a pulse.' The slide moved on. 'Now, when he stoops to move Franco to check on Paolo – see the flash of leather strapping? That's because he's wearing a shoulder holster *under* his right arm. Not his left arm. This is so he can pull a gun left-handed. Probably means it's a twin holster rig and this is his back-up gun. Only rednecks and real pros carry two weapons. And as you don't have too many rednecks out here, we can assume this guy is a pro and knows how to use them both. Most likely – *very* likely – this guy's carrying twin handguns.'

'Ten minutes' break everyone,' shouted Sylvia. Jack didn't have to say what he was thinking. Everyone was on the same wavelength. Find Sal the Snake. Find out if his guns are Glocks and whether the bullets match the murders.

The room emptied, but Jack hung back and asked for ten minutes. He wanted some time on his own. Time to figure out the link between Sal and Valsi.

He could hear the overhead neon strip lights buzzing as he forced himself to focus.

Nothing came.

He looked again at the victims' names. Their lives reduced to black ink on white boards. He dismissed the male victims. Sex was usually the key. Usually the area where offenders left their clearest psychological clues. He switched to the board listing all the murdered and missing women.

**Francesca Di Lauro (24) – dead (burned)**

**Gloria Pirandello (19) – dead (burned)**

**Patricia Calvi (19) – dead (burned)**

**Luisa Banotti (20) – dead (burned)**

**Kristen Petrov (24) – dead (burned)**

**Alberta Tortoricci (38) – dead (burned)**

**Donna Rizzi (19) – Missing, presumed dead**

No matter how hard Jack tried he couldn't see a connection to Salvatore Giacomo, or a reason for the burnings. And the only obvious connections to Valsi were Tortoricci, who'd testified against him, and Petrov, who worked for him and may well have had an affair with him. According to Lorenzo, Sal was fifty. It was unlikely he'd have moved in the same social circles as the women. *But, of course, it was possible that Valsi would have done.* Valsi was, what? Twenty-seven? At the time of their disappearances he could have been pretty much the same age.

There was another thing that couldn't be ignored. A gap of five years between the most recent murders – Tortoricci and Petrov – and the last victim, Francesca Di Lauro. That morning Sylvia had told him what Bernadetta Di Lauro had said about her daughter dating a married man. Was Valsi that man? A married man. The father of the unborn child she carried? There was no evidence to support it, but it was certainly possible. Sylvia said she could never have imagined Creed and Francesca together, but it wasn't so hard to picture the handsome Valsi with the beautiful Francesca. But why kill her? Jack was sure many Camorristi had bastard children all over the place. Hardly a killing matter.

And then it hit him.

The missing piece.

The mystery link that pulled it all together.

## 102

***Capo di Posillipo, La Baia di Napoli***

Gina Valsi arrived at her father's home at the same time that a police search team with a warrant was arresting a security guard who'd tried to stop them getting in.

Claudio Mancini had been dispatched with Jack in tow. Other search teams were crawling all over Valsi's home in Camaldoli and Sal's apartment in Napoli Capodichino.

'What's this? What the fuck's going on?' Gina barked at them as she slammed the driver's door of the X5.

'We've got a warrant.' Mancini pulled the paperwork from inside his jacket.

Gina waved him away. 'That won't be worth wiping your ass on when my father comes.' The look on his face pulled her up.

*It was true*. The stuff that Sal had been saying was really true. Her knees went weak, then buckled.

'Here, let me help you.' Mancini took her arm and steadied her.

Somehow she made it to a metal seat beneath a

window near the front door. She sat there in shock as the carabinieri officers filed into her father's home.

Mancini lowered himself down beside her. '*Signora* Valsi, your father and his driver have been killed. Their car was destroyed in an explosion, a car bomb, about three kilometres from here. I'm very sorry.'

Gina heard him through some kind of cotton wool. She knew what he was saying and knew that it was true, but the shock was so great, she felt nothing.

He'd *never* be killed, her father had promised her that. Everything would be all right. Everything would be fine. He'd reassured her so many times that she'd actually believed it.

And now? Now he was gone. Bam! As quick as that.

What next? What were she and Enzo to do?

*Enzo.*

'My child! Where's my child?'

Gina was in the house in seconds. 'Enzo! Enzo, where are you?' She hit the stairs two at a time. 'Elena! Elena, are you there?' Where was that damned childminder?

Mancini and Jack waited patiently in the hallway.

Eventually, Gina came down, her face grey with fear. 'Where's my son?'

Jack watched her every move. Watched her eyes settle on him and work out that he was the key to everything that happened next. It had been his suggestion to take her child away, keep the boy separated from his mother. Not nice. Not compassionate.

Jack knew all that. But he also knew he was going to need every ounce of leverage for what was going to come next.

The cops were still all over the Don's home when Sal drove up the hillside. There was just too much heat to go all the way up to the place and see for himself what had happened. He hit the brakes and did a U-turn. Thumped the steering wheel as he straightened up. His whole world was upside down. Crazy shit was happening now. And it would get crazier. It always did after a *Capo* had been killed. At times like this you either watched, or you played. Sal was a player.

Next stop, Valsi's place. The skunk would have his tail up and would be hiding there. Two miles from the Don's home, Sal became aware that he was being followed. Navy-blue Fiat Strada, new model, maybe a year old, but he couldn't make the plates. Thirty minutes later as he approached Valsi's home in Camaldoli, it was still in his rear-view mirror.

A white forensic tent jutted out from the frontage of Valsi's place. Carabinieri officers chatted and smoked in front of it. One peered skyward and hoped it wouldn't rain again. The scene confused Sal. He'd expected to see Camorristi outside, not carabinieri. There'd clearly been other casualties that he didn't yet know about.

The Fiat was three cars back as Sal rolled on past and, fifty metres later, took a right. Around the corner he floored the Merc and pulled a quick left. Tyres squealed. A glance in the mirror just before he finished the turn told him the Fiat was overtaking the second car back. Someone was definitely tailing him, and he had a feeling it wasn't the cops. The Merc straightened up and the smell of rubber wafted through the air con. Sal ripped through the gears along Via Terracina, his speed jumping from 60 to 80 to 120kph. In the rear-view mirror, the Fiat was struggling but still within sight. Ospedale San Paolo flashed past on his left. He was topping 160kph as he approached the sharp left-hander into Via Cupa Vicinale Terracina. Sal swung hard right and then cut left, hoping his racing line wasn't too tight. The Merc redlined and screamed as he changed down gears. The back end kicked out – but, despite what it looked like, Sal still had full control. He sighted the traffic parked up ahead, then deliberately slammed the brakes on and prepared for the Merc to plough into a parked car.

Sal flipped the driver's door open just before the impact. Air bags ballooned. He found just enough room to slip on to the sidewalk. He kicked the door shut and rolled up tight against the parked car. Seconds later the blue Fiat slid past and slammed on its brakes.

Lying on the hard stone, Sal slipped off the safeties on both Glocks. A clunk and grind of gears announced that the Fiat was reversing back up to the Merc. Sal had never seen the occupants, but he was sure he knew *who* they were and *what* they wanted. Engine still running, they got out.

Sal lay flat and watched them from beneath the Merc.

They were both square to the passenger door. The air bags meant they couldn't see anything inside the vehicle.

Someone tugged at the passenger-door handle to open up for a better view. Within half a second he was vertical, firing through the driver's window with both Glocks.

Within two beats of their hearts he'd emptied ten rounds from his fists. He stepped quickly on to the crunched nose of the Merc.

The men were already down. Wounded and bleeding. One was dead, face down, crimson jelly in the grime and grit. The other was on his back, twitching and gargling blood. The Glock in Sal's left hand jerked again, five more rounds. The gargling stopped.

He dropped over the other side of the Merc and chugged more shots into the bodies and heads of the men on the floor.

*Take no chances. Doubly sure equals doubly dead.*

The bodies didn't move.

He didn't recognize the guy on his back. He rolled the other stiff to look at him. Romano Ivetta. Dead as a fucking dodo. *Hoo-fucking-ray!*

Sal didn't waste any more time. He holstered the Glocks. Walked over Ivetta's body to the still-running Fiat, slipped inside and drove off.

# 103

***Stazione dei carabinieri, Castello di Cisterna***

The closest thing to sympathy that Gina Valsi got was a cup of tea. Even then it was cold. She'd been taken to the carabinieri headquarters on the east of the city where the Murder Squad was based.

Claudio Mancini spent an hour with her in the Interview Room, tape rolling, questions flying. He kicked off by asking about her father. Where had he been going that morning? Who'd known of his movements? The usual stuff. Then they moved on to the more exotic. His line of work, his enemies, who might have wanted him dead. Every ten minutes Gina demanded to see her son and each outburst got the same deadpan answer: she'd have to wait.

The door swung open and for the sake of the tape Mancini announced Jack King's entrance.

'*Signora*, may I add my own commiserations? I'm very sorry for your loss.' The profiler settled comfortably into a chair opposite her. Her eyes followed a brown folder that he placed on the table. Jack interlocked his fingers and rested his hands on top of it. 'I'm here helping the carabinieri to solve a series of murders of young women. I think you may have known some of them.'

'I don't think so.' Gina looked confused.

He opened up the folder, slid out a photograph and turned it towards her. 'This is Francesca Di Lauro. Name mean anything to you?'

Gina shook her head. 'No. Why, should it?'

Jack didn't say anything. He took out several other photographs and lined them up in a separate row. Luisa Banotti, Patricia Calvi, Donna Rizzi and Gloria Pirandello.

Gina's gaze slid over them, their dark eyes and mixed expressions looking back up from the table at her. She bit at a thumbnail then turned the picture of Francesca back towards Jack. 'I don't know her but I've seen her face. In the papers, right? On television. She's the woman they found somewhere out near Pompeii.'

Jack steepled his fingers again. 'A pretty young woman. Like all the others. Much prettier than you. Do you think that's why Bruno chose her?'

Gina looked away. She knew she looked stressed. She could feel her face flush, her heartbeat quicken. She understood what he was driving at. He hadn't said it, but she knew.

'Gina. Gina, look at me.'

Her eyes locked on his.

Defiance? Pressure? Certainly not complete innocence. Jack decoded the signals. 'Lady, the way you just reacted, the fact that you can't say anything, tells me that I'm right. You *do* know this woman.' He slapped his hand firmly down on Francesca's photograph. Gina flinched. 'You *know* her and you *know* all the others on this table. Francesca Di Lauro had an affair with your husband and you killed her.'

'No!' snapped Gina. 'That's ridiculous. I'm not going to say anything else until I have a lawyer. I want a lawyer here.' She chewed hard on another nail. Jack sat in silence and let her stew. 'I agreed to answer questions about my father, but not this. *This* is ridiculous.'

Still Jack said nothing. He leaned back, tilted his chair on to the rear legs, drummed his fingers on the edge of the table and watched the pressure grow. Only when Gina looked straight into his eyes did he play his final card.

'Kris-ten Pet-rov.' He said the name slowly as he put the photograph down. Watched the reaction in her eyes. The pain caused a twitch in the corner of her mouth. Gina couldn't help but glance down at the photograph. Her face said it all. So that's what she looked like. Bruno's latest. The little bitch he'd sent text messages to.

'I've no problem getting you that lawyer,' said Jack calmly, 'but here's the deal. If we stop now and he turns you into Sleeping Beauty, then I promise you, you'll never see your son again.'

Gina looked up from Kristen's picture and glared at him. Could he do that? *Would* he do that?

'Worse than that, Gina, your husband will get custody of Enzo, while you go to prison for a long time. A *very* long time.'

Gina's head was aching, throbbing like crazy. So much in one day. So much in the future – that she could lose.

Now Jack wouldn't rest. Wouldn't give her a moment to think. He just piled on the pressure. 'Listen, Gina. I know you were involved in the murders of Kristen and Francesca, just as you were involved in the murders of all the other women. But I also know you didn't actually take their lives. You had someone do it for you, didn't you? Give up the real killer and maybe you can come out of this with the kind of sentence that will give you a chance to see some of the rest of your son's life.'

Gina looked up at him. She was about to make the biggest decision of her life.

'What's it to be, Gina? You going to roll the dice and risk spending the rest of your life without Enzo? Or do we get the name?'

***Centro città, Napoli***

A navy-blue carabinieri squad car fell into the traffic behind the Lexus.

'Amateurs. They don't have a fucking clue.' Valsi scoffed at them as he watched in the passenger-door mirror. 'Fucking morons.'

'They *want* to be seen,' snapped Mazerelli. 'They've

been glued to us since Rocco's. Waited outside the tailor's until we came out.'

'I'll glue their heads to the top of their car, then they'll be able to see.'

Mazerelli ignored the remark. 'They want you to know that they're going to breathe down your neck every minute of your day now.' He checked the rear-view and could see the squad car had at least two officers in it. 'They'll turn up the pressure any chance they get. Hope you'll crack, make a mistake.'

Valsi turned towards the consigliere. 'I can't even *spell* mistake, let alone make one.'

'Seriously, Bruno, they're going to be all over you. Pisano will have taps on your phones. They'll have spooks with laser listening devices in every parked car you go past. You can trust no one.'

'And you, Ricardo?'

Mazerelli pretended not to understand. 'And me, what?'

Valsi smiled. 'You know what I mean. Can I trust you? But you choose to avoid answering. That means you haven't made your mind up yet. You're not quite sure where the balance of power truly lies. You're a cautious man, Ricardo. Maybe that makes you a good one to have around. Or maybe it makes you a danger – and one that should be quickly eliminated.'

Mazerelli swallowed. He knew Valsi was unarmed, but given his psychopathic tendencies anything was still possible. 'Like I just said, you're going to have to assume that the carabinieri are listening to everything you say, everywhere you say it. And that includes right here and right now. Those amateurs as you call them might be recording this conversation. This car might even be bugged.'

The *Capo* fell silent. The creepy lawyer was right. Pisano's nose was up and he was sniffing for a bitch like a dog on heat. He found himself patting the headrest, searching the visors, the dashboard, the door frames, the floor carpets.

Mazerelli pulled out his portable electronic bug detector. 'It's been swept. This thing beeps if there are bugs within a mile. We're safe.' He pulled the Lexus into the avenue where his penthouse was. The squad car was still on their tail. 'There's a security expert I use for the apartment; I will get him to give you one of these hand-helds as well.'

'Your place is safe to speak?'

'Safe as can be. Besides, we do have client-lawyer privilege, but I need to talk to you about that.'

Valsi relaxed as they pulled up to the security gates of the apartment block. Mazerelli thumbed the remote to open the gates. He felt reassured by seeing Ivetta's car parked outside on the street. He'd done a good job. Very soon he'd buy him a Ferrari or a Lamborghini.

The carabinieri patrol cruised level. Valsi leaned over and jammed down the horn on the Lexus. 'Fuck you all!' He flicked a finger at them as they carried on past. 'Fucking amateurs,' he said to a horrified Mazerelli.

The lawyer's eyes widened. Not out of shock at Valsi's outburst. But at the sight of the guns at his window.

Sal the Snake opened up with both Glocks.

Mazerelli and Valsi were dead before the gates had swung open. They were history long before the squad car screeched to a halt and jammed up the traffic as they tried to turn around.

Before he left, Sal pulled a third gun. The one Valsi had made fun of him with on his birthday. The bullet from the limited edition pearl-handled Ultimate Vaquero blew a hole right through the *Capo*'s viper tattoo and down through his heart.

# 104

***Stazione dei carabinieri, Castello di Cisterna***

The wall clock in the Interview Room made a deep bass clunk every time the minute hand moved on. It drummed several times before Gina Valsi gave up the name that everyone was waiting for.

'Salvatore Giacomo.'

There. She'd said it. It was over.

Somehow she felt better. Maybe there was a way out after all. 'He works for my father.' Gina bit her lip and corrected herself. '*Worked* for my father.'

'Tell me how.' Jack's voice was soft and sympathetic. 'What did you say to him?'

Gina looked left and right across the room, like she was about to cross a road. Her eyes seemed to be searching for some unseen danger that she sensed. 'Like you said, Bruno was having affairs with these women.' She gestured to them all but then pushed at the edge of Francesca's photograph, flicked it away as though it was contaminated. 'Bruno got the bitch pregnant.' Her eyes flared. 'And he'd done this so soon after I'd had our baby. Can you believe that?' She pinched the end of her nose with her thumb and forefinger and sniffed. 'He taunted me with it. Said it was good to have children everywhere. Lots of sons with lots of lovers, that's what he said.'

'And you turned to Salvatore?'

Gina nodded. 'He's always been like an uncle to me. No kids himself. I called him Uncle Sal, worshipped him when I was a child, and he knew it.' She sniffed again and looked embarrassed. 'You got a tissue?'

Mancini went to the back of the room and brought a box of Kleenex. She pulled one and took a minute sorting herself out. 'I told Sal about her. Told him I couldn't go to my father because it would cause trouble with Bruno. He asked me what I wanted him to do. Make her go away, I said. Just make the *puttana* go away.'

Jack placed a hand on Kristen's photograph. 'And you did the same with this girl?'

Gina nodded, then realized the full implication of her tiny body movement. 'But I didn't know how. I thought he'd just got her to leave Naples. Leave my husband alone and leave the city. That's what I thought Sal had made them all do.'

Jack wasn't buying it. He was sure Gina hadn't thought Sal had only carried the women's bags to the train station.

'*Scusi*,' said Mancini, pointing to the door. 'I'll be back in a moment.' He slipped outside and both Jack and Gina knew why. The information on Sal would be relayed to Sylvia and the teams hunting him.

'You had no idea any of these women had been *killed*?' asked Jack as the door closed.

Gina shook her head. 'No, none at all.' She looked as guilty as hell, but this wasn't the moment to push her. That time would come. He was also sure she'd had no say in *how* the women had been killed. The use of fire had been Sal's own invention. Purification, no doubt. In his sick mind he was probably using fire to cleanse them from the sin of adultery. And it undoubtedly turned him on as well. In the minds of sadists, *morality* and *sexuality* often got mixed up in the most monstrous of ways.

'I want to see my son,' said Gina. 'You have no right to keep me away from my child.'

Jack's calmness almost cracked. 'Hey, take a look down at the pictures of Francesca, Kristen and those other dead women in front of you, then tell me again about your rights.' He paused to let the sharpness cut through her indignation. 'Right, Gina, here's how we're going to play it. I'm going to get an Italian officer in here. You're going to give full verbal and written statements. First about Francesca, and then Kristen. Then about each and every one of these other women. And then – and only then – do we even discuss you getting to see Enzo.' He let the ultimatum sink in. 'Your boy's been on his own for quite a while now, Gina. You ready to get this done?'

She nodded. She was ready. Ready as she would ever be.

* * *

Sal was on a roll. Donatello, Ivetta and Valsi all dead. Shame about Mazerelli; he'd had him down as a good guy. Even bigger shame the Don hadn't let him clean house earlier. He'd have been alive if he had.

What now?

He asked himself the question as he threw the Fiat through a labyrinth of backstreets. The cop car was still caught up in the gridlock. But it wasn't too far away.

Sal was running but he wasn't sure where to. The Don was dead. The other *Capi Zona* were probably dead. And he was sure that the Cicerone clan had bodies on the street as well. He dialled Gina's number. That was dead too. There were no obvious allies, no longer any Camorra safe houses that he could trust to hide him.

He headed north towards Palazzo Reale, then east along the Tangenziale di Napoli towards Poggioreale. He cut off the A56 and wove back and forth through the backstreets, buying time, trying to think.

He lost his concentration round a corner off the Via della Stadera. The rear end drifted and slammed into a mountain of rubbish. Sacks and bottles crashed on to the trunk. He held it in third and threw a tight right on to the Autostrada del Sole, forcing a young couple on a scooter to bang into a barrier. In short, he was barely in control.

He'd outrun the carabinieri patrol car but he knew they'd be tracking the Fiat by now, relaying information to central control, young women peering into computer monitors in the dark, passing route info to other squad cars.

Sal hammered the horn as the Fiat redlined and screamed its guts out. Traffic moved over. He was doing close to 200kph as he flew past the signs for Ponticelli.

The fog that had haunted Naples for most of the day soon thickened again in the darkening evening sky. Off in the distance he thought he could hear horns and sirens, perhaps even the thud and thwack of helicopter blades. If the police had a chopper up it wouldn't last long. For once the bad weather would be a blessing. Minutes later the *if* was over. Nightsun searchlights blazed from a carabinieri helicopter. A pool of wobbling white light flooded black hillsides and roadsides.

They'd have thermal cameras too.

The bird in the sky was either the *Raggruppamento Operativo Speciale*, or maybe even the heavyweight *Gruppo Intervento Speciale*. It didn't matter which. Both were probably eight-man teams. Trained and eager to shoot to kill. Well, so was he.

And he was willing to bet he'd killed a lot more than any of them had.

# 105

***Stazione dei carabinieri, Castello di Cisterna***

Six-year-old Enzo Valsi ran down the grey carabinieri corridor and clung like a rugby player to his mother's legs. Clara Sofri, the social worker who'd been caring for him, looked disinterested at the emotional mother-and-child reunion. She'd seen it all before. Dozens of times. Young woman comes off the rails, commits a serious crime and her family life is suddenly shattered. The kid will be better off in care.

Gina cried as she held her son. Hugged and squeezed him tighter than she'd ever done.

'*Ti voglio bene, tesoro – Mamma* really loves you.' She kissed his face and his head. His skin soft against hers. It smelled warm. Tender. She'd miss it. Miss it so much, it would almost kill her.

Gina had been as careful as she could with her statement about Francesca and Kristen, but she knew there was enough there for them to hold her and charge her. Then they'd come back and pick her story to pieces. After that they'd make her talk about the other bitches that Bruno had fucked and taunted her with.

One question haunted her. Spooked her as much as it did most of the cops on the case. Why hadn't she killed Valsi? He was at the root of the problem. He was the guy causing all the humiliation and pain. So, why hadn't she killed him, or had him killed?

The answer was a complex one.

She'd loved him. She hated him, but she loved him too. Really, really loved him. And all she'd ever wanted was to be his wife and raise his children.

A cell-block guard pulled at her shoulder. '*Signora*, we must go now.'

Her world fell apart. She had to be dragged away. Enzo tried to struggle out of the grip of the social worker. Gina felt her heart break. Until her dying day she knew she'd never forget the look in her child's eyes as she left him in that corridor.

***ROS Quartiere Generale***
***(Anti-Camorra Unit), Napoli***

Jack stood in the shaded background of the carabinieri central control room as Lorenzo Pisano's eyes flicked from monitor to monitor as he directed the helicopter unit and regular ground patrols.

'The GIS unit *will* get him,' said Sylvia. 'They're the best in the country. There's no escape.'

Jack's attention was glued to the live pictures of the blue Fiat, picked out by a white spotlight from the helicopter. 'They're a front-line anti-terrorist command unit as well, aren't they?'

'*Sì*,' said Sylvia, watching the same feed. 'They're based in Tuscany but Lorenzo pulled them into a local barracks as soon as he heard of the hit on Finelli. He'd have used the local ROS unit but everyone's already deployed. So today we get the big boys.'

They listened while Lorenzo re-angled the metal coiled flex of a desk mic and ordered two pursuit cars to get in front of the Fiat.

'Rolling block?' asked Jack.

'I think so,' said Sylvia. 'If we can get two, maybe three cars in front of the Fiat, that will slow him down. Then we can feed another couple behind and alongside and force him to a stop.'

'Giacomo will shoot his way out,' said Jack. 'I'd hate to be in the front cars.'

'They're special ops vehicles. Bulletproofed. Not like the tin cans the rest of us drive.'

Lorenzo had headphones on. He slipped off the left cup and turned to face Sylvia and Jack. 'Word from the street teams, Valsi and Mazerelli are both confirmed dead. Crime Unit medic says it looks like JHP slugs in both bodies.'

***Autostrada del Sole***

Whatever happened, *surrender* was not an option. Salvatore Giacomo was not going to lie down and whimper like a dog. He glanced left and right in the wing mirrors. Through the fog he could see the full beams of the approaching carabinieri cars.

They would try to get past him. Try to block him in. And he knew he couldn't stop them all.

He glanced ahead and spotted an upcoming slip road, an exit just west of Trecasse.

The lights behind him glowed brighter. Engines roared closer.

He was going too fast to make it.

But he did.

The Fiat shed 20,000 kilometres' worth of rubber as he veered out of the grey haze of fog and headlight glare and off the autostrada.

He couldn't tell whether any of the pursuit cars had made it after him. He guessed not.

The Fiat clipped a barrier on the winding exit road. Spun sideways off the autostrada. Squealed to a stalled halt in an unlit street.

Sal started her up, found second gear and burned his way east, still parallel to the E45.

The helicopter's Nightsun was struggling to find him. It glowed in the fuzzy sky like a cobwebbed old light bulb in a vast dark cellar.

He pulled a left into Via Alessandro Manzoni. In his rear-view he could see two white dots in the far distance.

They were still on him.

Still.

But not close enough.

Oncoming headlights reflected in the road spray. It was raining now as well as foggy. He glanced up, squinted out of the driver's side window. The white belly of the GIS chopper was illuminated for a second, then vanished. They were breathing down his neck.

Sal pulled a hard right, then an even tighter left.

He was on Via Canarde San Pietro, heading north towards the darkness of the Mount Vesuvius National Park.

Soon they would be on his ground.

His *sacred* ground.

His killing ground.

# 106

***ROS Quartiere Generale (Anti-Camorra Unit), Napoli***

Lorenzo Pisano drove his fist into the surface of the control-room desk, '*Porco Dio!*' The mild-mannered Major was in full rage. '*Porca miseria! Porca puttana! Porca Madonna!*'

He turned and glared at Jack and Sylvia, as though it were their fault that the pursuit team had just found the Fiat abandoned after forking right at the end of Via Marsiglia.

Salvatore Giacomo was gone.

'The fog is so damn bad out there. I'm going to have to bring the chopper down. Fuck it!' He hit the desk again. 'The ground teams can barely see their own hands, let alone find this bastard.'

Lorenzo wheeled away from them and barked orders into desk mics. Slowly his voice settled down and he found his normal level of calmness. A bank of control-room monitors showed a live feed from the helicopter as it landed close to San Sebastiano. Traffic cameras were almost blacked out, picking up only occasional bursts of headlights. Foggy pictures swirled in from the armoured pursuit cars, now parked and awaiting instructions.

On a lower screen a real-time satellite map showed in vivid colours the whole area in which the chase had taken place. And the dead end where Sal had vanished. The dark-green vastness of the Mount Vesuvius National Park dominated the north of the picture. The orange ribbon of the A3/E45 ran west to east. The pale blue of the endless Bay of Naples sagged across the south.

Sylvia pointed to the map. 'There's a railway stop just there. Giacomo could be on a train by now – going in either direction.'

Lorenzo threw up his hands. 'Or on a motorway – or down any of a dozen other minor roads. Or who-knows-fucking-where. We've lost him!' The major dropped his head between his hands. Cover of fog, cover of darkness, cover of the Camorra – it was as though every element of evil had conspired against him.

Jack moved towards the monitors. 'He'll head north-east.'

'What?' Lorenzo looked up. 'Why? Why do you say that? North-east will run him round Vesuvius and out towards Ottaviano.'

'This guy is going where he feels comfortable. Believe me, you bury bodies somewhere for five or ten years you get pretty comfortable around that area.'

Lorenzo was unsure. He knew he had only one more throw of the dice before Sal was really gone.

Not just gone for now. Gone forever. He scratched his head. He could muster barely a hundred men, maybe ten to fifteen sets of cars from five different barracks. Time was ticking away. 'Why wouldn't he double back, do as Sylvia says, and catch the train? He could be up in Rome in a couple of hours.' Another thought hit Lorenzo. 'Worse still, if he rides the tracks fully east he could be in Sicily by the morning.'

'It's your call,' said Jack. 'But believe me, our boy is right here.' He ran his finger along the Parco Nazionale del Vesuvio. 'Get me out there and we've still got a good chance of finding him.'

The Nightsun was gone.

Salvatore Giacomo had watched it drop to earth like a dying firefly.

He guessed how much distance he had on his pursuers. A kilometre. Maybe two or three at the most. Better than that, though, they wouldn't have a clue in *which* direction he was heading. Three kilometres in one direction meant their search circle had to be six in diameter. He couldn't remember the exact formula for pi, but he knew that it meant the cops would have to set a dragnet perimeter more than eighteen kilometres long. And they'd have to do it lightning fast. Not a chance. Not at this time of night. Not in this weather. And with every further kilometre he gained, then it became less and less likely.

Without the dull thwack-thwack of the helicopter blades he could hear himself panting as he ran through the foothills of the parkland. The darkness of the hills swallowed him. He ran hard. Ran until he was breathless. Then he ran some more.

Finally he stopped. Not because he wanted to, but because he had to. His lungs were on fire. His heart rate was more than three times its resting beat. He had pains in his chest.

Twigs and branches cracked beneath his feet as he ground to a halt. One minute. One minute's rest, then he'd run again.

As his breathing slowed he noticed that his legs, arms and face had been ripped by brambles and branches. In the morning, trackers would be able to see traces. They'd pick him up easy. But not now. Right now they'd find nothing.

His minute was up.

He ran again.

Lorenzo rolled the dice and took his chance on Jack.

To be sure, though, he spread his bets. He sent search teams to the central train and metro station in Naples. He mobilized all the support he could from local carabinieri barracks. And he called in favours from the polizia, both state and municipal.

Four GIS members – the ones from the helicopter – continued tracking Sal from where he'd abandoned the Fiat. They fanned out in the thickening fog. Helmet and torch lights flickered on the sodden hillsides. Radio crackle broke the humid silence as they struggled to establish search patterns in the dense darkness.

Four more GIS members headed east with Jack and Sylvia. Two drove in the car with them, two rode on their own.

Neither of the GIS men had a name. Neither spoke unless spoken to. They'd been briefed to do whatever Jack and Sylvia wanted and beyond that they retained their normal high levels of security. Everyone had live radio links back to Lorenzo who still held ultimate operational command.

The faces of the GIS men were covered by full balaclavas and Jack used their eye colours to name them Blue and Brown. Blue was driving; he was taller and older, his baby blues sat on creases and bags that put him in his late forties. Brown squashed in the back with Jack and helped him into a GIS combat suit, complete with the unit insignia of an open parachute and vertical sword.

'Serial killers of this guy's calibre have *approach* and *escape* routes from their burial scenes,' explained Jack, as Blue hurtled them at a frighteningly high speed through the fog. 'And I mean *routes*, not route.'

Sylvia shut her eyes as the passenger-side mirror slapped that of a passing car. 'So this is all still a game of chance?' She clutched a grab handle as the Alfa zigzagged into the outer lane of the autostrada. Its siren wailed again and its blue roof lights flashed incessantly.

'To some degree. This particular squirrel in the

woods will have many routes, and they'll lie north, south, east and west of his burial site. He'll also have several safe points. Bolt-holes that he can hide in if he's really spooked.'

'The whole area's littered with old farms, disused cottages and outbuildings,' Sylvia added. 'I'll radio Lorenzo and see if we can get some bearings on them.'

Brown patted Jack's belt. 'This thing – it looks like a palmtop – is a tracking device. See – it registers your position here, but change the screen like this and you get full access to all real-time satellite imagery of the area.'

Jack was impressed. He saw their flashing dot exit the A3 and begin the ascent of the winding mountain road that he and Sylvia had taken the first time he'd visited the crime scene. He'd said at the time that he wanted to see it at night, needed to look at it in the same way the killer did. Now that late shift might just pay dividends.

'Okay?' checked Brown.

'Very. Very okay.'

'Good.' Brown handed him a balaclava and Jack rolled it down over his face.

'Now you look the part!' The GIS man's eyes smiled approval. 'You need these too. They're Gen 2 Night Vision goggles – are you familiar with them?'

'Pretty much. I've used them, but not this model.'

'It's simple. Usual head-mount strapping. Tell me if you can't work it. There's a Picatinny rail on both the handgun and the MP5 that I'm going to give you, and a second scope to fit it. Okay?'

Jack clamped the goggles on to his head and felt mildly claustrophobic. 'Forget the rifle. Up close I'm fine. Beyond twenty metres, the way I shoot, I've got more chance of bringing him down with a rock.'

'Should have brought him a shotgun and some buckshot,' shouted Blue from behind the wheel. Both GIS men laughed.

Sylvia switched from her radio to her phone. She picked up three missed messages from the Murder Incident Room. She called in and asked for Mancini. When she finally reached him, the update he gave her almost made her drop the phone.

One of her task forces had come up with an ID on victim Number One.

*Numero Uno.*

Jack's profiling was spot on.

There had indeed been a relationship between the killer and the victim.

A very special one.

The tailor's label had led them to an old family firm called Tombolini who'd made bespoke suits for city gents for more than a century. Their designs and attention to detail were legendary, and they still kept detailed accounts of every fitting and every suit they'd ever made. She clicked off the phone, let Jack finish giving directions to the driver, then updated him. '*Numero Uno* was *Luigi* Finelli.' Sylvia twisted in her seat so she could see the impact on Jack's face. 'Salvatore Giacomo had murdered Luigi, no doubt on the instructions of the Don's own son, Fredo Finelli. Like you said, there was a good reason why Fredo kept him around for so many years.'

Static burst from Jack's belt. 'Jack, this is Lorenzo, can you hear me?'

'I can hear you. Loud and clear.'

'What's your ETA?'

'How long?' Jack shouted to Blue.

The driver took one black-gloved hand off the wheel and held it up.

'Five minutes. We'll be there in five.'

The total blackness reduced Sal to a slow jog.

Arms outstretched, he felt like a blind man. Twigs and branches snapped back and sliced more ribbons of skin from his face. He licked his lips and tasted blood.

Clouds shifted in a sky as dense as iron filings. For a moment the curve of a pale moon shone like a scythe. Dim light hinted at the outline of a mountain track.

He knew where he was.

Close to safety.

The hesitant jog became a run. Uphill, eastwards, across the track, through a clearing he knew well. In the summer it would bloom with apricots and cherries. Geckos would fill the foliage; woodpeckers and turtle doves would warble and coo in the branches. It was near here that he'd walked with his mother after his father had gone. Near here that she'd told him he was never coming back and had explained why it was her fault. Near here that he'd sat for years and let his hatred for her fester.

Something caught his eye. The moon outlined a moving silhouette fifty metres ahead of him.

Sal dropped to the sodden earth.

His Glock jerked in his outstretched arms. The explosion flashed in his face. The boom barrelled across the open field.

The silhouette slumped.

Sal felt his heart bang. His finger stayed on the trigger. He wouldn't risk another shot unless he really had to.

The silhouette was grounded. Flat. Dead.

He got to his feet. Gun outstretched in classic pistol grip. He ran towards it. The moon slipped back into a sheath of rainy clouds. Damn it! He needed another two strides, to see the body.

'*Merda!*'

Barely two metres ahead of him lay the corpse.

A deer.

Nothing more than a fucking deer!

Sal cursed himself. He thought he'd known every animal that roamed the park. He'd been distracted and the thing had surprised him. It must have been a recent addition – damned conservationists.

He knew he should have been cooler. There was

no need to have fired so quickly. Risked giving away his position. He wiped sweat and water from his face and slowly turned 360 degrees. Nothing. He held his breath and honed his concentration. He couldn't hear anything either. They'd have heard *him*, though. He was sure of it. Way back there, in the dark, in the unseen distance, their little soldier ears would have pricked up and they'd have heard him.

# 107

***Parco Nazionale del Vesuvio***

Blue stopped the car on Jack's command. They were two kilometres south of the summit of Vesuvius, almost four kilometres west of the site where the bodies had been excavated. If his geographic profiling was accurate, Giacomo was following a cognitive map, homing in on a bolt-hole deep in his comfort zone. Lorenzo was right. If they didn't find him quickly, he'd be gone forever.

Sylvia stayed in the Alfa with Blue. They drifted another kilometre east of the drop point, into a fall-back position. If Giacomo slipped past Jack, then they'd be the last line of the dragnet.

Jack and the other three GIS men hit the ground running. Radios were choked to almost silent. Visual contact was maintained at all times and in the patchy, swirling fog that meant a spread of only fifteen to twenty metres.

They headed due west. Set a pace that would see a mile covered in about twelve minutes. Too slow to set personal bests for any of them, but just fast enough to make sure they didn't lose each other, miss anything, or make fatal mistakes.

Within minutes they pulled up sharp. Frozen to the spot. They listened like bats to the rolling echo of a single gunshot.

It came from in front of them.

Jack felt a jolt of excitement. He was right. Giacomo was heading home.

They jogged on. The combat suit and cumbersome goggles were already making them sweat. The NVD made the ground fluoresce an alien green as pounding feet crunched across the parkland. In Jack's hand was a semi-automatic Beretta 92. He knew the gun well – double action with no safety, a trigger as smooth and sweet to pull as a finger through melted chocolate.

He ran in the centre, alongside Brown, the two other GIS men flanking them. Up ahead, in the green foggy mist, he saw something that made them all spontaneously slow to a halt.

It was a large outbuilding of some sort. An ugly bunker of breeze-block concrete and corrugated iron, overgrown with ivy and lichen.

Maybe a forestry workers' tool shed.

Maybe a bolt-hole for a killer.

Sal heard them long before he saw them. Heard the squish of their soldier boots as they squelched through spongy turf. Heard the crack of twigs and rub of rocks beneath their heels. Heard their hot breath snorting in the cold night air.

It wasn't until they were up close, almost breath-on-his-face close, that he *saw* them.

Full combat gear – one, two, three of them with rifles, a fourth with a pistol. They were GIS, he could tell, even in the thin moonlight. The rifles were MP5s. Serious fucking business. Twenty-five rounds in a blink of an eye. Not that he intended blinking.

They buzzed round the forestry outhouse, shaking locks, sweeping their NVDs up and down, arcing their weapons left, right and centre. But for all their technology, they couldn't see him there – right there – right among them.

Sal lay motionless, his breath so shallow it took him twenty seconds to exhale and another twenty to breathe in again. The Glocks felt warm in his hands. Their sturdy stocks nestled against his palms and itched for action. But he'd got his caution back. There'd be no hasty mistakes. Not with those MP5s around. One of the GIS men – a tall one to the far right – waved a hand. He curled his fingers and beckoned someone over. Sal watched as two men lined up behind each other and two spread wide. They were going to storm the building. The forestry building rudely erected right next to the grave of his first victim. Not Luigi Finelli. His mother. Strangled with a length of chain, long before he'd learned to shoot a gun. Her body dumped in the parkland grave and then burned to cinders. Burned for her sins.

Sal sould have buried the others next to her, if he'd had the chance. Only they'd moved in with their shovels and their concrete and iron, and they'd built right alongside her. That's what had driven him further into the park. Still, tonight his mother would be getting company.

Sal moved his index fingers inside the trigger guards. With one movement he could be in position to make two good head shots. But that wouldn't be enough. The sub-machine gun was still unaccounted for. And just one spray of that MP5 would cut him in half. He couldn't risk it. Not yet.

Brown let off a burst of gunfire. The rough plank door splintered and its heavy steel padlock fell away. He and two GIS men were through the gap in a split second. Jack hung back. Adrenaline juiced him up and he swallowed hard. A helmet light burst on inside the hut. Even outside, the sudden intensity of white made him look away.

'Clear!' shouted a voice. The light was snuffed and the men shuffled out.

The four huddled close. 'Nothing,' said Brown, his voice muffled by the balaclava. 'We checked the floor for trapdoors, floor pits. It's clean.'

'Then let's regroup and go on,' urged the tall one.

They waited for Jack's okay. He wasn't sure. Giacomo plainly wasn't here. But given the closeness of the gunfire he couldn't be far away. The fog had lifted a little again and the moon partially reasserted itself. Jack wondered whether to spread the team further apart – maybe thirty metres between each man – and slow the pace to a walking stride.

Brown took the initiative. 'Let's do the outside of

this place once more. You stay centre and we'll make a slow sweep in three circles twenty metres apart. Then we'll move on. Right?'

Jack nodded and they were on the move before he could reproach himself for not taking command.

Sal heard them fan out. Saw the tall one take a starting position barely three metres in front of him and begin his lap. By the time he completed it they would be face to face.

How long did he have? Twenty seconds? Maybe a minute? Certainly no more.

He looked up. The fog was clearing. Soon he'd be exposed.

*When the moon hits your eye like a big pizza pie . . .*

*Blam!*

The Glock in his right hand kicked. The GIS man dropped dead in his tracks.

Sal rolled out of the overgrown stone well. *Blam! Blam!* He missed. Missed his second target. Fuck! He shifted behind the forestry building and sprinted east. If he was right then the other soldiers were still circling west. They'd have turned at the sound of gunfire, but he still had a head start.

*When the world seems to shine like . . .*

Jack whirled round. Saw the dark shape dashing into the mist. He levelled the Beretta and fired.

Missed.

He tried to sight again but even with the night-vision goggles he couldn't see clearly enough.

He tore into a sprint and prayed he wouldn't turn an ankle. Behind him the other GIS men broke their pattern. One rushed to his fallen colleague. The other raced after Jack.

A bullet sliced out of the darkness. A sharp pain erupted in Jack's kneecap. For a moment he thought he'd been hit. Then he realized the slug had hit volcanic rock directly in front of him and he'd been spiked by shards of stone.

A burst of automatic gunfire erupted behind him. Jack hit the ground.

Crossfire!

Christ almighty, he was going to die in crossfire!

More 9mm pistol fire came from in front of him. Jack rolled on his side. Pain stabbed through his left arm. Nerves twanged and sizzled – a painful reminder of his battle with the Black River Killer. He kept rolling. The pain kept coming, but he didn't stop until he was a good ten metres away.

He scrambled to his knees, kept his head down and tried to get his bearings. The moon backlit Vesuvius in front of him. The rocky ground opened up for as far as he could see. There was a hint of a path to his left. Shadows changed shapes. On it – he was sure – was Salvatore Giacomo.

Jack opened fire.

Sal the Snake took the bullet in his left wrist. It destroyed the birthday watch that Finelli had given him, sent the Glock spinning out of his hand. He twisted round, fell to his knees, opened fire with his other Glock.

Two shots missed Jack, by less than a metre.

He seized the moment. Dashed closer to Sal. Fired off several rounds as he moved.

Two missed.

The third hit Sal's hipbone.

The Camorrista crumpled and his weapon fell.

'He's down! He's down!' shouted Jack. 'Don't shoot!'

Giacomo was prostrate. Flat on his back. Staring at the stars.

Jack could see both hands. Empty.

The man's face was contorted. Jack levelled the pistol at his head. His eyes locked on the empty hands. He fought the urge to pull the trigger. Blow the murdering bastard's head off. Save the state a lot of time and money. Deal out the kind of justice the victims' families deserved.

Brown was first on the scene. He flipped the body over and cuffed him.

Sal felt the soldier's knee in the middle of his spine. Felt blood puddle around his chest and waist. Felt himself blacking out.

It was a good feeling. A peaceful feeling –

*When you walk in a dream, but you know you're not dreaming, signore.*

# 108

***ROS Quartiere Generale***
***(Anti-Camorra Unit), Napoli***

The fog lifted enough for Lorenzo to get the chopper in from San Sebastiano. The GIS man was dead. Giacomo's shot had hit him full in the back of the head.

Jack had been luckier. He picked rock out of his knee and was pleased it wasn't any worse than if he'd come off his mountain bike on a Tuscan trail.

They loaded their prisoner first. Then their dead colleague.

Finally, they helped Jack into the helicopter. Sat him with his back against the wall. Sal was at his feet. Flat out. Alongside the man he'd killed.

A GIS officer knelt and prepared to patch up Sal's wounds. Blue stuck his face in the middle of the action. 'You motherfucking cunt. I hope you bleed to death before we reach the hospital.' The Camorrista twisted a smile back at him.

The soldier's hands ripped off his blood-drenched shirt and trousers. Jabbed a hypo of morphine into the meat of his leg.

The GIS medic looked over to Jack. 'Three body wounds. Nice shooting, soldier.' Jack looked down. Giacomo had been hit in the stomach as well as the wrist and hip. The gut wound was pumping blood. Too much blood for him to make it.

He leaned over and took the dying man's head in his hand, turned it towards him. 'Why – why did you kill them all?'

The Snake's memory disgorged itself. A thousand images flooded out. His childhood. His first fight. His first suit. His first victim.

'Why?' pushed Jack.

Sal was slipping away. He could hear the music – *'scusa me, but you see* – he could see the men Fredo had asked him to kill – the women Gina had asked him to kill – he could see the fires he'd lit – *when you dance down the street, with a cloud at your feet.*

'*Perché?*' Jack dragged him back. 'Why?'

Giacomo's eyes rolled. Blood filled his throat. He coughed as he spoke. '*Affari e piacere.* Business and pleasure.' That was the only explanation he gave.

Jack felt Sal's head go heavy. Dead heavy. He was gone.

He removed his hand and let the killer's skull thump to the metal floor of the helicopter.

# Epilogue

*December 23rd*
*JFK airport, New York City*

The transatlantic flight ploughed through a field of cropped clouds and dipped in to land at JFK. The carabinieri had pulled strings and got Jack on the early bird from Capodichino. His knee had swollen up during the flight and would need a bag of ice and a truckload of Ibuprofen to bring it down again. But right now he wasn't feeling any pain. He was going home. Nothing else mattered.

Sylvia and Lorenzo had wanted him to stay for a longer debrief, a press conference and even an end-of-case party. But none of those were quite his thing. Besides, he had more important business to attend to – last minute, *very* last minute, Christmas shopping.

Rubber spun on the runway. A crowd at the back of the plane clapped as they touched down. Fresh snow was falling and Jack could all but feel the cool, crisp winter air of his hometown.

He picked up his messages while he waited at baggage reclaim. A drunken Sylvia thanked him for the thousandth time. Pietro added his best wishes and confided that Pisano was fixing for him to be promoted and assigned full-time to the Anti-Camorra Unit. He'd hear from them both again. He was sure of it. They'd find more bodies, probably at least ten, probably from the period that Valsi was in jail. Sal would have carried on killing during that time, only without Gina's orders he'd have indulged himself differently, possibly even buried his victims elsewhere. Maybe even created another necropolis.

Finally, there was a message from Howie. He and Annie planned to swing by tomorrow afternoon with a present for Zack. Who the hell was Annie? Then Jack remembered. It was the woman his buddy had saved from muggers in an alleyway – and been stabbed in the ass for his troubles. He was glad to see the big guy's heroics were being repaid in TLC.

Jack stopped at a sports shop on one of the main shopping drags through the terminal and found the very specific present he wanted for Zack. He picked up perfume for Nancy – Dior's Forever And Ever – followed by a magnum of champagne and a heavy slab of Belgian chocolate for her mother and father. Thank God for airport shopping.

As he filed through Customs he remembered that this was the airport he'd so famously collapsed in, burned out from overwork and the stress of hunting the Black River Killer. That was all a thing of the past now. Another lifetime ago. He'd bounced back and built a new career for himself. Had a wonderful new home in a new country. And to top it all, it was Christmas.

Zack flew at him as he came through the doors into Arrivals. 'Daddy! Daddy! Daddy!'

Within a second he was holding his son. Kissing the soft sweet skin of his face. 'How you doing, buddy? I swear you've grown up even more while I've been away.'

Zack clung to his neck, arms wrapped around his father like he was never going to let go.

'Man, you're getting heavy.'

And then – *there* was Nancy.

Even more beautiful than he'd remembered.

'Hello, sweetheart. Boy, have I missed you.'

'Me too, honey.' She squeezed herself into the family embrace – what Zack called 'a three hug'.

She smelled amazing. Fresh. Special. Exciting. Smelled like the love of his life.

For a minute they just stood there and held each other. A homecoming scene being repeated all around them. Finally they broke for air, laughed and walked to the car.

'It's nearly Christmas, Daddy. Santa's on his way, Gramps said so. Do you think he'll remember my glove and bat, Daddy? Do you?'

Jack covertly passed the plastic sports bag to Nancy and lifted his son on to his shoulders. 'Have you been good? If you've been good, then I think it's a dead cert that he'll have remembered.'

Zack kissed the top of his father's head and sat up tall on his shoulders.

Innocent days.

Precious days.

Jack was determined to make the most of them.

# Permissions Credits

**Lyrics from *That's Amore* by Warren and Brooks**



**Lyrics from *Per Amore* by Mariella Nava**

# Michael Morley

# About Michael Morley

Born in Manchester in 1957, Michael Morley was orphaned at birth and never knew his mother and father. He grew up in care, foster and adoption homes. His first job was as a trainee journalist with the Bury Times Newspaper Group and his subsequent journalistic career has seen him work for Radio City in Liverpool, Piccadilly Radio and BBC Radio Manchester. In TV he was a programme maker and newsreader for Border TV in Carlisle and Central/Carlton TV in the Midlands. He was Editor and Executive Producer of many ITV network productions, including the investigative current affairs show *The Cook Report*. He won numerous international awards, including several Royal Television Awards for his documentaries and current affairs work.

Michael's first marriage produced two sons, Damian and Elliott, who both share their father's life-long addiction to Manchester City FC. He is now married to Donna, a former TV news director, with whom he has one child, Billy. He divides his time between the family home in Derbyshire – a converted farm, complete with ducks, Canadian geese and a growing population of rabbits – and a house in Naarden Vesting, in the Netherlands, where for the past half decade he's worked as a senior TV executive for an international production company.

## The Camorra

During my career as an investigative crime journalist I've had close contact with many organized crime gangs. I've run secret filming operations on a variety of notoriously evil groups, ranging from heavily armed coke running Yardies to Indian mafia gangs who maimed babies and young children to make better street beggars out of them. Whatever nationality they are – whatever cool name the press have given them – they are all simply bullies. It's no more complicated than that. In the big, global playground of life they flex their prison-hardened muscles and use their awesome capacity for violence to scare normal, decent-minded people into doing what they want. And what they usually want is money. Money they don't have to stick in a long day's legitimate work to earn. Nowhere did I see extortion more prevalently and *professionally* practised than in Naples, the home of the highly complex and most feared organized crime gang in the world, the Camorra.

Everything about the Camorra is difficult to pin down, and that includes both the meaning of the word and the origin of the organization. In Spanish, the word *camorra* means fight/quarrel and the most popular belief is that the organization sprang up during the Spanish presence in Naples and therefore goes back more than two centuries. It seems to have become well rooted in Neapolitan prisons during the period of Bourbon misrule and then spread outwards, becoming both a social and political force as well as just a strong street-gang organization.

Locally, the Camorra is known as the System and to understand its power and longevity you have to keep in mind the poverty of the region and how badly the Italian government has fared in providing jobs, health care and social support for its citizens. The Camorra provides jobs – albeit illegal ones. It puts food on the tables of the poor and it restores respect to the faces of the downtrodden men and women who have become redundant as legitimate business and industries vanished over the years. They do this by being everywhere and taking a 'taste' of virtually everything. Not a big taste – not protection money so large that the business is choked to death – but five or ten percent – an affordable tax. Everything – from banking to boat building, garbage collection to gardening stores – pays its *taste* to the Camorra, and it's been that way for as long as anyone can remember. The gangs behind the System sometimes get greedy and take too much, but by and large they know just how much to cream off to keep the concern healthy. If the host prospers, then so do the parasites living on it.

The protection money is then used to fund their own enterprises (both legitimate and criminal) and these cover every aspect of life – everything from people trafficking, drug smuggling and gun running through to making cheap rip-offs of designer clothing that are often so well produced the designer labels buy them from the Camorra and stock their own outlets both in Italy and abroad. The port of Naples, one of the busiest in the world, is a smugglers' paradise and thrives because of it – at a time when countless international ports are experiencing severe difficulties. Many estimates say the Camorra provides somewhere around 20,000 jobs in the Campania region, and is therefore not only one of the most powerful employers in the region, it's one of the most powerful in Italy. It almost goes without saying that if you hold the reigns of mass employment in your hands, then you can wield enormous political force with the other fist. And they do.

The Camorra is markedly different to the Mafia. The Mafia has a classic pyramid structure, not unlike that of a big multinational. Each mafia Family has its own agreed area and is essentially an operating company paying its dues into a big Holding with a very strict reporting structure and many rules that dare not be broken. Conversely, Camorra gangs are all autonomous, working in their own different ways, keeping all their ill-gotten gains for themselves and frequently fighting murderous internecine turf wars with rival Family gangs. Of course there are some local agreements and collaborations, but these are few and far between and at some point most get broken when one of the parties feels strong enough to wipe out their neighbours and expand their empire. That's not to say that the Camorra lacks sophistication. Far from it.

In Naples, the Camorra is so deeply imbedded into every day life that some Neapolitans I talked to believe the Camorra does more for them than the local government ever will. One kid – a teenager who'd been working for the Camorra for just over two years – told me that he and his family were overjoyed when he got approached to do jobs for the local clan. He said *being chosen* was like being picked to play for his favourite soccer team (incidentally that was Barcelona, not Napoli).

Another strange fact about the Camorra is that unlike the Mafia (and many legitimate businesses and governmental bodies) it has a very open mind towards women and gives them masses of opportunity. Women not only run many Camorra business (especially in the garment, counterfeiting and exporting areas) but they also head some of the crime Families, and they are reported to be at least as brutal and merciless as the men.

And the violence can be truly ferocious. Much, much worse – and on a far, far greater scale than the Mafia has ever managed. Kids in their late teens stalk the inner-city streets – their zones – and will kill in the blink of an eye. Often the prize for shooting a rival Camorrista is as low as a new scooter. Sometimes even lower. All murders are brutal, but the Camorra go out of their way to flaunt their talent for violence. Even after death, victims are humiliated. Tongues are cut from the corpses of those who dared to speak against them; eyes are gouged from those who saw things they shouldn't. It's not unknown for victims to be decapitated and their heads placed between their naked legs. As one carabinieri officer told me, while the Mafia might leave a dead horse's head in your bed, the Camorra are more likely to leave your dead daughter's head in your bed.

Getting at someone's family or friends is a typical tactic designed to maximize leverage and it's become a trademark of Camorra dealings in the drugs sector, where their annual turnover is estimated to be at least 15 billion euros a year. Do a second take on that figure – 15 billion – then remind yourself that drugs are only one part of their portfolio.

Big money brings big problems and these problems are

usually outbreaks of assassinations and random shootings. Parts of Naples are now so bad they are known locally as the Third World. It's not unheard of for there to be more than 130 Camorra killings in a year – more than two a week.

Grandfathers, fathers, sons, brothers and cousins are all caught up in this giant spider of evil that has crawled from century to century and shows no signs of shrinking or being stopped. Those brave enough to cross it, chase it and try to crush it have often ended up being murdered.

# Naples

I've always loved Naples – probably always will. It's full of passion, energy and an earthy grit that reminds me of my upbringing in northern England. Think Moss Side, Manchester, think Toxteth, Liverpool, and you get the picture. No airs and graces to the locals, lots of down-to-earth humour and plenty of wholesome, filling food. Just as the north of England gave the world the likes of fish and chips, Lancashire hotpot and Yorkshire pudding, Naples gave it pizza, the great grandpapa of fast food. Okay, it's a real stretch to compare the climates – and the views – but hopefully you get the picture. Naples is no sociological showcase, but its people rise above its problems. They smile their way through its daily toll of murders and corruption.

Like any big city, if you come in as a tourist and use your holiday cash to skim over its polished veneer, your flying visit will leave you with a feeling that its main offerings are wonderful beaches and islands, fantastic food and usually pretty good weather (though during my last visit it seemed a monsoon season had been added).

However, that veneer is now wearing a little thin, and these days it's easier to see that beneath the polish of tourism lies a great city with immense difficulties. Youth unemployment, poverty and slum conditions are among the worst in Europe. Joblessness in Naples is often two to three times what it is in the north of Italy, while adult literacy rates are low and the birthrate is high. Overcrowding is also now a very serious social blight and is causing numerous health problems. In the backstreets of many towns, hope has been traded for survival. The social underclass is so large it is almost visible – skeletal and disaffected, downtrodden and dangerous. The struggle to find food, pay bills, keep a roof over your head is prevalent. Those with the ambition and opportunity to move to another part of Italy – or even emigrate – have already done so, or they will do so just as soon as they can get enough cash together. Those who can't escape are the unfortunate majority, and they have to stay in the mire and fight for the crumbs. Of course there are exceptions, and among the million inhabitants of Naples you'll certainly find its share of legitimate millionaires as well as the sharks of organized crime.

Naples is a real mishmash of cultures. It has a mix of Greek, French and Spanish in its genes, going back to 7BC when the Cumaeans, Greek settlers from Cumae, built Neapolis – meaning 'new city'. It became strategically important to the Romans as they fought several battles in the south of Italy and they eventually seized the region and made it their own. For several hundred years it was a kingdom, then became the capital of the Two Sicilies until Italian unification.

During the early sixteenth century the French briefly seized control of Naples and imprisoned its king, Frederick. The Spanish then won the city at the Battle of Garigliano and it actually flourished under them, at one point becoming the largest city in Europe after Paris. After the Second World War it fell into sharp decline and never really recovered. Walk its streets and you see decay on every corner, sale signs in every shop window. Pick up a daily or evening newspaper and you will read about the latest Camorra crimes.

Yet, despite all the horrors, it is in one of the most beautiful places on earth. The Amalfi Coast can match most resorts around the globe. The ever-rumbling Vesuvius is visited by tens of millions of tourists, while Pompeii and Herculaneum are so magical you have to check the walls to make sure Disney or Steven Spielberg haven't had a hand in shaping them. Capri and Capodimonte remain not only havens, they are international brands, while at Paestum you'll find some of the best-preserved Greek temples. On paper then, Naples should be able to use tourism as a tow rope to safety. But it can't. Pulling hard on the shoulders of the good, dragging them back into the mire, are the hands of the mob – a mob responsible for a crime rate that makes even the most hardened and smooth-tongued politician cringe.

If your social conscious will allow you, then you really can glide over and around the inner-city horrors that beset Italy's third-largest city, just as you can avoid the blackspots in England that have been the centre of fatal teenage stabbings, unbelievable car crime and open drug dealing. I stayed at the awkwardly named Hotel Grand Parker's and had precisely the experience Jack King had. In fairness to them, the staff were incredibly courteous and as charming as any I've ever come across in Italy – which is saying a lot.

I also visited the small town of Castello di Cisterna, which is home to the major carabinieri barracks near Pompeii. I stupidly walked two sides of the giant building taking photographs for research purposes and duly found myself being arrested and hauled inside the barracks. This was good in one way – I would never have got inside any other way – but bad in that they treated me as highly suspicious, bordering upon being a terrorist threat. Suspicion peaked when they insisted on downloading the memory card from my Nikon and found that I'd also been shooting a variety of close-ups and wide-shots of the high-security prison at Poggioreale. Not your usual tourist snaps by any stretch of the imagination! Only the previous day I had been with two very senior carabinieri officers based in the centre of Naples, but as they'd seen me 'unofficially' – meetings fixed through Italian friends – I couldn't give their names in return for my freedom. Finally, after checking my passport and phoning several numbers I gave as references in the Netherlands and the UK, the highly diligent carabinieri at Castello di Cisterna wiped the camera's memory chip and released me.

Despite this little brush with the law, and despite all the troubles that Naples has, I would unhesitatingly return there. You'd be mad not to want to wander down the ancient chariot-rutted streets of Pompeii, stare across the national parkland and wonder what the hell it was like when Vesuvius blew its top back in 79AD.

You'd be crazy not to want to visit the Duomo, the Anfiteatro Flavio (one of the largest amphitheatres in the world) and while away as many hours as possible in the fantastic restaurants and bars in the Borgo Marinari or Mergellina areas. You'd be criminally negligent not to taste the succulent local pastries, perfect pizzas and heavenly Neapolitan ice cream that the culinary magicians of Campania can conjure up for you. One thing, though, if you do go – *and you should* – you'd also be foolish not to forget that old saying: 'See Naples and die.'

# MICHAEL MORLEY

## SPIDER

'For a second she thinks she is dead. Then she opens her eyes and wishes she was.'

The press call him the Black River Killer and his stats are shocking: 16 murders; not captured in 20 years; the FBI's best profiler – Jack King – burned out and beaten, his career shattered.

Jack and his wife now run a hotel in Tuscany. And though he still gets nightmares, rural Italy is a whole world away from BRK's brutal crime scenes in Southern Carolina. Or so Jack thought . . .

As Italian cops discover the body of a young woman – her remains mutilated like BRK's victims – a gruesome package arrives at the FBI, twin events that conspire to lure the profiler back into the hunt.

But this time, who is the spider and who is the fly?

'*Spider* chillingly captures the harsh realities of a deteriorated mind' Lynda La Plant

'A terrifying read that will keep you hooked' Simon Kernick

# *He just wanted a decent book to read ...*

Not too much to ask, is it? It was in 1935 when Allen Lane, Managing Director of Bodley Head Publishers, stood on a platform at Exeter railway station looking for something good to read on his journey back to London. His choice was limited to popular magazines and poor-quality paperbacks – the same choice faced every day by the vast majority of readers, few of whom could afford hardbacks. Lane's disappointment and subsequent anger at the range of books generally available led him to found a company – and change the world.

*'We believed in the existence in this country of a vast reading public for intelligent books at a low price, and staked everything on it'*
***Sir Allen Lane, 1902–1970, founder of Penguin Books***

The quality paperback had arrived – and not just in bookshops. Lane was adamant that his Penguins should appear in chain stores and tobacconists, and should cost no more than a packet of cigarettes.

Reading habits (and cigarette prices) have changed since 1935, but Penguin still believes in publishing the best books for everybody to enjoy. We still believe that good design costs no more than bad design, and we still believe that quality books published passionately and responsibly make the world a better place.

So wherever you see the little bird – whether it's on a piece of prize-winning literary fiction or a celebrity autobiography, political tour de force or historical masterpiece, a serial-killer thriller, reference book, world classic or a piece of pure escapism – you can bet that it represents the very best that the genre has to offer.

**Whatever you like to read – trust Penguin.**

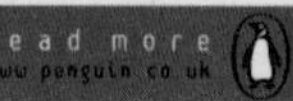